James Craig has worked as a jour thirty years. He lives in Central L ous Inspector Carlyle novels, *Lond Explain*; *Buckingham Palace Blue.* also available from Constable & R

For more information visit www.james-craig.co.uk, or follow him on Twitter: @byjamescraig.

Praise for *London Calling*

'A cracking read.' BBC Radio 4

'Fast paced and very easy to get quickly lost in.' Lovereading.com

Praise for *Never Apologise, Never Explain*

'Pacy and entertaining.' *The Times*

'Engaging, fast paced . . . a satisfying modern British crime novel.' *Shots*

'*Never Apologise, Never Explain* is as close as you can get to the heart-beat of London. It may even cause palpitations when reading.' *It's A Crime! Reviews*

Also by James Craig

Novels
London Calling
Never Apologise, Never Explain
Buckingham Palace Blues
The Circus
Then We Die

Short Stories
The Enemy Within
What Dies Inside
The Hand of God

A MAN OF SORROWS

James Craig

Constable & Robinson Ltd
55–56 Russell Square
London WC1B 4HP
www.constablerobinson.com

First published in the UK by C&R Crime,
an imprint of Constable & Robinson Ltd., 2014

A copy of the British Library Cataloguing in Publication Data is available from the
British Library

ISBN 978-1-147210-041-2 (paperback)
ISBN 978-1-47210-042-9 (ebook)

Typeset by TW Typesetting, Plymouth, Devon

Printed and bound in the UK by CPI Group (UK) Ltd, Croydon, CR0 4YY

1 3 5 7 9 10 8 6 4 2

ACKNOWLEDGEMENTS

This is the sixth John Carlyle novel. Thanks for help in getting it over the line go to: Polly James, Michael Doggart and Peter Lavery, as well as to Chris McVeigh and Beth McFarland at 451 for all their help in promoting the inspector online.

I also doff my cap to Krystyna Green, Rob Nichols, Martin Palmer, Colette Whitehouse, Saskia Angenent, Clive Hebard, Joan Deitch and all of the team at Constable.

As always, the greatest thanks are reserved for Catherine and Cate. This book, like all the others, is for them.

*'He is despised and rejected of men;
a man of sorrows.'*

Isaiah 53:3–5

'The road to hell is paved with priests' skulls.'

St John Chrysostom, Archbishop of Constantinople
(c. 347–407)

ONE

'Are you happy?'

'What?'

'Are you happy?' Helen Kennedy repeated. She lowered her copy of the *Independent* and shot an enquiring look at her husband. They were sitting in a branch of EAT, one of the dozens of café chains in London, this one situated at the top end of Kingsway, across the road from Holborn tube station. Taking a white cup from the table, she took a sip of green tea and allowed herself the smallest sigh of pleasure.

The two of them were enjoying a rare breakfast together before the working day got started in earnest. Gazing out of the window at a woman walking down the street with a miniature Schnauzer dog under her arm, Inspector John Carlyle – aka *Mr Kennedy*, insofar as Helen had never taken his surname – wondered how best to answer what was obviously some kind of trick question.

'Of course,' he said finally. Taking a cautious sip of his own green tea – citing unspecified health reasons, Helen was trying to wean him off coffee – he smiled at his wife, looking for a sign that he had come up with the right answer.

Not really interested in his reply, Helen stuck her head back in the paper. 'The Prime Minister,' she explained, adopting the scornful tone reserved for politicians and other dullards, 'yesterday launched his "happiness index".'

Outside, a couple of police cars roared past, heading south, sirens blaring.

'Nothing to do with me,' Carlyle shrugged, when she automatically looked at him. 'That's why I'm so bloody happy.' He took another sip of his tea; to his surprise he was getting quite into it. It was unlikely that it would lead to him cutting his relentless coffee intake by much, but it was a start. 'Ecstatic, in fact.'

'I'm sure the PM would be delighted to hear that.'

'Edgar Carlton.' Carlyle shook his head as he finished his tea. As an inspector in the Metropolitan Police, he had once dealt with the super-slippery Carlton and his 'chumocracy' cohorts in a professional capacity. 'What an over-privileged, under-achieving idiot!'

An elderly woman at the next table glowered at him from behind her copy of the *Daily Mail*. Returning the scowl with interest, Carlyle caught sight of the rag's front page. Princess Diana was back from the dead.

Or something.

Why don't all these stupid people just fuck off back to the Home Counties? he fulminated. *And leave London to people who can appreciate it.* Not for the first time, he wondered why no one had ever set up a London Independence Party. He would vote for it in a shot. London for Londoners – which included all the Scots, all the Poles, all the French . . . all the people who came here to get away from the fucking idiots in their own countries. Maybe even the odd Englishman, here and there.

Helen interrupted the political ranting in his head. '"*From next month*",' she continued, carefully enunciating each word in her best mock BBC English as if she was having a trial for Radio 4, '"*the Office for National Statistics will try to measure a range of key areas that are thought to matter most to people's wellbeing*".'

'Shoot some fucking politicians, for a start,' Carlyle snorted louder than was absolutely necessary, largely for the benefit of *Daily Mail* Woman. 'That would make everyone happy.'

Regarding him as the troublesome child that he was, Helen continued serenely, ' "*Such as health, education, inequalities in income and the environment*".'

'What a load of old bollocks,' Carlyle harrumphed. He was now resigned to working himself up into an indignant frenzy; any wellbeing that he *had* been enjoying now not even a distant memory. 'How can you measure bloody happiness?'

Helen sipped her tea demurely. 'Mr Carlton said, and I quote: "*I think this debate will help us think more carefully about how we are affecting the quality of people's lives*".'

'And *I* think that this kind of moronic pseudo-debate,' Carlyle hissed, 'is the sort of crap that bloody politicians spout instead of doing any work.'

The world was spared any more of the inspector's refined views by his mobile going off in the breast pocket of his jacket. Grabbing the phone, he peered at the screen. It took a moment for the numbers to come into focus so that he could see that the call was from his sergeant. *I really should go and get my eyes tested*, he thought as he answered it.

'Yeah?'

'Where are you?' Alison Roche rarely bothered with pleasantries. It was something they had in common and one of the many reasons he liked her.

'Near Holborn tube,' Carlyle explained. 'Why? Where am I supposed to be?'

'I'm at the north end of the Strand underpass,' said Roche, ignoring the question. 'You'd better get down here.'

'Sure.' Given that he was barely a minute away from her location, Carlyle didn't bother to ask why. Ending the call, he dropped the phone back into his pocket. Standing up, he stepped round the table and kissed Helen on the top of the head.

'Sorry. Looks like something's going on. Need to run.'

Roche met him at the entrance to the underpass, part of the former Kingsway tram subway. In her mid-thirties, she was a striking redhead with a sharp temper to match. Today, however, there was a lack of sparkle in her green eyes as she waited patiently for him.

Reaching the mouth of the tunnel, he could see traffic at a standstill and a bunch of uniforms running around with their Heckler & Koch G36s very much in evidence.

The days of unarmed coppers are long gone, he thought sadly. 'What's going on?'

'Security alert. SO15 have been tracking a sleeper cell.'

'Okay, but if Counter Terrorism Command are, indeed, on the case, then why are we here?'

Roche was already striding underground. 'Come and see.'

Thirty yards inside the tunnel a white Ford Transit Minibus had come to a halt in front of a pair of police Astras which were blocking off the exit.

'Police!' With his ID held high above his head, Carlyle shouted over the noise of the angry horns back down the tunnel as he walked towards the nearest uniform. Stepping past the police cars, he counted eight figures dressed in camouflage lying face down on the tarmac under the unyielding gaze of six armed officers who seemed completely unperturbed by his arrival. Twenty yards further back, another group of officers were trying to hold back gawkers who had got out of their cars to watch the show and film the action on their mobile phones.

Tapping him on the shoulder, Roche handed him a flyer. 'This was in their van.'

Carlyle frowned. 'The Eternity Dance Troupe?' Squinting, he looked at the prostrate figures, who, in fairness, were doing a very good impression of a bunch of frightened teenage kids. 'I know it's a scary old world and all that, but I'm assuming that they're not al-Qaeda's finest.'

'They were doing breakfast television at the studios on the South Bank this morning,' Roche explained. 'I saw the piece.'

'Were they any good?'

'Not really.'

'Maybe that's why they've been arrested,' Carlyle quipped. 'Seems fair enough to me.'

'SO15 are making dicks of themselves.' She nodded in the direction of the rubberneckers. 'And the media will be here soon to hoover up all this citizen journalism.'

Carlyle handed her back the flyer. 'That's hardly our problem.'

'It will be if they all get dragged back to Agar Street.'

Carlyle grunted. As usual, Roche had a point. The last thing he needed today was a full-blown circus descending on Charing Cross police station. Not when he had other fish to fry. 'What were you doing here anyway?'

Roche gestured down the tunnel. 'My car's back there. I was on my way in.'

'Fair enough.' Carlyle began marching towards the nearest G36-toting uniform. 'Let's go and find out who's in charge of today's fiasco.'

'*The tunnel was closed for more than an hour before anti-terrorist officers realized their blunder, which was blamed on a tip-off from an over-zealous member of the public. The troupe's manager, Cyril Bowles, says he will be suing the Metropolitan Police for wrongful arrest and emotional trauma . . .*'

'Ungrateful sod,' Carlyle grumbled as he switched off the TV and dropped the remote on his desk. 'He should think of all the free publicity.'

Roche handed him a Diet Coke she'd brought up from the canteen. 'We need to get downstairs.'

'Huh?' Carlyle cracked open the can and took a healthy slug.

'The priest.'

'Fuck.' *The fucking priest!* Carlyle had forgotten all about Father Francis McGowan. He jumped to his feet. 'How long has he been downstairs?'

'Since just after one this morning.'

'God! You didn't get much sleep then.'

Roche made a face. 'He started squealing for his lawyer straight away.'

'Sorry.'

A grin broke through her tiredness and he was suddenly struck by how good she looked. *Lose that thought right now*, he ordered himself.

'Unfortunately, we haven't been able to track her down yet.'

'Better get on with it then.'

Roche put a hand on his arm. 'There's one other thing. There was a bit of a scuffle when I brought him in. He's got a few cuts and bruises.'

5

Nothing he doesn't deserve, the inspector thought.

'I know, I know.' Roche held up a hand. 'It shouldn't have happened. But when we found his porn stash I just wanted to kill the old bastard.'

A not altogether unreasonable point of view. Carlyle nodded.

'When I told him he was coming down the station, he started mouthing off about a conspiracy against the Church. Then he told me I was going to hell and that's when—'

'You bounced his head off the wall a few times?'

'He had it coming.'

'This isn't the 1970s,' Carlyle laughed. 'We're not *The Sweeney.*'

Roche gave him a blank look.

'Sweeney Todd. Cockney rhyming slang – Flying Squad; it was a TV show, Regan and Carter.' He smiled as he recalled his underage self sneaking into the ABC Cinema on Fulham Broadway to see the X-certificate movie version of the show. In those days, no one bothered to kick you out at the end, so he'd stayed in to watch it three times in a row. Duality. '"*You're nicked*", that was their catchphrase.'

Roche couldn't have looked any less interested. 'Didn't they do a remake of that?'

'It was shit,' Carlyle told her, with all the authority of Pauline Kael on crack. 'Ray Winstone and some ten-year-old dickhead rapper. Utter shit.'

'Mm.'

'Not a patch on the original.'

'Aha.' Roche's interest edged another notch downwards.

I'm just a sad old bastard, Carlyle observed. *Move on.* 'When you were bashing the guy up, were there any witnesses? Any chance of any of the action being caught on a security camera?'

She shook her head. 'No. Nothing to worry about in that regard. I went into the flat alone.'

'Good.'

Roche gave him a meaningful look. 'But if it were to come back to us, I don't want to get into trouble over this.'

Meaning: *I don't want to get in trouble dealing with something that is your bloody crusade.*

'Fair enough. Are your union dues paid up?'

An expression of concern crept across her face. 'Yes. Why?'

'Always better to have the Federation on your side,' Carlyle advised, 'just in case. Frankly, there's nothing they can't get you out of, short of shooting the Commissioner. And you wouldn't do that, would you?' Roche just laughed.

Taking a final swig of his Diet Coke, the inspector thought about the situation for a moment. Then, opening the bottom drawer of his desk, he pulled out one of the tools of the trade, an extendable steel baton. It was barely a quarter of an inch in diameter and weighed only a few grams. But you could use it to break a bloke's arm with just a flick of the wrist.

'Where is he?' he asked.

'B3.'

'When we get down to the basement,' Carlyle smiled, 'just follow my lead.'

'Okay,' said Roche, without any conviction.

Sticking the baton under his jacket, he kicked the drawer closed with the toe of his shoe. 'Let's go.'

Under his shock of unruly snow-white hair, Father Francis McGowan looked like a man who had spent a night in a cell. He also looked like a man who had walked, face first, into a door – which, of course, he had. Carlyle noted the bruising on his left cheek and a cut under his right eye. The injuries were hardly serious, but there was no way that they would go unnoticed. At least Roche had given him a plaster and a cup of coffee.

'She hit me!' Shifting in his seat, McGowan pointed a bony finger at Roche, who was hovering half a yard behind the inspector.

Carlyle said nothing.

'Where's my lawyer?' the priest asked in a quavering voice.

'We're still trying to contact her.' Roche's voice sounded flat and bored.

Carlyle took out his baton and slowly extended it to its full twenty-six inches, trying not to grin as McGowan's eyes grew wide and he glanced at the security camera high on the wall behind Carlyle's head.

'I want my lawyer, now!'

His own eyes gleaming with mischief, Carlyle gently tapped the baton against the side of his leg. 'Tell me, Father, are you happy?'

'Huh?' The priest seemed genuinely confused by the question.

'Are you happy?'

McGowan looked at him suspiciously. 'You mean right now?'

'In general.'

The old man gazed around, as if searching for divine inspiration. Finding none, he stammered: 'I d-don't understand.'

'I'm not happy,' said Carlyle quietly.

'Me neither,' said Roche, quickly getting into the spirit of things.

The priest frowned. 'Are you asking for confession?'

'I'm angry,' said Carlyle, ignoring the question. 'In fact, I'm mad as hell and I'm not going to take it any more!' Laughing, he did a little shuffle, a skip and a hop, raising the baton above his head, in a vague approximation of a member of the Riot Squad. Despite having been out of service for three weeks, the WTC9SHR miniature bullet camera exploded with a satisfying bang, sending pieces of glass and plastic flying across the room, towards the elderly man cowering in his chair behind the desk.

Maybe now, the inspector thought, *someone will look into getting it fixed.*

Leaning against the far wall, Roche looked at him open-mouthed, as if genuinely surprised at the quality of his acting skills.

'It's a line from a film,' Carlyle shrugged, pulling a piece of glass from his hair. 'More or less.'

She glared at him and he recoiled slightly from the anger in her green eyes.

'*Network*,' he tried to explain. 'Peter Finch. Great movie.'

Still nothing, other than a slight shake of the head which sent a strand of red hair falling across her face. She pushed it away.

'Before your time, I suppose.' *Just like* The Sweeney. With a dismal grin, Carlyle threw the baton, backhanded, across the room. Bouncing off the table, it hit the wall about three inches from Father Francis McGowan's head.

The priest looked at Roche, eyes pleading. 'My lawyer,' he croaked. 'I want my lawyer.'

'You'll get your lawyer when I'm fucking ready,' Carlyle snarled. Grabbing the baton from the floor, he took one end in each hand and leaped at McGowan. Ramming the steel under the priest's chin, he forced him back in his chair until he was pinned against the wall.

A gurgling noise tried to fight its way out of McGowan's throat.

It's okay, Carlyle thought, *we're only pretending. Make it seem real but don't overdo it.*

Method acting. Like Paul Newman.

As he pushed harder, McGowan's face turned puce.

Al Pacino.

'John!' Roche grabbed him by the shoulder and tried to pull him away. 'For fuck's sake! You're going to kill him!'

Shrugging her off, Carlyle pushed even harder. 'Where's the boy?'

Robert DeNiro.

McGowan's lips moved but nothing came out. His eyes rolled back in his head as he started drifting out of consciousness.

'Where,' Carlyle screamed, 'is the fucking boy?'

'JOHN!!' Roche stuck an arm round his neck and finally managed to drag him backwards.

CUT! That's a wrap, everybody. Great scene.

Slumping forwards, McGowan vomited across the table.

Carlyle let Roche push him to the far side of the room. He was buzzing, as high as if he were 18 and he'd just done a line of his mate Dom Silver's Grade A, top-notch amphetamine sulphate.

Fucking BUZZING.

His brain overloaded, thinking about the victims, thinking about fantasies of revenge, thinking about this sad excuse for a man sitting in front of him. Letting the sour smell of sick fill his nostrils, Carlyle waited until McGowan had lifted his head and was breathing more normally. 'If you don't tell me exactly where the boy is,' he said, his voice calm now, 'I will kill you.'

Travis Bickle eat your heart out.

Wiping a tear from his eye, McGowan allowed himself the merest hint of a smile. '*Credo in Deum Patrem omnipotentem,*' he said quietly. '*Creatorem coeli et terrae. Et in Iesum Christum, Filium eius unicum, Dominum nostrum, qui conceptus est de Spiritu Sancto, natus ex Maria Virgine, passus sub Pontio Pilato, crucifixus, mortuus, et sepultus, descendit ad inferos, tertia die resurrexit a mortuis, ascendit ad caelos, sedet ad dexteram Dei Patris omnipotentis, inde venturus est iudicare vivos et mortuos. Credo in Spiritum Sanctum, sanctam Ecclesiam catholicam, sanctorum communionem, remissionem peccatorum, carnis resurrectionem, vitam aeternam. Amen.*'

Folding his arms, Carlyle waited for the priest to finish. 'Give me what I want or I will kill you,' he said finally. 'A-fucking-men to that.'

Max fucking Cady.

'I believe in God,' McGowan stated, his voice refusing to waver, 'the Father Almighty, Creator of Heaven and earth; and in Jesus Christ, His only Son, our Lord; Who was conceived of the Holy Ghost, born of the Virgin Mary, suffered under Pontius Pilate, was crucified, died, and was buried. He descended into Hell; the third day He arose again from the dead; He ascended into Heaven and sits at the right hand of God, the Father Almighty: from thence He shall come to judge the living and the dead. I believe in the Holy Ghost, the holy Catholic Church, the communion of saints, the forgiveness of sins, the resurrection of the body, and life everlasting. Amen.'

TWO

Checking that the store manager had turned his back, Paula Coulter raised her hands above her head and let out a massive yawn. Her legs ached and Paula was dying to sit down and have a cup of tea. It had been a shit day, nothing but tourists and window shoppers; pitiful sales that left them way down on their weekly target. After almost three years working at St James's Diamonds on New Bond Street, Paula could spot a timewaster as soon as they walked through the door. It never ceased to amaze and annoy her that people who didn't look like they had enough for a McDonald's would saunter in and expect you to treat them as if they were the Prince of bloody Wales or something. Almost as bad were the people who had the money but who just seemed to want to dangle it in front of you and never spend anything. Sighing, she glanced up at the clock above the till which read 4.57 p.m. Half an hour to go. Maybe tomorrow would be better.

The buzzer rang. Mohammed, St James's security guy, glanced at the CCTV monitor and stepped out from behind the counter. Unlocking the door, he pulled it open and stepped aside to let the customers enter.

'Good afternoon, gentlemen.'

'Good afternoon,' the two men smiled in unison, as Mohammed closed the door behind them.

'Nice,' Paula murmured under her breath, putting on a big smile and trying to make some eye-contact with the two guys approaching the counter.

They made a handsome pair, one black, one white, with tanned skin, both tall, with the black guy maybe a shade over six foot and the white guy a shade under. Both were dressed in expensive-looking grey suits and white shirts. The black guy had a green tie, while his friend wore his shirt open at the neck. Both were wearing oversized Ray-Bans, making them harder to age, but Paula put them at late twenties. Hopefully, City boys looking to blow their bonuses on something flash. Crash or no crash, those guys always had money to burn. She remembered reading something in that morning's *Metro* about bankers getting record bonuses this year. Paula couldn't work out why that was, given that bankers were supposed to be the people responsible for pushing everyone into recession, but she supposed it was one of those things. Bigger bonuses every year were just a fact of life. If that was the case, the least these two could do was spend some of their money in her store.

She watched as both of them checked her out and wondered if they might be interested in her phone number. She might even be able to wangle a double date with her mate Debbie. Debbie was a bit on the lardy side, but she scrubbed up well. *Business first though*, she told herself firmly, pulling back her shoulders and sticking out her chest, *so stop daydreaming*. Maybe today wouldn't be a total washout, after all.

The store manager, Martin Luckman, was obviously having similar thoughts as he appeared at her shoulder. *He's practically licking his lips*, Paula thought disgustedly.

'How can we help you gentlemen today?' Bouncing on the balls of his feet, Luckman almost did a little bow.

The black guy looked directly at Paula. 'We're interested in a selection of things,' he said pleasantly.

Uh oh. Paula's heart sank. *Timewasters.* If you were a serious buyer, you didn't walk into a place like St James's without a decent idea of what you wanted to buy.

Luckman gestured around the store, the sweep of his arm taking in tens of millions of pounds' worth of rings, watches, earrings, necklaces and other jewellery. 'Do you have anything particular in mind?' he asked, the tiniest change in the tone of his voice indicating to Paula that he had marked their cards as she had.

Trying not to let the smile fall from her face, Paula let her gaze drift from the customers to Mohammed at the door. The security guard was intently checking his watch; clearly he was as keen to get home as she was. Out of the corner of her eye, she caught a rapid movement and the glint of metal, followed by a gasp from Luckman.

'Huh?' Paula looked back at the two men to see the white guy pointing a pistol at her. The black guy also had a gun, with which he was gesturing to Mohammed to get away from the door.

'Hands where I can see 'em!' the white guy shouted. 'Stay well away from the panic button.' Luckman did as he was told in the blink of an eye. Paula felt stupid putting her hands in the air, but duly followed suit. 'Good,' the white guy smiled. 'Now we don't want to stay too long, so let's start with the expensive stuff, shall we?'

THREE

Keen to avoid Father McGowan's lawyer, Roche frogmarched Carlyle out of the station and took him off to do some interviews relating to a fraud case they had been ignoring for too long. Eventually, they ended up all the way across Covent Garden at Il Buffone, the tiny 1950s-style Italian café, on Macklin Street, at the north end of Drury Lane. It stood opposite the block of flats where Carlyle lived and was therefore deep in 'home' territory. At this time of the day, the place was empty.

As they walked in, Marcello Aversa looked up from behind the counter and smiled. Normally, the place would have been shut by now. But Marcello and his wife were having to work ever longer hours to try to keep the place afloat. 'Ciao!' their host shouted over the noise of the ancient Gaggia coffee machine which laboured behind the counter.

'Two espressos please, Marcello,' Roche said, pushing Carlyle into the back booth, under the poster of AC Milan's '94 Champions League winning team, a present from Roche which had place of honour on the wall, next to the counter.

'I'll have a green tea,' Carlyle corrected her.

Roche looked at the inspector then laughed. 'What? Are you ill or something?'

'Wife's orders,' Marcello chuckled.

Changing the subject, Carlyle pointed at Donadoni, Maldini and the rest. 'You got a new poster!' He had been quite impressed when Roche had found a copy for Marcello the first time. When that had been defaced by yobs, he was even more impressed by her ability to come up with a replacement.

'Si,' Marcello shouted happily. 'Otherwise, I was going to have to put up one of the Azzurri.'

'Jesus!' Carlyle threw up his hands in mock horror. 'That would simply not do.' The Italian national team, world champions not so long ago, was going through one of its periodic troughs. The star players had stayed on too long past their peak and stopped the next generation coming through.

'No, I know,' Marcello agreed with regret. 'They don't deserve the place of honour on my wall.'

Roche nodded. 'Too old.'

'I know the feeling,' Carlyle joked.

'Me too,' said Marcello. 'This job is getting too tough for me.'

Carlyle felt a ripple of panic in his chest. *Christ on a bike, not more change.* He had been coming to Il Buffone most days for more than a decade. The place was a delight, a throwback to the days when cafés had an individual identity. Walking five minutes in any direction, you could probably find close to a hundred other cafés, most of them part of big chains. Some franchises had maybe four or five branches in and around Covent Garden alone. But there was only one Il Buffone.

And, sadly, it was up for sale.

Carlyle looked at Marcello. The old man did appear more tired than usual. 'You haven't found a buyer, have you?' he asked warily.

'I wish,' Marcello sighed, wiping his hands on the dishcloth hanging over his left shoulder. 'Now it's getting to the point where I'm basically trying to pay someone to take it off my hands. There are a couple of people interested. We'll see.' He smiled at Roche. 'But don't worry, I've told 'em that the poster has to stay.'

'I'm glad to hear it, Marcello.' Reading the unhappiness on Carlyle's face, Roche slipped into the seat opposite him. 'We have to talk about what happened back at the station this morning,' she said quietly but firmly, 'and how it will never, ever happen again.'

Placing the drinks on the table, Marcello registered the tone of Roche's grim 'thank you' and beat a hasty retreat.

'What the hell do you think you were doing with McGowan?'

Carlyle stared into his mug.

'He's an old man,' Roche continued.

'He's a fucking paedophile,' Carlyle hissed, turning round to check that no one was listening to the conversation, almost embarrassed to say the word.

'Whatever he is,' Roche said icily, 'you cannot lose control like that. You could have bloody killed him.'

Carlyle grunted in a way that suggested the idea of a swift and violent end for Father Francis McGowan did not totally displease him. 'I didn't lose control,' he said, trying to keep his voice even, his words clipped and precise. 'He knows now that we are serious.'

'He knows that we are dangerous,' Roche snapped back.

I wasn't the one who smacked him about, bringing him into the station, Carlyle thought, his anger more than tempered by the knowledge that he should have done that job himself and not dumped it on his sergeant. 'Look, I want to find the boy,' he said. 'I know that I have dragged you into this and I'm sorry—'

Roche dismissed his apology with a curt shake of the head.

'– but if there are any repercussions, they will come back on me, not you.'

'His lawyer is bound to make a complaint.'

'Any complaint will focus on what happened in the interview room,' Carlyle insisted. 'That falls on me. You are in the clear, I promise.'

'It's not even our bloody case.'

Fumbling in his jacket pocket, Carlyle pulled out a small photograph, barely twice the size of a passport mug shot, and dropped it on the table. 'Simon Murphy.'

Roche sighed. 'I know who he is.'

'Twelve years old. He was taken into care when he was two.'

'I know the story.'

'Moved in and out of various foster-homes for more than twelve years. Expelled from three different Camden schools before he was ten. Dumped into a Boys' Club run by a sixty-three-year-old priest who has not one but two banning orders which are supposed to prevent him working with children.'

Roche smacked her fist on the table. 'John, I know all this – you've told me already.'

'Six complaints from children who have come into contact with McGowan in the last five years. Two have withdrawn their statements, three are pursuing civil claims against the Church and one committed suicide. Simon is the best, if not the only chance of bringing a criminal conviction against this scumbag. And now he's vanished.'

Pushing a strand of red hair behind her ear, she sat back on the bench and folded her arms. 'We have no evidence that McGowan has anything to do with his disappearance. The kid has run away before.'

'You saw that sick old bastard in there,' Carlyle said. 'He thinks he's untouchable. He thinks he's put the boy beyond our grasp.'

'Listen to yourself,' she scolded him. 'What happened to John Carlyle the arch pragmatist?'

Not meeting her gaze, the inspector looked to Marcel Desailly – on the wall behind Roche's head – for inspiration. None was forthcoming. He had put himself on the hook and she wasn't going to let him wriggle off. They had been working together for less than a year but Roche had quickly come to understand how his mind worked. He was getting used to her often disarmingly accurate commentaries on his moods and the contradictions in his behaviour.

'You have to get a grip – put the chimp back in its box.'

He looked up. 'Eh?'

'It's a psychological model,' she explained briskly. 'The chimp is your emotional side. In difficult situations you have to keep it under control or you will make mistakes. In a stressful situation, like the one with McGowan, you have to stop your chimp from preventing you dealing with the problem logically.'

'Sounds like a load of bollocks to me,' he snorted.

'Sports people use it.' She mentioned a few names, a couple of footballers, cyclists, even a snooker player.

'Good for them.'

'Maybe you should go and see a shrink,' Roche said gently, 'help you cage your chimp.'

'I am seeing a shrink,' Carlyle pointed out. 'Boss's orders.' He shook his head at the absurdity of it all. 'The silly old bugger couldn't cage a kitten.'

'Maybe you need to try someone else,' she persisted.

'Life's too short.'

'Life's too short for all this hopeless crusading,' she countered. 'Whatever happened to "don't fight battles you can't win"?'

Carlyle shrugged. 'Some battles you have to fight, even if you're going to lose. But this is one that I certainly don't want to lose. You can't give people who abuse children a free pass.'

'Well,' she replied, lifting her demitasse to her lips, 'there seem to be plenty of people who disagree with you.'

'Tell me about it.' Carlyle took a sip from his own mug and winced. Wherever Marcello got his supplies from, his green tea wasn't a patch on Helen's. 'This case has been knocking around for years now. No one wants to touch it with a barge-pole. It only ended up on our desk by accident.' That was literally true. Carlyle had been waiting for a file on the case of a local politician who had been burgled three times in six weeks. Instead, Archives had sent him the McGowan file. Once he'd read it, he'd dropped an email to his boss, Commander Carole Simpson, telling her that he was going to take another look at it. He knew that Simpson could be very hit and miss when it came to email communication, so there was every chance she would not try and stop him until he'd either made some progress or reached a dead end.

Roche gave him a look.

'Okay. It only ended up on *my* desk by accident.'

A sad smile spread across her face as she put a hand on his forearm. 'Your burden is my burden, Kimosabe.'

'Thank you, Tonto.'

Her smile vanished. 'But now McGowan's lawyer will have a field day – police harassment, brutality, assault with intent; you've really dropped yourself in the shit on this one.'

'I know. I'll speak to the boss about it.'

'Simpson? She's not around.'

'What?' In recent years, the Commander had a good track record when it came to watching his back. He relied on her network inside the

Met more than he cared to admit. If Simpson wasn't around, he could find himself very exposed indeed.

'I heard that she's been sent on some work experience jolly to Canada for three months.'

'Great.' Carlyle's heart sank. 'So who's replacing her?'

Roche shrugged. 'Dunno.'

'Okay.' Digging some change out of his pocket, he got up and walked over to the till. 'We'd better get back to the station then and see how bad things are.'

FOUR

Biting her bottom lip, Paula Coulter tried not to cry as she glanced at Luckman and Mohammed, spread-eagled on the floor in the middle of the store, guns to their heads. A pool of dark liquid was trickling across the wooden floor where one of the men – the manager, she presumed – had pissed himself. Squeezing her legs together, Paula swore to herself that she wouldn't lose control of her bodily functions, difficult though that might be. She glanced at the door, praying that someone might ring the buzzer and realize that something was wrong. The clock on the wall had just ticked past five, but the sign on the door clearly said that they stayed open until five thirty. She tried to clear the sour feeling in her throat. Someone had to come, surely? The window blinds had been drawn and she watched one shadow, illuminated by the late-afternoon sunshine, saunter past, quickly followed by another. She could hear a couple of women chatting outside.

'*I don't care if the silly old cunt buggers off with the au pair,*' one squawked in best estuary English, '*as long as I get the money.*'

'*Good for you!*' the other laughed hysterically.

Normal life was proceeding unhindered just a few feet away, on the other side of the glass. Paula thought she was going to vomit with disappointment and fear.

On the floor, Mohammed started wheezing. 'I've got asthma,' he gasped. 'I need my inhaler.'

The white guy gave him a kick and lowered his gun to where the security guard could see it. 'Shut up!' he hissed. 'We'll be gone in five minutes. You'll have to wait.'

20

Paula felt the tears welling up in her eyes and she let out a sob.

'Don't worry about them,' the black guy grinned, pulling a Harrods plastic bag out of his pocket and tossing it to her. 'Just start filling that up and no one's going to get hurt.'

The bag landed on the counter in front of her and she opened it up. Looking around, she had no idea where to begin.

'Start over there,' the black guy said impatiently, gesturing at the display of watches in one of the windows.

Paula stepped unsteadily from behind the counter and moved towards the window. Belatedly she realized that she needed to unlock the display.

'I need the key,' she wailed, bursting into tears.

'Oh, for fuck's sake,' the white guy screamed. Lifting his gun to shoulder height, he fired three times, into the centre of each of the store's main windows. Falling to her knees, Paula covered her ears. A split second of silence was instantly replaced by the sound of a dozen alarms going off at full blast.

'You fucking idiot,' the black guy spat at his companion as he hauled Paula to her feet. Thrusting the bag at her chest, he pushed her towards the display. 'You have three minutes to put as much stuff in that bag as possible,' he shouted, 'or I will blow your fucking head off!'

Jumping over to the window, Paula began grabbing at handfuls of watches, jewellery and broken glass. Ignoring the cuts to her hands and fingers, she shovelled handful after handful into the plastic bag. For the first time, she was conscious of her heart beating like crazy. But more than that, she was conscious that the fear had fled. Her ordeal was nearly over. Trying not to rush, she counted down the seconds as she dropped a tray of single stone diamond rings into the bag, followed by a *fin-de-siècle* dragonfly brooch and selection of gold charm bracelets. With every minute that slipped by, she grew more confident that these tossers were going to be caught. Smiling to herself, Paula had reached forty-three when she heard the first sirens in the distance.

The black guy roughly snatched the bag from her. 'That'll do!' Grabbing the collar of her blouse, he shoved her forward. 'Open the fucking door! Quickly!'

21

After fumbling with the lock, Paula pulled the door open. *Fuck off, you wankers, I hope that they gun you down in the street.* Trying to step aside, she felt a hand around her neck, pushing her out onto the pavement. When she tried to break free, the grip tightened.

'Get going, bitch!' She recognized the voice of the white guy behind her as they tumbled out on to New Bond Street. 'You're coming with us.'

Ducking through the back streets at a brisk pace, it took them less than five minutes to make it back to the station. Walking through the entrance lobby, Carlyle caught the eye of Desk Sergeant Kevin Price who was taking a break from reading the *Sun* in order to survey his domain. Price's grim expression suggested that the problem in B3 was growing.

'Trouble?' Carlyle asked.

Price nodded. 'Francis McGowan's lawyer, a woman called Abigail Slater.'

Oh, bloody hell. Carlyle made a face. 'I know her. At least, I know *of* her. Ambulance-chaser de luxe.'

'She's already asked for a doctor for her client and informed me that she will be making a formal complaint.'

Big surprise. 'Have you got one?'

'He's on his way.'

'Who is it?'

'Weber.'

'Okay.' That, at least, was a sliver of good news. Carlyle had known Dr Thomas Weber for three or four years. He was a stereotypical efficient German, with more than his fair share of good sense. At the very least, he would do nothing to make the situation worse. 'When he gets here, tell him to wait till we call him down.'

Price looked doubtfully at Carlyle but nodded.

Appearing at his shoulder, Roche ushered him past the desk and down the corridor leading to the basement. 'Let me deal with this,' she said, once Price was out of earshot.

Stopping at the top of the stairs, Carlyle looked at her, surprised.

'I'll handle Slater,' she said, a gentle insistence in her voice. 'You go upstairs and get going on your report.'

Carlyle started to protest, then thought better of it. 'Okay,' he said. 'Thanks.'

'It's no problem,' she said, slipping down the stairs and out of sight.

Sitting next to Father Francis McGowan, Abigail Slater cut an imperious figure. Even sitting down, it was clear that she was an unusually tall woman. At well over six foot, she towered over her client. Thin, but not too thin, in a well-cut black suit and pearl-white blouse buttoned at the neck, her hard grey eyes locked on Roche as the sergeant entered the interview room. Sipping from a small bottle of Evian, Slater suspiciously watched the policewoman take a seat at the table. Slouched in his seat, looking half-asleep, McGowan failed to acknowledge her arrival.

'Where is Inspector Carlyle?' the lawyer asked, replacing the cap on the plastic bottle. 'We have been waiting . . .' she glanced at an expensive-looking watch, 'a ridiculously long time.'

'The inspector,' said Roche primly, not offering her hand, 'is attending to other matters. I am his colleague, Alison Roche. I will be conducting this part of the interview.'

Taking a business card from the pocket of her jacket, Slater passed it across the table.

Roche picked up the card. *Abigail Slater, Director, Catholic Legal Network.* 'What's the Catholic Legal Network?'

'I am Father McGowan's legal representative,' Slater replied. She pointed at the priest. 'As you can see, my client has been viciously assaulted.'

Roche looked at McGowan's face. Happily, apart from some red marks on his neck, there was no sign of any bruising. She kept her expression studiously neutral and said nothing.

'I have asked for a doctor.'

'He's on his way.'

'And I want the tape of the interview,' Slater pointed at the remains of the security camera hanging from the wall, 'before your colleague went berserk and smashed the equipment.' Biting her lip, she tried to suppress a smirk. 'As you must be aware, this will signal the immediate end of his career in the police force.' She tapped the file of papers on the desk in front of her with a ruby-red nail. 'Criminal charges will undoubtedly follow.'

Roche took a deep breath and told herself to remain calm. 'The camera has been out of service for several weeks now,' she said evenly. 'Your allegations are extremely serious. They will, of course, be investigated thoroughly.'

Slater nodded, waiting politely for the '*but*'.

Roche, knowing that she was not going to disappoint, allowed herself the smallest of smiles. 'However,' she continued, 'I have been present when your client has been interviewed and I can confirm that he has been properly treated at all times.'

Rousing himself, McGowan started to protest but the lawyer put a firm hand on his arm. 'Has he now?' she said softly.

'Yes, he has.'

'I hope you're sure about that, Sergeant. Or maybe the inspector won't be the only one facing charges.'

'I would remind you,' Roche said sternly, 'that we are investigating the case of a young boy who has gone missing – a young boy who, along with several others, has made some extremely grave allegations against your client.'

'Petty gossip,' the lawyer said dismissively. 'Across the whole world, there is hardly a priest left who hasn't been accused of something. These days, we are just an easy target.'

Roche pulled her up. 'We?'

'The Church.'

'Ah.' Roche nodded, happy to move the conversation away from Carlyle.

'The Church gets the blame for everything.' Slater waved a careless hand in the air. 'Invariably, it's just people jumping on the bandwagon, trying to make some easy money.'

Roche looked at McGowan and then back to his lawyer. 'Your client, however, has a criminal record.'

'Which is unfortunate,' the lawyer conceded, 'but that was all a long time ago. It is a matter of historical interest only.'

'I see.'

'It does not,' Slater said angrily, 'justify this ongoing campaign of police harassment, culminating in his arrest last night and today's outrageous behaviour by your colleague.'

'Father McGowan is refusing to assist with our enquiries,' Roche said stiffly. 'What does he have to hide?'

'He is not in a position to help,' said Slater, ignoring the complaint. 'He knows nothing.'

Roche pocketed the lawyer's business card and got to her feet. 'I will send Dr Weber down when he arrives,' she said, pulling open the door. 'After he has examined your client, you are free to go. We will be in touch.'

The warning shot went off less than a foot from her head. When the ringing stopped, Paula realized that she was deaf in her left ear. Through the haze of an appalling headache, she watched people fleeing down the street from the advancing gunmen. They were heading south, moving steadily towards Piccadilly. Paula thought that she could hear the police sirens getting closer, but she wasn't sure. Suddenly, a hand grabbed her by the arm and pulled her down an empty alleyway. At the bottom was a cobbled courtyard, just off Avery Row. At the far end was a slightly wider exit, leading on to what Paula knew was Grosvenor Street. In the courtyard was a black London taxi cab and a navy Vespa 125 cc scooter.

The white guy pulled open the back of the taxi and poked her inside, jumping in behind her and closing the door. 'Act normal, bitch,' he ordered.

Paula glanced in the rearview mirror to see the black guy hand the plastic bag full of jewellery to a third guy in a crash helmet, who stuck it in the helmet box on the back of the scooter.

'Hey!' Sticking his gun into the waistband of his trousers, the white guy reached across the seat and gave her a slap around the back of the head. 'The less you see, the less trouble you're in.'

Paula obediently lowered her gaze.

'That's more like it.'

Keeping her eyes on the floor, Paula listened to the scooter move carefully out of the courtyard and into heavy traffic. Once she could no longer make out the sound of the scooter's engine above the general hum of traffic noise, she lifted her eyes. Despite the ringing in her ears, she could clearly hear the police and ambulance sirens now. They seemed to be coming from all directions. *The net's closing in*, Paula thought. She suddenly realized that might not be a good thing and felt her stomach do a somersault. Once again, she squeezed her legs together and hoped that her bladder would not give out.

'Just look fucking normal.' The white guy tried to smile, but all Paula could see was the tension etched across his face.

'Let's go.' Jumping behind the wheel, the black guy reached under the seat and pulled out a Chelsea baseball cap. Ramming it down on his head, the brim over his eyes, he started the ignition. There was a loud click as the passenger doors were locked. Switching off the 'For Hire' sign, he carefully steered the cab out of the courtyard.

FIVE

On the third floor the inspector sat at his desk and reread the email from his union, the Police Federation. Reading it for a third time, he shook his head in frustration.

'Wankers!' he said aloud. Ignoring the disapproving glance of a passing WPC, he hit the print button. After about five seconds, a printer called 'Vigilance' on the far side of the floor wheezed into action. With a groan, he pushed himself out of his chair and went to collect the two sheets of A4 that it had started to spew out.

As he returned to his desk, he saw Roche appearing out of the lift. Folding one copy of the email, he dropped it in the pocket of his jacket, which was hung on the back of his chair. The other he handed to his sergeant as she approached him.

'What's this?' Roche asked, taking the piece of paper.

'It's a memo from the Federation,' Carlyle said flatly, 'about voluntary redundancies.' It had been more than three months since the Commissioner, a political appointee unpopular with many officers, had announced that the Met would have to make sizeable job cuts in the wake of the never-ending financial crisis that was affecting the whole of the public sector. Since then, everyone had been waiting for information about numbers and, more importantly, what that might mean for their own job.

Roche screwed up her face. 'This won't affect us, will it?'

Carlyle shrugged. 'Who knows?'

Roche looked blankly at the paper in her hand. 'Jesus.'

Carlyle tried to offer what reassurance he could. 'I haven't really been through anything like this before,' he said, 'but I think it's very unlikely that you have got much to worry about.'

She looked at him doubtfully.

'Your career is clearly on an upward path,' he continued. 'They will definitely want to keep you.'

'What about you?'

That's a different equation altogether, he thought dolefully. 'Basically,' he said, pointing at the email, 'the Federation are saying, if you get anything from HR, do nothing without talking to them first.'

Roche folded the sheet of A4 and folded it again before stuffing it into the back pocket of her jeans. 'Thanks.'

'It's nothing. The important thing is not to worry about it. Just be aware of what the Federation are saying.'

'Makes sense,' she nodded, flopping into a nearby chair.

'So,' said Carlyle, as he sat back down at his desk, 'McGowan's lawyer. What's she like?'

Roche stuck a hand into the front pocket of her jeans and pulled out Abigail Slater's business card. 'She comes across as your bog standard corporate bitch,' she said, reaching forward and tossing the card onto Carlyle's desk.

Picking up the card, Carlyle laughed. 'Alpha female, you mean?'

'Whatever.' Roche sighed. 'They're ten a penny these days. All they do is show that, given the chance, women can be just as rubbish as men.'

Carlyle chuckled. 'You liked her then?'

Roche shot him a frosty look. 'She and the priest certainly made an odd couple. I need to see what I can find out about the Catholic Legal Network but, basically, she just seems like your average smug lawyer with God on her side.'

'And McGowan?'

'Father McGowan,' Roche glanced around the room and lowered her voice, 'looks like he's in reasonable shape, given you tried to beat the crap out of him not so long ago.'

'I didn't beat the crap out of him.' Carlyle wagged an admonishing finger at his sergeant. 'It was just a bit of role play to help him forget about the circumstances of his arrest.'

'Whatever,' Roche said, yawning. 'Anyway, I'm sure Weber will be able to write it up the right way and then basically it will be a case of our word against his.'

'Two upstanding police officers versus a bent priest.'

'Exactly,' Roche said. 'I think it'll be fine.'

The phone on Carlyle's desk started ringing. The inspector hesitated. On the one hand, he wanted to go home. This would be the first time he'd managed to have dinner with his wife and daughter in almost a week. On the other hand, getting one over on the pervert priest had given him a smidgeon of job satisfaction for the first time in a while. He picked up the phone on the sixth ring.

'Carlyle.'

'Inspector, it's Kevin Price downstairs.'

'Yes?' Carlyle's bonhomie, which rarely if ever extended to the front desk, evaporated. He looked at Roche warily.

'We've reports of shots fired at a jewellery store on New Bond Street,' said the desk sergeant matter-of-factly. 'Uniforms have left already.'

'Okay.' Carlyle jumped to his feet. 'I've got Roche here with me – we're on our way.'

The black cab gently nosed into the heavy rush-hour traffic on Grosvenor Street, heading west in the direction of Hyde Park. Paula held her breath as she watched a police Range Rover, siren blazing, racing towards them, forcing its way down the gap in the middle of the two-lane road as drivers pulled over to either kerb. As it sped past, she was just in time to see it turn into New Bond Street before she let out a whimper.

'Result!' The driver smacked a triumphant palm against the steering wheel.

Sitting next to her in the back, the white guy patted her thigh. 'Don't worry love,' he leered. 'It's almost over.'

SIX

Bond Street was named after Sir Thomas Bond, a follower of King Charles II. Old Bond Street was laid out in 1686 and was extended towards Oxford Street to the north in 1721, when it became New Bond Street. Once a street of private homes for the gentry of Georgian London, it had long since been home to a range of luxury retailers and art dealers. Specializing in 'the accessories of gracious living', St James's Diamonds had occupied the nineteenth-century stucco townhouse at number 122 since 1971. Now the place looked like a battle zone. Stepping carefully through the shattered glass on the pavement, Carlyle glanced up at the small Royal coat-of-arms above the door. Squinting, he made out the legend below the crest: *By Royal Appointment to Her Majesty the Queen and His Royal Highness the Prince of Wales. Buying and selling the loveliest jewellery for over two hundred years.* With a nod, the inspector flashed his warrant card at the uniform by the door and stepped inside.

They had finally made it on to Park Lane and, stuck behind a procession of tourist coaches, they were crawling north at an average speed of about four miles per hour. It was sweltering in the back of the cab and Paula moved to open her window. Immediately, the white guy reached over and smacked her hand away from the button.

'Leave it!' he said angrily. He was sweating heavily himself. She could see that he was wearing heavy make-up, like an actor or a TV presenter. As the temperature rose further, it looked as if his face was beginning to melt.

The traffic began edging slowly towards the next set of traffic-lights. Overhead, Paula could make out the steady thud of a helicopter. 'Where are we going?' she asked, her voice barely a whisper, as she pulled her skirt towards her knees.

'Don't worry about that,' the white guy grinned. 'Just sit back and enjoy the ride.'

After what seemed like an eternity, the last of the alarms fell silent. *Thank fuck for that.* Carlyle rubbed the back of his head, trying to forestall the headache that he knew was brewing. Folding his arms, he stood in the middle of St James's Diamonds and looked down at the protective powder-blue booties over his shoes. *Why did they have to be powder blue?* he wondered sourly. *It just makes you look like even more of a dick than is necessary.* Careful to avoid stepping on anything, he turned slowly through 360 degrees, taking in the scene. The store had been badly damaged, with glass and jewellery strewn across the floor, along with empty display cases. On first glance, the whole thing looked like an amateurish smash and grab raid. How much had actually been taken was far from clear.

The clock on the wall read 5.52 p.m. It was less than an hour since the alarms had been activated. The raiders had left on foot; if they were going to nab them red-handed, he would have expected it to have happened by now. At the very least, he would have expected them to have dumped the shop assistant. He listened to a police radio on the counter cackle with impotent activity. There had been no sightings since they dropped off New Bond Street – amazing in itself, given that there could hardly be an inch of the neighbourhood that wasn't covered by multiple CCTV cameras. Maybe they'd gone to ground. But where? Even if they had organized somewhere to hide out, that would require the kind of careful planning – not to mention balls of steel – that seemed at odds with the mess he was looking at in the store. So, what would that leave? Hiding in plain sight?

Carlyle was aware of the London rush-hour continuing undisturbed around him. *There are millions of people out there*, he told himself, *and you are looking for three of them.* They had to get them straight away or prepare for the long haul. It was looking like this was going to be taking over his life for the foreseeable future. Trying to recover some over-priced baubles that no real person could ever afford – these types of cases bored the shit out of him. Basically, you were working for the insurance company. Big fucking deal.

Catching a whiff of ammonia, Carlyle looked down at the pool of piss on the floor in front of him. Glancing over at Russell Blake, the chief forensic technician currently at the scene, he tried not to grin.

'Who pissed themselves?' he asked quietly.

Blake, a no-nonsense guy in his mid-thirties, who had worked for the West Yorkshire Police before transferring to the Met three years earlier, showed no such restraint. 'It were t'store manager,' he said, in a much louder voice than was necessary, his thick Bradford accent incongruous in the rarefied environs of W1. He nodded in the direction of an ashen-faced guy standing in the corner, trying to look as inconspicuous as possible. 'He lost it when they made him lie on t'floor and pointed a gun at his head.'

Carlyle caught the manager's eye and looked away, embarrassed. He felt a wave of sympathy for the guy, having to stand there in his damp trousers. 'That's fair enough,' he shrugged. 'No one wants to die on the job, after all.' Standing next to the manager, a huge, shaven-headed Asian guy was sucking on an inhaler. By Carlyle's estimate, he had to be at least six foot two and sixteen stone. He lowered his voice still further. 'Who's the giant?'

'Security guard,' Blake replied. 'He suffered an asthma attack during t'robbery.'

'No one's covering themselves in glory today,' Carlyle quipped. He smiled at Alison Roche, who had appeared at Blake's side.

Roche put her hands on her hips and sighed. 'They've lost them.'

Carlyle gritted his teeth and looked at Blake. 'Will you get much here?' he asked, gesturing at the chaos of the store interior.

'You bet,' Blake told him. 'We'll get plenty. The question is whether we'll get owt that's of any use. And it's gonna take ages.'

'Okay,' Carlyle nodded. 'Understood.' Carefully picking a path back towards the door, he gestured for Roche to join him outside.

A block of the street had been cordoned off and a couple of uniforms were marshalling curious onlookers at each end. Carlyle watched idly as a TV crew arrived at the north end of the cordon and began shooting some general views. Stepping away from the technicians on their hands and knees on the pavement in front of the store, he looked up at the police helicopter still hovering overhead. Pulling one of his mobiles out of the breast pocket of his jacket, he pulled up his recent call list and rang his wife. He listened to it ring, feeling a small sense of relief when it became apparent that Helen wasn't going to pick up.

Once the voicemail kicked in, he left a terse message. 'It's me. Something's come up and it looks like I'm going to be late tonight. Maybe very late. Sorry. Give Alice a kiss for me and I'll call you later when I've got a better idea about what's going on. Bye.'

Slipping on a pair of sunglasses, Roche waited for him to finish his call. 'Bit of a mess, eh?'

Carlyle said, 'Yup. Any idea how much they took?'

'Too early to tell. Millions maybe, assuming they can sell it at anything approaching a reasonable price.'

'What do we know about the missing shop assistant?'

Roche began reciting what she had gleaned so far from her preliminary chat with the manager. As always, Carlyle was impressed by her ability to retain all the key facts in her head without reference to notes. 'Paula Coulter, twenty-three. Worked there for almost three years. Lives in Theydon Bois with her parents. A couple of local uniforms have been sent to the house,' Roche gestured in the direction of the camera crew, which had just been joined by a second, 'so that they don't see it on the TV first.'

Carlyle snorted. 'I'm not sure most people wouldn't prefer getting the news from a bimbo reporter, rather than some pimply youth in a uniform. Anyway, we know for sure that she was taken against her will?'

Roche jerked a thumb at the shattered shopfront. 'That's what the other two said. Why? Are you thinking inside job?'

'Something like this, you've always got to look at the possibility.' Carlyle thrust his arms out wide and smiled. 'But, of course, we will never jump to any conclusions.'

33

Roche gave him a sharp *don't tell me how to suck eggs* look. 'Of course not, Inspector.'

'We need to go through the usual drill,' said Carlyle ignoring her irritation, 'check her bank records, phone calls, friends, et cetera, et cetera. Speak to the desk and see who else we can pull in to this.'

'Fine,' said Roche doubtfully, 'but he'll just try and palm me off with the new PCSOs.' Police Community Support Officers were volunteers known as 'plastic policemen'.

Carlyle adopted what he hoped was an imperious pose. 'Tell him that I will not tolerate any plastics on this case. No fucking way. This is far too serious.' He mentioned the names of a couple of regular constables. 'See if we can get them.'

'Yes, Inspector.'

'Right. Take the manager and the security guy back to Charing Cross and get the interviews started.'

'Okay.'

'And get someone with an attention span longer than that of a gold-fish started on going through the store's CCTV pictures.'

'Right.'

'And see if we can find the manager a clean pair of trousers or something,' Carlyle added, immediately wondering what the 'or something' might be.

Roche mumbled an indistinct reply, which he presumed was in the affirmative. But something further down the street had caught her eye and he no longer had her full attention. 'Oh Christ!' she breathed. 'What's *he* doing here?'

Carlyle spun round in time to see a rather overweight, fifty-something officer in full dress uniform heading towards them at an uncomfortable trot, followed by a young flunky who was struggling to keep up. He barely had time to remove any expression from his face before the man was upon him.

'Commander Dugdale.' Carlyle thrust out a pre-emptive hand and allowed it to be crushed in an equally pre-emptive show of excessive force.

'Inspector,' said Dugdale, his gaze on Roche. 'Sergeant.'

'Commander,' Roche nodded.

The flustered flunky appeared at Dugdale's side – a small blonde woman in a cheap grey trouser-suit and a white blouse who looked about twelve and, on first glance, had no distinguishing features whatsoever. 'Judith Mahon,' she smiled weakly. 'Met Press Office.'

Disregarding the PR woman, Carlyle eyed Dugdale suspiciously. Their paths had crossed once before, on a case where Carlyle had worked with one of Dugdale's officers in SO15, the Counter Terrorism Command Unit. Things hadn't ended happily, not least for the SO15 officer, David Ronan, who had been murdered in the line of duty. Externally, the Met had put a brave face on the whole thing, holding the usual enquiry to sweep as much as possible under the carpet. Internally, the matter was deemed a complete fiasco and Dugdale, who had been conspicuously behind the curve, had shouldered much of the blame. His career prospects had taken a serious hit and any lingering thoughts he might have had about reaching the dizzy heights of Assistant Commissioner had been destroyed. Carlyle, with no career prospects to begin with, simply shrugged the matter off. He knew perfectly well, however, that he had made another senior enemy in the process.

Dugdale's watery blue eyes flicked up and down the road before settling back on Carlyle. In his turn, the Inspector made no attempt to hide the fact that he was scrutinizing his superior carefully. Up close, Dugdale seemed to have aged a decade in less than a year. He was heavier than Carlyle remembered and the colour in his cheeks suggested a considerable taste for drink. His expression was that of a man with a bad case of piles.

'Is everything under control, Inspector?'

'Er, yes,' Carlyle said, trying to keep the bemusement out of his voice. 'But I'm not aware that there's anything here that will be of interest to SO15.'

Dugdale shot him a filthy look. 'I would have thought you knew . . .'

Carlyle gave a gesture signifying his complete absence of knowledge.

'I left SO15 at the beginning of the year,' Dugdale said stiffly. 'As of right now I will be standing in for Commander Simpson while she is in Canada.'

Oh fucking great, the perfect end to a perfect day.

'So I will need a full update on the situation here, as will Miss . . .'

'Mahon,' interjected the PR girl, making it sound like *Ma-on*.

'Miss Mahon,' Dugdale continued, 'will need to organize a press briefing.'

'No problem,' said Carlyle, grinning inanely. 'Sergeant Roche will get you up to speed while I proceed with the investigation.' Ignoring the annoyed look on Roche's face, he turned on his heel and began marching quickly down the street.

SEVEN

Carlyle stepped into interview room B3 and looked around as if he hadn't seen it in a while. His eye caught the remains of the bullet camera hanging from the wall in the corner and he let out a small laugh.

'What happened to that?'

Carlyle turned to Martin Luckman and shrugged. 'Dunno.'

Raising his eyebrows, the St James's Diamonds store manager took a sip from a can of Coke. Placing the can on the table next to an open packet of Benson & Hedges, he watched as Carlyle pulled out the chair on the opposite side of the desk and sat down.

'I'm Inspector John Carlyle,' he said in what he hoped was a reassuring manner as he took his first close look at the man. 'I will be leading the investigation into this afternoon's events.'

Luckman nodded. He was not particularly tall – it was hard to guess his height with him sitting down, but maybe five foot eight – with a slight build and curly, sandy hair that reached his shirt collar at the back but was receding at the temples. With a bland, oval face and a worried expression, he certainly didn't look like the kind of guy who you would go to, to spend a hundred grand on a watch.

Luckman dropped his gaze to the table and began playing with his cigarette packet.

'I'm sorry,' said Carlyle officiously. 'You can't smoke in here.'

'No, of course.' Luckman closed the lid on the Benson & Hedges and placed it back on the table.

'I work with Sergeant Roche,' Carlyle continued, 'who has already spoken to you at New Bond Street.' Resisting the urge to look under the table to see if Luckman had managed to change his trousers, he tried a surreptitious sniff. Unable to detect any lingering odour of piss coming from the witness, he pulled his chair closer to the table.

'Nice lady,' said Luckman, in a way that suggested he would rather continue that conversation than start a new one with the inspector.

'She is next door speaking to your security guard, Mohammed.'

'Mo,' Luckman smiled. 'Mo Hendricks. He's a lovely guy.' The smile mutated into a frown. 'I was really worried when he started wheezing like that. I knew he had asthma, but he'd never been as bad as that.'

'I presume,' said Carlyle, unencumbered by any knowledge about the condition, 'that the stress of the robbery will have brought on the attack. I'm sure he'll be okay after a good night's sleep.'

'Yes,' Luckman said, taking another swig of his Coke. 'But what about Paula?'

Carlyle made a face. 'No news yet. But we have a lot of people out looking for her.'

Luckman looked far from reassured. 'I can imagine.'

'And,' Carlyle lied with an easy smile, 'I'm sure that we'll find her sooner rather than later, safe and sound. Once the robbers have used her to help make their getaway, they'll let her go.'

'I hope so,' Luckman said limply.

'And how about you?' Carlyle asked. 'How are you feeling?'

Luckman finished the last of his Coke and sighed theatrically. 'Okay, I suppose.' He clasped his hands together and leaned forward in his chair. 'I think that after the initial shock wears off, you're just happy to have got through it alive, don't you think?'

'That seems reasonable,' said Carlyle, reaching over and switching on the Sony BX800 MP3 digital voice-recorder in the middle of the table. He looked at his watch and spoke to the machine. 'The time is now seven fifty-three p.m. Present in the room are Inspector John Carlyle and the witness Martin Luckman.' He looked back at the store manager. 'Now, Mr Luckman, why don't you just tell me, in your own words, what exactly happened this afternoon?'

* * *

It was after 9 p.m. when they had finished interviewing Luckman and Hendricks. Both men had been given the medical all-clear and sent home to get some rest. Realizing that he was starving hungry, Carlyle got hold of Roche and they went out of the building to get something to eat. He chose the Box café on Henrietta Street, barely a minute from the station, just down from the piazza, on the grounds that it would be cheap and relatively free of tourists. When they arrived, the place was empty and it was clear that the owner, a Ukrainian called Myron Sabo, was well on the way to shutting up for the night. He was just about to say, 'Closed' when he looked up from washing the floor and saw Carlyle. Nodding cautious acknowledgement of a semi-regular customer who was also a policeman, he put down his mop and gestured at a table by the window.

As Carlyle and Roche took their seats, Myron flipped over the Open sign to Closed on the door and shuffled over to take their order. Carlyle went for a cheese omelette and a Diet Coke, while Roche chose a pasta salad and an orange juice.

'Excuse me a second,' she said, as Myron disappeared into the kitchen. 'I just need to make a quick call.'

'No problem.' As Roche slipped out of the door and onto the pavement, Carlyle pulled out his own mobile to call Russell Blake. He let it ring and waited for the forensics technician's voicemail to kick in. 'Russell, it's John Carlyle. I was after an update on New Bond Street. Give me a call. Thanks.' He put the phone back in his pocket and watched Roche paw the kerbside with the toe of her left shoe. She had her back turned to him and her voice was raised slightly, suggesting a somewhat fractious conversation. Carlyle tried not to eavesdrop – but not very hard.

'I know,' Roche was saying apologetically. 'I'm sorry, but it's just one of those things.' Carlyle could see her pushing her hair back while listening to the person on the other end of the line. 'It comes with the job, I told you.'

Myron appeared with their drinks and Carlyle finally stopped snooping. He took a sip of his Diet Coke and smiled.

'Thanks.'

The café-owner nodded blankly and headed back to the kitchen. Carlyle heard the door open behind him and Roche plonked herself down in the chair opposite.

'Sorry about that,' she said tensely and lifted the glass of orange juice to her lips.

'Trouble at home?'

Roche put her juice down and looked at him warily. Carlyle was not really the kind of guy to show much interest in her private life and that was the way she liked it. She had introduced her previous boyfriend to Carlyle, SO15 Detective Inspector David Ronan, and he had ended up dead. From that moment, she had determined to keep her private life completely separate from work.

'Had to blow out the boyfriend for dinner,' she said, trying to inject a little levity into her voice. 'These things happen.'

'Comes with the job,' Carlyle parroted.

'Yes, it does,' Roche said, gazing out of the window in a manner that suggested that the conversation was closed.

Carlyle left Roche to her thoughts and flicked through some football websites on his BlackBerry for a couple of minutes until Myron appeared with his omelette.

Finishing his main course, Carlyle resisted the temptation to order an apple Danish from the selection under the counter and limited himself to a green tea.

'Still off the coffee, then?' Roche asked.

'More or less. Want anything else?'

Roche stopped pushing her half-eaten salad around her plate and sat back in her chair. 'No. I'm done.'

'Okay,' said Carlyle, once the café owner had stalked off with their plates. 'Let's compare notes.'

'Well,' Roche began, 'the security guard, Hendricks, seemed to be on the level. There's nothing complicated about his story: the two guys arrived just before five. They look kosher, he lets them in, and then all hell breaks loose. Once he started having his asthma attack, all he was worried about was continuing to breathe. The moment they'd left, he went to grab his inhaler and just waited for the police to arrive.'

A thought popped into Carlyle's head. 'Why did the call come in to us, rather than West End Central?'

'It's closed.'

'Closed?'

'Yeah,' Roche said. 'It closed at the end of last month. It's supposed to be being refurbished, but there's a rumour that it might not reopen, in order to save money.'

'Better that than losing jobs,' Carlyle murmured. There were seven police stations in Westminster; West End Central, in Savile Row, was one of the smaller ones. Over the years, several others had closed as operations had been centralized and uniformed coppers spent less time pounding the beat. It was the same all across London, just the way of the world.

'Anyway,' Roche continued, 'the alarm was supposed to go to Belgravia, but for some reason it came to us.' She watched as Myron arrived with Carlyle's tea. Placing the mug carefully on the table, along with the bill, the owner once again retreated behind his counter. 'I think he wants to get home,' Roche said, reaching into her bag for her purse.

'Don't worry,' said Carlyle, picking up the bill. 'I'll get this.'

'Are you sure?'

'Of course,' he told her, digging into his jacket pocket for his wallet. 'It's the least I can do for dragging you out here and making you miss your date.' Dropping a tenner and a fiver onto the table, he gulped down half his tea and jumped to his feet, nodding his thanks to Myron. The Ukrainian gave him a weary smile in reply and came out from behind the counter to unlock the door.

'Thank you,' Roche told him, hoisting her bag over her shoulder and following Carlyle out.

Standing on the pavement, Carlyle was torn between turning right and making the short walk through the piazza to his flat, or left and back to the station.

Roche, shivering in the cold night air, made her decision first. 'I'm going to call it a day,' she said.

'Which way are you going?' Carlyle asked.

'I'll get the Central line at Holborn.'

'Okay,' he said. 'You can walk me home and I'll tell you about my conversation with Luckman.' Just then, he felt his mobile vibrate in his pocket. Assuming it was Helen, he checked the number. 901. It was his answerphone. A message appeared, telling him he had four missed calls. 'Shit!' Carlyle gestured at the screen, which shone brightly in the gloom. 'How can that happen?' he moaned. 'We sat in the café. No one rang me. How can I have missed *four* bloody calls?'

Roche tutted sympathetically.

The phone started ringing again. 'For fuck's sake!'

'Work?'

Carlyle nodded, hitting the receive button. 'Yes?'

'Inspector? It's the desk here.'

'Yes?' said Carlyle, already waving goodnight to Roche. Changing direction, he set off wearily in the direction of Bedford Street.

'There is someone here who is demanding to speak to you, sir.'

EIGHT

As Carlyle approached the front desk, the night sergeant gave him a look that he couldn't decipher until the woman talking on the phone turned round. If the look on her face said that she was less than impressed, Carlyle's reaction was rather different. Dressed in what at first glance looked like a black leather cat-suit and biker boots, she was tall, easily a couple of inches taller than he was, and slim, with her blonde hair cut in an expensive-looking bob. Her face was classically beautiful and he doubted if she could have yet reached thirty. Still talking on the phone while she watched him gawp, an elbow propped casually on the desk, her blue eyes sparkled with mischief. Taking it all in, Carlyle's first thought was that she looked like Cameron Diaz's little sister or, rather, Cameron Diaz's *hotter* little sister.

'Look, I've got to go. The help has arrived. Ciao.' The woman poked a finger at her iPhone and stepped away from the desk. 'Inspector Carlyle?'

Temporarily dazed, Carlyle had to think about that one for a moment. 'Er,' he stammered, 'yes.'

The woman did not offer her hand. 'I am Katrin Lagerbäck, the owner of St James's Diamonds. I wondered if we could talk about today's . . . events.' Her English was perfect and betrayed no obvious accent, but it was clear that she wasn't a local.

Carlyle tried to regain his composure. 'Thank you for coming to see me.' Glancing around, he was aware that they – that *she* – was quickly attracting a crowd among the officers on duty, as well as the members of the public waiting to be seen. 'Please,' he said, leading her deeper into the station. 'Come this way.'

He showed her into a meeting room on the third floor. Dropping her bag on the table, Katrin Lagerbäck pulled out a seat and sat down. He could see now that she wasn't wearing a cat-suit but rather a matching leather jacket and trousers ensemble. Carlyle had never seen the attraction of leather trousers. To his mind, only Jim Morrison had been able to carry them off and even then it seemed a pretty much borderline thing. Lagerbäck unzipped the jacket and Carlyle was disappointed to find a very prim white blouse beneath, with just a single button undone at the neck.

'Inspector?'

'Yes?'

'I was wondering,' Lagerbäck said, the amused smirk on her face growing bigger by the second, 'if you could give me a report on what's happening.'

'Of course.' Clicking back into work mode, Carlyle remembered that he had still to update Dugdale. If it had been Simpson, he would have put it off until tomorrow; with the new Commander, however, he knew that such tardiness would be somewhat impolitic. He replaced the Dugdale note near the top of his mental 'to do' list as he locked onto Lagerbäck's gaze and gave her some good eye-contact.

'Well,' he said, 'the situation is like this. We responded to the alarm going off at St James's Diamonds in approximately six minutes' – this was important as he had checked the store's security plan and the police were expected under the terms of the insurance arrangements to respond within eight minutes – 'and found that the robbers had fled, apparently taking a member of staff as a hostage.'

'That poor woman,' Lagerbäck said, with no feeling whatsoever.

You might have Cameron Diaz's looks, Carlyle thought, *but you certainly don't have her acting skills.*

'The search for them is extensive and continuing,' Carlyle went on. 'Meanwhile, our forensic analysts have been going over the crime scene in great detail and we have been speaking to the other members of staff.'

'I hear that the store manager . . . lost control of himself.' She tossed him a look that perfectly balanced amusement and disgust.

Doubting that Lagerbäck was the easiest of employers, Carlyle felt obliged to jump to the unfortunate Luckman's defence. 'Your staff were subjected to a terrible ordeal,' he said. 'We have every reason to believe that they genuinely feared for their lives. In that situation, such a reaction is perfectly understandable.'

'Huh,' she snorted, playing with the strap on her bag. 'Whatever happened, *I* would not disgrace myself like that.'

Carlyle was bemused by her focus on such an irrelevant detail. 'What would be helpful,' he said, trying to move the conversation along, 'is whether you have any thoughts about who might have carried out the robbery.'

'No,' she said sharply. 'None at all.' Seeing his interest in the speed of her response, she added, 'As you can imagine, I've been thinking about this a lot in the last few hours. Obviously, any luxury goods store is a potential target, but,' she shrugged, 'as to why us specifically? And why now? I simply do not know.'

'Okay.' Carlyle stifled a yawn, happy at the thought of at least getting her out of the station in a fairly short order. 'One of my colleagues will come and take a formal statement in the next day or so, and I will let you know of any developments.'

'Good.' Unzipping the breast pocket of her jacket, Lagerbäck pulled out a business card and handed it to Carlyle. 'You can get me on any of these numbers.' Pushing back her chair, she got to her feet. 'I am a very easy woman to get hold of.'

Still in his seat, Carlyle looked down the list of two office numbers, three mobiles and two email addresses. 'Thank you. The other thing that we need is a detailed list of everything that was taken.'

'Of course,' she nodded. 'The insurance company will have it for you first thing in the morning.'

Here we go, bloody insurance companies. He made to stand and felt her hand on his shoulder, keeping him in his chair with some considerable strength. 'There's no need to get up, Inspector,' she purred. 'I can find my own way out.'

NINE

The young lad looked around to see if anyone was watching. Satisfied that he could proceed undetected, he pulled a half-bottle of Deer Park blended whisky from his jacket pocket, unscrewed the cap and took a cautious slug, grimacing as the cheap Scotch hit the back of his throat. Whisky wasn't his drink, but the Deer Park had been the first thing to hand when he'd gone into the off-licence on the promenade. He had slipped it into his pocket and walked out while the Asian owner was arguing with a stroppy wino over the price of four cans of Special Brew. It was a piece of cake. He took another long drink. Now the bottle was half-empty and, as well as ill, he felt suitably woozy.

Unsteadily, he got to his feet and moved across to the rail of the Palace Pier. A gust of wind hit him in the face and he shivered in the cold. In the failing light, he looked along the pier to check if anyone was in sight. They weren't, so he carefully climbed onto the railing. Swinging his legs over the side, he looked down into the darkness and the depth of the sea, and said a small prayer. Then he took a deep breath and jumped.

It took Carlyle the best part of two hours to write up his report. He kept things short and to the point, but still found himself rewriting it twice to make sure that his back was sufficiently covered. Once he was confident that it was as anodyne as possible, he attached the necessary forms to an email and sent it off into cyberspace. As he did so, he felt a familiar sense of unease in his gut. It came not from worries about the case itself but about the *politics* of the case.

It had taken Carlyle many years, and much goodwill on the Commander's part, to establish a good working relationship with Simpson. Now she was gone and he was worried that Dugdale might try to use the robbery as an opportunity for payback. The robbers were still on the run, with no expectation that they would be caught, at least not in the next few hours. There was bound to be an issue about the speed and effectiveness of the police cordon, even if that wasn't necessarily his responsibility. The main worry, however, was the woman. In a sense, it would be a lot easier if Paula Coulter was in on the robbery. Certainly, that would mean less chance of her being found dead by the side of a road somewhere. If that happened, the blame game would go into overdrive.

Sitting in the empty office, he castigated himself for being so self-indulgent. 'Solve the case,' he said out loud, getting slowly to his feet, 'and no one can touch you.'

It was after midnight when he opened the front door to his flat. Taking off his shoes, he stepped into the darkened hallway and closed the door gently behind him. A quick check of the bedrooms told him that Alice and Helen were both asleep and he crept carefully back to the kitchen. Opening the fridge, he pulled out a two-litre bottle of Evian, unscrewed the cap and took a long drink.

'Ahhh!'

Replacing the cap, he put the bottle back on the shelf inside the door and looked around for something to eat. Seeing nothing in the fridge that took his fancy, he checked out the rest of the kitchen. In the corner, next to the microwave, was a bunch of bananas. Crossing the tiny kitchen floor, he selected the largest banana and snapped it free. Unzipping it, he took a huge bite, gazing out of the kitchen window across the river to the London Eye, lit up in the darkness. When he'd finished, he dropped the skin in the bin beneath the sink. Yawning, he noticed a couple of letters on top of the microwave, one opened, one not. Carlyle made to pick them up then changed his mind. 'Fuck it,' he said quietly to himself. 'It's nothing that can't wait until tomorrow.'

After taking a quick shower, he eased himself into bed, careful not to disturb his wife, who was snoring softly, the duvet pulled up under her chin. Lying still, he stared up at the ceiling, trying to make sense of the day. Only too well aware that he had overstepped the mark with the priest McGowan – even if he *had* told himself it had all been an act – he felt genuine regret for putting Roche in a position where she had to lie in order to cover for her boss. But the feeling was fleeting, quickly overridden by a sense of huge injustice on behalf of the missing boy, Simon Murphy. Carlyle had never met Murphy, and if he ever did, the inspector was fairly sure that he wouldn't like the kid much. '*Give me a child until he is seven,*' said the Jesuits, '*and I will give you the man.*' On that basis, Simon Murphy, who had been abused and ignored for the first twelve years of his life, was pretty much a lost cause. *Well, maybe he was – but that didn't mean his abusers should be allowed a free pass.*

Was Father McGowan a Jesuit? Carlyle had no idea. As an avowed atheist, the inspector had no interest in what were really nothing more than fairy stories. As far as he was concerned, people could believe what they liked, as long as they respected the beliefs of others and obeyed the law. In his view, someone's religion was about as significant as the football team they supported and considerably less interesting.

Somewhere deep in his brain, he recalled another Jesuit motto: *Ad majorem Dei Gloriam* – 'for the Greater Glory of God'. *There* is *no fucking God*, Carlyle harrumphed silently in the darkness, wishing his brain would switch off and he could get some sleep. *And, even if there was, He wouldn't gain any glory from the buggering of little boys.*

TEN

He woke with a start. It was still dark and it took him a moment to focus on the LCD display on the alarm clock, which told him that it was 5.12 a.m. Carlyle looked over at Helen, who was still fast asleep. Yawning, he moved himself cautiously out of the bed and slipped into the bathroom. After a careful shave, he dressed quickly while running through a list of places where he might get some breakfast. At this early hour, Marcello would still be travelling into Town from his North London home, and Il Buffone would not open for another hour or so. However, there was a café at the Embankment end of Villiers Street, next to Charing Cross train station, that stayed open through the night, primarily for taxi drivers and, at weekends, for clubbers waiting for the first train home in the morning. Carlyle had been there a few times; the food was crap, but it would do.

Creeping into the kitchen, he found a pen in one of the drawers and scribbled a brief note on the back of one of the envelopes on top of the microwave: *Sorry I was so late, back early tonight. Give me a call when you get up. X.* Propping it up against the remaining bananas, he made his way out.

David Hogg yawned as he watched Boris, his bull-mastiff, race down the shingle of Brighton beach towards the sea. It was not yet 6 a.m. and there was no one else around, which was just the way Hogg liked it. Otherwise, Boris would have to stay on his leash. He was a good-natured animal, but the sight of 140 pounds of dog bearing down on them was enough to give most people the willies.

Covering his eyes against the bright light, Hogg gazed out towards the horizon. It was a beautiful morning, azure sky, bright sunshine but with a fresh, chill edge to the air. All the same, he'd rather be in bed. At the very least, he could do with some breakfast. Off to his right was the pier. If they headed that way, he could pop into Luigi's café on Old Steine. Looking round, he struggled to pick out the dog against the glare. 'Boris!' There was no reply, save for the gentle crashing of the waves against the beach. Grumbling to himself, Hogg began walking towards the water. *'Boris!'*

Twenty yards from the water's edge, Hogg finally caught sight of the dog. As he got closer, he heard a friendly yelp. Closer still, he saw that the dog was wagging his tail happily, standing over what looked like some kind of package that had been washed up on the beach. Pulling the leash out of his pocket, Hogg reached for the dog – who promptly ran off, in the opposite direction to which he wanted to go.

'Boris!' he shouted angrily. 'Come back here!' But the bull-mastiff had already raced away further down the beach.

'Blasted dog!' Annoyed, Hogg realized that he would have to wait for the animal to come back of his own volition. Meanwhile, he walked down to the water's edge to inspect the package. Squinting against the sun, he was almost on top of it before he understood what he was looking at. 'Bloody hell!' Dropping the dog's leash at his feet, Hogg fumbled in his pocket for his mobile. Ignoring the barking from down the beach, he quickly dialled 999.

It was way too early in the day to start on the green tea. After a terrible, weak mug of lukewarm coffee and a stale pastry in the all-night café under Charing Cross arches, Carlyle morosely made his way to the station. It was still barely 6.30 when he approached the front desk and he was insufficiently alert to acknowledge the man hovering at the corner of his vision.

'Inspector Carlyle?'

Frowning, Carlyle turned to face a dapper man of similar height and age to himself, with a rapidly receding hairline and a pair of glasses that were too big for his face. He was well turned out for the early hour, in a pinstripe suit, with a white shirt and red tie. In his left hand was an oversized black leather briefcase.

Not waiting for a reply, the man extended his free hand. 'Trevor Cole,' he smiled. 'Gotha Insurance. I'm here about the St James's Diamonds incident.'

Stifling a groan, Carlyle shook the insurance agent's hand. 'Come with me,' he said, gesturing towards the bowels of the building.

Parking the insurance assessor in interview room B3, the inspector went off in search of more coffee. After a few minutes, he returned with a couple of paper cups full of oily black liquid to find Cole happily ensconced behind a pile of paperwork three inches thick. On Carlyle's side of the table he had placed a business card, giving an office address in EC4.

'Sorry,' said Carlyle, placing the cups carefully on the table, 'there's no milk, but at least it's hot.'

'That's fine,' Cole said politely. 'Thank you.' He peered into his cup but made no effort to pick it up. With a nod of his head, he gestured at the remains of the bullet camera hanging from the ceiling in the corner. 'What happened to that?'

Carlyle shrugged. 'Dunno.' Taking a seat, he gingerly tasted the coffee and tried not to wince. 'Okay,' he said, once he'd regained his composure, 'where do you want to start?'

Cole picked the top document from his pile and handed it to Carlyle. 'This is a list of the items that are missing from St James's Diamonds following the robbery.'

'Thanks.' Carlyle counted eight sheets of A4 paper stapled together in the top left-hand corner. He scanned the neatly typed, single spaced list of jewellery, with their prices attached:

A single stone diamond ring, the round brilliant-cut diamond weighing 4.05 cts of H colour, SI1 clarity, with Gemmological Laboratory certificate number 3001518968, eight-claw set to a platinum crown collet, with tapered D-section shank, cheniered shoulders, hallmarked platinum London 2002, *gross weight 5.3 grams – £98,000.*

A fin-de-siècle *dragonfly brooch, the two pairs of wings encrusted with rose and old brilliant-cut diamonds, silver set to a pierced gold mount, wingspan 6.1 cm, a curved tail of nine graduated oval pearls, set in gold and measuring 3.9 cm, the body of an oval shape faceted emerald, eight-claw set to a gold mount, the head encrusted with rose-cut diamonds and cabochon-cut ruby eyes, the legs of carved gold, gross weight 15.1 grams, circa 1860 – £18,250.*

10 × Picos Chronograph Watch in stainless steel with black rubber and silver and black dial. Size large, 42 mm case, chronograph function, mechanical movement with automatic winding, date window, water resistant to 100 metres/328 feet (10 bars), Swiss-made – £5,300.

A single stone diamond ring, the round brilliant-cut diamond weighing 6.06 cts, of F colour, VVS1 clarity, Precious Stone Laboratory certificate number 4002318781, four double claw-set to a platinum collet, to a tapered D-section shank with tapered baguette-cut diamond-set shoulders, bearing the Evelyn Shaw *sponsor mark, gross weight 7.1 grams – £495,580.*

£495,580? It slowly dawned on him that the price was almost half a million pounds. For a fucking ring! *Holy shit!* Carlyle's brain went into overdrive, bombarding him with questions. How much had he spent on Helen's engagement ring? He couldn't remember. How many years would he have to work, to earn that kind of money? After tax? He couldn't work it out. Many, many decades was the best he could come up with. Resisting the urge to let out a low whistle, he looked up at Cole. 'How much in total?'

Cole pointed to the papers in Carlyle's hands. 'It's on page eight.'

Carlyle quickly flipped to the last page and the number in bold at the bottom. This time he did whistle. 'My God,' he said, dropping the list onto the table. 'You mean to tell me that these comedians got away with almost forty million quid's worth of gear?'

Cole clasped his hands together, as if in prayer. 'Not exactly, Inspector,' he said.

Carlyle frowned. 'What do you mean, "not exactly"?'

'Well,' Cole explained, 'a preliminary review of the security cameras seems to suggest that not all of the items went missing in the course of the robbery.'

How were you able to review the CCTV pictures already? Carlyle wondered. However, he let the point slide as he waited for Cole to spell it out.

'There are at least three items on that list,' Cole continued evenly, 'that we believe were in the store when the police arrived.'

Carlyle quickly held up a hand. The last thing he needed now was *two* cases of theft to deal with. 'If you let me have a copy of your report,' he said, sitting up straight to convey the seriousness with which he was taking the matter, 'I will look through all of this in detail. You can rest assured that it is my intention to recover all of your property as quickly as possible. In the meantime, I will keep you informed of all developments.'

'Thank you,' Cole smiled. 'Of course, these items are not the property of my company. We simply have a significant financial exposure . . .'

'How much?' Carlyle asked.

The smile drained from Cole's face, to be replaced by the kind of sadness that only money can bring. 'I believe,' he said quietly, 'that the items were insured for somewhere in excess of their retail value.'

'Is that common?'

'Not uncommon. Personally, I would not read anything into it.'

'So you don't think it was an inside job?'

'I would never express a view. That is for you to decide.'

Carlyle nodded, grateful that for once, someone was prepared to let him get on and do his job without telling him how to do it. He tapped the list with his index finger. 'How much do you think this stuff will fetch?'

'Once again,' Cole said weakly, 'I would not wish to be drawn on a matter that is not really my area of expertise.'

53

'We're just talking amongst ourselves,' Carlyle reassured him. 'It's not something that I'm going to hold you to.'

'Well,' Cole thought about it for a moment, 'some things may have been stolen to order, but from what we have been able to make out so far, it doesn't seem that they targeted particular pieces.'

'No,' Carlyle agreed, 'they just shot out the windows and grabbed what they could.'

'So,' Cole went on, 'assuming that they have to find a buyer, they might get ten or fifteen pence in the pound.'

'That's still six million quid. Not bad for an afternoon's work.'

'It might be less, of course. Some of the items, like the dragonfly brooch, for example, might well be unsaleable. In that case, pieces might get broken down and sold for little more than pennies.' Cole looked genuinely pained at the thought.

A question popped into Carlyle's head. 'Will you be offering a reward?'

'That is not our policy in cases like this.' Cole looked at him steadily. 'At least, not at this stage.'

'I understand.' Carlyle got to his feet and picked Cole's card off the desk, along with the list of stolen items. 'Thank you for these,' he said. 'I will be in touch.'

Cole carefully replaced the remainder of the papers in his bag and got to his feet, glancing apologetically at his untouched coffee.

'Don't worry about that,' Carlyle said. 'Let me show you out.'

Standing on the steps of the station, Carlyle shook Trevor Cole's hand with more enthusiasm than he had when they had first met. *It's funny*, he thought to himself, *how a little bit of respect goes a long way in terms of goodwill.* At that moment, the inspector actually wanted to get the stolen jewellery back – for Cole, if not for the store's owner.

As Cole disappeared round the corner, Carlyle turned and skipped up the steps of the station, running straight into a woman who had been standing behind him.

'Sorry.' Carlyle took a half-step backwards, trying not to fall.

'Good morning, Inspector,' the woman said imperiously.

Carlyle stared back blankly.

'Abigail Slater.'

'Ah, yes,' he mumbled, wondering just how she knew who he was. Taking another step backwards, he checked the lawyer out. She was dressed in an expensive-looking red jacket and skirt combination, with the skirt rather shorter than you might expect for a Catholic lawyer. Under heavy make-up, she looked tired but determined.

'I was looking for you,' Slater continued, reaching into her shoulder bag and pulling out an envelope.

'What's this?' Carlyle asked, making no effort to take it from her.

'It is a copy of the letter that has gone to your commanding officer,' Slater said, her tone almost gleeful, 'outlining your assault on Father McGowan and the legal action we will be taking, both against yourself, Sergeant Roche and the Metropolitan Police Force.' She pinned the letter to his chest with an index finger, forcing him to take it from her.

Why not the Prime Minister and the Queen as well? Carlyle thought sarcastically, but he managed not to say anything.

'I would start making plans for your post-police career if I were you.' Slater grinned maliciously as she began to pick her way down the steps.

On the pavement, Carlyle watched her pause, waiting to see if he had a reply. But he wasn't going to give her the pleasure. Instead, he stuffed the envelope into the back pocket of his jeans and walked slowly back inside.

From behind the counter, Myron Sabo nodded to Alison Roche as she walked into the Box café and headed for the table by the window.

'The desk told me I'd find you here,' she said, pulling out a chair and sitting down.

Looking up, Carlyle grunted. He signalled to Myron that he'd like another green tea, while Roche ordered an orange juice.

Picking up the sheet of paper on the table, she turned it round so that she could read it. 'What's this?'

Carlyle sat back in his chair and yawned. It wasn't yet 9 a.m. but he already felt exhausted. 'It's a letter from McGowan's lawyer to Dugdale saying that they're suing the Met and they want my head on a plate. The bitch hand-delivered me a copy at the station this morning. She knew exactly who I was, as well.'

'It's not that difficult,' Roche grinned. 'After all, how many dashing young inspectors are there in Charing Cross?'

Not in the mood to have his leg pulled, Carlyle shot her a dirty look.

Roche sighed. 'She probably Googled you.'

'But I'm not on fucking Google.'

'Everyone's on the internet, these days. All you can hope for is that you've got some of your clothes on.' Roche scanned the letter then read it again carefully from the top. 'So much for keeping me out of it.'

'Sorry.'

'Anyway,' she continued, dropping the letter back on the table, 'I spoke to Dr Weber last night. His report will be pure vanilla – it puts us in the clear.'

Carlyle smiled, appreciating her use of the word 'us'. Roche hadn't walked away from his stupidity and he would remember that. Myron appeared with the drinks. Carlyle nodded his thanks and took a sip of his tea; not as good as Helen's, but not bad. He gestured at the letter with his mug. 'Slater's got her own doctor to take a look at McGowan and he, of course, will take a different view.'

Roche shrugged. 'So, she pays some guy to say what she wants him to say, big deal. Let her go to the IPCC, let her sue, there's nothing there that you haven't dealt with before. The Met will handle it.'

'We'll see.' Carlyle drank some more of his tea. Roche was probably right, but he couldn't be sure. Certainly the Independent Police Complaints Commission was nothing to worry about. Still, he would be happier when Simpson was back from Canada and Dugdale was out of the picture. That meant dragging the process out for a couple of months, and the best way to do that would be to track down Simon Murphy. 'We need to find the kid.'

Roche knew as well as he did that they had no leads and no time to dig any up. 'Let's see if we can get this jewellery business sorted and then maybe we can try and find him,' she suggested.

'Okay,' Carlyle said, unconvinced. 'What have you got?'

Roche reached into her bag and took out a small notebook. Flicking through the pages, she found her notes and started reading: 'St James's Diamonds was started in 1805 and was first invited to supply jewellery to the Royal Family during Queen Victoria's reign. It was in the same family for four generations, before being bought by an American private equity firm in 2005.'

'That must be who Katrin Lagerbäck works for,' Carlyle mused, outlining his meeting with Lagerbäck, as well as Trevor Cole's list of stolen items. 'There's a suggestion that some of the missing items were not taken by the robbers. They might have been nicked at the scene in the aftermath of the robbery.'

Roche thought about that for a moment. 'Lifted from the crime scene. That would take some balls. Do you really think that's likely?'

Carlyle scratched his chin. 'It's possible. Have we checked out the CCTV?'

'Not yet,' Roche sighed. 'Not enough resources. I'll see what I can do this morning.'

'Thanks.'

'Any news on the shop assistant?' Roche asked.

'No, afraid not.'

A mobile phone started ringing loudly, to the tune of 'Breathe' by The Prodigy. 'Sorry,' said Roche, reaching into her bag and peering at her BlackBerry. 'Hello?'

Carlyle watched her face darken as she said, 'Where?'

Knowing what was coming, he reached into his pocket and pulled out a fiver and some change, gesturing to Myron as he dropped it on the table.

'No.' Roche raised her eyebrows and looked at Carlyle. 'It's okay. He's with me. We'll meet the car outside the station.'

Stuffing Abigail Slater's letter back in his pocket, Carlyle got to his feet and was at the door by the time Roche finished her call. Pulling it open, he let her lead him out onto the street.

'They've found the girl,' she said, deftly sidestepping a dawdling tourist.

'Great,' Carlyle responded, following in her slipstream, not needing to ask if Paula Coulter was still alive.

ELEVEN

It was a long way from home turf. Carlyle stood shading his eyes in the middle of a massive empty space, the size of maybe half a dozen soccer pitches, five minutes from the Westway, halfway to Heathrow. Poking at some rubble with the toe of his trainers, he scanned the site, which was bathed in bright sunlight. It had been completely cleared and fenced off but, aside from a couple of Portakabins in one corner, there was no sign of any impending building work. 'What is this place?' he asked.

Standing ten feet away, Alison Roche pushed her sunglasses back up her nose and said, 'This was going to be the Lex West Central Business Park. Then came the financial crash and its Arab backers pulled out. They're still arguing with the developers over who's responsible for it. The Mayor's been talking about letting local residents use it as an allotment.'

'The Mayor,' Carlyle snorted, shaking his head. 'Gawd bless him.' He looked across at the crumpled body of Paula Coulter, who was being fussed over by a pathologist, with a couple of technicians in tow. 'I guess it wasn't an inside job then.'

Roche wandered closer to the body. 'Not involving her, at least.'

Carlyle, squeamish at the best of times, had no intention of following his sergeant. He was near enough to see that Paula, face down, still in her work clothes, had been shot in the head. He was unlikely to gain any stunning insights into her demise by getting any closer to the corpse.

'What have we got?' Roche asked the pathologist, a fat, middle-aged guy called Evan Stone, who worked out of the Ealing station.

'Well . . .' Stone, on his haunches, tried to turn to face Roche and fell on his backside. Not bothering to get up, he pulled a handkerchief from his pocket and dabbed at the beads of sweat on his forehead. 'For some reason, her killer felt the need to shoot her both in the face and in the back of the head.'

'Idiots,' Carlyle grumbled, under his breath. 'Was it the same gun that was used in the robbery?'

From behind her sunglasses, Roche shot him a rather exasperated look. 'Too early to tell,' she replied for the pathologist.

'Fair enough,' Carlyle said, returning her glare in a way that suggested he did not think it a *totally* unreasonable question.

'Both shots were from close range,' Stone continued, ignoring their little spat. 'Either would have been more than enough to kill her.'

'So why shoot her twice?' Roche asked, still glaring at Carlyle.

The pathologist looked down at the corpse as if it might offer up the explanation. 'Maybe they thought they could try and delay identification of the body.'

Carlyle asked Roche, 'How *did* we identify her?'

Roche pointed to the girl's feet. 'She has a tattoo on her left ankle, a snake. It's an Indian King Cobra, according to her mum. Paula was very proud of it, apparently.'

Carlyle couldn't see anything but nodded anyway.

'Time of death was around ten hours ago,' said the pathologist in a monotone fashion as he ticked off the key points in his head. 'I'd say she died sometime before midnight last night. She was shot somewhere else,' he gestured across the empty ground, 'maybe at another location on this site, before being dumped here.' Pushing himself to his feet, he stuck his handkerchief in his pocket and brushed the dirt off his trousers. 'I'll let you have a preliminary report by the end of the day.'

'Thanks.' Head down, the inspector began marching back towards his waiting car.

Strains of Arcade Fire's 'Black Mirror' came from inside the police BMW. Sitting behind the wheel, the driver finished munching on an apple and tossed the core out of the window. Listening to his stomach rumble, Carlyle leaned against the bonnet and watched Roche finish her conversation with one of the technicians and begin to walk towards him. Off to his left, he saw an ambulance trundle over the uneven ground, heading for the little group clustered around the body. Pulling out his mobile, he called Helen. It went to voicemail immediately and he ended the call without leaving a message.

'They're taking her to the West Middlesex,' Roche said, stopping a couple of feet in front of him.

'Fair enough.' Carlyle had no intention of going there himself. He hated hospitals and he doubly hated morgues; he was quite happy to wait for Stone to email him a report. He jerked a thumb over Roche's left shoulder. 'What did the tech guys have to say?'

'Like Stone said, they presume someone drove in and dumped Paula's body after she'd been killed. But there are lots of different vehicle tracks, so that probably won't give us much.'

Carlyle looked around unhappily. 'No CCTV, of course?'

'No,' Roche told him. 'Since the money ran out, there's effectively been next to no site security. Anyone could have got in.'

'Witnesses?' Carlyle could hardly be bothered to ask the question.

'Nothing, so far.' Roche gave the impression that she could hardly be bothered to give the answer. 'The local uniforms are going door to door, but there isn't much residential round here; it's mainly small workshops and a few offices.'

Carlyle pushed himself off the car and signalled to the driver that they were ready to go. 'Let's get back to Charing Cross and start picking out some suspects.'

TWELVE

After three hours of going through the forensic reports and the CCTV footage of the St James's Diamonds raid, Carlyle was losing the will to live. Picking his mobile off the desk, he looked at the screen morosely. For once, it wasn't telling him that he had missed any calls. Why hadn't Helen tried to return his call? Most likely she was having a tough day at work too. Chief Operating Officer of a medical charity called Avalon, she was responsible for a growing team of several people in thirty countries, which meant that there was a crisis somewhere. Sighing, he looked at the clock on the wall. It was almost 7 p.m. and he knew that he should be heading home.

'Dugdale's on the TV.' Roche appeared from behind him with a remote in her hand, unmuting the monitor that hung from the ceiling above them.

'Again?' Carlyle frowned. He looked at the Commander, sitting next to his PR flunky, in front of a large Met logo, with the legend *Working together for a safer London* spelled out in foot-high letters, as he prepared to make a statement to the assembled journalists. Dugdale seemed tired, washed-out, like a man who was just going through the motions until someone unlocked his pension pot and put him out of his misery. Not for the first time, the inspector cursed Simpson for fucking off to Canada on some jolly when she should be in London watching his back. In other words, doing her job.

'He did an impromptu press conference on New Bond Street after you left yesterday,' Roche explained, gesturing at the screen with the remote.

'Where is he now?' Carlyle asked.

Roche shrugged. 'Dunno. Paddington Green, I suppose.'

'Makes sense,' Carlyle said. Dugdale had taken over Simpson's office in Paddington Green police station for the duration of his secondment.

'He's giving them some of the CCTV footage,' Roche added.

Carlyle grunted. As far as he was concerned, press conferences were the first refuge of the brainless and the desperate. He listened to Dudgale confirm that Paula Coulter's body had been found that morning and watched as a clip of the raid jerked across the screen in slow motion. Once it had finished, grainy stills of the two robbers flashed up on the screen.

'Maybe they've left the country,' Roche mused, muting the sound.

'Fuck it,' Carlyle yawned. 'What a shit day. Let's quit while we're ahead. We can start again tomorrow.' Standing up, he closed the file on his desk and dropped the mobile into his jacket pocket. The landline on his desk started ringing. He looked at it for a moment then reluctantly picked it up. 'Carlyle,' he said wearily.

'Inspector, Dugdale here.'

Carlyle smacked his hand on the desk. *Why did you pick up the phone, you fucking idiot?* 'Commander,' he said, trying to keep the annoyance from his voice, 'we've just seen you on the news.'

'I wasn't calling about that,' Dugdale said gruffly.

'Oh?' Carlyle looked at Roche, who was hovering by his desk. Shaking his head, he pointed to the door, signalling that he would call her later.

'No,' Dugdale replied, the anger rising in his voice. 'What the hell have you been doing?'

'Excuse me?' Carlyle watched Roche disappear into the lift, a sick feeling growing in this stomach.

'This woman . . .' down the line came the sound of papers being shuffled. '. . . Slater – she says that you assaulted a priest.'

'I've seen the letter,' Carlyle sighed. 'Father McGowan is under investigation in connection with the disappearance of—'

Dugdale cut him off. 'Did you or your sergeant assault this man, or not?'

'No, sir,' said Carlyle without hesitation.

'Well, you had better speak to the Federation about representation. There will have to be a disciplinary enquiry. They are going to sue.'

Carlyle gritted his teeth. 'Yes, sir.'

'If you did assault this man, Carlyle,' Dugdale said, with more than a hint of malice in his voice, 'I will have you straight out of the sodding door, without your deal.'

What deal?

'In the meantime, leave the bloody priest alone. This diamonds case has to be your priority, your *only* priority. It was bad enough even before that girl was killed. We need to demonstrate some immediate and substantive progress.'

'Yes, sir.'

'Keep me posted.'

'Yes—' Before Carlyle could finish, Dugdale ended the call and the line went dead. A righteous anger welled up inside him. 'Fuck you too, you timeserving cunt,' he hissed, slamming down the phone. A nearby cleaner gave him a curious look, but Carlyle ignored her as he skulked out of the building.

THIRTEEN

Arriving back at the flat, Carlyle heard the sound of the television playing in the living room. He vaguely remembered something about Alice being away on a sleepover, so he presumed it was Helen watching one of the crap 'reality' shows that she was partial to. Wanting to take the edge off his bad mood before engaging with his wife, he wandered into the kitchen and took a bottle of Heineken from the fridge. Pulling a bottle-opener from a drawer, he flicked off the cap and took a long swig. He wasn't much of a drinker, but after a day like the one he'd just had, the cold beer slipped down very nicely indeed.

Stepping over to the sink, he finished his beer as he watched an airliner heading towards Heathrow. Out of the corner of his eye, he noticed the letters from the previous evening still sitting on top of the microwave. Placing the empty beer bottle on the worktop, he reached over, picked up the top envelope and casually ripped it open. Inside was a single sheet of white A4 paper, with the Met logo at the top. Unfolding it, he scanned the contents.

This is to inform you that you could be eligible for voluntary redundancy and/or early retirement . . .

Scowling, he read the letter more carefully. Recalling the recent memo from the union, he felt his immediate angst subside. He already needed to speak to his Federation rep in the morning, so this was just something else for them to talk about.

Taking another beer from the fridge, he opened it and padded into the living room. Sitting on the sofa with her feet up on the coffee table, Helen was watching one of the news channels. Once again, he saw the

CCTV clip from the robbery that had been released to the media, jerk across the screen in slow motion. Helen muted the TV and smiled at him wanly. *You look absolutely shattered*, he thought, suddenly guilty at the lack of attention he had been paying to home matters recently.

'Busy day?' she enquired.

'I was just going to ask you the same thing,' he grinned, placing his beer bottle on the table. Plopping down on the sofa, he kissed her on the cheek and dropped the letter in her lap. 'Look at this.'

Reluctantly, Helen picked up the sheet of paper and looked it over expressionlessly. Carlyle found her reaction rather disconcerting. Normally, his wife was more exercised by his so-called 'career' than Carlyle was himself. Her obvious lack of interest this evening suggested that something was wrong.

'It's a pain in the arse,' he said, 'but the Union have already got it sorted. I'll speak to them tomorrow but basically I think we just have to sit it out and do nothing. They'll have plenty of people biting their hands off to go.'

'Did you see the other letter?' she asked, her gaze firmly trained on the television.

'The other letter?'

'It's in the kitchen.'

Grumbling to himself, Carlyle jumped to his feet and trotted back to the kitchen. The small envelope remaining on top of the microwave had already been opened. It was a bland, pale green colour. Helen's name and address had been carefully handwritten on the front. Noticing that the stamp had been stuck on the wrong way round, leaving the Queen's head upside down, Carlyle grinned as he pulled out the two sheets of blue notepaper inside and quickly scanned their contents.

Oh fuck.

He felt a terrible pressure on his skull and had to fight the strong urge to puke his beer into the sink. Placing the letter on the worktop, he stared blankly at the neat penmanship for a few seconds and then forced himself to reread the whole thing slowly and painstakingly, line by line. Reaching the bottom of the page for a second time, he realized that he had been holding his breath. Like a diver breaking the water's surface, he exhaled deeply. His mouth was dry and he could feel his heart going crazy inside his chest. *Calm down*, he told himself; *do not rant and rave. You have to walk next door and say exactly the right thing, do exactly the right thing.*

Picking up the letter, he headed out of the room feeling more scared than he had ever done in his entire life.

Sitting back down on the sofa, he put an arm round Helen, kissing her hard as he pulled her towards him.

'Oh, John!' she sobbed, burying her head in his chest.

'It's fine,' he said, squeezing her tenderly. 'It will be fine. We will handle this.' Gently stroking the back of her neck, he held up the letter with his free hand. Already, he felt as if he knew it off by heart:

Like me, you may be a carrier of a faulty breast cancer suscep-tibility gene, known as BRCA2. This means an increased risk of developing breast and / or ovarian cancer at an early age (i.e. before menopause). Blood tests are available to detect BRCA2 mutations. Not all people wish to get tested, but it is something to think about. Your GP can also tell you about counselling.

After a few minutes sitting in silence, he asked about the woman who had sent the letter: 'Who is Amanda Soames?'

Wiping her nose on his shirt, Helen sat up. 'She's my dad's younger sister. His mother and two of his sisters have all had breast cancer. One of the sisters died when she was thirty-eight.'

Jesus fucking Christ on a bike. It dawned on Carlyle that he knew next to nothing about Helen's family. Aside from her parents, he couldn't recall having ever met any of them. Her dad was long dead. He had keeled over with a massive heart attack in his early fifties, after her mum had dumped him and decamped to Brighton.

'I called her yesterday,' Helen continued. 'She was very nice. She has been part of a research project for the last two years, apparently. They suggested that she write to me. A letter is thought to be the best way to give someone the news. Mum gave her the address.'

'So what happens now?' Carlyle asked, trying to move the conversation on without sounding too brusque. *How do we make this shit go away?*

Helen took a deep breath. 'Well, I saw the GP this morning. Next week I go up to Great Ormond Street for the test. Then we have to wait for the results.'

'Great Ormond Street? I thought that was a kiddie hospital?'

Helen shrugged. 'That's where they've told me to go. Apparently, there's a guy there who is working just on this gene.'

'Fair enough. And if—'

Reaching up, she kissed him gently on the lips to shut him up. 'No ifs,' she said. 'Let's wait and see what the results say. It might be good news.'

Yeah, and it might not. 'What are the odds?'

'There's a twenty-five per cent chance that I've got it,' she said, giving him another kiss. 'They don't know if Dad had it. It would be fifty per cent if he did, zero if he didn't.'

Carlyle tried to do the maths, without success. 'So there's a more than fighting chance all this will prove to be a false alarm.'

She looked at him darkly. 'Speculating will only drive us round the bend. Let's just wait and see, shall we?'

'Okay,' he smiled, wiping away the tear from his eye.

Switching off the TV, Helen pushed herself up from the sofa and took his hand. 'C'mon,' she said, 'let's go to bed.'

FOURTEEN

Struggling to stifle a yawn, Christian Holyrod shifted in his chair and glared at his Special Adviser. Katya Morrison, a pert, twenty-something blonde Philosophy graduate from St Andrews University, gave him a quizzical look that the Mayor found intensely irritating. A powerful urge to sack her washed over him, but he knew that it would serve no purpose to do so. These political hacks were all the same – over-educated, over-privileged and over-confident. Sack Katya and another robot bimbo would just take her place. And she might not even be as well stacked.

Holyrod sighed. Really, it was all his own fault. He should never have stood for re-election; becoming Mayor of London was only ever supposed to have been a stepping stone to the Prime Minister gig. Now, after more than six years in the job, he had become hopelessly typecast. People knew him as the grinning idiot who promoted cycleways or allotments, his previous life as the warrior hero Major Holyrod, long since forgotten. Now he was just another politician – worse, a *local* politician – his chance of the top job receding even faster than his party's popularity in the polls.

Holyrod took a mouthful of coffee and tried to concentrate on the pale, puffy, bald guy in the dog collar sitting behind the desk in front of him. He looked twenty-five going on forty-five. *You need some sun and some exercise*, he thought, *not to mention a good shag*. To his bemusement, the priest had shown no interest whatsoever in Katya's tits, which had somehow been shoehorned into a completely inappropriate, see-through white cheesecloth blouse without the aid of a bra.

'There are around four and a half million Catholics in England and Wales,' Monsignor Joseph Wagner said, failing to hide his irritation at the Mayor's obvious lack of interest, 'and I know that each and every one of them is looking forward to the visit of the Holy Father next month.'

'As I am myself,' Holyrod smiled vacuously, 'which is why we are providing so much financial and logistical support for the Pope's visit.'

The Monsignor bowed graciously. 'For which we are truly very grateful.'

So you bloody should be, Holyrod thought meanly. *Millions that I don't have and extra overtime for God knows how many thousand police officers, not to mention the redeployment of the Diplomatic Protection Group, so that your guy can play two shows at Wembley. I'd better get to Heaven after all this.* 'It is just a shame that the Archbishop couldn't be with us today.'

Wagner raised his gaze to the heavens. 'I know that he would have very much liked to have been here; however, he is currently leading the annual pilgrimage to Lourdes.'

Katya started to titter and Holyrod glared at her even harder.

'As the Papal Visit Co-ordinator,' Wagner continued, ignoring the impolite young aide, 'I have just hosted a party of officials over from the Vatican for a final planning meeting. We have finalized the text for the handbook, the Missal, which will enable those who are participating in the gatherings with the Holy Father to follow the Visit, and also the merchandising and souvenirs that will be available in our online shop.'

'Very important,' Holyrod nodded.

'Of course, our work with you and with the security services is vital. We cannot allow any unauthorized access to any of the Masses or the Prayer Vigil.'

'No, no. Of course not.'

'People will be able to see that there are opportunities to greet the Pope as he is travelling around. Some of his movements will be in the Popemobile, precisely so that people can gather and greet him as he passes by, but everything has to be properly controlled.'

'As it will be.'

'Good.' Wagner hesitated. 'Of course, if it had been the case that the attitude of the British government had *always* been communicated clearly, we might have found ourselves in a somewhat better position today.'

Holyrod bridled at the reference, however oblique, to a facetious Foreign Office memo, written by some junior bureaucrat, which suggested, amongst other things, that a trip to an abortion clinic should be included on the Pope's itinerary. The leaking of the memo had been a gift to the Papal spin doctors in the Catholic Communications Network and had allowed the Church to chisel a formal apology from the Government, along with more taxpayers' money to pay for the trip.

'I think,' he said diplomatically, 'that the hundred million pounds or so – taking into account policing costs – that we are spending on this trip, at a time of great economic stress, sends a very clear message indeed as to our willingness to embrace the Pope's visit, as well as our understanding of the complexity and sophistication of the trip.'

'The Church has always made it clear that it would pay its fair share of the costs.'

'Indeed.' Holyrod smiled blandly, too polite to enquire of the Monsignor exactly how much cold, hard cash the Vatican had placed on the table so far.

'Not a penny is expected from public funds for those aspects of the visit which are an expression simply of the Catholic faith.'

'That is very fair.'

'The last Papal visit to the United Kingdom, thirty years ago, left the Church some six million pounds in debt.'

A tiny drop in the ocean for you, Holyrod observed. 'Was there anything else?' he asked, signalling to Katya that it was time to leave.

'Well, the Archbishop asked me to raise a couple of things.'

Get on with it then, Holyrod could feel his last reserves of patience and diplomacy evaporate. 'Yes?'

'Nothing can be allowed to spoil this visit.'

'Quite.'

'So we were wondering just what . . . arrangements were being made with regards to Roger Leyne?'

Holyrod glanced across at Katya, who stared back at him blankly. 'I'm sorry, Monsignor,' he said. 'Who?'

Wagner gave him a disappointed look. 'Leyne is the so-called "philosopher" who is leading a campaign to use international criminal rules to try to detain the Pontiff while he is in the UK.'

Holyrod shrugged.

Kayta suddenly perked up. 'Ah yes,' she smiled, relieved to finally have something vaguely relevant to contribute to the conversation. 'They want to bring a private prosecution in relation to the Pope's alleged cover-up of sexual abuse in the Catholic Church. The current rules are inadequate because the evidence required to get a warrant is far below the threshold that would be needed to bring a prosecution. The Justice Secretary was supposed to change the rules so that the Director of Public Prosecutions would need to give his consent to any arrest warrant issued under universal jurisdiction – the law that allows individuals to be prosecuted in the UK for crimes against humanity. Of course, the DPP would have nixed any attempt to arrest the Holy Father.'

Thank you, Miss Know It All. Holyrod glanced at his watch. A sense of despair crept up on him as he realized that he was already half an hour late for his next appointment, a school visit in Victoria. He never realized just how much he hated children until he'd started this job.

'But,' Katya continued, 'for some reason, it didn't happen. Some administrative mix-up, I think.'

'Sounds like the Justice Secretary to me,' Holyrod grunted.

A pained look swept across the Monsignor's face. 'So, therefore, the Archbishop was wondering what arrangements are in place for the Metropolitan Police to deal with Mr Leyne?'

Arrangements? Holyrod scoffed silently. *What the hell are you talking about? We're not a police state.* 'I'll look into it,' he said, slowly lifting himself out of his seat.

'Thank you,' said the Monsignor.

'My pleasure.'

Before he could make a bolt for the door, Katya piped up again. 'What was the other thing that the Archbishop wanted to raise?' she asked brightly.

Sitting back down, Holyrod wanted to throttle her.

'It's a rather delicate situation,' said Wagner.

Holyrod folded his arms and waited.

Wagner cleared his throat. 'It appears that one of our lawyers is suing the Metropolitan Police. The Archbishop would like the matter to be resolved before the Pope's visit.'

Holyrod sighed wearily. Putting the police under greater political control had been one of the great innovations of his first term. Overall, it had worked well, limiting the Met's ability to embarrass or annoy him. However, the downside was that everyone now felt that there was nothing he couldn't sort out personally, from arrests to parking tickets. Wagner and Katya both looked at him expectantly. With great reluctance, he asked the question: 'Why are you suing the police force?'

'One of our priests, Father Francis McGowan of St Boniface's in Farringdon, was assaulted in a police station,' said Wagner quietly, 'by a couple of your officers.'

My officers? Holyrod looked at Katya and frowned.

Wagner picked up a piece of paper from his desk and squinted at a name scribbled in the margin. 'The main one is an inspector by the name of . . . Carlyle.'

'Carlyle?' said Holyrod incredulously. 'John Carlyle?'

Wagner nodded.

'At Charing Cross?'

Wagner nodded again.

For a second, the Mayor sat there, stunned as a slew of unhappy memories flooded his brain. Then he jumped to his feet. 'Give Katya the details,' he said sharply as he bounded towards the door, 'and I will look into it immediately.' This time, he fled before the priest could ask for anything more.

FIFTEEN

Created by the Police Act 1919, a year after a controversial strike by the unrecognized National Union of Police and Prison Officers, the Police Federation was arguably one of the most effective trade unions in history, successfully looking after the interests of 140,000 police constables, sergeants, inspectors and chief inspectors for almost a century. One of the main reasons for its success was that it spent three-quarters of its annual budget on legal services for its members.

As far as John Carlyle was concerned, membership was £250 a year very well spent indeed. Sitting patiently in a nondescript office, just north of Oxford Street, he watched his union rep slowly sift through a handful of papers on the desk in front of him. The guy, a spotty, twenty-something called Geoff, with a stupid, over-gelled haircut, was 'his' rep, only in the sense that he had picked up the phone when Carlyle had rung to make the appointment the day before. On first impression, Carlyle seriously doubted that the young man would be much use in his fight against the forces of darkness, aka the Catholic Legal Network and Commander Dugdale. With everything else that was going on at the moment, the last thing the inspector needed was the office junior taking his case. However, given the mess he had dropped himself in this time, he realized that it was imperative to have the union on board. Anyway, if things got really tough, he could always ditch the kid and demand some grown-up support.

Finishing his reading, Geoff looked over at Carlyle nervously, as if he was worried that the Inspector might bite.

'And you're denying all these accusations?' he asked, letting the papers fall on the desk.

Carlyle smiled the smile of a gracious but wronged man. 'Absolutely.'

Geoff nodded uncertainly. 'Your line manager, Commander . . . Dugdale seems to be rather concerned.'

'Dugdale is filling in for my regular boss. He wants to play it by the book, which is fair enough.' Carlyle shrugged. 'I think he is spooked by the threat of legal action.'

'Unlike you,' Geoff deadpanned.

'I can only tell you what happened,' Carlyle said evenly. 'I cannot speculate as to the possible motivation of Father McGowan or his lawyer for these baseless accusations.'

The young man seemed disconcerted by Carlyle's apparent reasonableness. 'No, no,' he agreed, 'of course not.'

Carlyle gestured at the papers on the desk. 'So, how shall we proceed?'

'Well,' Geoff let out a deep breath, 'I will speak to Commander Dugdale's office and also to the Met's Legal Department, in order to ascertain where they intend going with this. Then I will report to our legal team here and contact you to discuss next steps.'

'Sounds good.'

A relieved look spread over Geoff's face as he could see the meeting drawing to a close. Scooping up the paperwork, he placed it carefully in a plastic folder. A sticker in the top left-hand corner had *Carlyle* written on it in a childish hand.

'There's one other thing,' Carlyle said.

'Oh?' Geoff looked worried again.

'Yes.' Carlyle pulled the redundancy letter out of his pocket, unfolded it and handed it across the table. 'I got one of these in the post yesterday.'

The union man gave it a quick once-over and handed it back. 'Ah yes,' he said, 'we've seen lots of these. If you're interested, give HR a call and see what they're offering, otherwise just ignore it.'

'Understood.' Carlyle stuffed the letter back in his pocket. 'Is it a good deal?'

Getting to his feet, Geoff grinned. 'That depends on the individual. They are legally obliged to offer everyone the same; it'll be a lump sum based on time served and a reduced pension. Whether it might work for you will depend on your circumstances. Given the squeeze on finances, the received wisdom is that any future offers won't be so generous, but you just don't know.'

'No, I suppose you don't.' Carlyle got to his feet and shook the young man's hand.

'My view,' said Geoff, as he showed him to the door, 'and it's not the Federation speaking, is that there's no harm in asking. They are not allowed to take that as an indication that you want to leave, so they can't hold it against you, but at least you get all the right information. If you're going to think about it, you have to have all the information at your fingertips.'

'Fair point,' said Carlyle, already wondering just how lumpy his lump sum might be.

Alison Roche sat in the corner of the One Eyed Serpent pub, just off the Bayswater Road in West London. Taking a sip from her pint of Hoegaarden, she placed her glass back down on the table and began flicking through the evening paper. Amid all the usual boring shit, a headline caught her eye: ENGLISH TEACHER QUITS CLASSROOM FOR PORN CAREER. Beneath a picture of a rather plain-looking woman, the text read: *Jennie Mills, a supply teacher in Fulham, will star in erotic films produced by Lewisham-based Jellybaby Pictures two days a week. Ms Mills, twenty-eight, said: 'I am only doing it part-time as there is not enough money in porn.'*

Roche started laughing. 'You have got to be joking!'

'Something amusing?'

Closing the paper and dropping it back in her bag, Roche looked up. 'Not really,' she sighed. 'More bizarre than funny.' She smiled but didn't get up. 'How are you, Sam?'

Samuel Smallbone placed his pint next to hers. Slipping off his leather biker jacket, he dropped it over the back of a chair. 'I'm good,' he said, taking a seat. 'Really good.' His sandy hair and youthful visage were the same as Roche remembered from the last time she'd arrested him, but the bags under his eyes were darker and his pupils were widely dilated. He looked wired.

The sergeant gave him a stern look. 'Are you using?'

Lifting the pint to his lips, Smallbone said. 'Nah.' He took a sip and coughed. 'I only do a cheeky line now and again, it's nothing serious.'

'Sam!'

A worried frown creased his forehead. 'It's nothing.' He looked around and mumbled, 'Anyway, I'm not carrying.'

'You'd better not be. It would be good if you could stay out of trouble for a while.'

Smallbone held up his hands in mock surrender. 'I'm doing my best!'

Having arrested Samuel Smallbone five times in as many years – four times for robbery and once for possession – Roche doubted that very much. Taking another drink, she looked at her watch. Her boyfriend had offered to cook dinner and she didn't want to be late. 'Still living with your mum?'

He blushed slightly, which, suspending disbelief for a second, she found almost endearing. 'Yeah.'

There was a lull in the conversation while each of them sipped their pints.

'You're looking nice,' Smallbone said finally.

'Sam,' she said patiently, 'I'm a police officer, you're a criminal. That's not a good combination, socially speaking. Don't try and hit on me.'

'I'm not! It's just . . .'

Roche took another mouthful of beer and placed the glass to one side. It was still almost half-full but she'd had enough. 'Look,' she said, reaching for her bag, annoyed at herself for agreeing to the meeting, 'what did you want to talk to me about?'

'That diamond robbery in the West End,' said Smallbone casually, chugging down the last of his beer.

'Yes?' Roche let her bag slip back to the floor and placed her hands in her lap.

'I'm assuming that there'll be a reward for information.'

'That depends on the information,' Roche said evenly, trying not to sound too keen. It was more than likely that the little weasel was going to give her a load of old tat, but it wasn't like they were making great progress on their own.

'If I tell you where they are,' Smallbone played with his empty glass, 'what do I get?'

Roche gritted her teeth and tried to smile. She hated being jerked around by idiots, but it was part of the job. 'Where *who* are?'

'The guys who did it.'

'What are their names?' she asked a tad too eagerly.

'Dunno,' he laughed, happy that she had taken the bait. 'What I *do* know is that a couple of berks are going round with a bag full of gear they don't know how to sell. And I know where they're holed up.'

'Mm.'

'So, what's it worth?'

Roche took a breath and exhaled deeply. 'If you help us catch them, I'm sure it will be a decent amount.'

Smallbone thought about it for a moment. It was almost as if she could see the cogs working in his brain. 'How much?'

Roche's mobile started ringing. Pulling it out of her pocket she glanced at the screen. *Martin*. Sadly, she concluded that the boyfriend would have to wait. Killing the call, she dropped the phone back in her pocket and looked up at Smallbone. 'The insurance company is on the hook for more than forty million,' she said, 'so it's bound to be a lot.'

'Give me a number.'

For God's sake, Roche fumed, *just tell me the bloody address*. Sighing, she got to her feet and pulled the phone back out of her pocket. 'Fair enough,' she said. 'Let me step outside and make a call. Why don't you go to the bar and get yourself another beer?'

Roche watched Smallbone slope off to the bar, picked up her bag and stepped outside. On the pavement, she put breathing distance between herself and the small knot of drinkers who had come outside for a smoke, and rang Carlyle. He picked up on the fourth ring.

'How's it going?'

You sound tired, Roche thought. *Maybe you should take a break.* 'I'm fine. I just need to run something past you.'

'Do you think this guy is genuine?' Carlyle asked when she'd finished explaining the situation.

'I think Sam's a complete tosser,' Roche reflected, 'and not the sharpest tool in the box. But he could know something. After all, he does mix in the right circles – he's done a couple of jewellery-store jobs in the past, albeit nothing remotely in this league, and one of his uncles is a known fence.'

'Criminal royalty,' Carlyle grunted.

'Hardly,' Roche replied, 'but he is potentially plausible.'

Carlyle laughed. '*Potentially* plausible – I love it.'

'Anyway,' Roche continued, 'it's not like we've got a whole lot else to chase down at the moment.'

'I suppose not.' Carlyle yawned. 'How much does he want?'

Roche watched a cab go slowly past. In the back, a young couple were arguing vigorously. 'Dunno,' she said. 'We don't know how much the insurance company will pay.'

'Tell him a million.'

'Yeah?'

'Fuck it, why not. If it comes to it, he can argue the toss with the insurance company. Just get the address and I'll round up the troops.'

SIXTEEN

Carlyle stood on the corner of Exeter Road as he watched the uniformed officers move slowly into place. Willesden Green wasn't a neighbourhood he was familiar with and the inspector felt slightly disconcerted at having to run such a high-profile operation so far away from what he would consider familiar turf. Roche appeared at his shoulder and pointed towards a black taxi parked about a hundred yards down St Gabriel's Road. 'That's 137, where that cab's parked. They've got the ground-floor flat, apparently.'

Carlyle sniggered. 'I hope your source hasn't started spending his reward yet.'

'The little sod made me write the offer out on a beer mat,' Roche laughed.

'Seriously?'

'Yeah,' Roche grinned. 'An IOU for a million quid.'

'I hope you didn't sign it.'

'I did what I had to do,' Roche said primly. 'But if you look closely, you might be able to make out that it says M. Mouse, rather than A. Roche.'

Carlyle chuckled. 'Good for you. Let's just hope it's not a Mickey Mouse tip.'

'Ha, very good, boss.'

Carlyle looked down the street. A small band of curious onlookers had gathered behind the police tape, mobile phones at the ready to record any drama. Worse were the cameras he couldn't see but knew were there all the same. To his left, a small tower block gave a great vantage-point for anyone wanting to film their operation. God knows how many cameras were trained on him right now. It was impossible to keep anything under wraps any more.

'This is going to be bollocks,' he hissed. 'I just know it.' But he was happy to be out and about, running around kicking in doors, rather than moping around worrying about everything under the sun.

Roche's phone went off in her hand. She opened up a text and sighed. 'Martin's pissed off because I blew out dinner.'

Carlyle watched a uniformed sergeant in a crash helmet and Kevlar body armour jog slowly towards them. 'Martin?'

Did Roche blush slightly? It was hard to tell as she gazed into the middle distance. 'The boyfriend.'

'A copper?'

'No,' she said firmly. 'No more coppers for me.'

'Smart thinking.'

The uniformed sergeant came to a halt in front of them. 'We're good to go.'

'Any sign of life inside?' Roche asked.

'Lights are on, but we haven't seen anyone so far.'

Roche looked at Carlyle. 'Do we want to wait?'

'Nah,' Carlyle shook his head. 'Let's get on with it before any TV shows up. I'll go in with the armed officers once they've gone through the door. Come in behind me but, remember, we have to assume that there are guys in there who are armed and dangerous.'

At the second time of asking, the door smashed open with a satisfying crash. Job done, the officer wielding the battering ram stepped aside and let the clearing party bound inside. Following on behind, the inspector stood patiently in the hallway and let the trio of officers brandishing Heckler & Koch P30 semi-automatic weapons check each room in the flat. According to his watch it took them approximately twelve seconds to establish that the flat was empty and jog back past him without even a nod of recognition. Slipping on a pair of latex gloves, he told the waiting forensics team that he wanted a couple of minutes before signalling for Roche to join him.

The flat was, he guessed, maybe about seven hundred square feet, five rooms off a central hall. He moved from the living room to the bedrooms, taking in the scene. The place was in complete disarray, with discarded fast-food wrappers and old newspapers everywhere. The kitchen was worse and the bathroom looked like it had been completely trashed.

'God!' Roche groaned once they had completed a quick tour of the premises. 'What a mess!'

'Plenty for the forensics boys to get their teeth into,' Carlyle observed, 'but nothing on first glance to suggest that your boy is going to be getting his million quid.' Carefully picking his way back outside, he signalled to the technicians that the place was all theirs.

Outside, the night air was chill and Carlyle suddenly had a hankering for some whiskey, just a little drink to take the edge off things and help him sleep. He pulled out his mobile and called home. Helen answered on the third ring.

'Hi,' she said sleepily, 'I knew it would be you.'

'I didn't wake you, did I?'

'No, no. I was just watching some TV. When will you be home?'

Carlyle explained the aborted raid. 'We're just finishing up here. I should be an hour or so. Don't wait up.'

Helen laughed. 'I won't. Don't be long.'

'I won't. Lots of love.'

'You too.'

As he ended the call, the phone immediately began vibrating in his hand.

'Carlyle.'

'Dugdale,' said a gruff voice. 'I hear you've been busy tonight.'

There was more than a hint of the Commander slurring his words. *Looks like I'm not the only one with a taste for the hard stuff,* Carlyle mused. 'Acting on a tipoff,' he said stiffly, 'we raided a house in Willesden Green about an hour ago, in connection with the St James's Diamonds robbery.'

'Any arrests?'

'No,' Carlyle said, trying to keep the defensiveness out of his voice. 'The place was empty. Forensics are in there now.'

There was a pause while Dugdale took a mouthful of whatever he was drinking. 'They'd better fucking find something,' he hissed, 'for your sake. The overtime for tonight will be astronomical.'

'It was a good lead.'

'For Christ's sake, Inspector!' Dugdale thundered. 'You know how tight money is at the moment.'

Carlyle counted to ten. 'Of course I understand the situation. I will let you know as quickly as possible what we turn up.' Without waiting for a reply, he ended the call as Roche stepped out onto the pavement. 'Wanker!' he said angrily, resisting the temptation to smash his phone against the kerb.

Ignoring Carlyle's ranting, the sergeant stepped in front of him and held up a small, clear plastic bag for his inspection. Inside was a single platinum raindrop earring. 'We've got a result,' she grinned. 'It looks like they were here and this got left behind.'

Carlyle felt all his frustration with Dugdale melt away in an instant. 'Out-*fucking*-standing.'

'I'll get back to the station and check it against the insurance company's inventory.'

Carlyle scratched his head. 'I'm fairly sure I can remember it being on the list. It can wait till tomorrow.'

'It's fine. We've got some progress at last. I want to get on with it.'

Carlyle shrugged. 'Okay, but it's getting late. What about the boyfriend?'

'He's happy to wait.' Roche's grin grew even wider. 'I promised him a good time when I finally get in.' She licked her lips suggestively.

Carlyle felt himself blush slightly. 'L-lucky bugger,' he stammered.

Roche raised her eyes to the heavens. 'He's got about as much chance of *that* as Sam Smallbone has of getting his million quid.'

'Oh,' said Carlyle, somewhat confused.

Tiring of explaining the psychology of relationships to her boss, Roche headed off down the street. 'Are you coming back to Charing Cross?'

Struggling to regain his composure, Carlyle hurried after her. 'I think I'll call it a night,' he said, 'but I fancy a whiskey. Let's go and get a drink first.'

SEVENTEEN

'Dad! Your phone! It's been going crazy.'

Yawning, Carlyle opened his eyes in time to see his mobile phone whizz past his head, bounce off the pillow and disappear over the far side of the bed.

'Shit!'

'Oops,' Alice giggled, beating a hasty retreat. 'Sorry.'

'Yeah, right.' Rolling over on to his wife's side of the bed, he stuck out an arm and groped for the handset. In the bathroom, he could hear Helen humming to herself as she got ready for work.

'I'm off to school now,' Alice shouted from the hallway. 'See you tonight.'

'Okay,' Carlyle called back, finally grasping the phone, which was buzzing away happily. Six missed calls. *Par for the course.* Sitting up in bed, he felt tired to the bone and had a vague headache which would need to be addressed with a couple of paracetamol before it had the chance to bloom into something worse. The two double whiskies on the way home from Willesden Green had maybe not been such a good idea after all, but it was rather too late to do anything about that now.

Helen appeared from the bathroom wearing jeans, a simple white blouse and a navy cardigan. Her hair was pulled back in a ponytail and she had applied minimal make-up. She looked at him and smiled. 'Want some tea?'

Gazing at her, he again felt the fear rising in his throat and in his heart. 'Thanks,' he told her. 'Green tea would be great.'

'Coming up.'

As she disappeared down the hall, he scratched his balls with one hand and pulled up his voicemail with the other. There were two new messages. The first was from Roche, who confirmed that the earring found in the flat on St Gabriel's Road had been stolen from St James's Diamonds and said that she would see him at the station later in the morning. The second was a gruff message that simply said: *Inspector Carlyle, this is Commander Dugdale. Be in my office at eight thirty this morning.* Carlyle checked the time on the alarm clock by the bed.

'Oops!'

The Central Line had better be working properly or he would never make it. Jumping out of bed, he pulled on some clothes and nipped into the bathroom to clean his teeth and splash some water on his face. Jogging down the hallway, he popped into the kitchen and kissed Helen on the forehead. 'Sorry,' he grimaced, 'got to go.'

She gestured at a mug on the worktop, a sliver of steam slowly rising from it. 'What about your tea . . .'

'Sorry.' He kissed her again, before turning on his heel and heading for the door. 'I'll see you tonight.'

By 8.39 he was sitting in an ante-room outside Dugdale's office in Paddington Green police station, sweating profusely. The underground had been working but after getting the tube to Marble Arch, he'd still had to run the length of the Edgware Road. Dugdale's PA eyed Carlyle suspiciously and made a point of neglecting to offer him anything to drink. Fiddling with his phone, all he could do was wait.

In the event, it was almost 9.15 when the door to Dugdale's office swung open and the Commander glared at him to come in. Slowly, Carlyle got to his feet and stepped inside. As the door clicked shut behind him, he registered the other man in the room.

'Inspector,' Dugdale said dully, 'I believe that you already know Mr Holyrod.'

Christian Holyrod got up from his chair and extended a languid hand. 'Inspector.'

What the hell? Carlyle took a deep breath. 'Good morning, Mr Mayor,' he said, shaking hands, 'very nice to see you again.'

'Sit.' Dugdale gestured to the empty chair in front of his desk.

Carlyle did as requested, his brain going into overdrive as he quickly ran through Holyrod's history of interfering with – and trying to block – police investigations.

Dugdale started to speak, but Holyrod held up a hand. The Commander looked peeved but sat back on his chair, arms folded, while the Mayor had the first word.

'Thank you for meeting with us this morning, Inspector,' he said mechanically, holding Carlyle's gaze with a casual stare. 'I am sure we do not need to take up much of your time.'

Carlyle glanced from one man to the other. 'What can I do for you?'

The Mayor launched into his pitch. 'I am responsible for helping to organize,' he glanced at Dugdale, 'and also for financing, the London leg of the Pope's upcoming visit to the UK.'

Carlyle, who neither knew nor cared that the Pope was coming to visit *his* city, nodded sagely. 'Uh-huh.'

'In that capacity,' Holyrod continued, 'it has come to my attention that the Catholic Church is currently considering taking legal action against the Metropolitan Police.'

'Because you couldn't keep your bloody hands off that priest,' Dugdale hissed, able to keep out of the conversation that was taking place in *his* office no longer.

Carlyle gave his boss a gimlet eye. 'The statements you have received from various members of staff,' he said tartly, 'make it clear that the McGowan arrest and interviews were conducted in an entirely proper manner.'

Dugdale's face started to redden and it looked like he might explode with annoyance. 'What is *clear*, Inspector, is that you have a problem with authority in general and with the Church in particular.'

'That is simply not the case,' Carlyle replied calmly.

'For whatever reason, you have jumped on the anti-clerical band-wagon. The Catholic Church is such an easy target, but it is a surprising and perverse attitude for a Metropolitan Police Officer to take, especially at a time when we have to be extremely focused on the threat of Muslim extremism.' Dugdale glanced at Holyrod. 'It's those buggers we need to chase! God knows, if they're not planning suicide bomb-ings, they're stoning women for having sex!'

For a second, Carlyle was thrown by Dugdale's grasp of current events. Then he allowed himself the smallest of grins. 'If I see anyone trying to organize a stoning in the Covent Garden piazza,' he said, 'I will, of course, take appropriate action.'

Holyrod raised his eyes to the ceiling as Dugdale smashed an impo-tent fist on to the desk. 'Don't be flip with me, Carlyle,' he snapped. 'Get on the right page here; fight the right enemy or you're out!'

Carlyle glared at his superior with ill-concealed loathing. 'I am not fighting any "enemy", *sir.* I am simply doing my job, which is to uphold the law. I take people, cases and institutions as I find them, and I do not let any political or other judgements get in the way of perform-ing my duties.'

For a moment, it looked as if Dugdale was having difficulty breath-ing. 'This is intolerable. You are the most conceited, arrogant bastard I have ever met in my entire life!'

Dismayed by the complete lack of professionalism on display in the room, the Mayor held up a hand: 'Gentlemen, please. This is no time for a philosophical debate. And I do not care what happened in that interview room. What I *do* care about is that this issue is resolved quickly and quietly, and that it does not interfere with the smooth run-ning of the Papal visit.' He ran a hand through his hair, which was considerably greyer and thinner than Carlyle remembered it from their previous encounters. 'It is incumbent on us to give the Catholic Church confidence in our good faith. If we can do that, we can resolve this issue and move on to everyone's satisfaction.' Holyrod contem-plated the inspector as if he could read the policeman's every thought. 'Knowing you as I do, Inspector, I would never dream of trying to get you to back down in the case of Father McGowan.'

'It's not as if we have much room for manoeuvre there, anyway,' Dugdale said sourly.

Folding his arms, Carlyle said nothing.

Holyrod picked an invisible piece of lint from the shoulder of his navy suit. 'So, what I am proposing is this: in order to demonstrate that we,' he pointed a crooked index finger at Carlyle, 'and in particular *you*, are not prejudiced in matters relating to the Church, you will take charge of the handling of the Roger Leyne situation.'

'I have agreed with the Mayor that you will take this on,' Dugdale interjected. 'Leyne is—'

'I know who he is,' Carlyle said quickly. He turned to face Holyrod. 'What I didn't realize was that he had anything to do with the Pope or that he was involved in any police investigation.'

'He is not, at the present time, subject to any enquiry,' Holyrod said carefully, as if talking to a rather slow child. 'However, his absurd plans to have His Holiness arrested for crimes against humanity relating to alleged child abuse by members of his Church are, inevitably, bound to fall foul of the law in due course.'

And what am I supposed to be? Carlyle thought angrily. *The fucking Stasi?* Staring at the worn carpet, he took his time before responding. Then he looked up at Holyrod. 'If you have any information, sir,' he said, deliberately aping the Mayor's condescending tone, 'regarding either a breach of the law or a potential breach of the law, then of course I will look into it as a matter of urgency.'

Glaring at Dugdale as if to say *this is your problem*, Holyrod got out of his chair. 'Deal with this matter properly, Inspector,' he said firmly, 'and I am sure that there will be no need for any party to pursue the McGowan complaint. Any alternative outcome will have very serious consequences . . . for both yourself and your colleague Sergeant Roche.' He nodded at Dugdale, who seemed glued to his seat. 'You can keep me posted on developments via the Commander.'

As the door closed behind Holyrod, Carlyle turned to Dugdale and quipped grimly: 'Who will rid me of this turbulent atheist?'

A blank look passed across Dugdale's face before it reverted to its usual expression of constipated disgust. 'You've got work to be getting on with, Carlyle,' he said angrily. 'I suggest that you stop being such a fucking smartarse and get on with it.'

EIGHTEEN

Looking up from her computer screen, Roche said. 'We've had another memo from the Police Federation.'

'Jolly good.' Carlyle thought about mentioning his letter offering voluntary redundancy, but decided against it.

Roche scanned down the text. 'It says . . . *"investment in policing has gone up by over 47 per cent in the last decade, but just over 10 per cent of police are visibly available to the public".'*

' "Visibly available",' Carlyle harrumphed. 'Meaning what, exactly?'

'Yada, yada, yada . . . *"We accept that in the current fiscal climate, economies need to be made, but everything must be done to protect frontline services which ensure the public gets the service the public wants – more police officers on their streets."* Yada, yada. *"There are challenging times ahead, and all those who have a genuine interest in ensuring that the British Police Service remains the envy of the world must work together; to ensure we do not make short-term rushed financial decisions to make small savings which could have a detrimental impact on the service we are able to provide. Losing police officers is not an option where public safety and security is concerned".'*

Carlyle started humming the tune of a long-forgotten punk song about the British police being the best in the world. Roche looked at him blankly before closing down the email with a click of her mouse. 'Did the Commander give you a hard time?'

'How did you know I'd been in to see Dugdale?' Why was it that everyone seemed to know what he was up to in real time?

'The front desk told me that he'd been looking for you,' Roche shrugged, 'so I assumed that's where you were.'

'Fair enough.' Perching on the side of her desk, he glanced around to check that no one was eavesdropping. 'But the meeting wasn't just with Dugdale.' Lowering his voice, he recounted the conversation with the Mayor.

When he'd finished, Roche said, 'I read a piece about Roger Leyne in one of the Sunday papers a couple of weeks ago. He seems a bit of a twat. I mean, who has a job as a "philosopher"? What do you do? Sit around all day with your hands down your trousers?'

Carlyle laughed.

'And as for arresting the Pope, come on, it's just a stupid publicity stunt.'

'Whatever.' Carlyle yawned, a wave of tiredness washing over him.

'It's not something we should be wasting our time on,' she chided him.

'Feel free to tell the Mayor that he can fuck right off,' Carlyle suggested tartly. 'We'll go and have a chat with this guy, keep it light and, hopefully, minimize the chance of any unpleasantness further down the line.'

'It's not like we don't have anything else to do,' Roche moaned, unconvinced by her boss's newly found willingness to do what he was told.

'I know. But Dugdale's interest in the diamonds case seems to have evaporated. He didn't even ask me about it.'

'Well,' Roche grinned, 'whether he's interested or not, we've made some progress.'

'I know,' Carlyle nodded, 'I got your voicemail about the earring.'

Roche's grin grew wider. 'I've got more than that. Much more.'

Carlyle raised an eyebrow. 'Oh?'

'Forensics gathered various hairs from the bathroom. One of them gave us a hit on the National DNA Database.'

Carlyle punched the air, all weariness gone. 'Thank You, God!'

'I thought you'd like that. We got a partial match to a woman who was done for drink-driving two years ago, name of Tracey Hearst. She drove her Mini into a tree near Clapham Common. Turns out she is the sister of Colin Dyer.'

Carlyle thought about it for a moment. 'Colin Dyer . . . Colin Dyer. Why does that name ring a bell?'

'Dyer has six previous convictions for robbery and assault. One of them was for his part in a raid on a jewellery store in Hatton Garden seven years ago.'

'Yes, I like it! Do we have an address?'

Roche gestured at the notepad on her desk. 'We have an address for his mother, a council flat in Somers Town.' Somers Town was a particularly unlovely part of Camden, just north of St Pancras station.

'Nice,' Carlyle snorted. 'When you go up there to see Mum, make sure you take a couple of uniforms with you.'

She gave him a questioning look. 'Are you not coming?'

Carlyle shook his head. 'No, I've got another meeting. I'll do that, then I'll go and pay a visit to the philosophical Mr Leyne. Let's meet back here and compare notes this afternoon.'

If Roche was put out at being sent to Somers Town, she didn't show it. 'All right,' she nodded.

'Good,' said Carlyle, heading for the lifts. 'Well done. I'll see you later.'

Sitting in another waiting room, the inspector listened to the traffic noise outside while his mind wandered. *What was Dr Wolf's first name?* He realized that he had no idea. Not that it really mattered.

Carlyle had been coming to see the psychiatrist roughly once a fortnight for over a year now, ever since Carde Simpson had insisted on him getting some 'help' when an earlier case had spiralled out of control. Once he'd got over the fact that it was a slovenly process, with no timetable and no specific goals, it was easy enough just to write the time off and play the game.

The door to Wolf's office opened and the shrink beckoned him inside. There being no couch, Carlyle took a seat in his usual armchair and smiled blandly.

'Good morning, Doctor.'

'Good morning to you, Inspector,' Wolf replied, somewhat uncertainly, as he plopped into the chair opposite. Opening a hardback A4 notebook, he flicked through the pages until he came to the notes of their last meeting. Running an index finger down the page, he scanned them carefully, as if they were ancient hieroglyphic texts from the tomb of some long-forgotten king.

Wolf was a short, wizened gent of indeterminate age, with long grey hair, and watery blue eyes that invariably displayed a mixture of amusement and disappointment. The wall clock showed that they were already more than ten minutes into their allotted hour, which, in reality was fifty minutes. Past experience suggested that most of the rest of the time would be taken up with the doctor reading his notes, making random observations, or staring at his brown brogues. Carlyle estimated that the amount of time he had to spend actually talking in each session rarely topped fifteen minutes.

Closing his notebook, the shrink looked up with a satisfied smile. 'So,' he said, in an accent that Carlyle had never been able to place, 'how are we today?'

'Fine,' said Carlyle noncommittally. 'You?'

'What shall we talk about?' Wolf asked, ignoring the question.

And so began another session. It was always the same. He doubted if Wolf had changed his patter for decades. Not for the first time, Carlyle wondered just how much these sessions cost; he had asked Simpson several times exactly how much the Met was paying to secure his mental health. She had always refused point blank to discuss it, which only served to strengthen his suspicion that where the good doctor was concerned, talk was definitely not cheap.

'There are some interesting things going on at work,' he said casually. It was one of the things he'd learned over the last year; always have a topic of conversation ready.

'Tell me about it.' Wolf stared at his shoes and his eyes began to droop. Carlyle allowed himself a wry smile; this wouldn't be the first time the shrink had fallen asleep in one of their sessions. Taking a deep breath, he began a short monologue about cost-cutting at the Met and the need for redundancies.

After he had finished talking, there was a pause before Wolf shook himself awake. 'Ah yes,' he said finally, 'very interesting. What do you make of it all?'

Carlyle shrugged. 'It is a very difficult situation. Money is obviously very tight. There is a need to cut back.'

After some rummaging, Wolf retrieved a pencil from down the side of the chair and pointed it at Carlyle. 'But what do you, yourself, make of it?'

'Nothing, really. I just have to get on with my job.'

Wolf scribbled something in his notebook with the pencil. 'The job is very important to you?' he asked, as awake now as Carlyle had ever known him.

'Of course.'

There was more scribbling, which made Carlyle feel increasingly uncomfortable. Looking up from his notes, Wolf smiled. 'What would you do,' he asked, 'if it was taken away, if you couldn't be a policeman any longer?'

'Well . . .' Carlyle looked at the clock on the wall; they still had more than half an hour to go.

Standing on the third floor of Phoenix Court, Alison Roche banged hard on the door of number 23. She could make out some movement behind the frosted glass and gave it another thump with the palm of her hand. 'Hurry up!' she shouted. 'This is the police!'

'Do you want us to kick it in?' asked one of the two constables on the landing beside her, a young giant by the name of Joe Lynch.

'Don't you fucking dare!' said a voice as the door opened a few inches.

'Carla Dyer?' Roche asked.

The crone behind the door said nothing.

'Open up,' Roche said imperiously.

'What do you bloody want?' the woman demanded.

'What do you think?' said Lynch, quickly sticking his foot in the door. 'We're looking for Colin.'

'He ain't here,' Carla said unconvincingly.

'We'll just check for ourselves, if you don't mind,' said Roche. She nodded at Lynch, who stepped forward and shouldered the door open, pushing the woman back down the hallway.

'You can't come in here,' the woman shouted. 'This is harassment!'

Grabbing the collar of Carla Dyer's sweatshirt, Lynch marched her into the living room and on to a mangy-looking sofa. 'Stay there,' he barked, before going off to join his colleague in a search of the other rooms.

Arriving in the room, Roche looked around. On top of a sideboard there were four framed pictures, including one of a smiling teenage boy holding a football. There was the sound of breaking glass in the kitchen. Roche's heart sank. She knew that Carlyle would go mental if they made a mess of this.

'You'll fucking pay for that,' hissed Carla Dyer.

Roche gestured at the photo. 'Is that Colin?'

Carla looked at the picture but said nothing.

'Where is he?'

'How should I know?' The woman shrugged theatrically. 'I'm not his keeper.'

There was another loud crash from the back of the flat, followed by shouting. Stepping into the doorway, Roche caught movement to her right. Instinctively, she stuck out a foot and sent the fleeing man sprawling. Bouncing down the hallway, Colin Dyer tried to get back to his feet but was put down again by Roche's swift kick. He lay there groaning, so she gave him another for good measure. 'Stay down, you little bugger!' She turned to see Lynch moving sheepishly towards her, holding his nose.

'The bastard sandbagged me,' Lynch whined. 'I think it's broken.'

Behind him, the other PC tried to stifle a grin. 'The stupid bastard was hiding under the bed.'

Unable to summon up any sympathy for her colleague, Roche gestured towards the prostrate Dyer. 'Get him back to the station,' she said, taking her mobile from the pocket of her jacket. 'Take his mother too. I'll get Forensics up here and we'll see what we can find.'

NINETEEN

Roger Leyne lived in an impressive four-storey Georgian house on John Street in Bloomsbury, a twenty-minute stroll from the office of Dr Wolf. By the time he turned off Theobald's Road, the inspector felt suitably refreshed, the meaningless prattle of his latest session with the shrink deleted from the recycling bin in his head. Stepping off the pavement and onto the doorstep of number 42, he pressed the doorbell and waited.

Knowing that he was expected, Carlyle tapped his shoe against the stone. Leyne's office at the London School of Economics had informed him that the professor was 'working from home' and had promised to ring ahead, to inform him of Carlyle's visit. However, there was no sign of any response to his arrival. After a minute or so, he rang the bell again, longer this time, giving it three extended, insistent bursts.

Still no one came.

Feeling somewhat peeved, Carlyle pulled out his mobile and called the LSE. While it rang, he peered over the railings into the basement void.

'London School of Economics, Professor Leyne's office, good morning.'

Using his free hand, Carlyle pulled himself up on the railings to get a better view.

'Good morning.'

'Shit!'

'Hello?'

Ending the call, Carlyle slipped the phone into his pocket and stepped back onto the pavement. A small gate in the railings gave access to a narrow metal stairway leading to the basement. Peering over the railings, the inspector could see a pair of French doors; the glass in one of them had been smashed. He gave the gate a push; annoyingly, it was padlocked. With some considerable effort, he hoisted himself over the railings. Standing at the top of the stairs, he wiped the sweat from his brow and took a moment to get his breath back. He caught the eye of a well-dressed young woman who had stopped three yards away to let her dachshund take a shit.

'I hope you're going to clean that up,' Carlyle said tartly as he watched the dog crouch down to perform its business.

Pretending not to hear him, the woman turned and dragged the dog off in the opposite direction while still in mid-dump.

Carlyle shook his head. 'Poor little bugger.' Returning to the matter in hand, he began descending the stairs. At the bottom, there was the smell of chlorine and the gentle hum of a generator. A quick rummage through his pockets confirmed that he wasn't carrying any latex gloves. Cursing under his breath, the inspector gave the door with the broken window a gentle tap with his shoe. Gratifyingly, it edged open and he slipped inside.

Under more normal circumstances, Carlyle would have been very taken by the forty-foot swimming pool, the pale blue water shimmering off the white ceiling and the limestone surround; doubtless all very *House & Garden*. Today, however, he was more taken by the body face down in the pool and the blood that was slowly leaking from it. Slowly, carefully, he moved down the side of the pool. When he approached the hot tub that sat beside it, he stopped and listened for any sounds coming from upstairs. Other than the occasional passing car on the street outside, there was nothing. Confident that the killer was long gone, Carlyle pulled out his mobile and called the station.

It was only after the call failed to connect that he realized he didn't have a signal. He looked at the floater then raised his eyes to the heavens. 'God,' he laughed, heading for the stairs, 'if this is Your idea of some kind of cosmic joke, it isn't fucking funny.'

Leaving the front door ajar, Carlyle sat on the step and called Roche.

The call went to voicemail and he left a message. His second call was to Susan Phillips.

Phillips picked up on the second ring. 'John,' she said cheerily, 'how are you?'

'Not too bad,' Carlyle said. 'Are you busy at the moment?'

'Right now?' she asked, quickly twigging that this was not a social call. 'Not especially. Why?'

Carlyle explained the situation.

'I'll organize reinforcements,' said Phillips, 'and we'll be right there.'

'And Susan?'

'Yes?'

'Bring me some latex gloves, will you?'

Standing by the edge of the pool, Carlyle snapped on his rubber gloves and wiggled his eyebrows suggestively.

Rolling up her shirt-sleeves, Susan Phillips gave him a stern look. 'Why don't you go and have a look around upstairs and we'll see about getting this guy out.' Phillips worked out of Holborn police station, on nearby Lamb's Conduit Street. A staff pathologist with the Met for more than twenty years, she was quick, no-nonsense and dependable.

'All right,' Carlyle smiled. 'See you later.' Deciding to start at the top of the house, he skipped merrily up the stairs.

By the time he reached the fourth floor, the spring in his step had long since disappeared. Somewhat embarrassed by his lack of puff, the inspector flopped into a leather sofa placed next to the top of the stairs and looked around. The whole of the fourth floor was an open space that Leyne had turned into his office. Despite the grey skies outside, the space was flooded by light from large windows front and back. Along the length of the far wall ran shelving from floor to ceiling, groaning with books. A pile of papers two foot high stood in one corner but, otherwise, the place looked very tidy.

After recovering his breath, Carlyle slipped off the sofa and went across to the window overlooking the street. Outside, an ambulance was double parked in front of the house, leading to a build-up of traffic. One of the delayed motorists gave an angry blast on his horn, causing a couple more to follow suit. *Why isn't one of the uniforms sorting that out?* Carlyle wondered, annoyed. His gaze turned to the large desk next to the window. Pride of place was given to a nineteen-inch monitor for a very expensive-looking Apple computer. Stepping in front of the desk, Carlyle looked at the keyboard for a moment, then carefully tapped the return key. With gratifying simplicity, the screen blinked into life.

Carlyle smiled. 'Not big on online security, are we?' Sitting on the chair by the desk, he scrolled down the page. Under the headline 'Draft Article', Leyne had started writing what looked like a piece for a newspaper or magazine:

> *Is the Pope responsible for clerical sexual abuse? In a word, yes. When his degenerate priests are caught in flagrante, centuries of exploitation have shown them how to cover up their crimes, silencing their young victims with threats of damnation and emotional violence. What other organization could get away with such behaviour? No amount of sweet incense, ceremony or saints should blind us to the truth of rampant child abuse. Once he steps out of his Vatican fiefdom and comes to this country, the Holy Father should be arrested and tried in a civil court . . .*

'Say what you think, why don't you?' Carlyle said to himself. Hearing footsteps on the stairs behind him, he turned to see Phillips looking rather red in the face.

'I should have known that you'd be all the way at the bloody top,' she wheezed, taking a seat on the sofa he had occupied only a few minutes earlier.

Getting to his feet, Carlyle paced the room. 'Have you fished him out yet?'

'Not yet,' Phillips said, 'but it's definitely Mr Leyne.' She stretched her arms above her head and yawned. 'God! This sofa is comfortable.'

Carlyle laughed. 'Now's not the time for a kip.' His eye caught a familiar book on one of the shelves. Helen had bought him Richard

Dawkins' *The God Delusion* as a birthday present and then proceeded to read it herself, so that he didn't have to. It was a not unfamiliar situation that they were both happy with. Dawkins, Helen had gleefully informed him, was known as 'Darwin's Rottweiler'. He wondered what that made Leyne.

'Cause of death?'

Phillips yawned again. 'I couldn't possibly say at this early stage.'

'But?'

'But I think that the two bullets in the chest may have had something to do with it.'

The first thing that Carlyle noticed when he walked into the interview room at Charing Cross police station was that the CCTV had been repaired. Smiling for the camera, he walked over to the desk and sat down.

Colin Dyer looked at him sullenly. His shaven head gleamed under the striplighting. His left cheek was badly grazed and there was a large bruise above his right eye. He scowled defiantly at Carlyle. 'What do you want? I'm waiting for my brief.'

Carlyle dropped a thin sheaf of papers on the table and folded his arms. 'What happened to you?'

Dyer looked at the camera and pointed an index finger at the bruise. 'Your bloody sergeant beat me up!'

Carlyle waited for him to restore eye-contact. 'Who is your lawyer?'

Dyer thought about it for a while, as if he were being asked to divulge some state secret. 'Jenkins,' he said finally, 'Kelvin Jenkins.'

Carlyle nodded. Jenkins was a well-known bottom-feeder who probably spent more time in police stations than the inspector did himself. 'I thought you might have managed someone a little bit more upmarket this time,' he grinned, 'given you nicked tens of millions of pounds' worth of diamonds. Then again, fencing them hasn't been so easy, has it?'

Grunting, Dyer shook his head.

'You didn't plan ahead properly.'

'Fuck off!' Dyer waved a hostile hand in front of Carlyle's face.

'Thinking never was your strong point, was it?'

'I'm a victim of police brutality.'

Carlyle laughed. 'Tell it to Kelvin,' he chuckled. 'You can have fifteen minutes when he arrives; then we need to get going.' He watched Dyer's face settle back into a look of sullen hostility. 'I'm just here to give you a quick heads-up. You are nailed on for this. I don't really give a fuck about the stones, but a girl died here and you are in deep shit.' He was almost embarrassed by how trite it all sounded, but he could see that Dyer was taking it in. Pushing back his chair, Carlyle lifted the papers off the desk and got to his feet. 'So, when I come back in here, I don't want to hear any whining "*I don't know nuthin'*" bullshit. I want names, places, and, above all, a precise explanation of how Paula Coulter was killed.' He glared at Dyer, whose gaze fell to the table. *I've got you, you wanker*, Carlyle thought happily as he walked out of the door. *I've fucking got you.*

He found Roche upstairs, typing up her report. 'I just popped in downstairs to see Mr Dyer,' he grinned.

'Uh-huh,' she said, not looking up.

'I see you're making a habit of losing your temper.'

Roche stopped typing and gave him a hard stare. 'I didn't lay a finger on him,' she said. 'He tripped up while trying to flee arrest.' She resumed her typing, hitting the keys a bit harder this time.

Carlyle couldn't resist winding her up a little more. 'That's not what Colin says.'

Tap, tap, tap. 'Colin is a thief and a fucking liar.' Tap, tap, tap. 'Not to mention a murder suspect.' Tap, tap, tap. 'He also broke the nose of one of the constables.'

'Yes, yes.' Carlyle held his hands up in mock surrender. He pulled up a chair and sat down. 'Where's the mother?'

'We didn't have the space, so she was taken to Shoreditch.'

Carlyle raised an eyebrow.

Roche shrugged. 'That's where they took her. We'll get a statement and hold her while the flat gets searched.'

'What's she like?'

Roche scratched her head. 'The usual white-trash nightmare. Exactly what you would expect from Colin's mum.'

'I told him he could have fifteen minutes with the lawyer and then we want him to talk. This is first and foremost a murder investigation and there is no way he is just going to sit there and deny everything.'

Roche nodded. 'Are we going to charge him if he tries to tough it out?'

Carlyle hadn't thought about that. 'Yes.'

The phone on her desk started ringing and she immediately picked up the handset. 'Yes, fine. Take him down. I will be there in a few minutes. Thanks.' She put down the phone and looked at Carlyle. 'That was the front desk. Dyer's lawyer is here.'

'It's a guy called Kelvin Jenkins. Know him?'

Roche shook her head.

'Kelvin's a little gobshite. Middle-aged journeyman, you know the type.'

'A middle-aged journeyman?' Roche laughed. 'You mean a bit like you?'

'Ha fucking ha,' Carlyle deadpanned. 'Thank you very much.'

Roche at least had the good grace to seem a little embarrassed at the rather flat joke. 'Sorry.'

'Anyway, he's nothing to worry about but he does like the sound of his own voice. He can drag things out forever if you let him, so don't let him. Let me know how it goes. I need to get started on the Leyne investigation.'

'I heard about that,' Roche said. 'Messy.'

'Not really,' Carlyle quipped. 'The professor had the good sense to fall in the pool. Clean that out and the place can go straight on the market.'

Roche tutted. 'You know what I mean. What do you think happened?'

Carlyle sighed. 'What happened is that someone shot him twice in the chest. Why? No idea.'

A *not my problem* look drifted across Roche's face and she returned to her typing. Taking the hint, he sloped off to pursue his enquiries about the dead man.

TWENTY

Courtesy of Wikipedia, it took Carlyle less than ten minutes to bone up on Roger William Leyne, Fellow of the Royal Society and Professor of Culture and Ethics at the London School of Economics. In his mid-fifties, Leyne had an impressive list of academic jobs on his CV. He also had three marriages under his belt, resulting in five children. Armed with this knowledge, Carlyle strolled out of the station and headed east along the Strand. Five minutes later, he was standing on the Aldwych, looking up Houghton Street towards the LSE's main entrance. Knots of students wandered along the pedestrianized thoroughfare, heading to and from lectures or generally just mooching about. Beneath the School's motto, *rerum cognoscere causas* – to know the causes of things – he skipped up the steps and headed inside.

Sitting under the logo of an industrious beaver, a bored receptionist eyed him suspiciously as he approached.

Carlyle couldn't be bothered to give her a smile. 'I am here to see Professor Webb.'

The young woman tapped on her computer. 'The Professor is giving a lecture at the moment,' she said, talking to the screen.

Carlyle looked at his watch. It was twenty to the hour. Presumably he wouldn't have to wait long. 'Where is the lecture taking place?' he asked, keeping the irritation from his voice.

She hesitated, reluctant to give up any more information.

Not wishing to cause the Professor any embarrassment, Carlyle kept his ID in his pocket. He gave the girl a hard stare. Finally she glanced back at the screen. 'It's in the New Theatre,' she pointed outside, 'in the East Building, across the street.'

'Thank you,' said Carlyle, already halfway to the door.

A notice pinned next to the door informed the inspector that the subject of the lecture was *Religion and Pluralism*. Slipping inside, he took a seat on the otherwise empty back row. It was warm in the theatre and lethargy descended on him almost immediately. He tried to shake his head clear and scanned the room. The theatre, which he guessed could take maybe 400 people, appeared barely 10 per cent full. Groups of tragically young-looking students were scattered across the front rows, with only a few antisocial types sitting further back. On a platform raised six inches off the floor, Professor Webb spoke with the aid of a lapel mike, which gave her voice a slightly distorted quality.

'. . . to this day,' she said slowly, with the air of a practised performer, 'there is an active debate about religion's ability to withstand a plurality of ideas.'

Even at this distance, he could see that the Professor was a striking woman. Easily six foot tall, with a mop of snow-white hair, she paced the stage, eyeing her students with piercing grey eyes as she moved steadily through her lecture without the aid of a script. Even so, to Carlyle's ear, her words quickly became just background noise. The clock on the wall behind her head showed that it was not yet quite ten to the hour and Carlyle had to clamp tight his jaw in order to stifle a yawn. Closing his eyes, he let his mind wander.

'Excuse me, young man?'

Slowly, Carlyle became aware, first of his own snoring, then of someone poking him on the arm. Pushing himself up in the chair, he shook himself awake and met Professor Webb's stern gaze. 'Ah . . .' he said, embarrassed.

'What are you doing,' she asked sharply, 'asleep in my lecture?' A couple of female students sniggered as they walked past.

Carlyle felt himself blush. 'Well, em . . .'

'I think that you have to leave now, or I will be forced to call

Security.' As if on cue, a uniformed guard appeared in the doorway. Webb signalled the way out.

Not yet sure whether he was more irritated with his own sleepiness or Webb's haughtiness, Carlyle got to his feet and held up a hand. The bouncer took a threatening step forward. With his free hand, Carlyle fumbled in his pocket. He managed to pull out his ID before facing the ignominy of getting his collar felt.

Webb reached for the spectacles resting on the top of her head. 'Good heavens,' she said with an amused smile. 'A sleeping policeman!'

'Sorry.'

The smile widened. 'Am I under arrest, Inspector?'

'Not at all,' Carlyle smiled, recovering a little graciousness, 'but I do need to speak with you quite urgently.' He glanced at the guard. 'In private.'

'Yes, yes, of course.' Webb addressed the guard. 'Thank you, Jonathan, I think we'll be fine now.' As the guard took his leave, Webb handed Carlyle the pile of books she had been carrying. 'Here, you can carry these for me,' she said, leading him out of the theatre, 'and we can go and get a drink.'

Webb had her office on the tenth floor of the imaginatively named Tower One on Clement's Inn. Showing Carlyle inside, she gestured to a bookcase by the window. 'Just drop the books over there, thanks, and make yourself at home.'

Putting the books down, he took in the panorama of the Royal Courts of Justice on the other side of the road. 'Nice view.'

'Isn't it,' Webb agreed, dropping into the chair behind her desk. 'I think it's the least I deserve after almost thirty years of living in a cupboard in the Old Building. They moved us here three years ago. It's heaven.' Pulling open a desk drawer, she took out a bottle of whisky and a couple of shot glasses.

Carlyle gave her a quizzical look.

Webb shrugged. 'After that lot, I need a little something. When you've been giving the same lecture for more than a quarter of a century you inevitably need some form of artificial stimulation.'

'What is it?'

'Glenfarclas. A twenty-one-year-old Highland single malt.' She handed him the bottle to inspect. 'Very nice.'

Turning the bottle in his hand, Carlyle read the back label: *A single malt with intense aromas of tropical fruit, almonds, nutmeg, citrus and vanilla* . . . to the end. Nodding appreciatively, he handed the bottle back. 'It looks very nice, but I'm afraid I'll have to pass.'

Pulling out the cork, she gave him a sly look. 'Does that mean you are on duty?'

'Sadly,' Carlyle replied with a wry smile.

'Shame.'

Carlyle watched enviously as Webb poured herself a generous measure.

'So,' she said, placing the glass on the desk without taking a sip, 'what is it you want to talk about?'

'Roger Leyne.'

Webb rolled her eyes. 'I see.'

'You're not a fan?'

Webb shrugged. 'The LSE likes to think of itself as "the place where the world comes to think", which is fair enough. After all, we are one of the foremost social science universities in the world, alongside Harvard, Berkeley and Stanford. In our world, Roger Leyne is something of a name. Not necessarily an A-lister like Dawkins, you understand, but a draw for some of our students.'

'But—'

'Professor Leyne isn't really an academic any more. For a long time, I've felt that he's been too focused on developing his own career to give his students the time and attention that they deserve.'

'So you weren't surprised when he launched his campaign to have the Pope arrested?'

'Is this what your visit is about?' Picking up her glass, she looked at him closely. 'You're not a *secret* policeman are you, Inspector?'

'Not at all,' Carlyle smiled. 'I'm just a regular member of the Met. Professor Leyne was found dead this morning.'

Webb's eyes widened as she took her first slug of whisky. 'Do I need to supply you with an alibi?'

Carlyle chuckled. 'No. Not at the moment, anyway. I just wanted to talk to you about the type of man he was.'

'And who his enemies were?'

'Quite.'

Webb gave him a grim smile. 'Roger Leyne was a shallow and vain man, Inspector. I should imagine that he had plenty of enemies.'

Carlyle nodded and waited for her to continue.

'He wanted to be the next Richard Dawkins, the new champion of rationalism. He wanted the book contracts and the lecture tours and all the side benefits that come with being a minor celebrity, the party invitations, the groupies and so on.'

Carlyle raised an eyebrow. 'Groupies?'

Webb laughed. 'Yes, I know. But to the extent that Leyne took an interest in his students, he focused on the attractive females. In many ways, he was a caricature of the louche academic.'

'So his death may have been a domestic incident of one sort or another?'

She gave him a funny look. 'Isn't that the case in most of these type of . . . situations, Inspector?'

'Yes,' he nodded. 'We will always take a close look at friends and family in any murder investigation.'

'That will keep you busy,' she said. 'Roger had three wives and God knows how many children, of all different ages. Then there were the various girlfriends and—'

'But I can't ignore the political angle to all this,' he interjected.

Webb drained her glass. 'Political?' Pouring herself another generous measure, she waved the bottle at Carlyle.

Reluctantly, he raised a hand to signal that he still couldn't partake. 'I mean his opposition to the Catholic Church and his campaign to have the Pope arrested when he visits the UK.'

'Hah!' Webb snorted. 'Such ridiculous posturing.'

'By whom?'

'By Roger, of course.'

'Presumably,' Carlyle said evenly, 'it was something that he took seriously.'

'Roger didn't take *anything* seriously, other than perhaps maintaining his levels of sexual conquest.' She looked at him, added: 'Anyway, what is religion?'

Knowing that he was not supposed to provide any kind of answer, Carlyle waited.

'I like to use the term "belief in the absence of data". There is absolutely no scientific proof that God exists, nor can He, or She, be defined. People who have faith simply believe in God. You might as well believe in fairies at the bottom of your garden. What is the point of trying to argue with people like that?'

'That doesn't mean you shouldn't take a stand against child abuse.'

'No, no, of course not. But Roger couldn't have cared less about the Church or about the Pope. And when you talk about taking advantage of children, some of his conquests were fairly, well, borderline.'

'I see.'

'No, Inspector, this was just the particular bandwagon that Roger had chosen to jump upon. The whole thing was just another vehicle for self-promotion. He liked to call it "feeding the media machine". It had nothing to do with justice, it was all about his ego.'

'That may be the case, but it is still a line of enquiry that I have to pursue.'

Webb put down her glass and gave him a stern look. 'Inspector, the Catholic Church has been going for hundreds of years. There have been two hundred and sixty-six Popes. This one, by the way, is only the fifty-fifth who is not Italian. He is also the oldest person to have been elected Pope since Clement XII in 1730 which is, perhaps, a factor in the current mess. Nevertheless, the Church is still, arguably, the most successful institution in the history of the world, and its senior members can get away with just about anything. Why would they care two hoots about a nobody like Roger Leyne?'

'He must have caused some concerns ahead of the Papal visit.'

'I very much doubt it,' Webb replied. 'They've got far bigger things to worry about.'

'Oh?'

'The Pope,' said Webb, slipping into lecture mode, 'advocates strict orthodoxy. He sees the Church as a citadel of truth and righteousness against the realms of atheism and deceit. Britain's Catholics are rather more liberal, and enthusiasm for his visit is, by all accounts, lukewarm at best. Of course, the child-abuse scandals have not helped either. Some relatively senior people in the Vatican, meanwhile, try to argue that it is a problem caused by gays.'

Carlyle frowned. 'How do you mean?'

Webb laughed. 'Cardinal Ignazio Acerbis, the Vatican Secretary of State, one of the Pope's most senior advisers, claimed last year that psychiatrists have demonstrated that there is no relationship between celibacy and paedophilia, but that there *is* a relationship between homosexuality and paedophilia.'

Carlyle felt a familiar anger rising in his throat. He had a brief flash-back to his performance with Father McGowan in the basement of the police station. 'These people . . .' he ground out.

Webb took another mouthful of Scotch and sighed appreciatively. 'You have to understand the mindset, Inspector. If you are the Pope, you see yourself as a descendant of the Apostle Peter.'

Carlyle, ever the happy, ignorant, atheist, stifled a yawn.

'Catholicism has set itself up as the Church Christ intended to build. This allows it to claim a monopoly of the deepest truths of humanity and the universe.'

'Jesus!' Carlyle mumbled.

'Quite.' Webb waved a hand airily in front of her face. 'This place can be annoying at times but we have a simple and decent goal, which is to improve society and to understand the causes of things.' Leaning forward, she gave Carlyle the kind of stern look that had doubtless put the fear of God into many a poor undergraduate over the years. 'The LSE has always been about engagement with the wider world. In that sense, we are an institution completely at odds with the ways of the Church.'

Carlyle said nothing, happy to let the Professor say her piece.

'There is an old joke,' Webb continued, 'that says everything is for-eign policy to the Vatican. It exists to do three things: maintain the primacy of the Pope, define and sustain doctrine, and appoint bishops.

The bishops do the rest. There is a widespread view that civil authority must be kept out of Church affairs, however criminal they might be. Obsolete canon law means that the Vatican appears in grave breach of the convention on the right of the child, and an enemy of human rights. This leads to lots of difficult questions. Is the Pope legally liable for the system that has allowed terrible crimes to go unpunished? Should the Holy See continue to enjoy immunity from prosecution in matters such as this?' Finally, she saw the glazed expression on Carlyle's face and eased off on the rhetoric. 'You see what a difficult situation it is.'

'Yes,' he lied.

'So you can also see,' Webb chuckled, 'why Roger Leyne doesn't really feature as a major player in this holy mess.'

Carlyle suddenly felt hugely weary.

'The good news,' Webb continued, 'is that it will crumble.'

'What do you mean?'

'The Church. It is most definitely on the way out, Roger Leyne or no Roger Leyne.'

'But,' Carlyle replied, 'I thought you were just telling me how successful it was?'

'Exactly!' Webb beamed. 'How successful it *was*. The future is a different matter entirely.'

'I guess it would be,' Carlyle said weakly. Never a man for the big picture, he wondered how much longer his little tutorial was going to go on for.

'When the last Pope came to Britain,' Webb continued, 'he drew large, enthusiastic crowds. This time, there will be sullen hostility, reflecting the widespread opposition to the Roman Catholic Church as a political entity. The Church's moral turpitude, its scandalous disregard for its victims, has stripped it of all moral authority. There is no chance that it will be able to get it back. The Vatican cannot accept that it does not have a monopoly on truth, that individuals have their own values. A changing moral code is part of social evolution. Meanwhile, the Church's own moral failings should induce more than a little humility.' She shook her head. 'It's not possible. You can take comfort in the fact that they will be swept away by history.'

That doesn't stop me from wanting to nail that bastard McGowan in the meantime, Carlyle thought as he pushed himself out of the chair. 'Yes.'

'Just remember one thing.' Webb's eyes sparkled with amusement.

'What's that?'

'If you ever do manage to get round to arresting the Pope,' she chuckled, 'you have to address him as either "Your Holiness" or "Holy Father".'

'Thanks,' Carlyle smiled. 'That's good to know.'

TWENTY-ONE

Wandering back through Covent Garden, the inspector tried to summon up some measure of enthusiasm for the Leyne case. In a vaguely dissatisfied mood, he allowed himself to be waylaid by a café called Coffee, Cake and Kink on Endell Street. Ignoring the selection of teas on offer, he ordered a latte and a slice of banana and cherry loaf. The place was full but he was able to nab a seat by the window, just as it was vacated by a disappointingly ordinary-looking customer. On the table was a copy of one of the comics CC&K had on sale. Carlyle flicked through it aimlessly; even *Fetishman 6 – Nuns* couldn't raise him from his torpor.

After a considerable wait, the waitress, dressed in a black leather cat-suit with matching cap gave him a smile as she brought him his order. The coffee had a sharp edge, which he liked, but it was not hot enough for his taste. He thought about asking the girl to heat it up for him, but couldn't be bothered. The cake, however, was delicious. Carlyle, conscious of the need for potential replacements for Il Buffone if – or, rather, when – Marcello called it a day, made a mental note to add this one to his list. Popping the last of the loaf into his mouth, he carefully returned *Fetishman 6* to the nearby magazine rack and pulled out his mobile. There was a text from his wife. Opening it, he frowned.

Don't forget the school at 2 x

What the hell? It took him several moments to remember that he had promised to give a talk on drugs to the sixth-formers at Alice's school. He had been bounced into it by the Headmaster, Dr Terence Myers.

Carlyle and Helen had been summoned to the Headmaster's office after Alice had been suspended for possession of cannabis. They had been so relieved that she hadn't been kicked out for good that he had happily signed up for the talk. That had been more than a year ago. It had been almost three months since Myers's office had confirmed the date. He had completely forgotten all about it.

'Bollocks,' he muttered, typing in a reply: *Sure. No problem. X.* As the message disappeared into the ether, the phone started ringing in his hand and Roche's name appeared on the screen. 'How's it going?' he asked.

'I'm just going in with Dyer now,' Roche said excitedly.

'Eh? I thought you would have been finished by now.'

'We've got a major result. Dyer's fingerprints were recovered from the scene and they've found some jewellery at his mum's flat.'

'That's the great thing about criminals,' Carlyle said. 'Some of them are so fucking stupid that it's unbelievable. God bless the cretinous little sod.'

'I've left him and his lawyer to stew for a while and I'm just about to go in and hit him with both barrels. I wondered if you might want me to wait for you?'

'I've got to do something else right now.'

'Okay,' Roche replied, some of the enthusiasm draining from her voice.

'Get as much out of him as you can, charge him and get him processed. In the meantime, can you get someone to do some basic background checks on the recently deceased Professor Leyne. He's been married three times apparently, so we need to track down the wives. Also, we need to check finances, et cetera, et cetera. I'll chase the autopsy report and forensics and we can compare notes at the end of the day.'

'Suppose so.' Roche sounded more than a little pissed off now, but Carlyle didn't have time to worry about that. Ending the call, he borrowed a pen from the waitress and began scribbling some notes for his talk on the back of a flyer advertising an exhibition of photographs of female bodybuilders at a gallery in Camden.

Gazing out across the rows of bored faces, careful not to make eye-contact with any of them, Carlyle stood at the front of the classroom, desperately trying not to feel intimidated. After a moment, he turned to the Headmaster and whispered: 'This is the sixth form, right?'

'No, no,' Dr Myers smiled apologetically. 'The sixth-formers are sitting exams this week. This is the fourth form.'

Good God. Carlyle's heart sank. Alice would be in this class soon enough, assuming she didn't get caught with any more drugs in the meantime. The twenty or so girls sitting in front of him oozed self-confidence and maturity. At least half of them could have passed for twenty-five at a casual glance. All of them looked like they could eat him alive. He glanced at his notes. Gibberish. What in God's name was he going to talk about?

Sensing his anxiety, Myers gave him a consoling pat on the shoulder. 'Don't worry, Inspector, they are all very interested in what you have to say.' Turning to face the group, he gave Carlyle a gentle push forward. 'Ladies, we are very fortunate to have with us today Inspector Carlyle from Charing Cross police station.'

Trying to smile, Carlyle nodded. 'Good afternoon.'

While a couple of the girls mumbled a desultory 'good afternoon' in reply, the majority sat in stony silence.

'Inspector Carlyle,' Myers continued, ignoring the lack of enthusiasm that had sucked all of the energy from the room, 'is here to talk about drugs.'

'Has he got any then?' a cheeky voice piped up from the back, precipitating a few giggles from her mates.

'Thank you for that, Tara,' Myers said stonily. 'I'm sure that the inspector will be happy to take any sensible questions you may have.' He gestured for Carlyle to take the floor. 'Inspector . . .'

'Thank you, Headmaster,' Carlyle replied, his mouth suddenly dry. 'It is very nice to be here this afternoon. Thank you for inviting me.' Finally realizing what he was going to say, he broke into a smile. 'I'm not going to talk for very long, I promise!' He scanned the blank looks. 'First, though, hands up anyone who has done drugs.'

His opening gambit got a few bemused looks, not least from the Headmaster, but no hands went up.

'No one?' Carlyle's smile went wider. 'Are you sure? Dr Myers?'

Blushing slightly, the Headmaster shook his head. There were a few laughs.

Carlyle gave him a quizzical look. 'Are *you* sure?'

'Quite sure, th-thank you,' Myers stammered.

'Okay.' Carlyle put his own hand up. 'Well, I have tried drugs,' he looked around his audience, 'and lived to tell the tale.'

There was more laughter and some whispering. Carlyle felt himself begin to relax, knowing that he was going to be fine after all. He put down his hand. 'I was a bit older than you, but not much. I experimented with them when I was at school and when I was a young copper.'

'What types of drugs?' asked a serious-looking girl near the front.

Carlyle shrugged. 'I did a bit of cannabis but I didn't like it much; I found it made me feel nauseous. Mainly speed was my thing – amphetamine sulphate. It was relatively cheap and easily available. I would buy it from a mate.'

A hand went up at the back.

Carlyle nodded. 'Yes?'

'Why did you give up?'

'I just kind of grew out of it, I suppose. I was never that into it. If it was there, I would do it; if it wasn't, I never really felt the need to go looking for it.' He spread his hands wide. 'The point is that I'm not here to lecture you that it's evil and that you should never do it. What you *should* do is be informed about the issues and the consequences of using and abusing restricted drugs. As a policeman, drugs are not a moral issue . . .' he paused, scanning the faces to see if they were taking in what he was saying . . . 'they are a *crime* issue. Drug dependency is an important factor in robberies, violent crime, people-trafficking, prostitution and money laundering. There are other important issues in terms of drug-related deaths, ill-health, unemployment and the break-up of families.'

A girl in the front row shot him an exasperate look. 'Isn't that why drugs should just be legalized?'

Carlyle glanced at the Headmaster. Dr Myers seemed to be getting unhappier by the minute. He turned back to the girl and said honestly, 'Maybe it is – I don't know. But it isn't going to happen. For whatever reason, politicians are just as addicted to the war on drugs as any junkie is to smack. There is some tweaking round the edges – Holland is famous for its liberal attitude towards soft drugs and there have been similar initiatives in Portugal. Even here, in the UK, there have been some attempts to reform the Misuse of Drugs Act, which dates back to 1971. Cannabis, for example, was downgraded to a Class C drug a few years ago and then changed back to Class B later on. However, the basic point that I want you to take away from our session today is that you really need to be aware of both the potential consequences of restricted drug use. You have to be clear about the *legal* consequences of using drugs. There are various types of drugs offences that might be committed in certain situations: mixing tobacco with another herbal substance in a roll-up cigarette, for example – that's called possession; carrying several small plastic bags containing a herbal substance is "possession with intent to supply"; smoking cannabis at home with friends is "allowing premises to be used". And so on . . .'

'Haven't the police got better things to do,' the blonde girl harrumphed, 'than harass people for smoking a joint?'

'My point is that you need to be aware of the potential consequences,' Carlyle repeated. 'You've heard of the phrase, *the law is an ass?*' Much nodding. 'Well, whether it is or not really doesn't matter. The law is the law. Under the Misuse of Drugs Act, you can go to jail. And lots of people do. Penalties range from life imprisonment for supply of Class A drugs like heroin, to two years for possession of less dangerous Class C drugs.'

'What a waste of our taxes,' someone complained.

Don't you mean 'our parents' taxes'? 'Our priority,' Carlyle said evenly, 'is to target the organized criminal groups involved in drug trafficking and confiscate their ill-gotten gains. Local dealers, crack-houses and cannabis factories are other targets. So, if you find yourself in a crack-house, watch out.'

As the girls started laughing, Dr Myers looked like he was about to have a coronary. In the corridor a bell sounded, followed almost immediately by the sound of hundreds of pairs of feet making a dash for freedom. The room emptied in barely five seconds, leaving Carlyle with the Headmaster, who was slowly regaining his composure.

'What a nice bunch of kids,' Carlyle smiled, relieved that it was all over. 'That was really interesting. Let me know if I can come again.'

'That is very kind of you, Inspector,' Myers said, leading him quickly towards the door. 'We will certainly bear it in mind.'

On his desk, back at the station, was a thick file of documents with a Post-it note stuck on the top. In blue biro, Roche had written neatly: *background reading on Leyne*. Moving the file to one side, Carlyle reached across the desk and picked up the phone. Dialling Roche's mobile, he let it ring six times, before hanging up and calling the front desk downstairs. The sergeant on duty confirmed that Dyer had given Roche a name for his accomplice. She had taken a team up to Wood Green to raid an address near Alexandra Palace.

Putting the phone down, Carlyle checked his mobile. There were no missed calls. He felt a pang of disappointment that she hadn't bothered to keep him in the loop, and had an unhappy sense of missing out on the action. But it quickly passed as he realized that she was more than capable of handling the situation without him. Anyway, there would be plenty of other doors to kick in; he could afford to miss out on this one.

'Fuck it,' he mumbled to himself, 'time to go home.' Sticking the Leyne file under his arm, he headed for the stairs.

TWENTY-TWO

At home, he found Helen on the sofa, sipping some *Rooibos* tea and doing *The Times* Sudoku puzzle. Making himself a cup of green tea, he flopped down beside her. 'Going well?'

She scribbled a couple of numbers on the page and tossed the paper and the pen on the floor with a satisfied smirk. 'Done it! The Super Fiendish, too.'

'Nice one,' Carlyle grinned, not having the remotest idea what the 'Super Fiendish' actually was.

'How did it go at the school?' Helen asked, cuddling up to him.

Sticking an arm round her, Carlyle recounted his triumph with the fourth form. 'All in all, I think it went rather well.'

Helen's face darkened and she pushed him away. 'Why did you have to be such a bloody smartarse?'

With a sinking feeling in his stomach, Carlyle placed his mug on the coffee table. Too late, he realized that he had made a terrible error of judgement. Trying not to panic, he played dumb. 'What do you mean?' he asked, smearing an approximation of a confused look across his face.

'Bloody hell, John,' she complained. 'All you had to do was go in and say the usual stuff about how drugs are dangerous and you could go to prison and so on. How difficult could it have been?'

'But—'

'Why did you have to go in and try to be like the *too cool for school* policeman?'

'I didn't.'

She looked as if she was about to cry. 'It was a bunch of teenage

117

girls and the bloody Headmaster! What will he think of Alice now? What will he think of our promise to keep her away from more dope?'

Carlyle took a deep breath. 'I tried to treat them like young adults.' Reaching over, he ignored her protests and kissed her on the forehead. 'We had an interesting discussion. *And* I offered to go back. I think the Headmaster felt it went well.'

She looked at him, unconvinced.

'Alice will be judged on whether she goes around carrying any more cannabis in her bag – which she won't – not because of what Dr Myers thinks of my talk. It will all be fine. We know that she's doing well.' Pulling his wife closer, he again put his arm round her shoulder. 'Anyway, we have other things to focus on.'

Helen dropped her head onto his shoulder. 'You don't have to come. All they will do is take some blood. We won't get any results.'

'I know,' he replied, giving her a gentle squeeze. 'But I want to be there. We can go for a coffee, or at least a green tea, afterwards.'

'Yeah.'

Carlyle smiled to himself. The promise of a decent cappuccino was usually a winner where Helen was concerned. For several minutes they sat there in silence, listening to each other's breathing. After a while, Carlyle found himself idly fondling Helen's right breast. She tut-tutted her displeasure but made no effort to push his hand away. Almost immediately, he felt himself begin to stiffen. With his free hand, he reached down and unbuttoned the top of her jeans.

'Hey,' she whispered, looking at her watch, 'Alice will be home in five minutes.'

'Five minutes,' Carlyle grinned, 'is gonna be more than enough.'

Feeling rather pleased with himself, Carlyle had been sitting on the sofa for almost ten minutes by the time the door went and Alice finally appeared in the doorway.

'Hi, Dad,' she smiled, 'where's Mum?'

Carlyle yawned. 'She's having a bath. How was school today?'

Alice's grin grew wider. 'I should be asking *you* that question. I hear you made quite an impression on 4G.'

'I did?'

'Yeah. One of the girls said you asked the Headmaster in front of the whole class if he'd ever done drugs. Old Myers wasn't happy at all.'

Oh shit, Carlyle thought, *please don't tell your mother that.* 'But did they think the talk was any good?'

'They liked the bit about you being, like, a *junkie* when you were younger,' Alice said, eyes wide in mock horror.

Carlyle's heart sank even further. 'I didn't—'

'I know,' she sighed, 'I know. You were just being a know-it-all, as usual.'

Conversation over, she skipped down the hall. Carlyle listened to her bedroom door slam shut, followed almost immediately by the strains of some anaemic pop music. He sat in silence, wondering how he could pull himself out of this latest hole. Failing to come up with a solution, he turned with some reluctance to the Leyne file.

On closer inspection it was basically a series of press cuttings that didn't really tell him anything that he hadn't learned from his trip to see Professor Webb at the LSE. The only new information was a single sheet of A4 paper containing the names and contact details of the academic's three wives. Next to two of the names, Roche had written in capitals: *NOT YET INFORMED*. However, the third, a Christine Donovan, had a big tick, which Carlyle presumed meant he could call with relative confidence.

Donovan had an overseas number with a 213 dialling code which he vaguely thought must be somewhere in America. It took what seemed like an eternity to get a connection but once the phone started ringing, someone picked up almost immediately.

'Donovan residence,' said a sleepy-sounding Hispanic voice. 'How may I help you?'

'Good afternoon,' said Carlyle in his most official manner. 'Could I speak to Ms Donovan, please?'

There was an extended pause. 'I'm sorry, sir,' the voice said finally. 'Could you repeat that, please?'

'I am calling from London,' Carlyle said slowly, trying not to shout. 'I would like to speak to Ms Christine Donovan.'

'Hold the line, please.'

After what seemed like an eternity, Carlyle was about to hang up when there was some rustling on the end of the line and someone picked up. 'Hi!' said a chirpy teenage voice. 'This is Christie.'

Confused, Carlyle was momentarily struck dumb. He looked at his notes: Christine Donovan and Roger Leyne were married almost twenty-five years ago, divorced after barely ten months, before this kid could even have been born.

'Hello?'

'Yes,' he said quickly, 'my name is Inspector John Carlyle from the Metropolitan Police in London. I am looking to speak to Christine Donovan.'

'Cool!' the girl squealed. 'Has Mom done something bad?'

'No, no,' he stammered, as the conversation spiralled out of control. With her usual immaculate timing, Helen wandered into the living room. With a big grin on her face, she pulled open her bathrobe and flashed him. Aroused and confused, he felt his brain melt.

He was saved by the American teenager more than five thousand miles away. 'Do you want to speak to her?'

'Yes,' he nodded, watching Helen cover herself up. 'Yes please, if she's around.'

'Is it about her ex-husband?'

Fuck me, Carlyle despaired, *does everybody have to know everything about my business?* 'Yes,' he sighed, 'it is. Is she available?'

He listened to the phone being put down again and a voice in the background shout: *'Mom! It's for you. It's the London po-lice. They want to talk to you about that guy's murder.'*

After a few moments, a rather haughty voice came on the line. 'This is Christine Donovan.'

'My name is—'

'My daughter explained who you are,' Donovan said sharply. 'What can I do for you?'

'I was wondering – when was the last time you saw your ex-husband?'

Her laughter cut through the time delay on the line. 'You're kidding, right? I mean, I'm in LA, for Christ sakes. How could I have killed the bum?'

Carlyle said nothing.

Donovan sighed. 'Twenty years ago, I would have happily killed Roger. Hell, even ten years ago I might have happily nailed his smug limey ass.'

Limey? 'How did you two meet?' he asked.

'I went to study in London in the eighties and Roger, quite literally, charmed the pants off me. Goodness, I was a right idiot. That phony took me to the cleaners. My dad went crazy because I refused to have a pre-nup agreement. In the end, that marriage cost me about five million dollars. But I got over it.'

Jeez, Carlyle thought, *why couldn't you have bumped into me back then?* 'Who do you think might er . . . want to kill Professor Leyne *now*?'

'Inspector,' she said firmly, 'I haven't seen Roger for more than twenty years. I haven't been to England for more than ten. How the hell would I know who wanted to kill him?'

'Fair point,' Carlyle admitted, 'but I have to ask.'

'Sure, sure. I found out soon enough that Roger was good at annoying people. No doubt if you dig around, you'll manage to find plenty of suspects.'

'That's extremely helpful,' Carlyle said sarcastically.

'He's been married twice since me,' Donovan said, apparently oblivious to his tone. 'I'm sure that would be a good place to start.'

'I will,' he said, crossing her name off the list. 'Thank you for your time.' He waited for her to say '*have a nice day*', or something similar, but after a moment, he realized that she had simply hung up. Tossing the mobile on to the sofa, he let out a massive yawn. It was time to call it a day.

Perched on the edge of a desk, Roche took a long, hard drag from her bottle of Budweiser as she watched the party mood around her grow. The raid had been a spectacular success, with Colin Dyer's partner, Damien Samuels, taken into custody, along with a quantity of jewellery and a Smith & Wesson Model 909. Tests on the automatic pistol wouldn't take place until the morning, but she was sure it would turn out to be the gun that killed Paula Coulter. Samuels was toast. It was a major fucking result.

Finishing the beer, Roche placed the bottle down on the desk beside her. The adrenaline rush from the raid was wearing off and she ached with tiredness. One of the grinning uniforms walked past, gave her a high five and handed her another beer. Roche nodded her thanks and took a swig from the new bottle. Getting a healthy beer buzz now, she knew she was going to get blasted. Her mobile buzzed angrily in the back pocket of her jeans. Assuming that it was Carlyle, she pulled it out and opened the message. However, it was only her boyfriend. *Gone to bed, don't wake me up when (if?) you get in.* Roche sighed. Martin's moaning was beginning to get on her nerves. More to the point, she wondered, where the hell was the inspector?

Out of the corner of her eye, she saw Dugdale in his uniform – did he ever wear anything else? – appear on the floor. She was surprised to see that he still had the PR woman – what was her name? Judith something – still in tow. Why would she still be following him around at this time of night? The idle thought that he might be fucking her drifted through Roche's brain as she finished the beer.

The Commander helped himself to a couple of beers and headed towards her. As he approached, she saw him sway alarmingly, his face flushed. *You're well ahead of me*, she thought, giving him a tired smile.

Dugdale handed her a fresh beer. 'Well done.' He tried to smile, but it was more like a leer. 'That was excellent work this evening.'

'Thanks.' She placed the beer on the table next to the empties. Seeing Dugdale had rather tempered her desire to get hammered. 'It's nice when things work out.'

Dugdale lifted the bottle to his lips. 'You've done a fantastic job on this one, Alison.'

Watching him empty half the bottle, Roche played with her mobile. 'I should give Inspector Carlyle a call.'

'Why?' Dugdale tried to stifle a belch. 'So he can run round and steal your glory?'

That's not his style, Roche thought, shoving the mobile back into her pocket.

Dugdale finished his beer and signalled to Judith Mahon, the PR woman, hovering on the other side of the room, to bring him another. 'Where is Carlyle anyway?'

'He's working on the Leyne case,' the sergeant said swiftly.

'That was a bloody result too!' Dugdale exulted.

'Presumably,' said Roche, trying to affect some insouciance, 'that means that the Church will now withdraw its complaint?'

Dugdale's brow furrowed. 'I wouldn't assume that,' he said quietly, glancing round the room to check that no one was overhearing their conversation. When Mahon appeared with his beer, the Commander grabbed it from her with a grunt of acknowledgement and took a healthy swig.

'But I thought that was the deal,' Roche said evenly.

'Deal?' Dugdale repeated. 'There is no "deal". Leyne and the Church's complaint are completely separate. I don't know what the inspector told you, but it is essential that we act – and are seen to act – properly and professionally in all matters. The investigation into the complaint against the inspector must be thorough.'

Roche felt a flash of annoyance at the fact that she had been omitted from the list of accused. 'You wouldn't be hanging him out to dry, sir, would you?'

'No, I would not.' Dugdale waved his bottle angrily in front of her face. 'If he hasn't done anything wrong, then he has nothing to worry about.'

'I made my statement,' Roche said firmly. 'The inspector acted entirely properly . . . and so have I.'

A sly grin crossed Dugdale's lips. 'In that case, like I said, he has nothing to worry about. And neither, for that matter, do you.'

Don't rise to the bait, Roche told herself. Dugdale put a paw on Mahon's shoulder. The PR smiled nervously. He took a sneaky peek down her blouse and the leer returned. *He's definitely screwing her*, Roche thought, *the dirty old bugger*.

'Judith is organizing a press conference for tomorrow morning at

Paddington Green,' Dugdale continued, 'so I want you to let her have the key details.'

'No problem.'

'And I want you to be there with me.'

Roche's heart sank. That was the last thing she needed. 'I've still got a lot to do on this—'

'Now is no time to be shy,' Dugdale trumpeted. 'I want you to get the recognition you deserve. This could be an important stepping-stone for your career. After closing such an important case, you could look to move on. Who knows? Maybe I could even help get you a move to SO15.'

Gazing at the floor, Roche shuddered as she thought about the price Dugdale might want for his help. On the other hand, SO15 was a very attractive proposition. Her murdered boyfriend, Detective Inspector David Ronan, had been with the Counter Terrorism Command Unit, and Roche had often wondered whether, one day, she might step into his shoes.

Forcing herself to make eye-contact with Dugdale, she somehow managed a smile. 'Okay,' she said, 'I will see you in the morning.'

TWENTY-THREE

Three men carried the coffin as it emerged from the parlour of A. France & Son into the pale late-morning sunlight. Two older guys took one side while a much younger man, a big bloke with a crew cut that highlighted his receding hairline, took the other. All were dressed immaculately in black suits, white shirts and black ties. Even from the other side of the road, Carlyle could see that their shoes were polished to a high shine. Taking a sip of his Brazilian Berries smoothie, the inspector watched as they slipped the coffin into the rear of the hearse with practised ease. After carefully closing the back door of the vehicle, the younger guy jumped into the driver's seat and started up the engine. Slowly, the black Mercedes moved off, heading north up Lambs Conduit Street.

Carlyle watched the two older guys go back inside and casually turned his attention to the two Goodfellas' regulars sitting nearby, discussing last night's football, struggling to complete their roll-ups while their cappuccinos went cold. Sitting beside him, Helen was fiddling with her mobile. He ran a finger gently up and down her upper arm. 'How are you feeling?'

She didn't look up from her phone. 'Stop asking me how I'm feeling!' Tossing the phone onto the table, she took a sip of her latte and scowled. 'This is cold, I'm going to ask them to heat it up.' Getting to her feet, she went back inside the café.

Watching a boy sail past on a bike, Carlyle finished his juice. Normally, sitting outside the Goodfellas café, idly watching the world go by, was one of life's little pleasures. This morning, however, the inspector was very much on edge. Their visit to Great Ormond Street Hospital had been quick and perfunctory – they had been in and out in barely half an hour – but it had forced him to face Helen's situation in a way that he had been happy to ignore for the past few days. The consultant, an amiable, featureless guy straight out of Central Casting, had talked to them briefly about the BRCA2 gene and his research project. Carlyle had nodded politely and even smiled in places, all the while knowing that the information was simply not entering his brain, which was screaming to him to get out of there. Helen had given a blood sample and they had made an appointment in two weeks' time to come back for the results. Then he had led her firmly by the arm, heading swiftly for the exit, avoiding eye-contact with the weary-looking kids and their parents hovering in reception, who were busy having to deal with crises of their own.

Helen reappeared with steam rising from her latte. Following behind her, the waitress placed a double macchiato and a large raisin Danish on the table.

'I thought you could do with some comfort food,' Helen smiled. Reaching over she gave him a kiss on the cheek. 'Thank you for coming.'

He took her hand and squeezed it tightly. 'I wasn't going to let you do it on your own.'

'I know. Thanks.'

Dropping her hand, he took a sip of his coffee and eyed the Danish hungrily. 'I suppose all we can do now is wait.'

'That's fine,' she shrugged. 'We'll know in a couple of weeks. There's no point in worrying about it until then.'

'No.' Taking a bite from his pastry, he chewed it mechanically.

Helen took a sip of her latte. 'Alice knows.'

Carlyle frowned. 'How?'

'She must have seen the letter, I suppose. She asked me if I was going to die.'

'Jesus! When was this?'

'The other day.'

'Fuck. She didn't talk to me about it.'

'You've been really busy.'

'Yeah,' he sighed. 'I suppose I have.'

Taking the Danish from him, she took a small nibble. 'It's not that bad. She's a sensible kid. We talked it through. She understands we have to wait for the results, and I explained that even if I do have it, there are things we can do.'

'Mm.' Carlyle didn't want to think about that.

'She was very grown up about it.'

'She's still a kid.'

Helen grinned. 'You were at the school. You see how quickly they grow up.'

'I suppose so,' Carlyle replied. 'Did she ask about herself?'

Helen's face darkened. 'About whether she might have it?'

'Yeah.'

'I explained that if I had it, she would need to consider getting tested when she was older.'

Carlyle finished his macchiato. 'If it comes to it, she should definitely get tested.'

Helen gave him a weary look. 'That will be a matter for her. Anyway, I don't think the Health Service would do it until she is eighteen.'

Carlyle gazed down the street. Next to the undertaker's was a flower shop. He watched as one of the assistants placed buckets of bright red and yellow roses on the pavement, under the front window. The caffeine in his system made him feel wired but he had a deep reluctance to move.

After a while, Helen got to her feet. 'Come on,' she said, 'it's time to get back to work.'

Katya Morrison took a sip of her tea and smiled at the priest. 'Well, Your, er, Holiness, how was the pilgrimage to Lourdes?'

The Archbishop of Westminster, Brian Crossley, eyed the young woman and smiled back.

Christian Holyrod cringed. His Special Adviser really would have to go. At least, this time, dressed demurely with a navy sweater over a white blouse, she didn't have her tits hanging out. But the girl's chronic inability to play the part of a grown-up really was beginning to try his patience.

The alpha female, on the other hand, looked quite a piece of work. Across the table, Abigail Slater sat demurely between the Archbishop and Monsignor Joseph Wagner, Papal Visit Co-ordinator. Even so, the look on her face suggested that she could eat him for breakfast, something which Holyrod found a by no means unappealing prospect.

Crossley glanced at the Mayor, who almost managed to tear his own gaze from the lawyer. 'One of the things that I saw in Lourdes is the great value of tapping into people's goodwill. If we can generate in our society that sense of fulfilment which comes from volunteering, then we would be much the better for it. It is important for society to not fall into the trap of thinking that everything is to be provided and that it is always somebody else's responsibility.'

'Oh,' Katya gushed, 'absolutely.'

Spare me, thought Holyrod.

Crossley looked patronizingly at the young aide. 'It is great that your boss respects the integrity of what faith-groups want to do, and respects our language and beliefs.'

God, how these people loved to talk! Holyrod allowed himself the smallest of smiles in Slater's direction. The amused look on her face suggested she was thinking something similar.

Tapping a pen on the table, Monsignor Joseph Wagner tried to get the meeting back on track. 'This visit is an opportunity to move away from seeing faith as a problem and seeing it as a resource to be discovered afresh. It will be a symbolic embrace by the leader of the Catholic Church, an embrace of Britain as it is today: multi-faith, multicultural, facing inner difficulties, but with great human resources which are strengthened by faith in God.'

'I think that we're all agreed on that,' said Slater somewhat brusquely.

'Will the Pope be meeting any child-abuse victims?' Morrison asked brightly.

The question caused Holyrod to momentarily choke on his coffee, to Slater's obvious amusement.

'In private,' Morrison added, when he'd finished coughing, 'of course.'

The smile on the Archbishop's face wavered only slightly. 'Child abuse is a dreadful scandal which is to be condemned, and it's something for which every Catholic feels ashamed and sorrowful. I think there are difficult issues in certain countries, but I don't get any sense of it here. If the Pope were to meet with victims of clerical sexual abuse,' he glanced at Wagner, who shook his head, 'and I am not aware of any plans for such a meeting at present, it would have to be done for the right reasons, not simply to satisfy a public agenda or curiosity.'

Those seem like pretty good reasons to me, thought Holyrod. 'It is a sidebar issue,' he said, however. 'Let us move on.'

'More than three hundred years after English priests were martyred by the anti-Catholic government of Elizabeth I,' Wagner said mechanically, as if reciting by rote, 'the Holy Father is to meet Elizabeth II as part of the first ever state visit by a Pope to Britain. That is what we need to focus on now.'

'That is what we *are* focused on,' said Holyrod, trying to keep the exasperation from his voice. He looked at the faces around the table. 'As you know, we have been working extremely hard to deal with the various different issues raised by the Monsignor at our last meeting. You will not be unaware that the specific matter relating to Professor Leyne appears to have, well, resolved itself. For which I am sure we are all grateful.' He paused, waiting for some sign of agreement but none was forthcoming. 'Which brings me to the second issue, that of Father McGowan.'

Crossley looked at Wagner. 'Where is the Father at present?'

A look of mild panic clouded the face of the Monsignor, who clearly did not have a clue. 'McGowan? He . . .'

'He is keeping a low profile,' Slater interjected, 'while continuing with his duties at St Boniface's.'

Crossley frowned. 'And what about the boy who made the complaint?'

'He has disappeared.' The lawyer gave Holyrod a look that bordered on a smirk. 'No one has been able to locate him. That, in itself, should give pause to anyone looking to give too much credence to his complaint.'

Holyrod felt himself bristle. Even by his standards, Abigail Slater was a hard bastard. He made a show of clearing his throat. 'All of this,' he said loudly, 'would seem to suggest that we have an opportunity to deal with the McGowan problem here and now.'

'The Inspector Carlyle problem,' Slater corrected him with a sly smile.

'*Our* collective problem,' said Holyrod, gesturing round the room, determined not to rise to the bait, 'however you want to label it.' He scanned the trio across the table, almost unable to believe that he had just tried to defend his nemesis.

There was an extended pause in which no one seemed prepared to speak. Finally, Slater scribbled a note on the sheet of paper in front of her and looked up. 'I am sorry, Mr Mayor,' she said, almost meekly, 'that will not be possible. Father McGowan deserves justice in this matter.'

Holyrod eyed the two Church functionaries, who had their eyes locked firmly on the table and were keeping their mouths shut. He fixed his gaze on Slater, trying not to lick his lips. 'I agree with you, of course, but—'

'But,' Slater interrupted, 'your officer is not above the law.'

'No,' said Holyrod through gritted teeth. 'Absolutely not. No one in the Metropolitan Police Force is above the law.'

'Well then,' the lawyer smiled, 'I suggest that, with the Papal visit barely a month away, we should deal with this matter as speedily as possible.'

TWENTY-FOUR

Striding towards the front desk, the inspector watched a familiar figure approaching and allowed himself a wry smile. Ambrose Watson must be pushing forty now; his hair was greyer than Carlyle remembered it and his hairline had receded further than the inspector would have thought possible. As usual, Ambrose was squeezed into a suit that seemed at least two sizes too small for him, and a garish tie hung limply from his neck.

The inspector stuck out a hand. 'How are you?'

'I am well, Inspector.' Shaking his hand, Watson returned the smile. 'And I see that you are keeping as busy as usual.'

'It's nice to know that the IIC carefully follows my progress.' Internal Investigations Command had looked into a couple of Carlyle's cases in recent years. Commander Simpson had seen to it that the fair and decent Watson had handled the enquiry, rather than one of his more aggressive colleagues. Watson knew that Carlyle sailed close to the wind, but that came with the territory: he wasn't going to go out of his way to destroy the inspector's career.

Watson dropped his gaze to the floor. 'Sadly, that is fairly inevitable, given past events.'

'Are you looking into this Catholic Legal Network thing?'

'No, that would be me.' From behind Watson's bulk appeared a sallow-looking woman of indeterminate age. With short blonde hair and dull brown eyes, she had an expression on her pinched face that could only be described as threatening. 'Superintendent Rebecca Buck.' She held out a hand. 'I will be coordinating both the IIC and IPCC investigations into this matter.'

Carlyle gave her hand the briefest of shakes. He glanced at Ambrose, who shrugged apologetically.

'Ambrose will provide me with administrative support.'

Seeing Dugdale's hand at work, Carlyle slipped a studiously neutral expression onto his face. 'Is it usual for you to manage what is primarily an IPCC matter?' he asked casually. Just as with the IIC, he was no stranger to investigations by the Independent Police Complaints Commission. But if the IIC could take away his job – and his pension – Carlyle was far less concerned about the prospects of the IPCC, which was run by a bunch of outsiders, ever doing the same.

'That is the way we are running this one,' Buck said stiffly.

'Your call,' Carlyle said, without enthusiasm.

Ambrose gestured in the direction of the desk. 'The sergeant is just finding us a room.'

'Good.' Carlyle smiled as he spied Roche walking down the corridor towards them. He signalled her over and made the necessary introductions. 'Now, if you'll excuse us, Sergeant Roche and I have to go and conduct a very important interview. Get yourselves installed here and I will be back as quickly as possible.'

Buck opened her mouth to protest but Carlyle had already wheeled away, dragging Roche towards the door.

Outside, he set a sharp pace along Bedford Street, heading north. Roche, struggling to keep up, broke into a jog. 'Where are we going?' she panted, annoyed.

Carlyle grinned. 'It's a surprise.'

'Fuck off,' Roche huffed. 'I'm not in the mood.'

'Okay, fine.' Carlyle held up his hands. 'FYI, just in case you *get* into to the mood, we're going fishing.'

'Caught anything yet?'

'Nothing, so far.' Trevor Cole, the agent from Gotha Insurance, placed his rod carefully on the towpath, with the line still in the water. Pushing himself up off his folding stool, he shook Carlyle by the hand.

Looking over the inspector's shoulder, he smiled at Roche. 'I thought you were good on TV this morning.'

Carlyle gave his sergeant a quizzical look which she returned with an *I'll tell you about it later* shrug. Moving swiftly on, she gestured at the murky waters of the Regent's Canal. 'Is there anything actually alive in there?'

'Oh yes,' Cole replied, checking his rod. 'This is one of the best spots.' From the far side of the canal came the rumble of a train heading into King's Cross. 'You can find bream, carp, perch, pike – all sorts.'

Carlyle peered into a small pot of maggots next to the stool. The attraction of fishing was something that he had never understood.

'As you get nearer to Camden,' Cole continued, 'there are so many shopping trolleys under the water that your line gets snagged all the time, but here it's fairly okay.'

'Interesting,' Carlyle yawned.

Roche gave him a meaningful elbow in the ribs. 'It must be very relaxing.'

'I enjoy it,' Cole agreed. 'You really do get a sense of being away from the hustle and bustle of London.'

Similar to what it might be like if they drop a neutron bomb, Carlyle mused – *kill all the people but leave the buildings standing*. An image flashed through his brain of radio-active mutant fish swimming up and down the canal between Limehouse and Little Venice, with no one to catch them.

Cole went to his knapsack and pulled out a small flask. Pouring some black coffee into a small plastic cup, he offered some to Carlyle and Roche, both of whom politely refused. Cole took a mouthful and let out a satisfied sigh. 'So,' he said, 'where have we got to?'

Roche jumped in before Carlyle could open his mouth. 'We've logged most of the stuff we've recovered,' she said matter-of-factly, 'and referenced it to your list.'

'Good job,' said Cole, glancing at his rod.

Carlyle watched a beer can float idly by.

'My best guess right now,' Roche continued, 'is that we've got maybe eighty per cent of the pieces. How much that will turn out to be by value, I don't know.'

Something started tugging on the line. Cole quickly stepped over and picked up the rod. After a couple of gentle pulls, he seemed satisfied that there was nothing there and placed it back on the ground.

What a bloody tedious carry-on, the inspector thought.

'It's like I said,' Cole told her. 'We're convinced that some of the items were taken *after* the robbery took place.'

'I have gone through the CCTV footage twice now,' said Roche, 'and we haven't come up with anything to support that idea.'

'The CCTV footage,' said Cole evenly, 'only covers the period up until an hour after the police arrived.'

'That's right,' said Roche rather defensively, knowing where this was going. 'Once the scene had been secured, checking the images on the camera's hard drive was one of the first things that we did.'

And you switched the camera off in the process, Carlyle thought, trying not to grimace. No point in worrying about that now. He turned to Cole. 'What do you think happened?'

Cole took another mouthful of coffee and poured the dregs into the canal. 'It's just a theory.'

'A theory that you want us to check out,' Carlyle said sharply.

Cole smiled. 'Indeed.'

Leaving Cole to his fishing, they walked slowly back along the towpath in the direction of King's Cross. 'I pulled someone out of there once,' said Carlyle as he watched a small barge chug slowly by, heading west.

Roche stared at the water, saying nothing.

He gestured over his shoulder with his thumb. 'A woman called Hayley Flood stuffed the body of her murdered five-year-old daughter, Danielle, in a suitcase weighed down with bricks, before dumping it about half a mile back that way. The mother's boyfriend had pushed the kid down a flight of stairs. She was too scared of him – so she said – to report it. When police divers found her, Danielle had been dead for three months.' Carlyle cleared his throat. 'The mother had continued to cash in her Child Benefit. The only reason it came out was that the boyfriend got drunk down the pub one night and started talking about what they'd done.'

'Unbelievable.'

'No,' said Carlyle sadly, 'no, it's not. People can be complete fucking animals. It doesn't take a lot.'

'At least you got them.'

'I suppose.' He was gripped by an overwhelming melancholy. 'The boyfriend got life. If I remember rightly, the mother got eight years. She'll be out by now for sure. Who knows? Maybe he is too.' Gritting his teeth, he fought back an embarrassing tear. 'Anyway,' he said grimly, 'cases like Danielle Flood are the ones that really get to you. Personally, I can't get too worked up about someone nicking a load of diamonds.'

'What about Paula Coulter?'

'Fair point,' Carlyle nodded. 'But it sounds like you've got that all sewn up.'

Coulter and her family deserved justice – of course they did. But, still, he knew that this was never going to be a case that emotionally engaged him the same way that the Danielle Flood case had done. It was always different when kids were involved. Adults could look after themselves.

Roche looked at him thoughtfully. An uneasy silence descended as they made their way back towards the dull, insistent hum of civilization.

TWENTY-FIVE

In no hurry to get back to Rebecca Buck and her IIC investigation, Carlyle decided that they should stop for lunch in the Venezia café on York Way. The lunchtime rush was still more than half an hour away and they had the place to themselves. Taking a table at the back, they settled down to choosing their food.

'What was this about a press conference?' Carlyle asked casually from behind the oversized laminated menu.

Roche talked him through Dugdale's appearance at the station the night before and the consequent press conference, which had taken place while the inspector was at Great Ormond Street with his wife.

'My, my,' Carlyle said meanly, 'we *are* flavour of the month, aren't we?'

'Look,' Roche shot back, tapping the back of his menu smartly with her own, 'don't give me any shit about this, all right? The whole thing was Dugdale's idea. Meanwhile, you had buggered off to God knows where.'

Placing the menu on the table, Carlyle looked her in the face. 'Did you talk to him about Leyne?'

Roche kept her gaze fixed on her menu. 'Let's order first. What are you having?'

'I think I'll go for the fried eggs, chips and beans and some black coffee,' decided Carlyle.

'Sounds good,' said Roche, getting to her feet. 'I'll have the same.'

Carlyle watched her move over to the counter and place their order. *Are you going to stitch me up?* he wondered. Given the way she had been handling the McGowan situation, he would have said not, but now he wasn't so sure. He watched her return to the table with some napkins and cutlery.

'I did ask Dugdale about Leyne,' she said, handing him a knife and fork as she sat back down. 'He denies that you were offered any "deal" and insists that the IIC investigation will have to run its course.'

Carlyle grimaced. 'The fucker!'

'He's a slimy bastard, all right,' Roche agreed.

'And what about you?'

'What about me?'

Carlyle held her gaze. 'Have you been offered a deal?'

Refusing to blink, Roche thought about it for a moment. 'I think,' she said finally, 'that they are much keener to get you. I'm not really relevant to this game.'

Carlyle nodded, acknowledging the back-handed compliment of sorts.

'But,' Roche continued, 'as long as we stick to our original statements, I don't see what they can do.' She placed a gentle hand on his forearm. 'Don't worry, I *am* sticking to what I said.'

He smiled wanly. 'Thanks.'

'Dugdale's really got it in for you, though.'

'I know.'

'I suppose he blames you for the shit storm that led to him getting kicked out of SO15.'

'As if that was my fault.'

'People like that always have to have someone to blame,' Roche shrugged. 'That's just the way they are.' She pulled a packet of Benson & Hedges out of her pocket and began turning it round in her hand.

'If you need a smoke,' Carlyle said, gesturing to the door, 'don't let me stop you.'

Roche shook her head. 'I'm trying to give up. But I like to know that they're there.'

'Does it work?'

She said unhappily, 'I haven't had one for almost two months.'

Carlyle changed the subject. 'I never thought I'd see the day when I would miss bloody Simpson.'

'I hear she's being lined up for the Presidency of the IAWP.'

'The what?'

Roche smiled. 'The International Association of Women Police.'

'Great,' said Carlyle flatly. 'What the fuck is that?'

'Dunno. Some kind of international association for women police, at a guess. Whatever it is, she seems set to be staying in Canada for a while.'

'In the meantime, we're stuck with Dudgale.'

'Yeah,' Roche said. 'He thinks he can buy me off, but I intend to give him the widest possible berth.'

Carlyle tried to affect a disinterested tone. 'So what's he offering?'

'He'll leave me out of the McGowan investigation.'

'Can he do that?'

'I suppose so.' Roche paused as their coffees arrived. 'He's also trying to dangle the carrot of a transfer to SO15.'

Carlyle tasted the coffee – it was truly terrible. 'And are you interested?' he asked, once he had recovered from the assault on his taste buds.

Roche gazed at the table. 'Yes, I'm interested.'

'Because of Ronan?'

She looked up at him. 'In the sense that he gave me a chance to see a bit of what it was like? Yes. Counter Terrorism Command would be great. In the sense of doing it for his memory? No. Just because he got shot, doesn't mean that I've forgotten that David was shagging his nineteen-year-old sister-in-law in our bed.'

'Fair enough.'

'I dumped him before he got shot, remember?'

'Yes.'

She gave him a harsh look while the café-owner placed their plates of food on the table. 'And he would have stayed dumped.'

Carlyle held up both hands. 'I don't doubt it for a second.'

'Anyway,' Roche sighed, 'Dugdale may or may not come through. But I won't leg you over to make it happen.'

'I appreciate it.' Picking up his cutlery, Carlyle started on his meal, wondering what he might be able to do, to try and keep her at Charing Cross.

It took him about two minutes to clear his plate. The terrible coffee didn't stop him ordering a second cup, drinking it slowly while watching Roche finish her meal. Inside his brain a dark mood was brewing, one that prevented him from being able to think through how he should progress the cases in front of them.

Roche finished her food, meticulously lining up her knife and fork on the plate and pushing it away from her. The place was filling up now and the owner eyed them expectantly, hoping to get the table back quickly. After serving a takeaway customer he came over to the table. Removing their plates, he dropped the bill on the table. Carlyle picked it up and reached for his wallet. 'I'll get this.'

Roche smiled. 'Thanks.'

'I'm going to take a couple of days off.'

Roche looked at him and shrugged. 'Fine.'

'I want to take Helen down to Brighton,' he added. It was as much elaboration as he was prepared to give.

'Sounds nice.'

'You stick with the St James's case. I need to talk to Roger Leyne's other wives and speak to Phillips about her report.'

'No problem.' Roche looked at him over the top of her cup as she sipped her coffee. 'What about McGowan?'

'We have to park him for the moment. At least until I get this investigation off my back.'

'And the boy?'

'Simon Murphy? Disappeared without a trace. Unless he turns up, we've got nothing.'

Roche placed her cup back in its saucer. 'So they get away with it?'

'Just for a change,' Carlyle said sarcastically.

Knowing better than to try and press on with a topic when he was in such a bad mood, Roche decided on a new topic. 'How much time do you want me to give chasing down Cole's theory?'

'Well,' Carlyle asked, 'what have we got?'

'Dyer and Samuels have both admitted to the robbery,' Roche replied. 'The Smith & Wesson is confirmed as the weapon that killed Paula Coulter. We have recovered the prints of both men and each says that the other pulled the trigger . . .'

139

'Let the CPS sort that out,' Carlyle advised. 'Even they can't fuck this one up.' The Crown Prosecution Service in London was a bad joke among many officers; it was widely believed that some CPS staff were being paid hundreds of thousands of pounds in bonuses while failing to get convictions. A much-discussed government report had claimed that people accused of offences were more likely to walk free in London than anywhere else in the country, thanks to weak preparation for court, poor supervision of cases, delays and inadequate protection for victims and witnesses.

'Yeah,' Roche laughed. 'Maybe they can earn their monster bonuses for once.'

'Still,' Carlyle sighed, 'I can't believe that those two muppets somehow did it on their own.'

'They are adamant that no one else put them up to it. Samuels used to go out with a cousin of Coulter. That's how they say they got the idea.'

'And anyway,' Carlyle added, 'if Cole is right, and some stuff was nicked after Dyer and Samuels legged it, presumably they had nothing to do with it.'

'Do you believe him?'

'I dunno. It seems more likely that we haven't been able to recover all the stuff from Dyer and Samuels.'

Roche laughed. 'They don't really have much of a clue one way or the other. They grabbed what they could and fled.'

'Fine,' Carlyle said, getting to his feet. 'Give it a little time to show willing, but don't bust a gut.'

'There is one thing . . .'

'Yeah?' Carlyle sat back down again, much to the café-owner's disgust.

'Hubaishi Dorning Klee. HDK Capital Management, the boutique asset management firm.'

'God! In my day, a boutique was somewhere where you bought a shirt.'

'They have two Nobel Laureates and a number of leading economics professors on the staff. Among other things, they own St James's

Diamonds. Katrin Lagerbäck is one of their Associates, responsible for the day-to-day running of the business. They have stores in London, LA, Mumbai, Shanghai, Moscow and Miami.'

'And?'

'And last year, St James's lost almost sixty million dollars.'

'So?' Carlyle shrugged. 'What's sixty million to a bunch of financial whiz kids. Don't these type of guys deal in tens of *billions*?'

'Yes, but HDK is reported to have lost something like thirty billion dollars of client money in the last three years.'

'Just as well they have the Nobel Laureates,' Carlyle chuckled. 'Otherwise they could have lost *a lot*.'

'It is currently being investigated by the authorities in both London and the US.'

Carlyle frowned. 'How do you know all this?'

Roche smiled. 'I have my sources.'

He gave her a *don't mess me about* stare.

'I have a good friend who works in the Financial Investigation Development Unit.'

Carlyle shrugged again. 'Never heard of that either.'

'They analyse Suspicious Activity Reports received by the Serious Organized Crime Agency from people working in the City. Apparently, HDK has been on their radar for more than two years.'

'So?'

'So, if HDK is going down the tubes, maybe Ms Lagerbäck saw this as a way of making some money before the whole thing collapsed.'

'Maybe,' Carlyle yawned.

'You don't sound too convinced.'

Getting to his feet for a second time, he stepped over to the counter to settle the bill. 'I'm convinced enough to go and pay her a visit,' he said, over his shoulder.

'When?'

'Now.' Taking his change, Carlyle shoved it into his pocket and stepped towards the door. Holding it open, he ushered Roche outside. 'We might as well go and have another chat with her,' he said. 'Apart from anything else, it keeps me out of the station.'

TWENTY-SIX

They were shown into a massive, minimalist office in Piccadilly, with views over Green Park. The back wall, behind a large cherrywood desk, was dominated by a black and white print three feet by one foot of a female nude. Shot from behind, the woman's face was turned slightly towards the camera, eyes lowered as if she was admiring her own muscular and sculpted behind. Conscious of Roche's gaze upon him, Carlyle tried not to stare. However, it was one hell of an arse and he found it simply impossible not to look.

'Do you like it?' Katrin Lagerbäck glided into the room, followed by a male assistant carrying a tray. On the tray was a cafetière filled with coffee, a plate of almond biscotti and three small cups. Lagerbäck was dressed far more demurely than on their previous meeting, the leather outfit and biker boots replaced by a grey business suit with a skirt that ended just above the knee. Her hair was perhaps slightly blonder than he remembered it, and she was wearing minimal make-up. Even so, she still looked very much like Cameron Diaz's hotter little sister.

With Roche grinning at him, Carlyle felt himself blush. 'It's quite something,' he agreed.

Lagerbäck let the assistant place the tray on the desk and waited for him to make his exit. 'Thank you, Rupert.'

Half-bowing, half-running, the young assistant made his exit. As the door closed behind him, she glanced at Roche before smiling at Carlyle. 'I'm glad you think my backside looks good.'

The inspector had no idea what to say to that. 'Ah.'

'Well,' Lagerbäck corrected herself, 'my backside as it was more than fifteen years ago.' She patted her right buttock. 'Although, I think it's held up pretty well since then.'

Carlyle lowered his gaze to the carpet.

'Please.' Lagerbäck gestured to a pair of leather armchairs in front of the desk. 'Take a seat.'

While they waited for her to pour the coffee, Roche gestured at the photograph. 'Doesn't it make you uncomfortable to have that up there?'

'Not at all.' Lagerbäck handed her a cup. 'As you can see, it's quite a talking-point. It's a great icebreaker with clients.'

I can imagine, Carlyle thought.

'I was very lucky,' said Lagerbäck, passing Carlyle his coffee. 'I was seventeen and still in Berlin—'

'You're German?' Roche asked.

Lagerbäck offered them the biscotti. Roche declined, so Carlyle felt at liberty to take two. He felt his mobile buzz in the breast pocket of his jacket. Sticking one of the biscotti in his mouth, he lifted it out and glanced at the screen. Seeing it was Ambrose Watson, he let it fall back into the pocket.

'My mother was Danish,' said Lagerbäck, pouring herself some coffee and taking a sip, 'and my father Spanish. I was born in Copenhagen, but we moved to Berlin when I was three. Anyway, I was in the Kaisersaal of the Staatliche Museen looking at photographs when this old guy approached me and said he wanted to take my picture. By then, I was getting quite used to being pestered by dirty old men and told him to fuck off.' She laughed at the memory of it. 'Turns out it was Helmut Newton. I had no idea who he was but, once I realized he was a great photographer and he wanted to shoot me, it was like, "let's do it!"'

'Interesting,' the inspector nodded, nibbling the second biscotti and wondering if it would be too rude to snaffle a third.

'It was great fun,' Lagerbäck agreed. 'Helmut was an incredible guy. I was so fortunate to get the chance to work with him.'

This is the standard patter that you dish out to your clients, Carlyle thought, giving in to his impulse and reaching for another biscuit.

'His family was Jewish. They spent the Second World War in Australia before he came back to Europe.'

'I really like the work of his wife,' said Roche.

Carlyle gave her a look, but she ignored him.

'Yes, indeed.' Lagerbäck seemed somewhat nonplussed at having her spiel turned into a dialogue.

'Apart from anything else,' Roche continued, 'anyone who calls themselves Alice Springs has got to have a lot going for them.'

Carlyle laughed. 'What a great name!'

'She chose it by sticking a pin in a map, apparently,' Roche explained.

'Anyway,' said Lagerbäck, suddenly now all business, 'what did you want to see me about?'

Carlyle wiped a stray crumb from his mouth. 'How did you get from there,' he gestured at the photo, 'to here?'

'I left Berlin to study at the Sorbonne in Paris. After that, I came to London to make some money. I worked for an American bank for a while, but I've been at HDK for, God, almost eight years now.'

'Forgive my ignorance,' said Carlyle, 'but what does Hub . . .'

'Hubaishi Dorning Klee,' Roche helpfully reminded him.

'What do you actually do?'

The first sign of annoyance crept across Lagerbäck's face. 'We are a boutique asset management firm.'

Carlyle smiled. 'Yes, but in layman's terms, what does that mean?'

'It means,' Lagerbäck sighed, 'that we invest in companies—'

'Like St James's Diamonds,' Roche interjected.

'We invest in companies like St James's Diamonds,' Lagerbäck repeated, 'that we believe are either significantly undervalued, for one reason or another, or have great upside potential.'

'And it pays well?' Roche asked.

Lagerbäck gestured around the office, as if the answer was obvious. 'Sure. Of course it's not *just* about the money.'

Of course not, Carlyle thought.

'I also want to go to bed at night and feel like I'm doing a good job.'

'And are you doing a good job,' Carlyle asked, 'with St James's?'

Lagerbäck raised her eyes skywards and laughed. 'You sound like my Board!'

Carlyle shrugged apologetically.

'Actually,' she smiled, sitting back in her chair, 'I think we're doing satisfactorily, under the circumstances. The business was struggling under too much leverage when we came in but it was fundamentally sound and there was scope to expand in key markets. We did a deal on the debt, kicked out the old management and invested in targeted expansion. The downturn hasn't helped, of course, but our high net-worth customers still like to shop and we can afford to see it through. All in all, I think we have a good chance of achieving a satisfactory exit in an acceptable timeframe.'

'I see,' said Carlyle, not having a clue what she was talking about.

'Presumably, something like the robbery can put a bit of a spanner in the works,' Roche mused.

Lagerbäck frowned. 'Spanner?'

'Cause you problems,' Carlyle translated.

Lagerbäck made a face. 'Not really. It's a matter for the insurance company, isn't it?' She looked from one officer to the other. 'I mean, of course, we were very upset that one of our staff colleagues was killed.' Her brow furrowed, as if on cue.

Her acting skills seem to have improved somewhat, Carlyle observed.

'The Board has written to Paula's family,' Lagerbäck continued. 'We will offer them any assistance we can.'

'Unfortunately,' Roche said, her head slightly bowed in apology, 'we have not been able to recover all of the stolen items.'

'So far, at least,' Carlyle added.

Lagerbäck smiled graciously at the limited but willing public servants in front of her. 'I think you have done an amazing job.' She focused her gaze on Roche. 'Especially you, Sergeant, if I understand correctly.'

'Thank you.' Roche tried not to smile in the presence of her boss.

'We will also be writing to your superiors to make sure that they understand how impressed we have been with the way in which the Metropolitan Police have handled this very difficult matter.'

If only Paula Coulter's parents could say the same, Carlyle thought ruefully. Crossing his legs, he sat up in his chair. 'There is just one final thing.'

Lagerbäck arched an inquisitive eyebrow in the inspector's direction. 'Yes?'

'There has been a suggestion,' Carlyle said, 'that some of the missing items were taken *after* the robbery.'

Lagerbäck didn't miss a beat. 'By whom?' she asked.

'That,' said Roche evenly, 'is something that we were wondering if you might be able to help us with.'

'Are you telling me,' Lagerbäck's voice had taken on a much harder edge, 'that I need a lawyer?'

'No, no, no,' said Carlyle cheerily, getting to his feet. Taking one last peek at Lagerbäck's nude bum in all its glory, he brushed some biscotti crumbs from his trousers. 'We are simply looking into the possibility. Most likely, the two geniuses who robbed the place have it stashed somewhere. However, if anything comes to mind, please let me know.'

Already out from behind the desk, Lagerbäck gave him a clipped 'of course' as she led them to the door.

TWENTY-SEVEN

Still in no hurry to return to the police station, Carlyle ushered Roche into Green Park. After buying two bottles of water from the kiosk on Queen's Walk, they found a free bench and sat down. For a few moments Carlyle sat in silent contemplation, thinking through the details of their meeting with Lagerbäck. Finally, he turned to Roche, who was fiddling with her mobile phone. 'What do you think?'

'I think I wish I had her arse,' Roche laughed.

'The picture was taken quite a while ago.'

'Yeah, but still.' Roche took a sip from her bottle. 'What kind of person has a larger than life-size picture of their bum hanging on the wall in their office?'

'Mm.'

'I don't think she nicked anything though.'

'Oh?' Carlyle watched a couple wobble past on rollerblades. 'Why not?'

'People like that,' Roche replied, following his gaze, 'they don't need to *steal* anything. They're all set up to get people to give them money willingly.'

Carlyle scratched his head. 'I suppose.'

'The woman is what, in her mid-thirties? She appears very well-off. She's definitely very sure of herself and has a smooth business operation going. If people like that need cash, they don't rob their own store; they just go and tap up a few rich investors.'

'But if her firm is in trouble . . .'

'If HDK is floundering, the numbers being talked about dwarf the value of the goods stolen in the raid, even at retail price. It would not make the slightest difference.' She shrugged. 'Anyway, firms go bust all the time. All you do is set up another one.'

Carlyle knew that was true, although the idea of just walking away from your debts was something at odds with the Calvinist DNA that his parents had brought down to London from Scotland almost half a century earlier.

'That's the thing,' Roche continued. 'You always hear stories about these people who make millions, billions even. But where does all the money come from? Not everyone can be a winner. The losers keep their mouths shut.'

'If they've got any sense,' Carlyle grunted. Taking the cap off the bottle, he drained the contents in three quick gulps.

'These kinds of people are definitely not stupid.'

'No,' Carlyle agreed. Crushing the plastic bottle in his fist, he tossed it in the direction of the trash can at the end of the bench. When it missed, he cursed, got to his feet, picked it up and dropped it in the bin. 'So what do we do now?' he asked, looking down at Roche.

'I would leave Lagerbäck for now,' she advised. 'The store manager and the security guy were on CCTV all the time until the first units arrived. Then they were with officers all the time until they came back to the station. So I would rule them out. And I can't believe any of our people would do that. The most likely scenario is still that Dyer and Samuels took the stuff and we haven't found it yet. I'll talk to them again.'

'Good.'

'I won't waste too much time on it though. Those two are toast anyway. If we don't get the stuff back, like you say, the insurance can take care of it.'

'Don't let Trevor Cole hear you say that,' Carlyle laughed.

'He seems a reasonable enough guy.'

'I think he is.'

Roche got to her feet. Putting the cap back on her bottle, she dropped it in the rubbish even though it was still more than half-full. 'You can't do his kind of job without being pragmatic. We've got a result for him on this one.'

148

'Yes, we have.' Carlyle's mobile started ringing. Checking the name on the screen, he decided this time to answer it. 'Ambrose,' he said cheerily, 'how's it going?'

'Inspector!' said a low, hoarse voice. 'What has happened to you?'

'Apologies,' said Carlyle, turning away from Roche, 'but we have been tied up on a rather pressing investigation.'

'Superintendent Buck,' said Ambrose, lowering his voice further, 'is extremely unhappy. She was expecting to talk to you today. And your sergeant.'

Stepping further away from Roche, Carlyle scanned the horizon in search of some tranquillity. 'Give the superintendent my apologies, but remind her that I did not consent to any meeting today. Moreover, I will not be taking part in any interview without my Federation representative being present.'

'She has complained to Commander Dugdale.'

'About what?' Carlyle snapped.

'About your lack of cooperation.'

'Look, Ambrose,' Carlyle sighed, 'I apologize if you've been placed in a difficult situation here. I know that you are trying to help me and you have always been very fair in our previous dealings.'

'Yes.' For Ambrose, that now sounded like that was a matter of some considerable regret.

'But you don't have to get involved this time. I will, of course, cooperate fully and promptly with any IIC and IPCC enquiry. I do, however, expect that my own rights will be respected, along with those of Sergeant Roche.'

'Of course.'

'Innocent until proven guilty and all that.'

'Indeed.' Ambrose seemed even less sure of that than Carlyle did himself.

'So give the superintendent my *sincere* apologies and tell her that I look forward to meeting with her soon.'

'Okay.'

'And Ambrose?'

'Yes?'

'Thanks again for all your help. I really mean it. But you don't have to go out on a limb for me.'

'Just be careful, Inspector. Once these investigations get up a head of steam they can be very difficult to stop.'

'I will. Thank you.' He ended the call and turned to face Roche.

The sergeant made no effort to hide the fact that she had been listening intently. 'More problems?' she asked.

'Just the usual,' Carlyle sighed. Minded to walk back to the station via The Mall, he started walking in the direction of the Queen Victoria Memorial.

Behind him, Roche groaned as her phone started buzzing. The next thing he knew, the handset was flying past his left ear before bouncing off the grass five yards away.

'Hey!'

'Sorry.' Roche held up a hand in apology. Her face was a picture of annoyance. He could almost see the steam coming out of her ears.

'The bastard!'

Carlyle stepped over to the phone, which had narrowly avoided landing in a fresh-looking pile of dog shit. Wrinkling his nose, he picked it up and moved quickly away. On the screen was a text from 'Martin' that simply said: *It's over x*

Handing the phone back to his sergeant, he somehow managed to keep his mouth shut.

'What a total wanker!' Roche hissed. 'Imagine dumping someone by fucking text!'

'That's men for you,' Carlyle said, affecting the air of someone who knew what he was talking about.

Roche shook her head.

'At least he sent you a kiss.'

She shot him an angry look. 'Don't try and be fucking funny.'

'No. Sorry.' Dropping his gaze to the grass, the chastened look on his face was real; something that he had had ample opportunity to perfect at home over the years.

They resumed walking. 'It wasn't like it was working out,' Roche said after a while. 'But it's always better to do the dumping, rather than be dumped.'

'I suppose so,' said Carlyle, conscious that he didn't have much experience of either.

'And to be dumped by bloody text!' Holding up the phone, she deleted the message with a flourish. 'Well, fuck you.'

'A commendably healthy attitude,' Carlyle smiled.

He waited until they had almost reached the ICA before returning to work-related matters. 'Have there been any more developments regarding SO15?'

Roche swerved a dawdling tourist. 'Not really. I would be interested though. I hear that CTC are investigating the guy in the holdall.'

Carlyle grunted. The 'guy in the holdall' was a Secret Intelligence Service officer whose decomposing body had been found a few days earlier in a sports bag in the bath of an expensive Pimlico apartment. The media were, of course, loving it, happily speculating that he had been brutally murdered because of his job. Was the poor victim the first 'spy' to be killed in Britain since former KGB man Alexander Litvinenko was poisoned in a sushi bar in Piccadilly? Carlyle knew that the reality was likely to be more mundane – sex, money, whatever. However, Homicide and Serious Crime Command were still having to work with Counter Terrorism Command and domestic intelligence agency MI5 looking over their shoulder. He knew, from personal experience, what a pain in the arse that could be.

Reading the concerned look on his face, Roche gave him a gentle punch on the shoulder. 'It's not a done deal,' she smiled. 'We can worry about it if it happens.'

He nodded. 'Fine by me.'

Neatly stacked on his desk at the station were two letters. On top, someone had stuck a Post-it note on which an unknown hand had simply scrawled: *call Dugdale. Maybe later*, Carlyle thought, picking up the first envelope. It was no great surprise to find that it was a formal notice from the IIC, signed by Buck, informing him of the date of his complaint hearing. Of more interest was the second, from one

Jayne Smith, Personnel Administrator, in HR, outlining the redundancy terms that they were prepared to offer him. Carlyle stared at the numbers on the page, trying to work out whether they offered him even the remotest chance of walking away from the Met.

Unable to come up with any conclusions one way or another, he stuffed the letter in his pocket and reached for the desk phone. It was past the time he expected anyone from the Federation to still be in the office and, sure enough, Geoff the Rep's voicemail kicked in after a few token rings. Carlyle left him a message asking him to call in the morning. Pulling a sheaf of papers out of the top drawer of his desk, he quickly went through his 'to do' list on the Leyne killing.

First, he called Phillips. She picked up on the second ring, but it sounded like Carlyle had caught her at a bad moment as she curtly informed him that her report into Leyne's death had been sent to him the day before.

'But it's not on my desk,' he complained, repaying her irritable tone with interest.

'That's because I emailed it to you,' she sighed. 'Call me if you've got any questions.'

'Okay,' he replied. 'Sorry.' But she had already hung up on him. With a heavy heart, he switched on his PC. Bitter experience told him that it would take at least five minutes for the thing to warm up, before crashing again almost immediately. After typing in his user name and password, he ignored the somersaulting sand-timer and tried ringing another of Leyne's former wives.

Sally Jones, wife number two, had a London phone number but wasn't answering it. Carlyle left a message. Undeterred, he moved swiftly on to number three. Next to Rachel Gilbert's name was a mobile number which he proceeded to misdial three times. However, when he finally got the number right, the call was picked up instantly.

'Hi!' said an impossibly chirpy voice that sounded like it was coming from the middle of a disco. 'This is Rachel . . .'

Confused, Carlyle frowned. Was this another mother-daughter situation, like his call to LA?

'Hello?'

'Is that—'

But the call was terminated before he could get any further.

Cursing, he dialled the number yet again.

'Hi! This is—'

'This is Inspector John Carlyle of the Metropolitan Police in London,' he said quickly and firmly, 'and I am looking to speak to Rachel Gilbert.'

There was a pause.

'Hello?' Carlyle shouted, feeling like an idiot.

'This is Rachel,' said a now not so chirpy voice.

TWENTY-EIGHT

Once they had mastered the art of conducting a basic telephone conversation, it was established that Rachel Gilbert was sitting in a bar called Stearn's in Golden Square, walking distance from the station. Always preferring to do these things face-to-face, Carlyle proposed heading over there straight away. With some reluctance, she agreed.

Ending the call, Carlyle realized that his PC had finally sprung into life. Opening Phillips' email, he scanned her report. Not surprisingly, the cause of Roger Leyne's death was given as the two 9mm hollow-point parabellum rounds that had been fired into his chest at close range. It was estimated that Leyne had been face down in his swimming pool for eight or nine hours before Carlyle had found him. The retrograde extrapolation of Leyne's blood-alcohol content suggested it was approaching 0.20 per cent at the time of his death, representing very serious intoxication. Unless Leyne had developed a very high tolerance for drink, such a high BAC would result in emotional swings, impaired judgement and poor gross motor control. In other words, he was quite an easy target. Phillips had also found traces of cocaine in his bloodstream, but it wasn't clear if the professor had been partaking immediately before his death. '*Quite the party animal*,' Carlyle said to himself. Printing off a copy of the report, he stuck it in the inside pocket of his jacket and headed for the door.

Twenty minutes later, he walked into the funky, if largely empty, bar, to be greeted almost immediately by a nervous-looking waif, whose short, pixie haircut only served to accentuate the fact that she looked about twelve years old. She was dressed in black jeans and a Kylie T-shirt. A pair of pink Converse All Stars rounded off the ensemble, further enhancing the childish look.

'Inspector Carlyle?'

'Yes.'

Rachel Gilbert offered him a limp hand. 'I thought it was you. Most of the people who come in here are a lot younger.'

Thanks, thought Carlyle, as he let her usher him to a table near the door.

'Would you like something to drink?' she asked. 'They have the biggest gin collection in the country and the cocktails are great.'

Carlyle took a seat and gestured for her to follow. Thankfully, someone had turned the music off. 'I'm fine,' he said. 'This shouldn't take too long.' He scanned the Stearn's early-evening crowd, wondering who she was with. 'Just a couple of quick questions and you can get back to your . . . er . . . friends.'

'Oh, I'm here working,' she smiled.

'Ah, okay.'

'Just a bit of pocket-money really. And something to do. It gets me out and about and stops me being terminally anti-social.'

'I see.'

'So,' she said pleasantly, 'what can I do for you?'

'First of all, please accept my condolences about your former husband.'

Rachel placed her hands in her lap, intertwining the fingers. 'Thank you,' she smiled awkwardly. 'But I have to say that I haven't really been able to feel anything about Roger's death.'

This guy really was Mr Popular, Carlyle noted. 'Why is that?' he asked gently.

'The marriage . . . well, it seems like it was decades, hundreds of years ago – another lifetime, in fact.' She gave him a searching look. 'I'm twenty-six years old. We married when I was twenty-two and I was twenty-three when I walked out. I haven't seen him since. The divorce was finalized three days after my twenty-fourth birthday.' She gazed vacantly into the middle distance. 'It turned out he had been sleeping with other students all the time we were married.'

'Professor Leyne didn't seem to stay married for very long,' Carlyle commented.

Rachel shrugged. 'I think his second marriage lasted for a decade or so. I know they had kids. She must have been good at looking the other way.'

'So he was a serial philanderer?'

She laughed. 'He was a serial everything . . . Roger thought that everything and everyone that crossed his path had somehow been put on this earth for his benefit.'

'How did you two meet?'

She sighed so deeply that Carlyle felt a wave of sadness wash over him. 'I was one of his students. He taught me ethics.'

Carlyle raised an eyebrow.

'Not an unfamiliar story.'

'No,' said Carlyle, not wishing to pry into the prurient details, 'I suppose not. The question is, why would anyone want to kill him?'

Sticking her elbows on the table, she leaned forward. 'Surely,' she said primly, 'the question is *who* killed him? And then *why*?'

'Yes, but—'

'Presumably,' Rachel grinned mischievously, 'you have discovered by now that lots of people may have *wanted* to kill him. I quite often thought about it myself, when we were together. My inclination would have been to have given him a quick shove down the stairs and hope he ended up with a broken neck.' She took in the rather bemused look on Carlyle's face. 'What are the chances of getting away with that?'

Carlyle shrugged vaguely. Unbidden, his brain summoned up the memory of yet another abused child. This one was called Josie Parrish. It had been a case six or maybe seven years before. Five-year-old Josie had died from head injuries that Carlyle was convinced had been inflicted on her by her stepfather. Both the stepfather and the mother insisted that the child had accidentally fallen. The investigation had dragged on for months before finally coming to court. At the trial, pathologists squabbled publicly over whether Josie had been

156

killed by an 'accelerated impact' as a result of being pushed. When the parents had walked out of the Old Bailey, having been acquitted of child cruelty and manslaughter charges, it was one of the worst days of Carlyle's professional life. 'It can be hard to prove,' he admitted.

There was a sparkle in her brown eyes now. 'Just a harmless little fantasy I used to have from time to time.'

'Yes.' Carlyle wondered if Helen ever had similar thoughts about him; surely not?

'That's not a crime, is it?' she asked, and when the inspector shook his head: 'Just as well. But, to go back to the *precise* question, I don't know why someone finally decided to shoot him, or who that someone was, but I do have some ideas.'

Carlyle sat back in his chair and opened his arms wide. 'Go ahead,' he said, 'let's hear them.'

Daintily sipping his green tea, the inspector yawned as he watched the television news. A spokesman for the Archdiocese of Birmingham was complaining about the 'draconian' security plans for the Pope's visit. Alcohol, barbecues, gazebos and musical instruments were all banned, along with bicycles, whistles, candles and animals.

Gazebos? Carlyle wondered. *These guys really know how to have a good time.*

Helen wandered in from the kitchen and sat down beside him.

Carlyle gestured at the screen. 'Have you seen this?'

'Yeah,' she grinned, 'it's hilarious.'

'Do you think the Popemobile will be going past here?'

'Let's hope not,' she said. 'The crowds will be a real pain.'

'Apparently you have to have a "pilgrim pass" to get into one of his gigs.'

'You're kidding!'

Carlyle shrugged. 'That's what it says.'

'Different world,' Helen murmured.

'Each to their own.' Carlyle muted the TV and took another sip of his tea. 'People can do what they like, as long as they respect the law.'

Helen stretched out on the sofa and placed her head in his lap. 'So,

157

how is the plan to arrest His Holiness for crimes against humanity going?'

'It's not, as far as I know.'

'It was always a cheap publicity stunt, anyway.'

'Absolutely. But finding one of the prime movers in the campaign face down in his swimming pool with two bullets in his chest has given people other things to worry about.'

'Maybe the Pope did it?'

Carlyle laughed. 'I very much doubt that the Pope has ever heard of Roger Leyne.'

'No,' Helen agreed. 'Anyway, I suppose that murder would be a bit over the top.'

'Yeah. Abusing little boys is more their thing.'

Helen yawned. 'So, why do you think that Roger Leyne was shot?'

Carlyle stroked the top of her head, happy to be talking about work rather than . . . other things. On the TV news, they had moved on to a story about flooding in Pakistan – people with *real* problems. 'That,' he said quietly, 'is a very good question. No one seems to have liked the bloke, but equally, no one's claiming to have hated him enough to have actually killed him.' He recounted his conversation with Rachel Gilbert and her admission that she'd daydreamed about pushing her husband down the stairs.

Helen thought about that for a minute. 'I would have thought fantasies about killing your spouse are fairly common.'

Carlyle looked down at her. 'Have you ever thought about pushing *me* down the stairs?'

A look of mock surprise fell across Helen's face. 'Oh no!' she grinned.

'Glad to hear it.'

'I'd never do anything like that. My preference would be to brain you with the frying pan.'

'Ha bloody ha,' Carlyle said sourly. 'Hardly an inspired choice.'

'It would do for me.'

'It would be much harder to get away with that, *my dear*.'

'Who says I would want to get away with it?' Helen pushed herself

158

up, giving him a kiss on the cheek as she slipped off the sofa. 'If I actually did it, I would want everyone to know that it was me.'

Not knowing quite what to make of that, he watched her sashay into the kitchen.

Five minutes later, she returned with a cup of steaming rooibos tea. 'So what does wife number three think lies behind the slaying of her ex-husband?' she asked, carefully lowering herself back down onto the sofa.

'Well,' Carlyle switched off the television, 'she says Leyne was fond of recreational drugs, which would tally with the coke that we found in his system. She also says he was a bit of a gambler.'

'Horses?'

'No, cards. Apparently he liked poker.'

'Would that have got him killed?'

'I've no idea. Maybe – if he fell in with the wrong people and had money problems. We'll have to check it out. I thought I might talk to Dom about it.' Dom was Dominic Silver, policeman turned drug dealer and longtime family friend. Theirs was a relationship that went back thirty years, to Hendon Police Training College in North London. Once Dom had left the force and changed sides, as it were, the two men had eventually established a workable if often uneasy relationship.

'Shit!' A look of horror swept across Helen's face. 'I forgot to tell you. I heard the other day – Marina died.' Marina was the youngest child of Dom and his partner, Eva Hollander. A year before, she had been diagnosed with a genetic disorder called Cockayne Syndrome. It was so rare that barely twenty other kids in the country had it. Carlyle and Dom had talked it over many times. But with no cure and no treatment, there was nothing that they, or anyone else, could do. The disease had been a death sentence from day one.

'Fuck,' Carlyle grimaced. 'How old was she?'

'Six, I think.'

'Jesus.'

'I put a call in to Eva,' Helen said, 'but she hasn't got back to me.'

'I'll try and get hold of Dom tomorrow,' Carlyle sighed, knowing

159

that it would be a tortured conversation. Dom might want to talk about it, but he certainly didn't. In situations such as this, Carlyle felt over-whelmed by a sense of uselessness and the futility of words. How could you do or say anything that would give a bereaved parent any comfort whatsoever?

TWENTY-NINE

Ignoring his mug of green tea, the inspector sat at a window table in the Box Café flicking through the pages of the morning edition of *The Times*. On the Home News pages, he scanned a story by the Crime Editor about what had been dubbed the 'spy in the bag' case. The death of an MI6 man found padlocked inside a sports holdall remained unexplained. The police were appealing for any witnesses. *Good luck with that*, Carlyle thought as the waitress appeared at his shoulder and placed his bill on the table.

After some protracted fumbling in his various jacket pockets, he pulled out a couple of mobile phones and placed them on top of the newspaper. Sitting next to his official issue BlackBerry Pearl, the Alcatel OT-206 Candybar handset was his current private, pay-as-you-go phone. Carlyle liked to buy a new one every three to four months. He didn't flash it around and gave the number out to very few people. The contacts list contained less than thirty numbers. None of this guaranteed complete secrecy, but it gave him some comfort that no one was checking his calls as a matter of routine. Pulling up Dominic Silver's number, he let his thumb hover over the button for several seconds before hitting 'call'. Willing it to go to voicemail, he rehearsed his message.

Dom picked up on the sixth ring. 'John. How's it going?'

Carlyle could hear the strain of recent events in his voice. 'Mate,' he said, with feeling, 'Helen told me about Marina. We're really sorry.'

'Thank you. I'll let Eva know. Appreciate the call.' The awkward pause was punctuated by the sound of voices in the background. 'Look, sorry, but some folk have just arrived. I've got to go.'

'If there's anything we can do,' Carlyle stammered, forcing the words out despite the fact that they sounded lamer than anything he'd ever heard in his whole life.

'Thank you,' Dom repeated. 'I'll let you know. I think the funeral is going to be small, just family.'

'Understood.'

'I'll be in touch later, all right?'

'Sure. Speak soon.' The call ended and Carlyle realized that he had been holding his breath. Exhaling, he watched the BlackBerry start vibrating with an incoming call. Happy for the distraction, he quickly picked it up with his free hand.

'Yes?'

'Inspector Carlyle?' asked a voice he didn't recognize.

'Yes.'

'This is Brian Sutherland, Crime Editor at *The Times*.'

The inspector felt himself tense. Dealing with journalists was part of the job but they made him uncomfortable. 'I've just been reading your story in this morning's paper.'

Sutherland seemed thrown for a moment. 'What? Oh yes, of course. Very strange carry-on. Not one of yours?'

'No, no,' said Carlyle. 'That's nothing to do with me.'

'Lucky you,' the journalist laughed.

'Quite.'

'Anyway,' Sutherland said briskly, 'that wasn't why I was calling. I am writing a story for tomorrow about Father McGowan of St Boniface's Roman Catholic Church and the suit that has been launched against you, in connection with your alleged assault against him.' Sutherland paused, waiting to see what immediate reaction might be forthcoming. When Carlyle said nothing, he continued: 'I just wanted to get your response to the allegations. This is your chance to put your side of the story.'

Looking down at the BlackBerry, Carlyle hit the end button. Almost immediately, the handset started vibrating in his hand. On the screen it simply said 'call' but he knew it would be Sutherland chasing him for an unguarded reaction. Letting it go to voicemail, he got to his feet and shuffled over to the counter to pay his bill. Then, with the phone still demanding his attention, he headed for the station.

Turning into Agar Street, he almost walked straight into Abigail Slater. 'What are *you* doing here?' he mumbled, in no mood for any fake pleasantries.

'How are preparations going for your hearing?' Slater asked, ignoring his question.

'I have nothing to worry about on that score,' Carlyle replied defensively. 'Not that it matters now.'

'Oh?' Her face was a mixture of amusement and curiosity. 'Why do you say that?'

'Well,' said Carlyle, just about holding on to his temper, 'now that you've leaked the story to the media, I'm sure that the matter will be done and dusted before we get anywhere near a formal hearing.'

'I wouldn't say that,' Slater smirked. 'I wouldn't say that at all.' Without waiting for a reply, she turned away from him and jogged up the front steps of the station.

'Bitch,' Carlyle hissed under his breath.

'What?' From nowhere, Roche appeared at his shoulder. In her hand was an outsized latte and a packet of cigarettes.

'Nothing.'

'Was that McGowan's lawyer?' Roche asked.

'Yeah.'

'What did she have to say for herself?'

'Nothing really.' Carlyle told her about his call from the Crime Editor of *The Times*.

Roche sucked greedily on her coffee. 'Did he mention me?'

'No.'

'Good. Anyway, I wouldn't think Slater would have leaked that story.'

'Why not?'

'Too risky. A Catholic priest accused of child abuse is one of the few people with less public credibility than a copper. Even a copper like you.'

Carlyle gave her a funny look. 'Is that supposed to make me feel better?'

'It's supposed to make you think that having this in the papers might not be altogether unhelpful.'

'Slater didn't deny that it was her.'

Roche shook her head. 'Why would she? Lawyers will never confirm or deny anything if they don't have to. Ambiguity and bullshit is in their DNA.'

'Anyway,' said Carlyle, bored with the whole thing, 'she likes winding me up.'

'For God's sake,' Roche said, 'don't let her get to you. Sticks and stones and all that.'

'We *are* in a cheery mood today,' Carlyle said sarcastically.

'Come on,' said Roche, leading him towards the station. 'I've got something that will definitely cheer you up.'

Letting her go on ahead, Carlyle watched a tourist almost get run over by a refuse truck. A drop of rain fell on his head, followed by another. With some reluctance, he headed inside.

Roche had reached the front desk when the opening bars of Eminem's 'Love The Way You Lie' started up. Sighing, she stopped and began rummaging around inside her bag. After a few moments, she found her mobile.

'Roche.' A confused look spread across her face as she listened to the voice on the other end of the line. 'What?'

Carlyle hovered a respectful distance away. Looking up, she gave him an angry glare. *What have I done now?* he wondered.

'What was he doing there?' Roche demanded down the phone. 'Oh, for fuck's sake! When did this happen? Okay, we'll be right there.' Ending the call, she shoved the phone back in her bag. 'Come on,' she said, half-jogging back towards the door. 'We need to get up to UCH. Colin Dyer's escaped.'

Carlyle firmly believed that you should never get ill. If you did, seeing a doctor, any kind of doctor, should only be an absolute last resort. He had never, in his entire life, encountered a medical professional who had inspired confidence. The motley crew currently on duty at A&E in University College Hospital did nothing to change that deeply held view.

'We are very busy here, you know.' The inspector glanced at the name-tag on the young man's white coat, resisting the temptation to give the little berk a good slap.

'I understand that, Dr Higgins,' he replied through clenched teeth, 'but this is a very important matter. The man who has disappeared had been arrested in relation to an extremely serious crime.'

Higgins looked like he was in his mid-thirties. He was short, plump and well on the way to being completely bald. His florid complexion more than hinted at a taste for drink. The overriding impression was of a heart attack on legs. 'Well,' he pouted, folding his arms, 'it might have been helpful if your colleagues had explained that to us at the time.'

Carlyle looked around for the two constables who had brought Dyer to the hospital but they had wisely made themselves scarce. He turned his gaze back to Higgins. 'Just tell me what happened.'

'Like I said,' Higgins sighed, 'the man was brought in about an hour and a half ago. We were very busy, but the officers insisted that he was seen straight away.' Higgins gestured at a row of curtained-off cubicles to his right. 'I took him into the nearest one of those and had a look at him.'

'And?' Roche asked.

'Before I could say anything, the man dropped his trousers and showed me his penis,' said Higgins matter-of-factly, as if this was an everyday occurrence, which, in reflection, Carlyle supposed it might well be. 'He said that he had some "flesh-eating bacteria" that was going to kill him if he wasn't treated immediately.'

If only, thought Carlyle. He glanced at Roche, who simply shrugged.

'He seemed quite distressed,' Higgins continued. 'I could see some inflammation and possibly a discharge. There was certainly a very strong odour – although, of course, that could simply be poor personal hygiene.'

'Did you give him an examination?' Roche asked.

Higgins shook his head. 'I went to find some latex gloves. When I got back, he had disappeared.'

'The CCTV shows he just walked out of A&E,' Roche confirmed. 'The constables had gone to get coffee.'

Carlyle rubbed his temples. 'Okay.' He looked at Higgins. 'Thank you, Doctor. We'll let you get back to your patients. Let's hope you've had your quota of member-munching bugs for the day.'

Higgins grunted and scuttled off.

'What do we do now?' Roche asked, as she watched the doctor move away.

'Apart from rip the shit out of the idiots who brought him here?'

'Yes,' Roche muttered. 'Apart from that.'

The inspector looked at his watch. The day was slipping away and he had things to do. He took a moment, sorting their priorities in his head. 'Get back to the station and make a list of all the places he might have gone,' he said finally, 'and get uniforms started on checking them out. Speak to Dyer's lawyer, Kelvin Jenkins. Make sure he knows that if his client doesn't turn himself in immediately, we will go after him for assisting a fugitive.'

Roche frowned. 'But we don't know that he was involved.'

'Doesn't matter,' Carlyle said firmly. 'Kelvin needs to understand that we will take this chance to fuck him up if he doesn't help us out. Then go and talk to Damien Samuels, let him think he might get a better deal if he helps us find Colin – see if that loosens his tongue.'

'Will do,' Roche nodded.

'No need to tell Dugdale yet,' Carlyle added. 'Dyer's an idiot. He won't stay free long, so let's see if we can get him back in custody before the Commander gets to hear about it.'

'Yes.'

'We don't want to damage your chances of getting into SO15,' he added cheekily, 'if we don't have to.'

'Very funny.' She shot him a dirty look. 'Where are you going?'

Carlyle watched a wizened old woman shuffle past them with the aid of a Zimmer frame. 'I think,' he said quietly, 'I'll go and have a word with Colin's dear old mum.'

THIRTY

On the third floor of Phoenix Court, Carlyle gave Carla Dyer's front door one last thump and turned away. Either the woman wasn't in or she was hiding in a back room. He might be pissed off at the antics of the Dyer family but he wasn't going to kick the door down on the off-chance that she was under the bed. Roche could come back later. His stomach rumbled and he wondered what his chances were of finding a decent café in Somers Town; probably not that bad, as long as he didn't set the bar too high.

Reaching the top of the stairs, he paused to let an old woman pass on the way up. She was carrying a plastic bag filled with groceries and moving slowly. Making eye-contact, Carlyle gave her a friendly nod.

'Are you a copper?' she asked suspiciously, struggling on the landing.

Carlyle laughed. 'Is it that obvious?'

The woman took a moment to catch her breath. 'No one round here would be so polite as to let me past,' she said finally.

'I'm looking for Carla Dyer.'

'Now, that is a big surprise.' The woman continued on her way. 'Try the Cock Tavern on Chalton Street.'

'Thanks,' said Carlyle as he headed down the stairs. Five minutes later he was standing in the Cock Tavern, eyeing a large early-lunch-time crowd. The haggard woman sitting at a table in the corner could, at first glance, have been anything from between forty and sixty-five. Wearing a replica Arsenal away shirt from four or five seasons previously, she held a bottle of Beck's lager to her lips while contemplating the *Sun* crossword.

'Carla Dyer?'

The woman barely glanced up from her paper. 'Who are you?'

Carlyle pulled up a stool. 'John Carlyle,' he said quietly. 'Metropolitan Police.'

Carla took a swig of her beer and lowered her eyes still further. 'I don't know where he is, so fuck off.'

Carlyle laughed.

'What's so funny?'

'Colin did a runner a couple of hours ago. How did you know we were looking for him?'

She took another mouthful of beer and let the newspaper fall on the table. 'So he phoned me. Big deal. I don't know where he is.' Her eyes flitted around the room. 'If you don't fuck off and leave me alone, I'll scream the place down. There's plenty of folk in here who would happily give you a good shoeing, copper.'

'It is surprisingly busy,' Carlyle persevered, 'for the time of day.'

'We're all refugees from the Coffee House, down the road,' Carla scowled. 'Some fucking Frogs took it upmarket and banned loads of regulars. They only want professional people in suits in there now.'

And who can blame them? Carlyle wondered, eyeing up the motley crew of refugees from Gastropub Land who had been washed up in the Cock.

'It's a disgrace.'

'Look, Carla,' said Carlyle, tiring of her musings on the evils of gentrification, 'Colin is in deep shit. You either help us find him now, or the whole thing gets prolonged and, when we catch him, we throw the book at him.'

'All over again, you mean?'

Carlyle nodded. 'All over again.'

Draining the last of her beer, Carla let out a belch as she picked up her purse and got to her feet. 'I'm going to the bar for another,' she said, waving the bottle in his face. 'Make sure you fuck off before I get back.'

As he watched her walk over to the bar, Carlyle caught a glimpse of her large red shoulder bag, doubtless some designer knock-off from a nearby street market, sitting open on the floor under the table with a mobile phone sticking out of a side pocket. He glanced at the bar. With her back to him, Carla was waiting for her drink. Taking his chance, he reached under the table and grabbed the phone. As he did so, he realized that there was something else in the pocket. Pulling it out with the mobile, he saw it was a photograph. After a moment's hesitation, he slipped them both inside his coat.

Getting to his feet, he moved sharply to the door. Out on the street, he paused for a moment and tasted the air, a foul mix of exhaust fumes and cooking smells coming from a kebab shop two doors down. Then with a backward glance towards the Cock, he marched off at a brisk pace, heading towards Covent Garden.

At Il Buffone, the lunchtime rush was still in full swing. Squeezing into the last available seat by the bench in front of the window, the inspector found himself next to a fat man in a suit who was slowly eating a plate of lasagne while reading a story in that morning's *Metro*; a couple of policemen had arrested the driver of a Mitsubishi Lancer Evolution VIII high-performance sports car on the Embankment and then decided to take it for a test drive around Central London. The end result was a collision with two trees on The Mall at 2 a.m. The £30,000 car was a write-off and the policemen were suspended. *More fantastic PR for the Met*, Carlyle mused. *You couldn't make it up.*

The newspaper story didn't give the names of the officers involved but everyone at the station knew who they were. Carlyle knew one of the coppers reasonably well. The guy had always struck him as quite sensible and he hoped that his career wasn't now as totalled as the car. Turning in his seat, he watched Marcello trying to toast a sandwich and make a latte at the same time. Catching the owner's eye, he signalled that he was in no great hurry to be served.

Just as well I'm not that hungry, he thought, as he idly counted eight people waiting to be fed, the queue spilling out along the street. As one departed, lunch in hand, another one joined the back of the line. By a quirk of the licensing laws, Marcello was not supposed to be running a takeaway business, just operating an eat-in café. But Carlyle was well aware that, without the additional trade, the place would be even more unprofitable than it already was.

Marcello took the money from one customer with a perfunctory '*Grazie!*' and moved on to the next. *What a tough job*, Carlyle thought. Marcello had often complained to him that he couldn't afford to bring in any help. As he watched his friend rushing around from Gaggia to grill like a madman, Carlyle hoped that he would get the place sold soon. Casting aside his selfish concerns, he knew that Marcello deserved better than this daily slog.

With a sigh, he pulled Carla Dyer's mobile out of his pocket. A quick glance showed him that it was a cheap Samsung handset, presumably a pay-as-you-go model. The tiny battery in the top left-hand corner of the screen revealed that the battery was two-thirds charged. Happily, Carla had left the thing switched on, so he could easily check the voicemail box (empty) and the call lists. The latter showed that there had been a couple of calls received since Colin did a runner, but both were from unknown numbers. Carla had made one outgoing call, to another mobile. Carlyle looked at the screen for a few moments. *Sod it*, he thought. *Maybe I should just ring it and see what happens.* Before he could press the call button, however, the handset started vibrating in his hand.

Finishing his lasagne, the fat man struggled out of his chair. Tossing his newspaper on the seat, he waddled out of the door. Carlyle watched him disappear down Drury Lane and pulled up the incoming text message on Carla's phone. It came from the same number that Carla had called earlier and simply said: *Need £££ now.*

'Ah, Colin,' Carlyle smiled to himself, 'how nice of you to get in touch.' He laboriously typed in a reply – *how much?* – and hit 'send'.

Placing the phone on the bench, he picked up the discarded *Metro* and flicked through the news pages. The reply came when he was enjoying a story about the trial of a couple of conmen accused of trying to sell the Ritz Hotel for two hundred and fifty million pounds. The duo even managed to sucker a property developer into handing over a one-million down payment. '*In that competitive world of secretive, multi-million-pound deals,*' the prosecutor told the court, '*some people*

are prepared to take risks that might seem breathtaking to most of us.'
No shit, thought Carlyle. Laughing to himself, he opened up the new message.

£500

'You're having a laugh,' Carlyle muttered, as he began typing back. *Only got £200.* Hitting 'send', he glanced at the queue in front of Marcello. It was down to two people now and he wondered about what he might want to eat. No decision had been reached by the time the handset started vibrating again.

OK. Meet @ Coffe House @4

What kind of spelling is that? And the Coffee House? Don't you realize that's been yuppified, so that wankers like you won't want to go there any more? Shaking his head, Carlyle typed a response.

OK, c u there, luv mum x

He looked at the last bit and decided it would be taking the piss just a bit too much, so deleted the 'luv mum x' before sending the shorter version.

Job done, he called Roche on his BlackBerry. She picked up on the fifth ring.

'Colin Dyer will be at the Coffee House in Somers Town at four this afternoon,' he said, by way of introduction, 'which, incidentally, is a pub, not a café.'

'I've heard of it,' said Roche, who sounded as if she was in a pub herself. 'How do you know this?'

'The result of my investigations,' Carlyle said cryptically. 'Just make sure that the place is properly watched and that he's caught. He thinks he's picking up some cash from his mum.'

'Should we bring her in too?'

'Nah. She's getting pissed in another pub up the road. Doesn't know anything about it. We'll deal with her later.'

'I haven't spoken to Samuels yet.'

'Don't worry about it,' Carlyle snapped, annoyed at her inability to focus on the matter in hand. 'Fingers crossed the problem is solved.'

'Okay,' Roche replied wearily. 'Let's hope he turns up. I've already had Dugdale on my case.'

'Fuck him,' Carlyle spat. 'It's hardly your fault that Dyer was allowed to walk out of the damn hospital.'

'No, but—'

'No buts,' Carlyle ordered. 'Get Dyer back in custody and then we'll deal with Dugdale. I'll see you back at the station this evening. Watch out for the flesh-eating bacteria!'

'Don't worry,' Roche laughed. 'The only thing that will be going anywhere near Colin's crotch is the toe of my boot.'

'That's the spirit!' He ended the call as Marcello appeared at his shoulder. 'Rush over?' Carlyle asked.

'Just about.' Wiping the sweat from his forehead with the corner of the tea-towel draped over his shoulder, Marcello blew out a breath. 'What're you havin'?'

By the time he had nibbled his way through a toasted cheese sandwich, the lunchtime rush had finished and the café largely emptied. Retreating into a now empty booth at the back, Carlyle asked Marcello for a green tea. He took out the photograph that he had stolen from Carla Dyer's bag and placed it on the table just as Marcello appeared with his drink. The café-owner glanced at the photograph by Carlyle's plate. 'Brighton, yes?'

'Could be.'

'It is.' Marcello tapped the picture with his index finger. 'I know it well. We used to take the kids there every year.' The old man smiled as he shuffled back behind the counter. 'They loved the pier.'

Carlyle sipped his tea and peered at the picture of Carla Dyer standing at the entrance to Brighton Pier. It was, he guessed, an image from maybe fifteen or possibly twenty years ago. Even smiling in an ancient holiday snap, Carla looked like a mean-spirited piece of white trash, but at least back then she had youth on her side; as did the guy who was standing at her side. Maybe he was Colin's dad, maybe not. Either way, he was long gone.

Carlyle glanced at the clock behind the counter, which told him it was almost two thirty. What to do with his afternoon? Nothing immediately sprang to mind. He had no desire to return to the station, but at the same time, it would be premature to have another chat with Carla

Dyer before her arsehole son was safely back in custody. Finishing his drink, he tried to ignore the selection of pastries on offer. 'Marcello!'

'Yeah?'

'Let me have the bill, please. I need to get off.'

THIRTY-ONE

In the event, after leaving Il Buffone, Carlyle headed back towards King's Cross. Despite what he'd told Roche, he felt that he might as well see Colin Dyer's arrest for himself. Coming out of Euston tube station, he took a left up Eversholt Street. Ten or so yards in front of him, a refuse truck was slowly making its rounds. Taking the stolen Samsung from his pocket, he slid off the battery and removed the SIM card. Catching up with the truck, he casually tossed the two parts of the handset into the crusher in the back. Skipping across the road, he dropped the SIM card into the nearest drain and carried on his way.

Slipping into Polygon Road, a block from the Coffee House, he glanced at his watch. It was almost quarter to four but he knew that he had plenty of time. Scumbags like Colin Dyer were never on time. Pulling out his BlackBerry, he called Roche. The call went straight to voicemail and he hung up. From round the corner, there was the blare of a horn and the familiar refrain of a pissed-off cabbie.

'Hey! What the fuck do you think you're doing?'

Carlyle laughed to himself but the smirk was immediately wiped from his face as a body came hurtling round the corner and smacked straight into him, knocking him on his arse. 'Hey!' Carlyle shouted, winded. His surprise was compounded by the realization that he was staring at the equally shocked face of Colin Dyer.

'Shit!' Dyer tried to scramble to his feet but Carlyle grabbed him by the leg, taking a kick in the mouth for his trouble.

'You fucker!' Carlyle hissed, hanging on for dear life. 'You're nicked!'

'Fuck off!' Dyer shouted, kicking out as best as he could manage. Carlyle took a sharp blow to his left ear and felt his grip weaken. Dyer made it to his feet, caught in two minds about whether to leg it or give the inspector a good kicking. He seemed to be veering towards the latter when two uniforms rushed round the corner and took him out with a no-nonsense rugby tackle.

Carlyle struggled to his feet as Dyer was cuffed and pulled back upright. 'About bloody time,' he snarled at one of the constables.

The officer looked at him suspiciously. 'And who would you be, *sir*?' he asked, in an officious, *don't fuck with me* tone. Dyer let out a shrill laugh. Spitting blood into the gutter, Carlyle pulled out his warrant card and shoved it towards the constable's face. He could feel a bastard headache developing and his mood was black. 'I would be the officer,' he said darkly, 'who apprehended this little shit while you fat fucks were waddling down the road, failing to stop his escape.'

Both constables gave him a hostile glare, causing Dyer to snigger again. This time, however, his amusement was cut short when Carlyle stepped forward and gave him a swift boot in the balls for his trouble. Dyer sagged backwards but didn't collapse. 'That might give the flesh-eating bugs something to think about,' Carlyle said maliciously, resisting the temptation to give the worthless tosser another kick.

The constables exchanged confused looks.

'It wasn't you fuckwits that let him walk out of UCH, was it?' Carlyle demanded.

'No, sir,' they replied in unison.

'What's going on?' Barely out of breath, Roche appeared from round the corner, followed by another uniform.

'Shouldn't I be asking you that?'

'He turned up early,' Roche explained. 'That was the one thing we weren't suspecting.'

'I suppose not,' Carlyle sighed, his headache now in full swing. 'Try and get him back to the station without any more drama. I'll see you back there later.'

'Christ! What do you want now?' Carla Dyer gripped her front door tightly, ready to smash it into the inspector's face at the first sign that he would try and come inside.

'I'm here to tell you that Colin's been re-arrested,' Carlyle said, trying not to sound too smug about it.

Carla Dyer gestured at the bruise on Carlyle's cheek. 'Did he give you that?'

'He's in deep trouble, Carla,' Carlyle replied, ignoring the question.

'That's his problem,' the woman shrugged.

'You're his mother.'

'So what?' Her eyes narrowed. 'What can I do for him? He's fucked.'

'Where can I find his father?'

Carla Dyer looked at him suspiciously. 'What would you want to do that for?'

Carlyle saw the red light blinking on the side of the WTC9SHR miniature bullet camera and looked straight down the lens and smiled. 'Nice to see we are all together again,' he said, pulling up a chair and offering his hand to Kelvin Jenkins.

'Inspector,' the lawyer nodded, managing a relatively firm handshake under the circumstances.

'This needn't take long, Kelvin,' Carlyle said affably, pointedly ignoring Jenkins' client, Colin Dyer, who was staring zombie-like into the middle distance. There were a couple of fresh bruises on his face and it looked as if he had been given a few more slaps before reaching the station, which only served to improve Carlyle's mood further.

Roche, on the other hand, was wearing the kind of standard, pissed-off expression that he was very familiar with from home.

Tossing his A4 notepad on the desk, Carlyle sat down, turning to look at Roche as he did so. Conscious of his good mood, he tried to sound solicitous. 'Are you okay?'

'I'm fine,' she said sharply. 'But do I need to sit in on this?'

Carlyle glanced at Kelvin, who was clearly as confused by Roche's mood as Carlyle. He turned back to Roche and smiled. 'Nah. It's fine. I can cope.'

'Good.' She was out of her seat and almost through the door before adding a perfunctory, 'See you upstairs.'

Carlyle listened to the door close behind her and pulled himself together. 'Right!' he said, tapping his empty notepad. 'This shouldn't take too long.'

'No,' Kelvin agreed.

Colin Dyer continued to stare into space.

'Your client has had it,' Carlyle said cheerily. 'He's totally fucked.'

'What do you want?' Jenkins said wearily.

'What do I want?' Carlyle frowned. 'I don't want anything. Colin is going down for robbery, abduction and murder. Personally, I would just throw him in the Thames in a sack full of bricks, but it's not my decision. He'll be in jail for a long time; that's good enough.'

'So why are we having this conversation?' Dyer put in, his gaze still focused on a point over Carlyle's left shoulder.

'Because we're still missing some of the stuff you nicked from the St James's Diamonds store. We'd like to get everything back so that we can put this thing to bed.'

'You got all the stuff *we* took.' A smirk spread across Dyer's face. 'I heard that maybe some coppers were a bit naughty after we scarpered.'

Carlyle had a strong urge to smack the little twat in the face. Then he remembered the WTC9SHR blinking at his back. 'We've checked it out,' he said. 'You two took everything.'

Dyer looked at his lawyer and folded his arms. 'Bollocks.'

Taking a pencil from inside the spiral rings of the spine, Carlyle scribbled a small smiley face on his notepad. 'Either you help me,' he said, not looking up, 'or Carla will go to prison too. And the only way she'll ever come out is in a box.'

'Fuck off!'

'She is in a cell round the corner right now,' Carlyle lied. 'And if I walk out of here unsatisfied with your level of cooperation, she will be charged as an accessory both to the robbery and to the murder.' Looking up, he smiled maliciously. 'Twenty-five years minimum, even before I make it my business to put in a bad word for her with the judge.'

Dyer glared at him angrily, tears in his eyes.

Now it was Jenkins' turn to stare into space like a zombie.

'Well, Colin, what do you have to say for yourself?' Carlyle dropped his pencil on the pad and sat back in his chair, folding his arms. 'I know what you did. I know who put you up to it. All I need to know is where the stuff is being stashed.' He watched the cogs turning in Colin Dyer's head. *Here we go*, Carlyle thought. *He's going to fold.*

Kelvin Jenkins carefully watched his client as he waited for his response.

If you really know who put us up to it,' Colin snarled at Carlyle, 'go and ask *him* where the fucking stuff is, you stupid cunt.'

Up on the third floor, sitting at her desk, Roche munched grimly on a cheese sandwich while sifting through 123 unread emails. Carlyle's habit of dipping in and out of *her* case was becoming profoundly annoying. One moment he would give every impression of not giving a toss, the next he would be fighting in the street. Why he couldn't just be a bit more consistent was beyond her. Lots of coppers could be temperamental, but Inspector John Carlyle took the fucking biscuit. It was another reason why she wanted to make the move to SO15; when you were running around with a Heckler & Koch G36 assault rifle under your arm, you couldn't afford to be so egotistical.

The inspector didn't seem particularly bothered whether she left Charing Cross or not, which was just one more thing that really pissed her off. They had been working together for well over a year now and, despite his obvious shortcomings, were quite a good team. She was surprised that he appeared so insouciant about her desire to move on. Her mobile started vibrating across the desk, no number displayed on the screen. She looked at it for a moment then picked it up. 'Yes?'

'It's me.'

Not having a clue who was on the other end of the line sent her to a new level of grumpiness. 'Who is this?'

'It's me,' the voice pleaded. 'Sam.' It was noisy in the background, as if the guy was calling from a pub. 'Samuel Smallbone.'

Fuck, why did I answer the bloody phone? 'What do you want?'

'I was wondering,' Smallbone said, the self-confidence draining from his voice with every word, 'if you might fancy a drink?'

Yeah, right. 'I'm busy.' Roche flicked open an email from the Police

Federation complaining about a leaked paper on the future of policing by the Association of Chief Police Officers. '*We are extremely disappointed*,' said the Federation Chairman, '*that such an important paper has been leaked into the public domain, causing much anger and distress amongst police officers.*' *Yeah, right*, she thought. *We're all crapping ourselves.*

'I was wondering,' Smallbone persisted gamely, 'where I stand at the moment with the reward?'

'Reward?' She scrolled further down the Federation email. '*There are many areas of very real concern which we strongly oppose and will seek to address on behalf of our members. It is intrinsic that at a time of great uncertainty and constraint, all policing bodies work together openly and transparently to ensure that the future of policing in England and Wales is shaped by police officers, not individuals, for the benefit and safety of the public.*'

Well, fucking well do something about it then, you tossers, she thought angrily. *And while you're at it, it would be good to know just how safe my bloody job is.* Stabbing the delete key, she sent the missive heading for the cyber-trash.

'For helping catch the guys who did that diamond store.'

Roche gritted her teeth. 'I told you; you need to speak to the insurance company.'

'But you said you'd help me with that.'

Did I? 'No, I didn't.'

'Anyway,' said Smallbone, lowering his voice so that Roche had to strain to hear him against the background hubbub. 'There's more I can tell you . . . about the stuff that's still missing.'

Roche sat forward in her chair and simulated banging her head on the desk.

'Hello?'

'Yeah, yeah,' she said, 'I'm still here. Where are you?'

Carlyle appeared by the desk as she ended the call. 'Are you okay?'

She gave him a blank look. 'How did you get on downstairs?'

'Some morons cannot be helped.' Carlyle shook his head. 'We should leave Colin to the lawyers.'

'What about the missing gear?'

He looked at her carefully. 'How much is still unaccounted for?'

Roche consulted a print-out on her desk. 'Almost ten million.'

'I think we've probably taken this as far as we can.'

'Probably,' Roche nodded.

'I'm going to call it a night.'

'Me too.'

'We can formally charge Dyer in the morning.'

'Yes.'

'Fine.' Carlyle turned and headed for the stairs. 'Have a good one.'

'You too.' She watched him disappear and slowly began counting in her head. Reaching thirty, she grabbed her bag and followed him out.

THIRTY-TWO

'Are you here for another peek at my bum?' Katrin Lagerbäck grinned at Carlyle and gestured for him to sit down.

Carlyle's eyes fell on the photo on the wall behind her head. The image was just as memorable as he recalled. 'Not just that,' he said, slipping into the empty chair in front of her desk.

'Oh.' She returned her attention to a stack of papers under her nose. 'It must be important for you to come and see me at this time of night.'

You're not the only one who works long hours, Carlyle thought resentfully. *And at least you get paid for it.* 'I thought I'd come by on the off-chance that you'd still be here.'

'I'm always here,' she sighed, picking up a couple of sheets of A4 and tearing them in half before dropping them on the floor by her chair. She gave him a thin smile. 'I'm not a hard person to track down.'

'So,' Carlyle remarked blandly, 'if you're busy, business must be finally improving.'

She shook her head. 'Hardly. If it was any good, it would be parties, networking events and "business trips" to Milan, Barcelona and New York. Now it's a question of poring over spreadsheets trying to recover every last penny.'

'Ah.'

She sat back in her chair and went on: 'Mayfair is awash with that *fin de siècle* feeling. Fund managers are burned-out, world-weary. We are handing back investors' cash with a polite "thanks, but no thanks". Everyone thinks our best days have been and gone. Markets are flat and directionless. Making money is either easy or it's a terminal bore.

No one can summon up any enthusiasm. More to the point, investors won't pay big fees for mediocre performance. We might as well leave it all to the computers. The party has come to an end.'

'So, are you closing Hubaishi Dorning Klee?'

'That's not my call, but I suspect that it's only going to be a matter of time.'

'What will you do?'

She drummed her immaculately groomed fingernails on the desk. 'I've been thinking about that for some time, without reaching any firm conclusion. Maybe go back to Berlin.'

'And what would happen to St James's Diamonds?'

She shrugged. 'It'll get sold.'

'Is it worth much?'

'Not as much as if we were to finish executing the current strategy,' she said. 'Maybe someone would take it on as a business; maybe they would just want the stock.'

'In terms of the robbery . . .'

'Yes?' She gave him a *nice to see you're finally getting to the point* smile.

'Have you had any insurance payment yet?'

'No. That will take a while. The insurance company will want to be sure that you are unable to recover all of the items before making a payout. Why do you ask?'

'I was wondering,' said Carlyle, 'if you might be able to help me with something.'

'Here you go.' Roche placed a pint of Strongbow cider on the table in front of Samuel Smallbone and pulled up a chair.

'Thanks.' Smallbone quickly finished the last of his old pint and took a sip of the new one.

Roche scanned the dingy pub, full of grubby people, and wished she was at home in a nice warm bath. She took a large mouthful of Stolichnaya vodka and felt it hit her empty stomach. *Just the one*, she told herself. *You are leaving after just the one drink*. She caught Smallbone eyeing her up and shuddered. He looked as sallow, nondescript and feckless as ever. 'What have you got?' she asked.

'About the reward . . .'

Roche finished her drink and smacked the empty glass down on the table. 'Look, I will make sure that you get anything you're due, all right?'

Looking a little hurt, Smallbone gestured at her empty glass. 'Want another?'

'No,' said Roche with self-control. 'Just tell me what you've got and I can crack on with trying to track down your money.'

Smallbone took a wary sip of his pint. 'Colin Dyer . . .'

Why can't you just speak in sentences, Roche wondered, *like a normal person?* 'Yes?'

'He didn't do the job on his own.'

'We know that,' said Roche wearily. 'Damien Samuels is also in custody.'

'Yeah. But apart from him . . .'

The sergeant yawned. 'Name,' she said. 'Give me a name.'

Extricating herself from the wretched Smallbone, Roche hovered on the kerb, scanning the road for an available taxi. She ached to be home. She wanted that bloody bath. As usual in these situations, a procession of black cabs rolled past, already occupied with their lights off. It was one of the immutable facts of London life – you could never get a taxi when you needed one.

'Wanna cab?' Roche turned to face a small Indian guy, waving a set of keys in his left hand. He gestured towards a beaten-up Vauxhall Corsa parked across the street.

'Are you licensed?'

The guy gave her a funny look and laughed. 'Where you wanna go?'

'Show me your ID,' Roche demanded. Without a licence from the Public Carriage Office or local authority, the guy in front of her was breaking the law. Not only was it illegal for minicabs to pick up or tout for passengers off the street, but the risks associated with getting in a vehicle with one of these cowboys was considerable. Random and excessive fares were bad enough. Much worse, on average, eleven women were attacked in London each month after taking an unlicensed minicab. A staggering 80 per cent of stranger rapes were committed by unlicensed cab drivers.

The guy waved again at his piece of shit motor. 'Come . . .'

The guy looked as decrepit as his car. If he tried anything funny, the sergeant could doubtless take him out with both hands behind her back. Even so, she wasn't going to get in the Corsa. 'I'm fine,' she said, walking away in the direction of the bus stop twenty yards down the road. She was halfway there when a bus glided past her and headed on without stopping. 'Shit!' Her mobile started ringing and she pulled it out of her bag.

'Roche.'

'Sergeant, this is Commander Dugdale.'

'Yes, sir.'

'Can you talk?'

'Yes.' Roche reached the bus shelter and looked up at the indicator board, which told her that the next bus wasn't due for another twelve minutes. *It's just not my day*, Roche thought as she squeezed onto the bench inside, next to a massive black woman laden with groceries.

'Good job recovering Colin Dyer.' Not for the first time, Dugdale sounded like he had partaken of some strong drink. There was music playing in the background. Roche thought she could make out the voice of Marvin Gaye, but she may have been mistaken. The thought of the Commander getting down to 'What's Going On' was just too horrible to contemplate.

'It was Carlyle who tracked him down,' she replied casually.

Dugdale grunted. 'Just don't lose him again.'

'No. We won't.'

'Has he been charged yet?'

'In the morning.'

'Good. Once that's done, come up to Paddington.' Dugdale stopped to take a slurp of whatever he was drinking. 'Let's say eleven.'

Roche sighed. The schlep would waste half her day. She took a deep breath. 'Of course. What is it about?'

184

'I want you to meet my number two at SO15.'

Your former *number two*, she thought snidely, *before you were kicked out.*

'I've given you a big write-up,' Dugdale smarmed. 'I think we're making some progress on your transfer.'

Roche squirmed. 'Great. Thanks.'

'It's my pleasure,' Dugdale replied, his voice becoming oilier by the second. 'It is hugely important that talented young officers like yourself are carefully . . . *nurtured* through the ranks.'

Roche glanced up at the indicator board. There were still nine bloody minutes before her bus was due. Peering optimistically into the middle distance, she saw the Indian cabbie lead a passenger towards the Corsa. She was relieved to note that the customer was a bloke; the worst that could happen would be a row over the fare.

'There is one other thing . . .'

'Huh?' Roche belatedly tuned back into the conversation.

'Another issue,' Dugdale repeated.

'Yes?'

'The Carlyle hearing.'

'Oh,' said Roche warily.

'The date is next week.'

I am perfectly well aware of that, she thought angrily. 'Yes.'

'I will be conducting the hearing, alongside Superintendent Buck.'

Roche frowned. 'Is it normal for an officer to be directly investigated by his commanding officer?'

Dugdale coughed. 'It is . . . allowable. A considerable amount of discretion is permitted in the way these things are set up.'

'But is there not a conflict of interest? Surely the Federation will protest?'

'The Federation,' Dugdale said breezily, 'can go fuck themselves. I have agreed the format with the IIC and also the PCC. What we want is for the matter to be dealt with swiftly, discreetly and with a minimum of fuss.'

It sounded like a kangaroo court to Roche.

More slurping noises came down the line and Dugdale turned his attention to someone at his end. 'Get me another, will you . . .'

The Corsa drove slowly past the bus stop. Still seven minutes to wait.

Dugdale came back on the line. 'So, I wanted to check on what you were planning to say at the hearing.'

As of right now, Roche thought, *it's none of your fucking business.* This thing was getting out of hand and she made a mental note to contact her own Federation rep in the morning. 'I think, sir,' she said, trying and failing to keep the anger from her voice, 'that it is reasonable to assume that I will be repeating what I said in my original statement.'

'I see,' said Dugdale. 'Maybe we could look at ways in which your submission could be more constructive.'

You have got to be fucking kidding, Roche fumed. Gritting her teeth, she said nothing.

'Anyway,' Dugdale continued, 'I won't detain you any longer this evening. Have a think about it. We can have another chat tomorrow.'

Roche waited for him to end the call and let out a deep breath. Her fucking bus was still five minutes away, but all thoughts of home and a luxurious bath had evaporated. Instead, she was resigned to heading back to the office. There was work to be done.

THIRTY-THREE

It was not shaping up as a green tea kind of day. The fact that Carlyle had eight missed calls on his mobile told him that *The Times* had indeed run their story. Picking up a copy of the newspaper from his newsagent on Drury Lane, he repaired to the relative sanctuary of the Box café for breakfast. He had barely taken a seat when Myron Sabo appeared at his shoulder and placed a double macchiato on the table. Carlyle smiled appreciatively. 'Thanks.'

With the merest of grunts, the café-owner wandered back behind the counter. The coffee was sharp and hot, just the way Carlyle liked it, and he paused to savour the moment, watching a refuse truck slowly move along Henrietta Street, a trio of bin men following behind it, dumping yesterday's waste into the compactor at the back. To his mind, these guys did the most under-appreciated job in the whole of London. *Without them*, he thought, *we would drown in our own shit in less than a week*. Picking up his paper, he resisted the temptation to start at the back with the sports pages, as he usually did, and flicked through the home news, looking for Brian Sutherland's piece about the Catholic Legal Network's lawsuit. He had to go through the paper twice before he found it, halfway down page twenty-three: CHURCH SUES MET AHEAD OF POPE'S VISIT. He read it and then read it again. There was a brief explanation of the situation and the comment that: *The dispute has the potential to embarrass the government as the Pope's visit looms*. Abigail Slater was quoted as saying: '*This is just another example of how the basic rights of members of the Catholic Church are being eroded. It is essential that this matter is dealt with properly*.'

The Met, according to Sutherland, declined to comment. Happily, Carlyle's name was not mentioned.

Finishing his coffee, Carlyle went over to the counter and picked out an iced doughnut to go with a second coffee. Returning to his table, he checked his calls. He had four messages. There was a curt *Call me* text from Dugdale and a voicemail from Roche explaining that she would be out for most of the morning. Carlyle drummed his fingers on the table in annoyance; he had wanted her to chase up some of the lines of enquiry on the Leyne investigation. Roche was getting into the habit of never being around when he needed her – something that annoyed Carlyle immensely. He was feeling increasingly out of synch with his sergeant, and wondered if her mooted move to SO15 might not be best all round.

The second voicemail message was from the Headmaster's office at Alice's school. *'Inspector Carlyle, this is Judith Atkinson from Dr Myers' office . . .'* Carlyle's heart sank. What on earth had happened now? If Alice had gotten into more trouble, there would be hell to pay. And why hadn't Helen told him about it? *'Dr Myers wanted me to thank you for the recent talk you gave at the school. The girls found it very stimulating. He was wondering if you might be able to come in and give us another one.'*

What? Relieved, Carlyle laughed out loud, prompting Myron to give him a bemused look. 'Stimulating'? Whatever next? He replayed the message, a broad grin spreading across his face. 'You have got to be kidding,' he said aloud. Alice was going to love this.

The final message was from Katrin Lagerbäck. *'I think we are on,'* she said. *'Call me this afternoon.' Blimey,* Carlyle thought, *that was quick.* His mood was further improved by Myron placing the doughnut in front of him. Dropping the phone back into his pocket, he took a large bite, before returning to his newspaper and the all-important sports pages.

Taking its name from one of the popular saints of the day, St Boniface's Church was built in 1290. The oldest Catholic church in England, it was one of only two remaining buildings in London dating back to the reign of Edward I. It had survived the Great Fire of London and the Blitz – despite a bomb tearing a six-foot hole in the roof – and was still much used for baptisms, weddings and funerals more than seven hundred years after being built. But at this time of the day, it was his and his alone. Scanning the sheet of paper in his hand, Francis McGowan wondered how much the Holy Father knew about his church.

I am very much looking forward to my visit to the United Kingdom and I send heartfelt greetings to all the people of Great Britain. I am aware that a vast amount of work has gone into the preparations for the visit, not only by the Catholic community but by the government, the local authorities in London, the communications media and the security services, and I want to say how much I appreciate the efforts that have been made to ensure that the various events planned will be truly joyful celebrations. Above all, I thank the countless people who have been praying for the success of the visit and for a great outpouring of God's grace upon the Church and the people of your nation. While I regret that there are many places and people I shall not have the opportunity to visit, I want you to know that you are all remembered in my prayers. God bless the people of the United Kingdom!'

Francis McGowan carefully folded his copy of the Pope's letter to the people of Britain and placed it in his pocket. Switching on the PA system, he let the sound of the choir's 'Ave verum corpus' fill the church. Turning the sound down to a modest level, he moved slowly towards the main doors. It was already almost twenty minutes past the due opening time, but it was rare for anyone to seek the solace of St Boniface's at this time of the morning. And those that did were used to waiting patiently and suffering delays in silence.

Unlocking the door, he stepped outside and sniffed the cold morning air. As he had anticipated, there was no one waiting and he decided to have a swift cigarette before getting started on the business of the day. Lighting up a Benson & Hedges King Size, he took a hearty drag, glancing up at the church noticeboard as he did so. Next to a newsletter covering various aspects of the church restoration programme was a poster advertising the Catholic Children's Society Parish Family Day on the coming Saturday. *I should probably give that a miss*, McGowan thought. Finishing his cigarette, he tossed the stub down a nearby drain and headed back inside. As he did so, the phone in his pocket started ringing, to the tune of '*Salve Regina*'. Sighing, he answered it. 'This is Father McGowan.'

'Father?' The voice was young and nervous. 'It's me.'

Oh sweet Jesus. McGowan closed his eyes and swallowed. 'Simon?'

'No, Father, it's Eddie – Edward Wood.'

McGowan felt a wave of relief wash over him. Concentrating hard, he tried to put a face to the boy's name.

'Father?'

'Ah, yes, Edward.' A thought struck him. 'How did you get this phone number?' he asked gently.

'I'm a friend of Simon's. We came to your drop-in centre. He gave it to me.'

'I see.' McGowan felt his relief begin to recede. 'Do you know where he is?'

'No,' said the boy. 'I have been looking for him. I wondered if you might be able to help me.'

McGowan stuck another cigarette between his lips. 'I can try,' he said dreamily. 'Why don't you come and see me? We can talk it over.'

Chief Superintendent Nicholas Tett looked at Roche and scowled. A tall man with pinched features and short curly hair that appeared dyed, he looked like a banker in a uniform rather than a copper. Taking a sip from the cup of coffee that he had been cradling for the last twenty minutes and which by now would be stone cold, he returned his gaze to a spot high on the wall of Dugdale's office. Since saying 'hello' at the start of the meeting, Tett had not spoken a single word. He was clearly out of the loop regarding his former boss's agenda vis-à-vis Carlyle and struggled to muster a level of interest in the conversation. If this was what the top team in SO15 was like, Roche was beginning to wonder if she might not be better off staying at Charing Cross.

Dugdale checked his watch and smiled. 'So,' he said, glancing at Tett, 'I think we're all on the same page.'

The Chief Superintendent hasn't even opened the book, Roche thought bitterly. She nodded.

Tett smiled vacuously. 'Always.'

'Good.' Dugdale struggled to his feet and gestured towards the door. 'I'll see you at the hearing.'

'Yes.' With some effort, Roche stopped herself from breaking into a jog as she headed for the door.

It was one of those days when no one was answering their phone. The inspector had called Katrin Lagerbäck, as instructed, only to get her voicemail. It was a similar story with Sally Jones, the second wife of Roger Leyne. Sighing, he left another message and wondered what he should do with the rest of his afternoon. After a moment's thought, he called Trevor Cole. 'Third time unlucky,' he mumbled to himself as a robotic voice told him, once again, that he should leave a message. Quickly ending the call, he sifted through various bits of paper on his desk until he found Cole's office number. It took him three attempts to dial it correctly and then he was passed between various secretaries before finally finding himself talking to Cole's PA.

'Mr Cole is on holiday this week,' the woman said chirpily, as if this made her life a happier one. 'Do you want to leave him a message?'

'Do you know where he went?' Carlyle asked.

The woman's tone turned frostier. 'I'm not sure we would disclose that kind of information, sir. Would you like me to take a message for Mr Cole?'

'It's all right,' said Carlyle. 'It can wait.' Ending the call, he tossed the handset onto his desk, on top of a copy of Roger Leyne's bank records. Rubbing his eyes, he wondered if there was more that he could be doing on that front. The professor's bank statements made very interesting reading, showing that he had withdrawn almost fifty thousand pounds over the last year and was seriously in debt. But, unless he could work out what had happened to the cash, the inspector knew that he wasn't going to get very far.

He was contemplating heading out for something to eat when his mobile started ringing and Helen's number popped up on the screen. Lifting it off the desk, he immediately said 'Hi.'

'How's it going?' she asked.

'Fine,' he yawned, 'a bit of a boring day, not making much progress. You?'

'Hectic. Work is crazy – but it's good to be busy.'

'I know what you mean,' Carlyle said gently. They were due to get the results of the BRCA2 cancer gene test in less than a week and the thought of it made him feel sick to his stomach. The different scenarios played out in his head endlessly. The hospital; the doctor. Good news; bad news. The relief; the fear. It was all bollocks. Work was a blessed relief.

'Anyway,' said Helen, 'are you going to Fulham tonight?'

Shit, thought Carlyle. He'd forgotten about his promise to take Alice to see his mother. 'Yes.'

'Good,' said Helen. 'In that case I'll work a bit later.'

'Don't overdo it.'

'I won't. Now, the other thing is that *my* mother has agreed to come up for the weekend.' Carlyle's mother-in-law had dumped Helen's father (now deceased) years ago, about a week after Helen had left school. She now lived in Brighton, which was the usual destination for their family holidays. As Alice got older, Helen's mother would occasionally come up to Town to babysit, allowing Carlyle and Helen to spend some time in her flat.

'Great.'

'So we can go to Brighton for a bit of time to ourselves.'

'Yes. That will be good.' He was looking forward to it, but nervous too.

'But you have to make sure work doesn't cause a problem.'

'Don't worry,' said Carlyle, 'I'm not due to be working. And I won't let anything get in the way.'

'Make sure you don't,' she said firmly. 'I'll speak to you later.'

'Okay,' said Carlyle.

'Lots of love.'

Glancing around the office, he lowered his voice. 'You too.'

THIRTY-FOUR

Ahead of a trip across Town to see his mother, Carlyle decided he needed a workout to build up his reserves of physical and mental energy. The Jubilee Hall Gym, next to the Transport Museum in the south-east corner of Covent Garden's piazza, halfway between the station and the flat in Winter Garden House, was where Helen did her yoga and Alice had a weekly karate class. Carlyle himself tried to do some exercise now and again, although his efforts had become increasingly sporadic in recent years.

Looking across the largely empty floor, Carlyle stepped onto a Life Fitness cross-trainer and switched on his Sony Walkman MP3 player, flicking through the random selection of tracks until he found Nirvana's 'Smells Like Teen Spirit' and started off on a modest hill programme. Fighting against the machine, he took a minute or so to get into a decent rhythm before turning his attention to the TV screen on the wall in front of him. One of the news channels was running and, helped by the subtitles, he was amused to see that the reporter was doing a piece from Britain's only 'gay mass' at the Church of Our Lady of the Assumption and St Gregory in Soho. *'Anybody who is trying to cast a judgement on the people who come forward for communion,'* said a priest, *'really ought to learn to hold their tongue.'*

Shaking his head at the absurdity of it all, Carlyle's thoughts turned to Father McGowan and the upcoming disciplinary hearing. He belatedly realized that the hearing was the day before Helen's results were due. *'Next week,'* he said to himself grimly, *'is gonna be a big week for you, Johnny boy. A big fucking week, indeed.'*

An hour later, showered and slightly more relaxed, Carlyle walked out of the changing rooms, ready to face his mother.

Almost.

Wandering into the gym's café, he ordered a latte and a plate of scrambled eggs and mushrooms on toast from the tired-looking girl in a Bruce Lee T-shirt behind the counter. Dropping his Adidas holdall on the floor next to a display for bodybuilding supplements, he took a seat at a table under a poster advertising Russian Military Fitness sessions – *Train the Red Army way, with genuine Spetsnaz instructors!* – and checked out a very attractive woman in tight shorts and a vest working out on a punchbag. Catching him staring, she gave Carlyle a hard glare and started kicking the bag in a way that suggested she would be happy to give him some similar treatment. Embarrassed, he turned his attention to his mobile and checked his messages. The first was from Katrin Lagerbäck, informing him that she was heading off early for the weekend and would call him when she got back. Carlyle tried calling her back anyway but only got her voicemail.

The second message was more of a surprise. *'Inspector, this is Rose Scripps. Long time no speak. I hope you are well. Give me a call. It would be good to catch up. I'm still at CEOP. I think you might be able to help me with one of our investigations.'* Shamelessly, Carlyle let his gaze slip back to the woman at the punch bag; she was working up quite a sweat.

'Here you go.' The girl placed his coffee on the table. 'The eggs are just coming.'

'Thanks,' Carlyle took a sip of his drink and made a face. It was cooler than he liked but he couldn't be bothered to make a fuss. He thought about Rose Scripps, a child protection social worker for the NSPCC, the National Society for the Prevention of Cruelty to Children, who had been seconded to the Child Exploitation and Online Protection Victim ID Team. CEOP was the police unit responsible for chasing down many of the three thousand people a year prosecuted for committing sex offences against children, including rape, assault and grooming. Over the years, Carlyle couldn't really say that he had been inundated with colleagues that he liked or admired – but Rose was definitely one of them. They had worked together a couple of years before on a nasty people-trafficking case, and he held her in high esteem.

The girl reappeared with the food and placed it in front of him. Nodding his thanks, Carlyle added some ketchup and shovelled a forkful of egg into his mouth. It was too hot for him to taste properly and he swallowed quickly. The woman in the gym gave the punch-bag one last kick and stalked off to attack some free weights. The place was beginning to fill up now as the post-work crowd arrived and Carlyle began to feel somewhat undersized as a procession of over-developed guys with shaven heads made their way past him en route to the changing rooms. Glancing at the clock on the wall, he realized that he was already late. Attacking his plate with gusto, he slipped the phone back into his pocket. Rose would have to wait until tomorrow.

'Jesus!' Leaning against the frame of the living-room door, Carla Dyer placed a hand on her chest. 'You gave me a hell of a fright! I almost didn't recognize you.'

Standing in the hallway, the man in the Arsenal baseball cap smiled. 'Have the police been round?'

Folding her arms, Carla nodded.

'Did you speak to them about Colin?'

Carla looked at her visitor carefully. 'What do *you* think?' Her face broke into a scowl. 'I didn't tell them nuffin'. I'm looking at a charge of obstruction, or summink worse. Fuck 'em.'

The man nodded thoughtfully. 'Good.'

'Is that why you're here?'

Of course that's why I'm here, you silly cow. 'I just wanted to speak to you and understand where we are with all of this.' Sticking his hands into his trouser pockets, he forced himself to smile. 'It's always better to do these things face-to-face.'

The woman shrugged; like she could give a shit.

'It would be a shame to blow it now,' the man said, 'not when it looks like we could be getting away with it.'

'Getting away with it?' Carla laughed. 'You're taking the piss, ain't you?'

'Things are going . . . relatively well.'

'Don't talk bollocks. Colin's going down, for sure.'

The man spread his arms wide. 'At least there'll be something put aside for him when he gets out.'

'Which ain't gonna be for a helluva long time, not with that girl getting killed.'

'That,' the man sighed, 'was very stupid.'

Standing up straight, Carla jabbed an angry finger at the man's chest. 'Well, maybe you should have planned it a bit better, shouldn't ya?'

'Maybe,' the man shrugged.

Carla's eyes narrowed. 'So, what are you gonna do about it now?'

'That's a good question.' Taking another step forward, he pulled a heavy sap from his pocket and gave her a firm backhand across the face.

Carla's knees buckled but she didn't go down. 'Awww!' she squealed. 'You bastard!'

'We can't have you talking now, can we?' On top of her now, he grabbed her by the arm, grunting as he smashed the sap across her skull, once, twice, three times. Finally she went down, blood oozing from her scalp, a long moan rising from her chest as she lay on the grubby carpet. 'Shut up!' he hissed, giving her a sharp kick in the ribs. 'Keep your gob shut or there'll be more where that came from.' There were some more indistinguishable groans and finally she fell silent.

Wiping the sweat from his brow, he put the sap back in his pocket and waited for his heart-rate to return to normal. Had he made his point? Had she got the message? Looking down at the body in front of him, Carla's breathing seemed shallow but regular, the wound on her head superficial. In the distance, he heard a siren, but he knew that it wasn't for him. In a dump like this, you could commit bloody murder and no one would lift a finger.

In a sudden moment of clarity, he knew what he should do. Turning round, he headed to the front door; once out on the landing, he looked around in the gloom. The place was deserted. He could see only one CCTV camera and that was pointing away from where he was standing. Returning inside, he left the front door open, marched down the hallway and stood over the prostrate Carla Dyer. Reaching down, he grabbed her by the hair.

'Argh!' she cried weakly.

'Shut it!' he hissed, giving her another kick for her trouble as he tried to pull her towards the door. Grunting with effort, he pulled too hard and went stumbling backwards, left holding nothing but a fistful of her badly bleached locks. 'Shit!' Regaining his footing, he grabbed Carla by the collar of her polo shirt and dragged her small frame along the hall at a reasonable speed.

Out on the landing, he propped her up against the low wall and quickly looked round again to check that there were no witnesses. As he started to lever her over the edge, Carla's eyes popped open.

'No!' she wailed. 'What are you doing?'

Despite himself, he had to laugh. 'What do you think I'm doing?'

'I won't say anything,' she whimpered. 'Not to any copper. You know I won't.'

With a grunt, he gave her a final push and she disappeared over the wall. He paused, waiting for a scream, or at least a thud. *'I do now,'* he said to himself, not looking down.

Sitting at the kitchen table, picking at a plate of spaghetti, Alice looked up from her vampire novel and smiled sweetly. 'Gran, is it true that Dad was a junkie when he was a teenager?'

'What?' With her back to the sink, Lorna Gordon took a mouthful of tea and glanced over at her son.

Standing in the kitchen of the small Fulham flat where he had grown up, Carlyle sipped his own mug of green tea. 'It's your granddaughter's idea of a joke,' he told her.

'No, it's not,' said Alice sternly. 'Dad gave a talk at school and said that he used to do drugs.'

'I was just making the point,' Carlyle said, equally sternly, 'that not everyone who tries drugs becomes an addict.'

Lorna shook her head. Thirty-odd years ago, she would have given him a firm clip round the ear and stopped him going out for a month. Now she just sighed.

'Anyway,' said Carlyle, 'my talk was a great success.'

'Yeah, right,' said Alice sarcastically.

'They've asked me back to do another one,' he grinned.

'What?' Alice screamed in mock horror. 'You have to be kidding!'

'Not at all. I got a call from the Headmaster's office asking me if I would be happy to do it again.'

'And are you going to?' Alice asked.

'I don't see why not.'

'Great,' Alice groaned, returning to her book. 'At least try not to be so embarrassing next time.'

'I'll see what I can do,' Carlyle laughed.

'Maybe,' said Lorna, 'you could be a bit more circumspect about your own misspent youth.'

'Yes, Ma.' Well into her seventies, she retained the steely determination that had always been at the core of her being. His mother never let anyone put her down; she was the first in a long line of strong women who had kept Carlyle in his place all his life and he knew that it had been the same for his father too. Which was why his dad was currently living in a bedsit a couple of miles away, having been kicked out of the family home after a row over a decades-old infidelity with a neighbour.

'So,' he said, trying to affect an air of insouciance, 'Helen tells me that the divorce finally came through.'

Lorna glanced over at Alice. 'Do we need to talk about that in front of the child?' she asked.

'It's fine, Gran,' said Alice, not looking up from her book. 'I know all about it.' She shovelled another mouthful of pasta into her mouth. 'Anyway, it's not a big deal. Two of my best friends at school – their parents are divorced.'

'We don't know about the grandparents though,' Carlyle quipped. His mother shot him a sharp look and he involuntarily dropped his gaze to the floor. He had long since given up trying to make some sense of the mess that his parents had got themselves into; it was their business. 'What will you do now?' he asked.

Alice artlessly looked over the top of the book, clearly interested in the answer.

Lorna frowned. 'What do you mean?'

'Will you and Ken . . . ?' Ken Walton, an amiable if rather dull pensioner, had appeared on the scene the year before as his mother's new companion.

His mother let out a snort of derision. 'I intend to remain resolutely single,' she harrumphed.

'You could still live together,' Alice suggested helpfully.

'Ken and I,' Lorna turned to face her son, lowering her voice. 'Ken and I are no longer seeing each other.'

Jesus Christ, Carlyle thought glumly. *The soap opera continues.*

'Ooh!' Alice squealed, dropping her fork onto the plate, 'Did you dump him?'

'No – well . . .'

Carlyle was amazed to see his mother blush.

After a moment, she regained her composure. 'Let's just say we have parted company and leave it at that, shall we?' Placing her mug in the sink, she forced a smile onto her face. 'Anyway, young lady, what are you up to these days?'

'Nothing exciting,' Alice sighed, 'just the usual.'

'Come on,' Carlyle chided her, 'you've got lots going on.'

Alice shot him a dirty look and turned to her grandmother. 'Well, of course, Mum's got cancer.'

What? thought Carlyle.

'What?' asked Lorna.

'Mum's got cancer,' Alice repeated.

'No, she hasn't,' Carlyle said hastily, wondering just where all this had come from. Taking a deep breath, he gave his mother a quick summary of the letter from Helen's aunt and the visit to Great Ormond Street to have the test for the BRCA2 gene.

When he had finished, Lorna reached over and squeezed him on the arm. 'I'm sorry, John.'

'It's not something to worry about,' he said, talking more to Alice than to his mother. 'When we get the test results, either it's a false alarm or it's an early warning and we can do something about it.'

They both looked at him. 'Like what?' Alice asked.

Carlyle took a mouthful of cold tea. 'We'll cross that bridge if and when we get to it,' he said resolutely.

THIRTY-FIVE

Cradling a mug of green tea in both hands, he watched her cross the street, heading towards the café.

You're looking good, girl.

Pushing the door open, she saw him sitting near the window and smiled. 'What happened to Il Buffone?' she asked, taking an oversized bag from her shoulder.

Carlyle got to his feet and let Rose Scripps give him a kiss on his cheek. 'Marcello's packing it in,' he said sadly, 'so I feel it's time for a change.'

'That's a shame,' she said, pulling out a chair and sitting down.

'These things happen.' Carlyle gestured around the Box café. 'This place is growing on me. Want a drink?'

'I'll have a latte.'

Carlyle gestured at the hovering Myron, and ordered the coffee. 'So, how's CEOP?'

'We're doing okay.' She smiled wanly. 'You know what it's like; an ongoing struggle against the perverts. But we do our bit. We tracked down a guy in Bromley last week who was on the run from the Canadian authorities. I put him on the plane myself.'

'Shame they didn't throw him out halfway across the Atlantic.'

Rose grinned. 'Interesting point of view, Inspector, as always.'

Carlyle shrugged. 'I try.'

'It's not easy.'

'Well, you're looking good on it,' said Carlyle, meaning it. Rose must be well into her thirties by now, but could have passed for ten years younger which, given what she did for a living, was quite something. Her long dark hair, which he presumed was dyed, was pulled back into a ponytail and she wore minimal make-up. He wondered if she was still single but didn't feel comfortable asking.

Rose lowered her eyes, trying not to blush. 'Thank you.'

'How's your daughter?'

'Louise is doing great. She's almost ten now, so we're worrying about secondary schools.'

'You should talk to my wife about that,' Carlyle said. 'Alice goes to City, but Helen's checked out just about every possible school in London.'

'I might do that, thanks.'

Myron arrived with the coffee. 'So,' the inspector said, 'you mentioned something about one of your investigations?'

Rose took a sip of coffee and nodded her approval. 'Father Francis McGowan.'

Carlyle's eyes widened. 'What?'

'Yep.' Rose beamed.

'You have got to be fucking kidding me!'

'No. We have been tracking Father McGowan for almost two years now.'

'And you haven't come a cropper with the Catholic Legal Network?'

Rose arched her left eyebrow. 'Well, like I said, we've been tracking him. No one from CEOP has tried to beat him to death in a police station.'

Carlyle frowned. 'You've spoken to Alison Roche?'

Rose nodded. 'She seems very switched on.'

'She is,' he admitted grudgingly.

'She likes you.'

'Everybody does,' Carlyle quipped.

Rose's expression turned serious. 'You could have blown it for us.'

'Sorry,' Carlyle held up a hand. 'But, obviously, I had no idea you were on the case. There was no mention of CEOP in any of the stuff that I read in McGowan's file.'

'That's the Met for you. The left hand rarely knows what the right hand is up to.'

'Yeah,' said Carlyle, knowing just how true that was.

'I only knew about your problem with McGowan because of *The Times* story.'

Carlyle took a sip of his coffee. 'I wasn't named in that.'

'Your little . . . moment,' Rose laughed, 'is hardly much of a secret. Anyway, I was able to find out because of our own CEOP investigation.'

'Does Commander Dugdale know about this?'

Rose shook her head. 'No. I wanted to talk to you first.'

'Good. Keep him in the dark. He would like nothing better than to use this to get me fired.'

A look of concern swept across her face. 'Is there any chance of that?'

'Nah. I don't think so. But it would be nice to save my arse and nail McGowan at the same time.'

'*That*,' she told him, 'is where a kid called Eddie Wood comes in . . .'

Just then, the BlackBerry went off in his pocket. Taking it out, Carlyle looked at the screen. It was Roche. 'Sorry,' he said to Rose, 'I've got to take this.'

'No problem.' Rose started playing with her own phone.

'Where are you?' As ever, Alison Roche sounded all business.

'I'm just about to walk into the station.'

'Well, you'd better head up here to Somers Town instead. Carla Dyer took a dive off the third-floor landing last night.'

'Interesting.' Carlyle made a face across the table at Rose. 'Suicide?'

'Nah,' said Roche. 'Looks like someone attacked her in her flat and then threw her off.'

'A sad loss for our great city.'

'Are you going to come up here?' she asked sharply.

'Of course,' he sighed. 'Give me about half an hour.' Ending the call, he told Rose, 'Sorry, I've got to go.'

'Problem?'

'Just some chav who's taken a dive off a block of flats.'

'Nice.'

'One of my other investigations,' Carlyle said. 'Not the end of the world.' He signalled to Myron for the bill. 'Thanks for coming to see me.'

'I think we can nail this bastard,' Rose said earnestly.

Carlyle patted her on the arm. 'I think we *will* nail this bastard.' Getting up, he walked over to the counter, dug a tenner out of his pocket and handed it over to the café-owner.

'Thanks for the coffee,' said Rose.

'My pleasure.'

'It's a shame about Il Buffone, but this place is nice.'

Carlyle took his change and dropped a pound coin into the tips bowl. 'Yeah, it's fine.'

'Say hi to Marcello for me.'

'I will.'

'I'll let you know when we have the McGowan meeting set up. It should be some time next week.'

'Good,' said Carlyle, hoping that when the time came, he would be able to make it. 'I'm definitely up for that.'

The chorus of R Kelly's 'I believe I Can Fly' had started playing in his head and Carlyle found it impossible to completely stifle a laugh.

Standing a few feet away, Roche looked at him disdainfully. 'What's so funny?'

'Nothing.' Carlyle peered at the chalk outline already fading on the concrete in the middle of the deserted courtyard. 'RIP Carla,' he said quietly, trying and failing to summon up an ounce of sympathy for the dead woman. 'Where have they taken her?'

'She's gone to St Pancras Mortuary.' Roche pointed up at the third-floor balcony. 'She broke her neck – among other things – as a result of the fall. As I said, it looks like she was beaten up inside the flat and then pushed over the wall. The forensics crew are still up there, but they haven't found anything interesting so far.'

'That's hardly surprising, given you went through it just the other day.'

Roche shook her head. 'Maybe we should have taken the poor cow back into custody, after all.'

Carlyle grunted. As far as he was concerned, Carla Dyer's death was neither here nor there. What *was* of interest was the fact that someone had found the 'poor cow' worth killing.

'No witnesses, of course,' Roche sighed.

'Of course.'

'Some of the neighbours reckon they heard some shouting, but that's not exactly unusual in a place like this.'

'No, it's not.' Having had more than his fair share of anti-social neighbours over the years, Carlyle knew exactly what she meant. He gestured at the various cameras looking down on them. 'What about the CCTV?'

'None of them covers the spot in front of Dyer's flat. Even if they had, none of the cameras on the estate have been working for over a year.'

'Fucking CCTV,' grumbled Carlyle. 'What is the point of having all this fucking surveillance if it never works?'

Immune to his moaning, Roche informed him, 'We've checked some of the others nearby, and there are some images of a guy walking away from the estate about the time Carla was killed. He was wearing a baseball cap though, so there's not much to go on. We think he went to King's Cross, but we're not sure.'

Stands to reason, Carlyle thought, *given that we're dealing with such a careful bastard*. Pulling out his mobile, he scrolled through his contacts until he found the number he needed and pressed the call button. When, as expected, the voicemail kicked in, he said simply and clearly: 'This is Carlyle. You have to hold off on what we were discussing. Call me as soon as you can. Thanks.' Ending the call, he slipped the phone back in his pocket and stared down at Roche, who was looking at him suspiciously.

'What was all that about?'

'Nothing,' he said firmly. 'Look, what I want you to do is get Colin Dyer to identify his mother's body.' Clearly not happy at being fobbed off, Roche gave him the briefest of nods. 'Make the whole thing as unpleasant as possible,' he continued. 'Lay it on with a trowel about how his mum died a horrible, agonizing death, et cetera, et cetera.

Wind him up good and proper, and see if he's got anything else he wants to tell us.'

'I can do that,' she said, brightening a little.

'I'm going to be out of Town for the weekend. I might be hard to get hold of, but keep me informed of any developments.'

'Will do.'

'Good,' said Carlyle, as he turned towards the exit to the street. 'I'll see you on Monday.'

There was one final thing that Carlyle had to do before heading off to Victoria to catch a train to the coast. Thanks to the joys of the number 27 bus, it took him more than an hour to get over to the Queen and Artichoke pub near his father's shabby bedsit in Westbourne Green. As promised, his father was sitting at a table in the corner, a pint of Grolsch in front of him, while contemplating the sports pages of the *Daily Mirror*.

For a man who had gone through a full-scale marital crisis well into his seventies, Alexander Carlyle appeared to be in rather good shape. Short and wiry, he was cleanshaven, with his white hair neatly trimmed and a sharp intelligence in his eyes. Wearing jeans and a navy jacket over an open-neck, button-down grey shirt and a black V-neck jumper, he looked younger than his years.

Carlyle forced a grin on his face as he approached. 'Hi, Dad.' He nodded at the half-empty glass. 'Can I get you another?'

'Just a half, thank you,' said Alexander with a swift nod, barely looking up from his paper.

Carlyle went to the bar and returned with the half-pint and a single Jameson for himself. 'Here we go.' Placing the glasses on the table, he took a seat opposite his father.

'Thanks.' Alexander folded the paper and placed it on the bench beside him. Pouring the half into his pint glass, he took a mouthful. 'Aahh!'

Carlyle took a sip of his whiskey and wished he'd gone for a double. 'So,' he asked, 'how are things?'

'Oh, you know . . . the usual.'

'Uh-huh.' Carlyle felt a familiar frustration bubble through his guts. For a long time, he had been very supportive of his dad. It was true that his father had played away. But, as far as Carlyle could tell, it had been a one-off, decades ago, that should have had no impact on the family's current life. As the split became more permanent, his father's unwillingness to fight for what was the defining relationship in his life left his son feeling deflated. Increasingly, he felt that the old fella was just too ready to embrace victimhood.

'How's the family?'

'Good, good.' Carlyle took another sip of his drink. 'Alice and I saw Mum yesterday.'

The old man looked warily at him over his pint. 'Oh yes?'

'She's dumped Ken.' Carlyle didn't know if that was true, but it sounded better. He took a deep breath. 'I think you should go and talk to her.'

Alexander picked up his paper and reopened it at the television pages. He glowered at his son with a mixture of anger and hurt. 'And *I* think you should mind your own damn business.'

THIRTY-SIX

Sitting in the otherwise deserted Yellowave café on Brighton beach, Carlyle looked out across the flat water in search of the horizon. Somewhere out in the Channel, the pale grey sky merged into the pale grey sea. Featureless, colourless, it fitted with his mood perfectly. After a couple of days away from London, it was time to go home. The trip had been great – dinner at Food for Friends, a late showing of *Five Easy Pieces* at the Duke of York's Picturehouse and long walks on the beach. Now he wondered how many more times like this they would have. Helen would get her test results in three days. Whatever the outcome, Carlyle was more conscious than ever that time was limited. He felt nervous as hell about it.

Sensing his unease, Helen took his hand and gave it a squeeze. 'Worried about next week?'

'Oh, you know,' he smiled weakly. 'It would be good to get on with it.'

Putting down her coffee cup, she gave him a peck on the cheek. 'We'll know soon enough.'

Carlyle watched a dog take a crap on the beach and wander off with a satisfied look on its face while its owner struggled to remove the mess from the shingle. 'Yes.'

'Anyway,' Helen continued, 'we know that we can deal with whatever comes our way.'

'Yes.'

'It's like we've always said – it's not worth worrying about it until we know what's going on. Even if it is the wrong result, I'm not going to make a meal of it.'

That's my girl, thought Carlyle, a lump rapidly forming in his throat.

'They offered me counselling, but I said "no thanks".'

Carlyle watched the dog-owner drop his plastic bag full of shit into a nearby bin. 'Are you sure?'

'Yeah,' she said softly. 'Medical advice is one thing. A bunch of strangers telling me what I should feel like is quite another.'

'Fair point,' Carlyle smiled.

'We're very lucky.'

It was a familiar refrain. He leaned over and kissed her on the forehead. 'Yes, we are.'

'I've been speaking a lot to our people in the Congo in the last couple of weeks,' Helen said, 'and when you hear about what families have to go through there – no houses, no clean water, no sanitation, the threat of cholera, diarrhoea and malaria – it really puts things in perspective. Once we get next week out of the way, I was thinking about going out there to take a look for myself.'

Jesus, thought Carlyle. *Cholera? Diarrhoea? Malaria?* 'If that's what you want to do.'

'I do,' she said firmly. 'And maybe you and Alice should come too.'

Whoa, tiger! Carlyle sucked in a deep breath. 'I don't know about that. Isn't she a bit young?'

'Yeah,' Helen smiled. 'Maybe. And it would be a bit hardcore. But I want us to take her on a trip somewhere soon. I think it would be a good wake-up call for her.'

'Does she need one?' Carlyle asked. Alice's problems at school were, he thought, largely sorted.

'Everybody needs one,' Helen said. 'Alice leads a relatively sheltered life . . .'

'Sheltered? In the middle of Central London?'

'Her world is home, school, friends. That's fair enough, she's still only a child, after all, but she could do with seeing a bit more of the world.' Helen grinned. 'So could you, for that matter.'

'I don't know about that,' Carlyle mumbled. He glanced at his watch. 'We need to get going if we want to catch our train.'

'Okey dokey.' Helen got to her feet. 'I'm just off to the loo.'

As she headed towards the back of the café, Carlyle took a copy of the local paper from the rack above his head and read the front-page headline: POLICE TO SHED A THOUSAND JOBS. The story was depressingly familiar, with the Sussex force looking to save more than fifty million pounds. The Chief Constable was quoted as saying: '*There are some very tough decisions that have had to be made in order to achieve necessary savings, and further difficult choices are still to come. Job cuts are inevitable for both police officers and staff, but we're working hard to ensure that improving the way we police is our driving principle, not desperate cost-cutting.*'

'Good luck with that, sunshine,' Carlyle mumbled to himself, as he turned to the inside pages.

On page four, his attention was drawn to a story proclaiming that Brighton and Hove had been named 'Britain's drugs death capital' for the second year in a row, with almost one drug-related fatality a week being reported. *Nice*, he thought. *That's something for the tourist people to work with.* Below the article was a single paragraph, part of the News in Brief section:

A boy who had been drinking on the Palace Pier, before jumping into the sea and drowning, has been identified, police reports said. The body of Simon Murphy, 12, of London, washed up on Brighton beach two weeks ago. The grisly discovery was made by a man walking his dog. Police said there did not appear to be any suspicious circumstances. They stated that they would not make any further comment until the boy's next-of-kin had been informed. Council chiefs today expressed their sadness over the death – the first on Brighton's seafront this year – and stressed the importance of sea safety. Chris Sidwell, Brighton Council's Head of Quality Standards, said: 'It is always so upsetting when someone loses their life in the sea. My thoughts are with the family and friends of this young man.'

How many Simon Murphys could there be? Well, how many drunk, suicidal twelve-year-old Simon Murphys? Carlyle reread the story and punched the air in triumph. 'Thank You, God!' Ignoring the funny look from the girl behind the counter, he carefully tore the story out of the paper and reached for his mobile.

St Pancras Mortuary was a grim-looking place, located in a hidden part of London only a short walk from the Eurostar Terminus. Buttoning up her jacket against the cold, Roche wished that she'd dressed more appropriately for her visit. Skipping breakfast might have been a good idea as well. Carlyle had told her to make it as horrible as possible, but she wasn't sure how you could make looking at a dead body more unpleasant than it already was. Roche wasn't squeamish like the inspector, but still, there were plenty of other things that she'd rather be doing than this. And she couldn't even begin to imagine how terrible it must be to have to identify a family member. Even a recidivist scumbag like Colin Dyer managed to elicit a twinge of sympathy from the sergeant under the circumstances.

Not waiting for the mortuary attendant, Colin Dyer stepped up to the trolley and pulled back the sheet. Looking up, he nodded at Roche. 'Job done. Let's go.' Dropping the sheet, he turned and headed towards the two uniforms standing by the door.

'Colin!' Cold and annoyed, Roche hurried after him. 'Don't you want us to find who did this to your mum?'

'Fuck off,' he said hoarsely as he reached the door, his voice cracking.

Roche followed him into the corridor and out to the car park. 'Want a cigarette?' She was trying to give up for good, but still had some in her bag.

Dyer shrugged. 'Yeah, why not?'

Roche glanced at the guards for their approval, only to find both of them lighting up themselves. Pulling out a packet of Marlboro, she handed one to Dyer, who stuck it in his mouth and took her lighter to fire it up. Inhaling deeply, he let out a long stream of smoke while giving her the eye. 'You not having one?'

Roche shook her head. 'Trying to give up.'

Dyer nodded at the packet. 'Why don't you let me keep those, then.'

Roche tossed him the packet, which bounced off his handcuffs and onto the damp tarmac. 'Sorry.'

Grunting, Dyer bent down and picked up the cigarettes and pushed them in his pocket. Looking around, he took another drag, letting the cigarette burn two-thirds of the way down before dropping it on the ground and stubbing it out vigorously. 'Will I get to go to the funeral?'

'I would have thought so,' Roche replied. 'Given what happened though, the pathologist may want to keep her for a while.'

Colin looked over at the van waiting to take him back to prison. The guards were still chatting away, in no apparent hurry to crack on. 'Fair enough.'

When he glanced back at her, Roche tried to maintain some kind of eye-contact. 'We do want to catch the guy who did this, you know.'

Dyer snorted. 'Yeah, right.'

'We know it's connected to the diamonds job,' Roche persisted.

'Look.' Dyer stepped forward, gesturing at her angrily with his handcuffed mitts. 'You know fuck all.'

Roche took an involuntary step backwards as the guards tossed their fag ends and looked over to see what the fuss was about.

'I know who did it,' Dyer hissed, lowering his voice. 'I'm not fucking stupid. Unlike you lot.'

'But—'

'You couldn't catch a fucking cold!' Dyer started laughing at his truly super joke.

Roche took a deep breath and stared at the sky. *You know what?* she thought. *Suit your-fucking-self. It was only your mother, after all.* 'Okay, Colin, we get the message.'

'About fucking time,' Dyer cackled. He turned and headed for the van. 'Let's get going,' he shouted, gesturing at the guards.

Sitting on the train on the way back to London, Carlyle pulled a letter from his travel bag and read through it for the umpteenth time. It was from the Met's HR Department, outlining the terms that he could expect to be offered if he were to go ahead and apply for voluntary redundancy. He showed it to Helen, who glanced up from her copy of *More* magazine and grunted.

'I've seen it already.'

'Maybe we could make the numbers work,' Carlyle mused, gazing out of the train window. Watching the countryside slide past, he realized just how much he was looking forward to getting back to London. 'Just about.'

'Don't be silly,' Helen laughed. 'What would you do?'

'I dunno,' Carlyle shrugged. 'But with the pay-off, and your salary, I wouldn't need to earn that much, as long as I cover the school fees.'

Helen reluctantly tore her attention away from a story about a washed-up pop singer who'd been jailed for driving under the influence of cannabis. 'If you think I'm going out to work so that you can lounge about the flat all day, you're sorely mistaken.'

'I wouldn't do that,' Carlyle protested unconvincingly.

'Anyway, we couldn't afford it. The price of everything's going up; we're hardly flush as it is.'

'But maybe it's just time for a change.' Carlyle winced at how lame the words sounded.

'Only if you know what you want to change *to*,' Helen said firmly. With a sigh, she closed her magazine and threaded her arm through his. 'Why the angst? Are you worried about the hearing?'

'Nah.'

She looked at him again. 'Are you sure?'

'Yeah. Roche's statement puts me in the clear. So does the police doctor.'

'But will they stick to it when the time comes?'

'Yeah,' Carlyle nodded. Despite the current wrinkles in their working relationship, he still had faith in his colleagues.

'They better had,' said Helen grimly, returning to her magazine.

THIRTY-SEVEN

Home sweet home.

Walking down the platform at Victoria station, the inspector felt a familiar sense of relief at being reconnected to the kinetic energy of the capital. The world had speeded up to a pace he was more comfortable with. Somehow, he felt that life was no longer passing him by.

As he cleared the ticket barriers and crossed the main concourse, his mobile started vibrating in his pocket. He answered without checking the identity of the caller. 'Carlyle.'

'Inspector, it's Rose Scripps.'

He had left her a message about the Murphy boy before leaving Brighton. 'Thanks for calling back, but I'm just about to head into the tube.'

'I'll be brief then. We've tracked down Simon.'

Bloody hell, Carlyle thought, *that was quick*.

'But there was no record of any next-of-kin, so the body was cremated three days ago.'

'Ah.'

'On the other hand,' Rose continued, 'McGowan probably doesn't know that Simon is dead.'

'Does that help us?' Carlyle asked, weaving his way through a sea of people.

'McGowan is meeting with Eddie Wood tonight because he thinks Simon is still out there, able to nail him.'

Shit, thought Carlyle, *it's tonight?*

'Now is gonna be our last chance to get something on him.'

Taking Helen by the arm, Carlyle stopped by the entrance to the tube station. 'Okay. Where and when?'

Rose gave him a time and a place. 'Let's meet up an hour before, and I can take you through it all.'

'Sounds like a plan,' said Carlyle. 'I'll see you then.' Ending the call, he turned to his wife. 'Sorry about that.'

'Work?' Helen asked.

'What else?' he sighed. Together, they headed down into the underground, homeward bound.

'We're back!' Carlyle dumped his bag in the hallway and went into the living room where Patricia, Helen's mother, was sitting on the sofa with a mug of coffee and the *Daily Mail* crossword. 'Hi Pat,' he said as cheerily as he could manage. 'Alice gone to school?'

'Yeah,' Patricia nodded. 'She left about half an hour ago.' Dressed in jeans and a grey T-shirt, she looked even more gaunt than usual. He could see by the look on her face that her weekend hadn't been as relaxing as theirs. In fact, the last couple of days looked as if they had aged her by about ten years.

Helen appeared at his shoulder. 'Good weekend?' she asked.

'Not really,' her mother said tartly, gesturing at half-a-dozen roll-ups lined up on the coffee table next to a green Bic lighter. 'I found her smoking one of these in her bedroom. When I told her to put it out, the cheeky little bugger told me to "fuck off".'

Helen shot Carlyle a look that said: *I wonder where she gets that kind of language from?*

'Then I tried to confiscate these,' she gestured again at the roll-ups, 'and she went crazy.'

Carlyle's heart sank as he stepped over and picked up one of the homemade cigarettes, rolling it between his fingers as he gave it a sniff. Another visit to the Headmaster's office loomed. Dr Myers had made it very clear that Alice had already been given her second chance. This time she could be out.

Patricia gave him a stern look. 'Did you know she was smoking dope?'

Carlyle looked at Helen, who had turned red with embarrassment. 'Well,' she said, 'we were aware of an issue . . . but that was a while ago.'

'She's a kid,' Patricia scolded them. 'She shouldn't be smoking at all, never mind doing drugs, for God's sake.'

Helen folded her arms, her embarrassment turning into defensive anger. 'Now look, Mum, I don't think we need a lecture on parenting.'

Oh Christ, Carlyle thought, *here we go*. Patricia had split with Helen's dad and run off to Brighton not long after Helen had finished school. Family life had, by all accounts, been strained long before that. Anyway, he knew from his own experience that the mother-daughter relationship was a tricky one at the best of times. If this was going to develop into a full-blown row, he wanted to have the chance to run for the hills before things got too nasty.

He held up a hand. 'Look,' he said, giving Helen a firm stare, 'we will sort this out.' Letting his face soften, he turned to Patricia. 'A while ago, Alice was caught with some dope in her possession at school. But it wasn't hers and she wasn't using it. At least that's what she said. And, to be fair, I believed her.'

'Well,' Patricia interjected, 'she certainly seems to have developed a taste for it now.'

'She's a sensible girl,' Carlyle continued, 'and we had a perfectly decent conversation about it at the time. Okay, so she's a bit young, but she'll have to experiment at some stage.'

Helen shot him a horrified look. 'I'm going to make some tea,' she said, slipping out of the room.

Patricia said accusingly, 'She did tell me that you did a lot of drugs when you were young.'

This is fucking ridiculous. 'I did not "do a lot of drugs",' he protested. 'I simply tried a few things – as a lot of people did – at an age when I was considerably older than Alice is now. It was never really a big deal.' He gestured in the direction of the kitchen. 'By the time I met Helen, I hadn't done anything for years.'

'It's a different world now,' Patricia said vacuously.

'Yeah,' Carlyle said, 'but we'll get it sorted.' *I hope*, he thought. 'I'm going to get a cup of tea.'

In the kitchen, while the kettle was coming to the boil, Carlyle stepped behind Helen and put his arms round her waist. Kissing her gently on the neck, he wiped a tear from the corner of her eye.

'Bloody hell, John.'

'Don't worry,' he said, 'we *will* get this sorted. When I find the little bastard that's supplying her, I'll fucking kill him.'

Helen gestured back towards the living room. 'That's not what you were saying in there, to my mother.'

'Sod your mother,' Carlyle whispered, with feeling.

It was a relief to get back to work, even if that meant standing in the cold for four hours on the windowless second floor of an office block currently being gutted by builders. He turned to Rose Scripps, wrapped in a navy coat that reached down to her knees; she was gazing down at St Boniface's Church on the opposite side of the street. 'How long?'

'Here's our boy now.' Rose pointed at the gangly figure of Eddie Wood who had just appeared in Ely Place. Turning off Charterhouse Street, he ducked through the gates at the end of the road and ambled slowly towards the church.

'Do you think he's up to it?' Carlyle had wondered about the wisdom of putting a wire on a fifteen year old but had come to the conclusion that it was worth a punt.

'We're just about to find out.'

Opening hours at St Boniface's had ended more than three hours earlier, but when Eddie stepped up to the door and gave it a gentle push, he found it unlocked and was able to slip inside. Carlyle held his breath as he stared at the Motorola Tetra digital radio handset placed on a bench in front of them, switched to loudspeaker mode. For a few moments, there was nothing but the sound of Wood humming tunelessly to himself and then a whisper. '*He's here.*'

'For fuck's sake,' Carlyle hissed, 'don't give us a running commentary.'

Rose shrugged. There was nothing they could do about it now.

'Edward.' Carlyle recognized McGowan's lazy drawl immediately. 'You are intolerably late.'

'Sorry,' Eddie apologized. 'My bus took ages to show up.'

'Come this way. We can talk in the crypt.'

There was another delay and a burst of static that left Carlyle worried that the boy's mike might have malfunctioned.

'So,' McGowan's voice finally reappeared, 'what do you think has happened to young Simon?'

'I asked around,' Eddie said casually. 'Someone said he went to Brighton.'

Carlyle looked at Rose. 'I told him to dangle that in front of McGowan,' she said. 'Give him something to say.'

Carlyle shrugged.

'He's doing fine,' she said.

'So far.'

'Ever the optimist,' Rose grinned.

'Do you think you could find him for me?' McGowan asked.

'Maybe. Why?'

'I need to talk to him,' McGowan said smoothly.

'Because he went to the police?'

Careful, thought Carlyle.

'Because he is telling lies,' McGowan said sternly. 'Dangerous lies that could get him into trouble. I have spoken to the police and they recognize that he was not telling the truth. I just want to prevent Simon from getting himself into trouble.'

'That's one way of looking at it,' Rose laughed. She glanced at her watch and gazed out into the night. 'I hope my mum's put Louise to bed by now.'

'Handy to have the help.'

'Yeah,' Rose nodded, 'I suppose so. But you know what it's like when you've got to depend on the grandparents.'

'Sure do,' Carlyle agreed, safe in the knowledge that Helen's mum should be back in Brighton by now. If that solved the problem of wife-mother-in-law relations, there was still the slight problem of wife-daughter relations. He had forced Helen to promise that she would leave Alice to him. At the same time, he was pretty sure the two of them would have some kind of row while he was out. A familiar mixture of guilt and relief spread through him at the thought of leaving them to it.

McGowan's voice reappeared out of the radio receiver. 'Do you understand?'

'I suppose so,' said Eddie. 'It wasn't like you forced him to do those things. He usually quite likes it.'

Carlyle tensed. They were getting down to the sharp end of the conversation. Moving onto the balls of his feet he began rocking backwards and forwards, ready for a dash down the stairs and across the road. He looked at Rose. 'Once he's got everything out of McGowan that he can, he's just gonna walk out of there?'

'Yeah,' she said, peering out of the empty window at the brightly lit facade of the church. 'That's the plan.'

'Great plan.'

She gave him a sharp look. 'Thanks.'

'What about you?' McGowan asked. 'Do *you* like it?'

'Do I like what?'

'Good boy!' said Carlyle under his breath.

'Do you like . . . those things?'

'Why?' Eddie asked coyly. 'You want me to suck your cock, like Simon did?'

Holding their breath, Carlyle and Rose stared at the receiver.

McGowan said nothing.

'It's all about the money for me,' said Eddie breezily. 'Give me thirty quid and I'll clean your pipes, no problem. Won't even make you wear a johnny.'

There was the sound of what seemed like McGowan clearing his throat.

'Cash in advance, of course.'

'Of course.' There was a further pause and then McGowan spoke again. 'I only seem to have twenty-five.'

'That'll do,' Eddie replied. 'You can give me the rest next time.'

'Thank you, my son.'

'Shit!' Carlyle hissed, already heading for the door. 'Looks like he's changed the plan.' With Rose close behind, he rushed through the open doorway and down the stairs, carefully sidestepping various work tools and building materials that had been left strewn about the site. Outside, they ran across the empty road and approached the main entrance to the church. Carefully pulling open the door, Carlyle let Rose go in first then followed her inside. 'Where's the crypt?'

Rose shrugged her shoulders. 'No idea.'

'Fuck! Let's hope Eddie takes his time.'

'I get the impression he knows what he's doing,' Rose replied. 'He won't drag it out.'

'Okay,' Carlyle sighed. 'Come on.'

THIRTY-EIGHT

Standing in the middle of the church, Carlyle looked up at the west window, the largest stained-glass window in London, depicting martyrs hung down the road at Tyburn gallows, under the gaze of a triumphant Christ. Even in the gloom, the window was truly impressive but he was focusing on his hearing, trying to distinguish any internal noises from the background traffic hum outside. Finally he heard what might have been a grunt off to his left. Slipping between the pews, he saw there was a half-open door behind one of the pillars that ran down the length of the building. As he approached, the groans became more distinct. Checking that Rose was following him, Carlyle pulled out his mobile and bounced through the doorway. 'Father McGowan,' he said cheerily, shooting the scene in front of him using the video mode on his handset. 'We meet again!'

With his trousers around his ankles, the priest struggled to turn to face the inspector. The look of horror on his face was unmistakable. His member, however, showed no sign of wilting as Eddie continued diligently about his task while caressing the priest's balls with his thumbs. As Rose had said, it looked like the boy knew what he was doing. It was impossible to tell whether the croaking sound that caught in McGowan's throat signalled pleasure or pain. Either way, he was unable to step away from the boy's ministrations before Eddie jerked his head back, allowing an arc of semen to hit a pile of Bibles stacked against a nearby wall.

'Oh my God!' said Rose, appearing at Carlyle's shoulder. 'That is so gross!'

'Phew!' said Eddie as he bounced to his feet. 'That was a close one!' He grinned at the two police officers. 'You don't want to get a faceful, if you can help it.'

'No,' said Carlyle, trying not to laugh. 'I suppose not.'

Eddie patted McGowan on the shoulder. 'Don't forget, you owe me a fiver.'

'Might take him a while to earn that,' Carlyle said, all humour gone. 'You can only make about twenty pence a day in prison.'

With trembling hands, McGowan pulled up his Y-fronts and then his trousers. Rose waited for the priest to sort himself out before reading him his rights and calling for a car to take them to nearby Holborn station.

'Let's see if you can wriggle out of it this time, you piece of shit,' Carlyle snarled. For once, he felt no desire to smack the old bastard about, even as part of an act. Maybe it was the scent of victory in his nostrils; surely now the job was done and McGowan would be put away for a reasonable stretch. It was something that should have happened long ago; maybe it *would* have happened long ago if the degenerate criminal hadn't been wearing a dog collar.

The squad car arrived in less than five minutes. McGowan was bundled into the back. Rose got in beside him, letting Eddie ride up in front. As she went to close the door, she looked up at Carlyle, still standing on the pavement. 'Do you wanna come too?'

'Nah.' Carlyle shook his head. 'I've got stuff to do. Let's talk in the morning.'

'Okay.' Rose nodded.

He gave her a thumbs-up. 'Well done!'

'Thanks.'

Smiling, he slammed the door shut and watched them pull out into the light traffic on Charterhouse Street. Then he started out on the short walk home.

Christian Holyrod watched Abigail Slater pull the Durex Pleasuremax out of its packet and licked his lips. 'I didn't think you lot used condoms.' A sly smile spread across his face. 'Whatever would the Catholic Legal Network say?'

'Me?' Slater tossed the wrapper onto the carpet and flicked an imaginary piece of fluff from her puce-coloured Stella McCartney bra. 'I'm not a Catholic.' Glancing down at his erect, glistening member, she smiled lasciviously. 'I'll use anything if it gives me pleasure.'

'But—'

'The CLN? It's just a career thing.'

'Ah.' Holyrod knew all about the things one had to do to climb the greasy pole.

'I only got into it through a boyfriend. He was really old-school. No penetrative sex before marriage, and all that.'

'Really?'

'Yes.' Slater ran a cool hand along the length of his penis, causing Holyrod to gasp. 'He liked me to give him hand relief dressed as a traffic warden.' She giggled at the memory of it.

'How very unimaginative of him.'

'He had a thing about wardens . . . meters too.'

'Meters?'

'I know. We never did get to the bottom of it, but he liked to jerk off over them,' Slater explained. 'He regularly left his seed over the parking meters of Highgate.'

'Urgh.' Finding it hard to breathe and talk at the same time, Holyrod let out a small grunt of approval as he watched Slater unroll the Pleasuremax with her tongue. His admiration for this woman was reaching new heights. He hadn't known sex as good as this since his university days. Idly, he wondered how much a divorce might cost. With his cock poised to explode, however, his brain simply couldn't handle anything as prosaic as maths.

'Lie down.' Pushing him backwards onto the bed, she caressed his balls before taking him in her mouth, slipping the condom on to him as she did so.

'God!' he cried, 'I'm going to—'

'Not so fast!' Lifting her head, Slater gave the tip of his penis an expert flick with the index finger of her left hand. Instantly there was a slight relaxation in his groin as he backed away from the point of no return.

'Better than Viagra,' she laughed, crawling up the bed on all fours and kissing him deeply on the mouth. Given where Abigail's tongue had just been, Holyrod was less than keen but, pinned to the sheets, he was powerless to resist. Sitting up, she straddled his waist. Pulling her panties aside, she eased him inside her and started moving, slowly, up and down his cock. 'Now,' she said, waving an admonishing finger at him, 'you take your time.'

I'll try, thought Holyrod, gritting his teeth. Closing his eyes, he tried to focus his mind on something – English footballers, British prime ministers, his wife – that would stop him from prematurely shooting his load. It was no good. 'Argh.'

'Steady,' Abigail whispered, the amusement in her voice obvious, as she slowed the grinding of her hips almost to a stop.

'I can't . . .'

Holyrod's complaint was drowned out by the opening bars of Coldplay's 'God Put a Smile on your Face'. Without dismounting, Abigail reached over and pulled an iPhone from the Hermès Birkin Black Palladium at the side of the bed. Taking the call, she stuck the phone to her ear. 'Yes?' Grinning, she gave a firm thrust that made his knees buckle. 'What is it?' Holyrod tried to thrust back but she simply shifted her weight so that he couldn't establish any momentum. Listening to someone on the other end of the phone, she responded: 'Yes. Say nothing – nothing at all. I do the talking, remember? I'll be right there.' Ending the call, she tossed the phone back into the bag.

'Problem?' Holyrod croaked.

'Isn't it always?' Pushing herself half off him, she grabbed the shaft of his cock with her left hand and finished him off with a couple of swift tugs.

'Thanks.' Overcome with gratitude, he tried to pull her towards him, but she slid away, off the bed.

'At least you got what you wanted,' Slater said drily, already half-way to the bathroom. 'You'll have to sort me out later.'

'It will be my pleasure,' Holyrod grinned, stripping off the used condom and dropping it on to the bedside table.

* * *

With a theatrical sigh, Alice tossed her copy of *Bleak House* onto the duvet. 'I don't want to bloody talk about it!' Reaching across to the iPod dock on the bedside table, she steadily turned up the volume on The Clash's 'I Fought The Law' until Joe Strummer's vocals filled the room.

'Well,' said Carlyle, turning it down again, 'I do.' He retreated to the end of the bed and sat down. 'Grandma wasn't very happy – and neither is your mother, for that matter.'

Folding her arms, she gave him a hard stare. Wearing one of her mother's old grey Gap T-shirts, with her hair pulled back, she looked frighteningly mature. 'Tell me about it.'

'We have to sort this out,' said Carlyle gently.

'It's only a bit of dope,' Alice complained. 'No big deal.'

'I don't suppose you're going to tell me who you got it from?'

She shook her head. 'No.'

'I will find out.'

She looked at him defiantly. 'Give it your best shot, copper.'

Despite everything, he burst out laughing. He wanted to grab her and have a play fight, tickling her under the arms like they did when she was a kid. But as he had to keep reminding himself, she wasn't a kid any more.

'Anyway,' she grinned, happy that the tension had been broken, 'it's not like there's just one guy.'

Fucking great, Carlyle thought.

'And I've kept my side of the deal.'

Carlyle frowned. 'What deal?'

'I'm doing well at school.'

Feeling completely powerless, he gazed at the ceiling. 'Well, look,' he said finally, 'all I can tell you is that you're a bit young for this kind of thing. And . . .' Alice began to protest, but he held up a hand. 'And, whatever your grades, there is the issue of school. If Myers thinks you are smoking dope, they could kick you out.'

'There are plenty of other schools.'

Carlyle gritted his teeth. After all the time and effort, not to mention money, that they'd thrown in over the years, first to get her in and then to keep her there, his daughter's *laissez faire* attitude was totally soul-destroying. 'Look,' he told her, 'if you get into a problem at City, I *will* track down every little dope-dealing scumbag and I *will* break their legs.'

'Dad!'

'If you get kicked out, your card will be well and truly marked. Other schools will have the same issues. If you get on a downward slope, it's that much harder to get back on track.'

Alice frowned. 'Back on *what* track?'

'Back on the *not-fucking-things-up* track,' he said, frustrated at his inability to put together an argument that sounded convincing, even to himself. 'So that you don't end up a dickhead loser.'

Alice smiled malevolently. 'Are you going to use that line in your next talk at the school?'

Despite himself, Carlyle let out a small laugh. 'Maybe. What do you think? Would it go down well?'

Alice sniggered. 'I'm sure it could only add to the legend.'

'What legend?'

'My dad – the drug-using cop with borderline Tourette's.'

'Ha bloody ha.'

'See what I mean?' Reaching over, she gave him a peck on the cheek. 'Time for me to go to sleep. I've got school in the morning, remember?'

'Sure.' Carlyle got to his feet, stifling a yawn as he did so.

'Tell Mum not to worry, it'll be okay. You've just got to remember you can't tell me what to do all the time.'

'But—'

This time, it was she who cut him off with a sharp wave of the hand. 'After all, I'm only doing what you did, when you were at school.'

Christ, thought Carlyle sadly, *me and my big fucking mouth*. John Carlyle, Idiot Parent of the Year. 'I was a lot older then.'

'Not much.'

'Relatively speaking.'

'It's different now, everybody does it.'

'No.' He shook his head. 'No, they don't.'

'Well, I am,' she said, looking him straight in the eye. 'And you're going to have to trust me to be sensible about it.'

Like I have an alternative, Carlyle thought unhappily. 'Okay,' he said, stepping forward and kissing her on the forehead. 'I'll trust you.'

'Thanks, Dad.'

She sounded so young, Carlyle had to turn away quickly for fear of tearing up. He moved quickly to the door.

'And I never got kicked out of school.'

'Neither will I.'

'Fine,' he said wearily. 'We'll see how it goes.'

THIRTY-NINE

Abigail Slater took a mouthful of coffee, eyeing Rose Scripps suspiciously as she did so. 'Where is Inspector Carlyle?'

Rose returned the stare with interest. Female defence lawyers were not something you came across very often working in CEOP, certainly not one dressed like this. In a skirt that barely got halfway to her knees and a silk blouse with the top four buttons undone, Slater looked less like a brief and more like a high-class escort. *Were you on a hot date*, Rose wondered, *or is that your normal style?* When McGowan had made the call, it was disappointing that Slater had picked it up. Even more disappointingly, she had made it over to the station – albeit looking like a tramp – in barely twenty minutes, during which time McGowan had remained resolutely mute. Together, they made quite a pair. 'He is not here,' she said finally. 'This is my arrest.'

'What exactly is your relationship with the inspector?' Slater asked, placing the paper cup carefully on the table.

Taking a deep breath, Rose told herself that she was not going to take any nonsense from this one. 'The inspector and I have worked together on several occasions,' she said coolly, 'where there has proved to be an overlap in our investigations.'

Sitting next to the lawyer, McGowan started to say something. Slater cut him off. 'I've told you, Father,' she said sharply, 'leave the talking to me. We'll have you back in your bed in no time.' She smiled patronizingly at Rose. 'You understand that the inspector, along with his sergeant, is under investigation regarding a brutal and unprovoked assault on my client.' She placed a comforting hand on McGowan's shoulder as if to ease the priest's pain at being reminded of such a sordid affair.

'Oh yes, I understand that there are various unsubstantiated allegations that have been made against the two officers, by a suspect who has consistently refused to assist the police in their enquiries,' Rose gestured towards McGowan, who studiously avoided any eye-contact, 'and who, earlier this evening, was caught paying a minor for sexual services.'

'That was entrapment,' Slater snapped, 'and you know it.' Getting to her feet, she placed the lid on her coffee and hoisted her bag onto her shoulder. 'I will be upstairs. I expect the paperwork to be processed within thirty minutes, so that I can escort my client home. Rest assured, I will be speaking to your superior officer in the morning.'

Tired and hungry, Rose fought to contain her anger. Then the thought popped into her head that Carlyle might have done better to smack the lawyer, rather than the priest, and she couldn't help but smile.

'What's so funny?' Slater asked immediately.

'Nothing.' Rose cleared her throat. 'Nothing at all.'

'Good.'

'You can wait in reception if you wish,' Rose said, her eyes twinkling with mischief, 'but your client will not be released tonight.' She gestured at the clock on the wall behind Slater's head. 'My shift finished almost an hour ago.' Now it was her turn to grin maliciously. 'You may have heard that the Federation is asking all officers to restrict their overtime in protest at the proposed job cuts.'

Slater shot her an angry look.

'Father McGowan,' Rose continued, 'will have to wait until the morning to be charged.' Getting to her feet, Rose nodded at the uniform standing by the door. 'Take him to the cells, please.'

With a look of weary resignation, McGowan got to his feet.

Slater grabbed Rose by the arm. 'You can't do this!' she hissed.

'Take your hand off me,' Rose said quietly, 'or *you* will be the one facing the assault charge. And this time there will be witnesses.'

Helen looked up from her copy of *The Times* as Carlyle slipped under the duvet. 'How did you get on?'

'Fine,' Carlyle said glumly. 'She told me that I had to mind my own business and that we had to trust her.'

'And?' Helen dropped the newspaper onto the bedside table and took off her reading glasses.

'And . . . nothing.' Carlyle switched off the light on his side of the bed and pulled the duvet under his chin. 'I guess we have to trust her. I think she understands the point about not getting into more trouble at school, but we have to play it cool. What else can we do? We obviously can't micro-manage what she does; she's already proved that.'

'So we give up?'

'No, of course not. We just need to help her through this phase. She went into it early, so hopefully she'll come out of it early too.'

'Maybe,' said Helen, unconvinced.

Pulling her towards him, Carlyle gave her a firm hug. 'Look,' he said, kissing her on the nose, 'we've got a big couple of days coming up. Let's get through those and then we can take stock.'

'Okay,' she said unhappily.

He reached over and turned off Helen's light, leaving them in the orange-grey semi-darkness of the city that seeped in through the bedroom window. 'At least she didn't ask for her stash back.'

'That's just as well,' said Helen, squirming away from him as she fought to get comfortable. 'Mum took it back to Brighton with her.'

Sitting on the floor in his Calvin Klein trunks, Christian Holyrod had worked his way through the best part of a bottle of Vega Sicilia Valbuena by the time Abigail Slater reappeared. Even in his somewhat intoxicated state, he could see that she was less than pleased. 'What happened?' he asked, trying not to sound too drunk.

Kicking off her shoes, Slater dropped her bag on the carpet and slipped out of her jacket. 'Some fucking CEOP bitch refused to release McGowan.'

'Huh?'

Grabbing his wine glass, Slater took a large mouthful before demanding a refill. Once the last of the wine was gone, she began pacing the room, explaining the detail of her unsuccessful trip to Holborn police station as she did so.

'I see.' Holyrod forced himself to try and sound sympathetic but Slater had started unbuttoning her blouse and it was impossible to concentrate.

'You have to sort these people out!' she said angrily.

'Mm,' he replied, sticking a hand inside his Calvins.

'Seriously.'

Holyrod grinned. There was definitely life down there. 'Quite.'

Tossing the blouse on the bed, Slater unzipped her skirt. 'The whole thing is completely ridiculous.'

Holyrod grunted his agreement. 'It would help though, if your guy didn't go round paying fifteen-year-old boys for blowjobs.' Pulling down his shorts, he grinned. 'Speaking of which . . .'

A look of disgust spread across Slater's face. 'Forget it,' she said, heading for the bathroom. 'I'm going to take a shower.'

Standing in the semi-darkness of her unlit office, Katrin Lagerbäck looked at the portrait of her younger self and sighed. What was she going to do with it when she left Hubaishi Dorning Klee? She didn't want to take it, but she didn't want to leave it either. The girl with the impossibly pert bottom and, if she remembered correctly, the rather empty brain just wasn't her any more, hadn't been for a long time. Maybe she should just take it into the park and burn it, although that would doubtless break various bylaws.

The picture wasn't the only thing she had to worry about. HDK Capital Management had announced that the business was to be wound down and there was a lot to do. Above all, it meant she had to oversee the sale of St James's Diamonds and transition the business over to new ownership. Various bankers had already started sounding her out about the possibility of leading a management buyout, but she knew that her heart wasn't in it. An MBO would commit her to staying in London for the next couple of years at least and that wasn't going to happen. One thing she had decided was that she'd had enough of the capital. Berlin beckoned; it was time to go home.

The door of her office was pushed open.

'I thought I might find you here.'

Frowning, Lagerbäck turned to face her visitor. 'How did you get in?'

The man smiled. 'I thought that you wanted a meeting?'

'*I* thought,' Lagerbäck said tartly, 'that we had something in the diary for later in the week.' She made a move to switch on the lights but he stepped in front of her, pulling a gun from his pocket as he did so.

'No need for that,' he said. 'Move back in front of the desk.'

'What the hell are you doing?' Lagerbäck asked, more annoyed than scared.

'Just do as I say,' the man replied, the smile draining from his face. 'This is an M-1911, apparently.' He looked at the pistol in his hand as if he'd never seen it before. 'A round has been fed from the magazine and placed in the chamber. Firing occurs when the grip safety is depressed; the trigger is squeezed; and the released hammer transfers its energy to the firing pin which, in turn, strikes the primer. As the primer ignites the propellant charge in the chambered cartridge, the hot powder gases expand, building pressure that forces the bullet down the barrel.'

'What?' Lagerbäck had tuned out. This guy could make even murder sound boring.

'Like this.'

Lagerbäck felt the round tear into her abdomen. Thrown backwards across the desk, she looked up enquiringly at the image of her younger self on the wall, wondering how it had all come to this.

FORTY

Christian Holyrod looked over at Abigail Slater and smiled, getting only a frown in return. Noticing the exchange of looks, Katya Morrison grinned. Irritated, the Mayor sent his Special Adviser off to Starbucks to get him a Venti Caramel Macchiato and a chocolate muffin. Once she had taken everyone's order and flounced out of the room, he turned to Archbishop Brian Crossley and said, 'The situation we have been monitoring has taken an unfortunate turn.'

Crossley nodded. 'So I understand.'

'So,' said Holyrod, trying to sound diplomatic, 'I wonder if it might be timely to revisit my office's previous advice.'

Sitting next to the Archbishop, a look of pain passed across the face of Monsignor Joseph Wagner. 'The state visit is less than a week away. I do not see how we can, in all conscience, back down now.'

'I agree with the Papal Visit Coordinator.' Sitting at the end of the table, Gavin Dugdale eyed Holyrod carefully. 'We have the Carlyle hearing tomorrow.'

'What about the sergeant?' the Mayor asked.

'That can wait,' Slater said sharply. 'She's not a big deal. If we see off the inspector, Sergeant Roche will barely merit an afterthought.'

'I suppose not,' Holyrod agreed.

'The judgement,' Dugdale continued, clearly irritated by the interruption, 'will be reserved until after the Pope's visit has ended. Doubtless there will be an appeal, which will drag things out a bit longer, but,' he smiled at Slater, 'hopefully things have progressed sufficiently for the Catholic Legal Network to quietly drop its legal action.'

Nice to know you're going into this with an open mind, Holyrod noted sourly. He had never thought he'd see the day when he felt a twinge of sympathy for that upstart, Inspector Carlyle, but the blatant railroading of a police officer – one of *his* police officers, after all – stuck in his craw. 'I understand, Commander,' he said stiffly, 'but all of this seems to overlook the fact that Father . . .'

'McGowan,' Slater interjected.

'Yes,' said Holyrod politely, 'thank you. All of this seems to overlook the fact that Father McGowan was arrested last night for further offences.'

Slater jumped in again. '*Alleged* offences.'

Holyrod raised his eyes to the heavens. 'Further *alleged* offences, where there seems to be some pretty damning evidence that it will, in all likelihood, not be possible to wish away.'

Leaning forward slightly, he tapped his copy of that morning's *Financial Times*, his index finger landing next to the VATICAN BANKERS IN MONEY LAUNDERING PROBE story on the front page. 'We are all working towards a successful and trouble-free trip,' he said, and paused, giving everyone on the opposite side of the table the opportunity to nod in agreement. 'But it is not the case that you are making things as easy as they could be.'

He picked up the paper and squinted at the type. 'It says here: *Police have seized forty million euro while the Pope's top two bankers have been placed under investigation for suspected money laundering.*' He waved a hand in the air, ignoring the discomfort of the Church officials. 'And so on. *The Vatican's bank, the Institute for Religious Works, has been under pressure to fall into line with international norms and regulations on tax havens and money laundering. Originally founded in 1887 and housed within a medieval bastion within the Vatican, IOR was thrown into crisis following the suspected murder of the so-called "God's banker", Roberto Calvi, who was found hanging from London's Blackfriars Bridge in June 1982.*' Letting his exasperation get the better of him, Holyrod burst out: 'How you people manage it, I simply don't know! If it's not child abuse, it's bloody money laundering! You really are your own worst enemies.'

234

Crossley angrily scribbled a note on an A5 pad on the table in front of him and looked up. 'What precisely is your advice, Mr Mayor?'

'Just drop the legal action. We will cancel the hearing,' Dugdale made to protest but Holyrod cut him off with a wave of his hand, 'and we will sit on this McGowan thing until after the visit is over.'

'Will McGowan be released?' Wagner asked.

'He is already out on bail,' said Slater. 'He has been charged with sexually assaulting a minor and is due to report back to Holborn police station at the end of the week.'

'We will get that pushed back for at least seven days,' Holyrod said.

Wagner gazed out of the window. 'Can't you just get it dropped?'

Dugdale looked at the Mayor. 'No,' said Holyrod firmly. 'The matter is far too serious.'

'I think,' said Crossley, 'that the situation has to be dealt with in the proper manner, both in terms of Father McGowan and in terms of your officer.' He gestured at Slater. 'We have taken the necessary legal advice and we have every confidence in the CLN to handle this matter properly. Now, as you know, we still have a huge amount of work to do ahead of the visit. We cannot waste any more time on this unfortunate distraction.' Getting to his feet, he handed his notepad to Wagner. 'Now, you will have to forgive us, but we have work to do.'

Without getting up, Holyrod watched them leave, swiftly followed by Katya reappearing with a tray of outsized coffees. 'What happened?' she asked, handing Holyrod his Venti Caramel Macchiato.

Rising from her chair, Slater smiled grimly as she loaded papers into her bag. 'Your boss just got told where to get off.' She nodded at Dugdale. 'I will see you at the Carlyle hearing tomorrow, Commander.'

Dugdale grunted as he grabbed one of the coffees.

'It looks as if,' said Slater airily, heading for the door, 'that will be the last chance for you guys to avoid getting your arses sued off.'

The inspector let his gaze wander from the body covered with a plastic sheet up to the picture on the wall. The young Katrin Lagerbäck looked down, uncomprehending, on the dead Katrin Lagerbäck. Noticing a small amount of blood-splatter on the bottom left-hand corner of the photo, he idly wondered what would happen to it now. Probably, it would end up in the trash, which would be a shame.

'Don't forget it's a Helmut Newton,' said Roche, appearing at his shoulder. 'It's probably worth thousands.'

'What?'

'The portrait.' She pointed with a latex-sheathed finger, 'It will make some money for the estate.'

'Practical as always,' Carlyle observed. 'Does she have any next-of-kin?'

'Parents, maybe?' Roche shrugged. 'As far as I know, she wasn't married. Certainly no kids. Not that kind of girl.'

'No,' Carlyle said. 'I suppose not.'

Roche nodded at a badly dressed man, about Carlyle's age, talking on a mobile in a low voice. 'That's Chief Inspector Arbuthnot.'

Carlyle checked the guy out. 'Haven't come across him before.'

'*Archibald* Arbuthnot. Archie to his friends.'

'That won't include me.'

'No, I guess not. Anyway, this is his investigation. He'll want to talk to you about the background to what happened.'

'Fine,' said Carlyle wearily.

'I've already talked him through what we were up to,' Roche said, 'so he's up to speed.'

'Thanks.'

'So,' she went on, 'unless you've got other plans for me, I'm gonna head back to Charing Cross. I thought I could chase up some of the loose ends on the Roger Leyne investigation.'

I'd forgotten all about that, Carlyle realized. 'Good idea.'

'There doesn't seem to be a lot to go on.'

'No.'

'Maybe we should do a proper case review.'

'Makes sense. I'll see you there. We can have a catch-up.'

She grinned. 'I hear that you managed to catch McGowan with his trousers down.'

'Yeah,' Carlyle laughed. 'I'll tell you all about it.'

'Will it affect the hearing?'

236

'Nah. I wouldn't have thought so. Dugdale's out to get me. If that means protecting a child-abusing pervert along the way – hey, that's a small price to pay.'

'Don't worry, it'll be fine,' Roche said kindly. Then: 'I'll see you later.'

'Okay.' As Roche disappeared through the door, it came to him that he had forgotten to ask her about SO15. If the transfer was still on, he needed to start thinking about a replacement – assuming he still had a job, that is. Dying for a coffee, he hopped from foot to foot while he waited for Arbuthnot to finish his phone conversation before stepping up to introduce himself.

'Carlyle.'

Tall, thin and balding, Chief Inspector Archie Arbuthnot had the air of a man who was easily inconvenienced by things like dead bodies. 'Ah yes. I've spoken to your sergeant.' He smiled lecherously. 'She's an impressive woman.'

You mean she's got a nice arse, Carlyle thought. 'Yes, she is.'

'She was explaining to me about the St James's Diamonds situation. Do you think that had anything to do with this?' Arbuthnot gestured towards the body and Carlyle shuddered as his usual squeamishness came to the fore. 'Presumably the two things are interrelated.'

'It seems a perfectly reasonable assumption,' said Carlyle, 'but we don't have any evidence of that, so far.'

'I will need to see your files,' Arbuthnot said next.

Carlyle nodded. 'Of course.'

'Is there anything else you think might be useful for me to know?'

'Nothing immediately comes to mind.' Carlyle tried to look thoughtful.

Arbuthnot pulled a business card out of his jacket pocket and handed it over. 'Well, call me if you can think of anything.'

'I will.' Carlyle held the card carefully between his thumb and his index finger. 'We'll speak soon.' With one last glance at Katrin Lagerbäck's body, he made for the door.

Head down, deep in thought, the inspector dived into the constant chaos of Piccadilly. He had barely put one foot on the pavement, when he walked straight into someone coming the other way. 'Sorry,' he mumbled, barely breaking his stride.

'John! I was just coming to find you.'

Slamming on the brakes, Carlyle finally looked up and did a double-take. The woman in front of him looked tanned, relaxed and ten years younger than he remembered. In jeans, a white blouse and a fawn jacket, Carole Simpson looked more like a Euro-Sloane tourist than a police officer heading for the scene of the crime.

'Commander!' he explained. 'You're looking good.'

'I wish I could say the same for you,' replied Simpson.

Carlyle held his hands from his sides and shrugged. 'It seems like it's been a long day already.' He gestured towards the lobby of the HDK office building. 'The body's upstairs.'

'I'm not here for that,' Simpson told him. 'I'm here to see you.'

'Oh?'

'Yes,' she said, surprising him by taking his arm. 'Let's go and get a coffee.'

By the time they'd reached the relative calm of Lansdowne Row, a couple of blocks to the north, Simpson had explained that she was in London for a few days' catch-up with family matters and to spend some time with her new boyfriend. Carlyle hadn't been aware that she had resumed dating since the death of her husband, but didn't pry. In turn, he filled her in on selected developments at home, giving her a quick run-through of the problems with Alice, while steering clear of Helen's medical issues. Although their relationship had become a lot closer in recent years, he still didn't feel the need to share everything.

It was a mild morning, so they took a table on the street outside the Nightingale café, Carlyle ordering a green tea while Simpson went for a black Americano. 'Are you coming back?' Carlyle asked, having run out of small talk, as they waited for their drinks to arrive.

'Oh, yes,' she said immediately. 'My life is in London – and I miss it. But the secondment has been interesting. And it's got a few months still to run.'

'Okay.'

'How are you getting on with Dugdale?'

Carlyle let out a long breath. 'Fine. He's a time-serving drunk bastard on the way out who wants to get me sacked. What's not to like?'

The waitress arrived and placed their drinks on the table. Simpson nodded her thanks, waiting for her to retreat from their table before continuing. 'I hear you've been getting into trouble again.'

Carlyle took the tea bag from the cup and placed it on his saucer. 'So that's why you're here?'

'I took a call from Ambrose Watson last week.' She waited for the look of exasperation to finish spreading across Carlyle's face. 'He's a good guy.'

Carlyle daintily sipped his tea. 'I know.' It was true. By now he had featured in an unfortunate number of investigations involving the fat IIC man, and it would have been more than churlish not to recognize Ambrose's efforts to try and help him out of several tricky situations.

'Ambrose suggested that it might be a good idea for me to look you up if I was in London. He explained the situation with the priest.'

'McGowan is a nasty individual. We caught him with his trousers down, literally, a couple of days ago.'

'That's as maybe,' Simpson retorted, 'but the IIC hearing is still going ahead.'

'Yeah.' Carlyle shrugged. 'Dugdale wants me out – no pension, no nothing. He blames me for getting kicked out of SO15, and this is payback.'

'He didn't get kicked out of SO15,' Simpson corrected him.

'He got kicked sideways, whatever. No offence, but I'm sure he would still be rather running round after terrorists than keeping your seat warm for you.'

'Yes, well.'

'And, realistically, what chance has he got of ever getting back to Counter Terrorism Command?'

Playing with her cup, Simpson said nothing.

'He's a waste of space,' Carlyle continued. 'But he's not going to be able to kick me out. My Federation rep is very relaxed.'

'Perhaps,' Simpson acknowledged. 'But it's not *his* job on the line.'

'Fair point,' Carlyle agreed, 'but my sergeant and I are consistent in what we're saying and there are no other witnesses. Plus, a doctor looked McGowan over and gave him the all clear.'

Simpson gave him a careful look but said nothing.

'It'll be fine.' Carlyle took another mouthful of tea. 'Anyway, with the redundancy terms on offer, I might want to walk anyway.'

Simpson watched a thin man struggling to return one of the Mayor's rent-by-the-hour bikes to its docking station. 'I'm not sure I believe that.'

'I've talked to Helen about it,' Carlyle divulged. 'The numbers just about add up.'

Leaning across the table, Simpson pointed a crooked index finger at him. 'John Carlyle, do not try and kid me. There is bugger all chance of you walking away from the job before you have to.'

'Maybe,' said Carlyle, staring vacantly into the middle distance.

'I recall you saying something similar to me when Joshua died and I was thinking of packing it in.'

'Yes.'

'And you were right,' she said briskly. 'I didn't mean it then, just like you don't mean it now.' Reaching into her bag, Simpson pulled out her purse, signalling to the waitress for the bill. 'Both of us will be dragged out, kicking and screaming, at the latest possible opportunity.'

'I suppose you are right,' he conceded.

The waitress appeared and Simpson handed her a ten-pound note, waving away the change. 'One of the things you do realize, though,' she sighed, 'when you are away, is just how bloody expensive this place is.'

'Tell me about it.'

'Even with a strong Canadian dollar,' Simpson mused, 'the cost of living is so much cheaper over there.'

Grunting, Carlyle got to his feet. Currency movements were not his strong point. 'Thanks for the tea.'

'My pleasure.' Simpson gestured north. 'I'm heading up to Oxford Street, so I'll leave you here. But I thought I might come to the hearing tomorrow, just to observe.'

Carlyle thought about that for a moment. 'That would be great,' he said finally. 'I'd appreciate it.'

'Good.' She patted him on the shoulder. 'I'll see you tomorrow then.'

'Yes. See you tomorrow.' Feeling rather happier about things than he had for a while, the inspector watched her cross the road and disappear into Curzon Street.

Walking along Pall Mall, in no hurry to get back to the station, he felt his mobile go off in his pocket. He didn't recognize the number on the screen but answered it anyway.

'Carlyle.'

'Inspector,' the voice on the other end of the line sounded tired and distant, 'this is Sally Jones.'

On the far side of the road, a workman helpfully started up with a pneumatic drill. 'Who?' he shouted.

'Sally Jones,' the woman said patiently. 'You rang me about Roger Leyne.'

Shit! He'd forgotten all about wife number two. 'Ah y-yes,' he stammered, 'sorry. Thank you for calling me back. I'm investigating your husband's – sorry, your *ex*-husband's – death.'

'Yes,' Sally Jones replied, waiting for him to tell her something that she didn't already know.

Carlyle began jogging down the road, trying to get as far away from the man with the drill as possible. 'I was wondering,' he wheezed, 'if I could come and see you.'

There was a pause. *It's not a bloody question, madam*, he thought, irritated.

'I think,' she said finally, 'that would be a good idea.'

'Oh?'

'Yes,' said Sally Jones. 'You see, I think I know who might have killed Roger.'

FORTY-ONE

'Hey, stranger.' Marcello looked up from the Gaggia and grinned. 'You've been avoiding us!'

Entering the empty café, Carlyle held up a hand. 'Nah,' he said, injecting some weariness into his voice for effect, 'just busy.'

'Yeah, right,' said Marcello sarcastically. 'I hear you've been going to the Box café, the other side of the piazza.'

Christ, thought Carlyle as he slipped into the back booth, *how did you know about that?* 'I've been going there for years,' he said somewhat defensively. 'It's near the station.'

'The guy who runs it,' Marcello grumbled, 'he's a proper nutter.'

Carlyle shrugged. 'His pastries certainly aren't up to Il Buffone standard, that's for sure.'

Marcello gestured at a plate of large raisin Danishes, smothered in icing, behind the glass-fronted counter. 'Want one?'

'Don't tempt me.' Carlyle patted his stomach and winced. He seemed increasingly well-upholstered these days. 'Just a green tea.'

'Green tea.' Marcello tutted. 'That's all you drink these days.'

'Hardly. Anyway, Helen says it's good for me.'

'Suit yourself.' Marcello filled a mug with boiling water and dropped in a tea bag. Slipping round the counter, he placed it on the table in front of the inspector.

'Thanks,' Carlyle smiled, mildly surprised when the owner sat down opposite him.

'It's done,' said Marcello quietly, looking at the table.

Carlyle nodded. 'Congratulations.'

'Yeah.' Marcello wiped his hands on the tea-towel draped over his left shoulder. 'The family are happy – Cathy in particular. She says we should have retired years ago.'

Carlyle forced himself to smile. 'I hope you guys have a long and happy retirement.'

'I'm sure that the kids and the grandkids will keep us busy.'

'That's the way it should be, Marcello,' said Carlyle, offering his hand to shake. 'But you'll still come and see us, won't you? I know that Alice and Helen will want to keep in touch . . . and me too.'

'Of course,' Marcello nodded. 'Definitely.' Both of them knew, however, that it wouldn't happen. At that moment, the door behind them opened and a couple of office workers in search of an early lunch shuffled towards the counter, staring at the menu on the wall. With a sigh, Marcello got to his feet. '*Buon giorno*, gentlemen! What can I get you?'

Back at Charing Cross, Carlyle put a call in to Rose. She informed him that statements had been taken from McGowan and Eddie, and the priest had been bailed to reappear at Holborn police station in three weeks' time. 'That's convenient,' Carlyle noted. 'Nothing will be done till after the Pope's been and gone.'

'These things happen,' she said philosophically. 'There is pressure coming down from the higher-ups to keep this thing under wraps. I've been told that if there are any more stories about McGowan in the papers, I'll be shipped right back to the NSPCC.'

'Subtle,' Carlyle mused. There was a time when he wouldn't have thought twice about picking up the phone and tipping off some friendly journalist, if only to annoy the brass. Now, however, he had more important things to worry about. 'How did McGowan react when you told him that Simon Murphy was dead?'

Rose thought about it for a moment. 'He looked relieved, to be honest,' she said. 'Then he started mumbling about suicide being a mortal sin and the incumbent obligation on man to preserve his own life.'

'Good God!' Carlyle moaned. 'These people really know how to talk shit.'

'Yeah,' Rose agreed. 'His lawyer quickly made him shut up. That Slater woman is quite a piece of work.'

Carlyle laughed. 'She certainly is.'

'Anyway,' said Rose, 'the whole thing will progress at its own pace. One thing that would be helpful is if you could send me the video you shot on your phone of Eddie "in action", as it were.'

'Sure,' said Carlyle, not having a clue how he would get the video off his phone and into an email.

'Great. I've got to run. Speak soon.'

'Bye.' Ending the call, Carlyle looked at the handset, trying to find the images he had recorded in the crypt of the church. For a while, he was worried that he hadn't actually recorded anything, but eventually he found it in a folder marked 'Gallery'. Playing it back, he was surprised at the quality of the images, not to mention his own camera-work. Now all he had to do was send the damn thing to Rose. He was still grappling with this problem when, a few moments later, the phone started vibrating in his hand. He answered. 'Hello?'

'Inspector Carlyle?'

'Yes?'

'It's Terence Myers.'

'Ah, Headmaster, how are you?'

'I'm very well, thank you.'

'Apologies for not responding to the message from your office but I would be happy to come in and give another talk to some of the girls.'

There was a pause. 'Good, good,' said Myers finally. 'Thank you. But that wasn't what I was ringing about.'

Carlyle's heart sank. 'No?'

'No. It's about Alice . . .'

Taking a deep breath, Carlyle opened the door of 3C and walked inside. Alice, sitting by the window, looked up as he entered the classroom. The deep scowl etched on her face did nothing to diminish her beauty in the eyes of her father. Listening to the beating of his heart, he walked down the row of desks and gave her a tender kiss on the top of her head. 'C'mon,' he said, picking her bag off the floor. 'Let's go.'

'But I'm in detention,' she said sullenly.

'I've spoken to Myers,' he said, his voice gentle, 'and you've served your time. He is releasing you into my care.'

With a grunt of displeasure, Alice pushed back her chair and got to her feet.

Carlyle handed her the bag. 'Let's go and get something to drink. We need to work out what to tell your mum.'

Ten minutes later, they were sitting in a Starbucks just north of Smithfield Market. Alice was sipping from a can of Diet Coke and Carlyle had already downed a double espresso. He tried to count up the total number of shots he'd had already that day. Reckoning that he was probably well into double figures, he vowed to try and stick to green tea from now on. 'So,' he said, staring into his empty paper cup, 'let me make sure I've got this right. You spliffed up at lunchtime and ended up falling asleep in Double French.'

Alice let out a disaffected belch. 'I hate French.'

'Everyone hates French,' Carlyle grinned, amazed that his sense of humour was holding up. 'Get over it.'

She gave him a sour look.

'I thought we had a deal,' Carlyle whined, angry at how lame he sounded.

'I only smoked the damn thing because you lectured me about not being in possession on the school premises. They had a free concert in the Barbican – Mendelssohn's Trio in D Minor – it was cool.' She grinned maliciously, knowing full well that his knowledge of classical music was less than zero.

Makes a change from The Clash, I suppose, Carlyle thought. He took a deep breath, exhaling slowly. 'Okay,' he said, 'so you took on board my point about not getting kicked out of school. That's good.'

Alice smacked her can down on the table. 'Don't laugh at me, Dad!'

Carlyle looked around nervously, but the place was almost empty and none of the other customers showed any interest in their conversation. 'I'm not laughing at you.'

'Dad!'

'Look,' Carlyle snapped, his good humour rapidly evaporating, 'you

245

need to experiment. Fine, it's part of growing up. But it's like anything else, there's a smart way to do it and a stupid way to do it. Your mother and I are not going to fight battles we can't win but we know that you are canny enough to understand the advice that we're trying to give.'

Alice looked at him blankly.

'Keep clear blue water between school and non-school activities.'

Alice finished the last of her Coke. 'Huh?'

For fuck's sake! Carlyle fought against a sense of despair. 'Three simple rules,' he said firmly, 'that will help us all get along okay.'

She shrugged.

'No drugs in school. No going to school intoxicated. No spliffing up at lunchtime – or on a school night, for that matter. No getting off your face so that you can't think straight.'

Folding her arms, she gave him a stern look. 'Is this what you and Mum have agreed?'

'Yes,' Carlyle lied, sticking out a hand. 'Do we, finally, have a deal?'

After thinking about it for a few moments, she offered up the limpest of handshakes. 'Deal.'

'Good.' Carlyle kissed her on the forehead as he got to his feet. 'Now, I've gotta go.'

Alice lifted her bag from the floor. 'Aren't you coming home?'

' 'Fraid not. I've got a meeting. I'll see you there later.' After they stepped out into the street, he watched Alice saunter off towards Holborn Circus before turning away and heading north, past Farringdon tube. He had agreed to meet Sally Jones at her home in Islington, and the twenty-five-minute walk was easier than trying to use public transport.

Waiting to cross at the lights on Clerkenwell Road, he checked his mobile and was irritated to find that he had four missed calls. One was from an unknown caller who had not left a message; the other was from Roche, who had. Somehow, his answerphone had gone off twice without him noticing it. With a disgusted shake of his head, he hit 901 and listened to what Roche had to say: *'Where are you? I've found something interesting regarding Roger Leyne. Might be important, might not. Give me a call.'*

How very cryptic, Carlyle thought sarkily. The lights changed and he skipped across the road. Reaching the other side, he phoned his wife. The number one priority was getting his story about Alice straight. His sergeant could wait.

Helen picked up on the third ring. 'Is everything okay?'

'Yeah, fine, fine.' He braced himself. 'I've just been over at the school . . .' Quickly, before she could jump in and rip his head off, he told her about Alice's detention, their subsequent coffee-shop conversation and the deal he had struck with their daughter.

There was an ominous pause that told him he was in deep trouble. 'Don't you think,' she said finally, the anger clear in her voice, 'that we should have discussed this first?'

'I felt that I had to seize the moment,' he replied feebly, a sense of panic rising inside him.

'And, of course, what I think doesn't matter,' she said venomously.

'No, n-no, of course not,' he stammered, dodging an onrushing cyclist zooming down the pavement towards him. By the time Carlyle was able to flip him the finger, the wanker was ten yards down the block.

'And why didn't you tell me about this when you got the call from the Headmaster?'

'Well . . .' Outflanked, he felt his brain begin to seize up and his mouth go dry. 'I just thought I could handle it. You've got a lot on your plate and—'

'Just . . . fuck off!' she screamed, ending the call.

Turning into St John Street, Carlyle stared unhappily at the handset. 'Well,' he muttered to himself, anticipating the hostile atmosphere that would doubtless await when he got home, 'that went well.' After waiting a few moments to see if Helen would call back, he tried Roche. The call went straight to voicemail and he couldn't be bothered to leave a message. Shoving the phone in his pocket, he kicked on towards Angel.

'Would you like some tea, Inspector? Or a coffee?' Sally Jones lived in an imposing four-storey Georgian house on Gibson Square, just off

Upper Street. Sitting in the kitchen, he could see a couple of kids, a boy and a girl about the same age as Alice, mooching about in a large garden.

'No, thanks,' he smiled. 'I'm fine. Thank you for seeing me.'

Leaning against a workbench, Jones held a steaming mug of chamomile tea in her hand. She was a slim, elegant woman, whom he took to be in her mid-to-late forties. Wearing jeans and a cream blouse under a fawn V-neck cashmere sweater, she lazily drew a circle on the ceramic floor tiles with the ruby-painted nail of her big toe. 'I'm sorry it has taken so long, but we were away.'

'That's okay.'

Jones gestured towards the garden. 'We took the kids to Tuscany for a couple of weeks. To be honest, I have to admit that we did know about Roger.' She sighed. 'My mother called me about it and we checked the story on the internet.'

Carlyle shrugged.

'But this was one holiday he simply wasn't going to be allowed to disrupt,' she went on determinedly. 'Even by dying.'

Carlyle laughed. 'That's fair enough. He certainly seems to have been a guy who managed to annoy a lot of people.'

'Oh, he was,' she said grimly. 'Roger was the most self-centred man I think I've ever met. And that's saying something.'

'You said in your message that you might have an idea who killed him?'

'Well, yes.' She took a mouthful of tea. 'I would have thought that it was quite obvious.'

Carlyle smiled indulgently.

'I mean,' Jones continued, 'you've spoken to Rachel, haven't you?'

'Rachel Gilbert?' Carlyle felt his phone go off and pulled it out of his jacket pocket. 'Yes.' He looked at the screen, it was Roche. Waving the handset in the air, he shrugged apologetically. 'Excuse me a moment.'

Jones nodded. 'Go ahead.'

Carlyle pushed open the sliding patio doors and stepped into the garden, waving at the children who eyed him warily and promptly ran inside to their mother. *Bloody kids*, Carlyle thought, irritated.

'Inspector?'

'Yeah.'

'I tried to get hold of you earlier on,' said Roche, with more than a hint of exasperation in her voice.

God Almighty, Carlyle thought dolefully, *is there anyone at all who isn't annoyed with me today?* You might not be able to please all of the people all of the time, but you certainly can piss all of the bastards off. At least he could. 'Sorry,' he mumbled. 'Busy afternoon.'

'Anyway,' Roche went on, 'I've been doing some digging into where the money from Roger Leyne's bank accounts went.'

'Wife number three – Rachel Gilbert,' Carlyle interrupted. It should have been a question but he made it sound like a statement.

There was a moment's silence on the other end of the line. 'How did you know that?' Roche asked, sounding even more irritated than before.

'I've been doing my own digging,' Carlyle lied. 'I think we need to go and have another chat with Ms Gilbert. She should be at work, so meet me at a bar called Stearns' in Golden Square in an hour.'

Ending the call, he stepped back inside, saying, 'Sorry about that.'

'It's not a problem,' Sally Jones told him, still leaning against her workbench. The kids had disappeared to some other part of the house.

'So,' said Carlyle, 'tell me what you know about Rachel.'

FORTY-TWO

'Where's Rachel tonight?'

The bartender, a large bloke, young and athletic-looking, gave him a bored stare. 'Who's asking?'

After digging around in his pockets for a few moments, Carlyle fished out his ID. 'I am,' he said flatly.

The bartender's frown deepened. With some amusement, Carlyle watched the cogs going round in his head as he tried to work out his best course of action. Finally, he gestured to a door off to the left. 'She's in the office.'

'Thanks,' said Carlyle, signalling for Roche to follow him.

The door was ajar and he kicked it open with the toe of his shoe and marched straight in, capturing the scene in front of him in the blink of an eye. 'Good evening, Rachel,' he said smoothly. 'How are you?'

'Shit!' On her knees, Rachel Gilbert looked up at her unwelcome visitor, sending the line of cocaine that she had been about to inhale across the coffee table and onto the grubby-looking carpet. The table itself was covered in empty beer bottles, amongst which sat a small bag containing maybe ten grams' worth of coke. On the opposite side to Gilbert, a podgy red-haired girl in a Ramones T-shirt shrank back into the fake green leather sofa on which she was sitting.

'Who are you?' Carlyle demanded.

The girl glanced at Rachel, who shrugged. 'I'm Sam,' she said nervously. 'I work here.'

'Step outside, Sam,' said Roche, who already had Gilbert by an arm and was lifting her to her feet. 'But do not move from outside that door. We will want to speak with you in a minute.'

Nodding, the girl slid off the sofa and, careful to avoid trampling any of the coke into the carpet, tiptoed out.

'Close the door behind you,' said Carlyle, grimacing as he caught a sniff of her all-too-pungent body odour. 'And if anyone tries to come in, tell them they have to wait with you.'

Head down, the girl trooped out without another word. As the door clicked shut, Carlyle watched Roche deposit Gilbert onto the seat vacated by Sam. Looking around the room, he realized that the sofa was out of keeping with everything else in the room, which was either black or a grubby grey. At the far end of the room was a desk, on which sat a computer and various sheets of paper. Behind the desk was a large poster for a film called *Drag Me to Hell*. The place was lit by an underpowered lamp sitting in the corner. He looked down on Rachel Gilbert. Tired and wired, in black jeans and a short black leather jacket, and with too much mascara, she looked almost unrecognizable from the girl he had spoken to on his last visit. 'Is this your office?'

Slumped on the sofa, Gilbert stared vacantly at the wall behind his head.

'Rachel?'

'I just work here,' she said, struggling to get the words out.

'You lied to me once,' said Carlyle sharply. 'Don't do it again.'

'We know you took this place over,' Roche told her. 'We've gone through your bank accounts and I've checked the contract you signed.'

Gilbert gave her a bemused look. 'Is that legal? Snooping around like that?'

'It is when you are a fucking murder suspect!' Carlyle laughed.

'What?' Gilbert slowly shook her head. 'I didn't kill anyone.'

'You needed more money from Roger Leyne,' said Roche.

'Yes, but—'

'And when he couldn't come up with any more,' the sergeant continued, 'you threatened him.'

Sitting up, Gilbert finally shook off her torpor. 'Yes,' she squealed, 'but I didn't bloody shoot him!'

'Then who did?' Carlyle asked.

By way of answer, the door came crashing open and the beefcake barman stumbled into the room, a small semi-automatic pistol in his hand.

'Shit!' Gilbert screamed. 'Julian!'

'Fuck!' Taking a step backwards, Carlyle picked up a bottle from the table and threw it at the guy's head. Then he picked up another, ran forward and began clubbing him around the head with it. The barman sagged under Carlyle's repeated blows but refused to go down.

'For fuck's sake,' Carlyle hissed at Roche, who was just standing there with an amused look on her face, 'fucking brain the fucker!' With a grunt, he again smacked the bottle across the side of Julian's skull, this time hitting him so hard that it smashed, leaving the inspector holding nothing but the jagged remains of the neck.

Reluctant to stab the bastard, Carlyle threw his weapon to the floor, turning to grab another bottle just as the barman pumped a round into the side of the sofa. The shot deafened Carlyle and sent Gilbert jumping about three feet in the air.

'Fucking hurry up!' the inspector roared at his sergeant.

Finally grabbing a weapon of her own, Roche jumped into action and smacked the gunman twice over the head with a beer bottle, to no obvious effect. 'Bollocks!' she panted, switching target and kicking him repeatedly in the balls.

Happily, Roche's boot had the desired effect where Carlyle had singularly failed. Groaning, Julian dropped his weapon as he sank to his knees. Another kick from Roche, this time to the base of his spine, sent him falling face first, across the coffee table, sending the remaining bottles rolling across the floor.

Carlyle booted the semi-automatic under the sofa. Pulling out a set of handcuffs, he gave Roche a sour look. 'Better late than never.'

'I thought you had it all under control.'

'Yeah, right,' Carlyle huffed. 'The fucker could have shot me.' Pulling Julian's hands behind his back, he snapped on the cuffs. 'You, mate, are fucking nicked.'

'I'll go and call for back-up,' said Roche, heading for the door.

Carlyle turned to Gilbert. 'Are you okay?' he asked, unable to spot any obvious sign of injury.

Shivering, she managed half a nod while pointing at the large hole in the sofa.

'Don't worry,' Carlyle joked. 'A couple of strips of duct tape and it will be good as new.' He turned to the door. 'Sam! Are you still there?' Gratifyingly, the malodorous barmaid stuck her head round the door-frame, her eyes growing wide at the chaos in front of her. 'Hey!' Carlyle gestured for her to pay attention. 'Go get me an espresso.'

The girl nodded.

'On second thoughts,' Carlyle amended, 'make it a double.'

Those patrons who didn't immediately take the hint when two dozen uniforms descended on Stearns' were finally shooed out of the door about half an hour after Roche had taken Gilbert and Julian off in a police van, heading for Charing Cross. After finishing his coffee and double-checking that the place was now empty, Carlyle locked up with a set of keys that he'd found in the office. Earlier that afternoon, there had been a triple murder in a gentleman's club called Heaven's Gate – some gangland shooting bollocks where a couple of strip-pers had been caught in the crossfire – and he had been informed by the desk that all the available forensics resources were currently on their knees in Stoke Newington's finest lap-dancing emporium. A detailed search of the bar would therefore have to wait at least until tomorrow.

For once, the thought of a delay didn't dismay Carlyle one bit. As he walked through Golden Square, he was convinced that Roger Leyne's murder would be wrapped up long before then.

Turning into Brewer Street, he called home. Alice answered. 'Hi, Dad!' she said cheerily, with no hint of the day's dramas in her voice.

'How's it going?' Carlyle asked warily, wondering if his daughter had been spliffing up again.

'Fine.'

'Is your mum there?'

'She's having a bath.'

'Okay.'

'And,' Alice said cheerily, 'before you ask – *no*, we haven't had a row.'

'I didn't think—'

'She is mad with *you* though.'

'Me?' Carlyle stepped off the crowded Soho pavement and straight into the path of an onrushing taxi. He only just managed to jump back out of the gutter as the cab shot past.

'*Watch where you're going, you fucking wanker!*' shouted the cabbie.

'Fuck you too!' Carlyle growled.

'What?' said Alice.

'Nothing.'

'Mum always said you're the reason I've got a foul mouth.'

'Why's she mad at me?'

'You'll have to ask her yourself,' Alice chided him. 'I'm not a marriage guidance counsellor, you know!'

'Okay, smartypants,' Carlyle laughed. This time he checked the traffic before stepping onto the road. 'Tell her we made some important arrests in one of my cases. I have to go back to the station to sit in on a couple of interviews, so I may be a while.'

'Will do.'

'And you make sure you get a good night's sleep. School tomorrow.'

'Sometimes,' Alice sighed, 'I think it would be easier just to get expelled.'

'Alice!'

'Only joking. See ya!'

'Okay. Lots of love.' But she had already put down the phone. Reaching the corner of Old Compton Street, his mind was a jumble of competing, confusing thoughts. Then Pâtisserie Valerie hoved into view and he was happy to be distracted by the prospect of Eggs Benedict and a pot of Organic Green Leaf tea.

'We've got them in separate interview rooms.' Roche looked down at some notes she had scribbled on a pad. 'The guy is called Julian . . .

Vine. Julian Vine. Australian. Been in London for almost three years. Been Gilbert's boyfriend for the last eighteen months or so.'

'He told you that?' Carlyle asked.

Roche shook her head. 'Nah. Samantha Bramble did.' And when Carlyle gave her a blank look: 'Sam – the barmaid. She's downstairs as well.'

Carlyle shuddered. 'I'm not going anywhere near her, not with that BO.'

Roche lifted her eyes to the ceiling. 'Why don't we start with Gilbert?'

'Okay.'

'She's the only one who hasn't lawyered up.'

A grin spread across Carlyle's face. '*Perfect*. What are we waiting for then?'

Sipping a cup of black coffee, Rachel Gilbert looked up nervously as Carlyle and Roche entered the interview room. She'd been crying. Wiping her nose on the sleeve of her jacket, she wailed, 'I didn't kill him.'

Carlyle took a seat on the opposite side of the table and waited for Roche to do the same.

'I didn't . . .'

Carlyle held up a hand for her to shut up. 'This was a brutal murder of a defenceless man,' he said quietly, in a matter-of-fact tone. 'We know that you and . . .'

'Julian,' Roche interjected.

'Yes. We know that you and Julian were responsible for the shooting.' He sighed. 'All we need now is for you to fill in some of the details. You need to be as clear and honest as possible. What you tell us now could mean the difference between being sent to prison for life or maybe as little as five years.' He paused, watching the last vestiges of her resistance crumble. 'Do you understand?'

Gilbert nodded.

'Good.' Pushing himself away from the desk, Carlyle got to his feet. 'Make sure you include everything in your statement to Sergeant

Roche. We can review it in the morning. This is your last chance.'
Without waiting for a reply, he headed for the door.

By the time he got home, Carlyle was relieved to find calm had descended in the flat. When he walked through the door, he was not greeted either by the smell of dope or by the sound of Alice and Helen going at each other, hammer and tongs. Carefully confirming that wife and daughter had both gone to bed, he tiptoed stealthily into the kitchen and made a cup of green tea. Then, repairing to the living room, he slumped onto the sofa and vegged out in front of Sky Sports News for half an hour, the volume kept down low to avoid waking anyone up. When he finally crawled under the duvet, Helen was snoring soundly. Giving her a gentle kiss on the back of the head, he waited for sleep to come.

FORTY-THREE

Carlyle placed the large takeaway coffee on Roche's desk and took a step back, waiting to see if the peace-offering would be accepted.

'Thanks for staying around last night,' Roche said sarcastically, not looking up from the screen of her computer as she typed out her report, hitting each key on the keyboard with unnecessary venom.

'Marcello sends his regards,' said Carlyle, nodding at the coffee.

Roche cursed as she made a typo and began bashing the backspace key.

'He's finally gone and sold the place,' Carlyle continued, 'so there won't be many more where that came from.'

Roche grunted. 'There are plenty of other cafés.'

For fuck's sake, thought Carlyle, his reserves of grovelling all used up, *give me a break*. 'Look,' he said, 'I'm sorry if you think I left you in it last night . . .'

Still typing furiously, Roche finally looked up. 'You *did* leave me in it last night.'

'But you had it all under control,' Carlyle protested. 'And I had some domestic stuff to take care of.'

'I can't wait to get out of here,' Roche mumbled to herself.

'What?'

'Nothing.' She hit the print button on her computer and a few moments later a nearby printer rumbled into action. 'There's the Gilbert report.'

'Enough to charge them?'

Reaching for the coffee, Roche nodded. Removing the lid, she took

257

a tentative sip. 'Basically, Gilbert says that she was still shagging Roger Leyne.'

Carlyle made a face. As a man who was only ever going to be married the once, the etiquette regarding sexual relations with ex-spouses was not something he felt the need to have a view on.

'Leyne also liked to party with the girls who worked at the bar.'

'Like Sam?' he asked.

'Who knows?' Roche took another mouthful of coffee. 'Maybe he liked the pungent aroma of BO.'

'Fair enough,' Carlyle shrugged. It would by no means be the strangest peccadillo he'd ever come across.

'Anyway, Gilbert's boyfriend, Julian, was happy enough with this arrangement while Leyne continued to bankroll the bar's losses.'

Carlyle stepped over to the printer and picked up Roche's report. 'How can a bar in bloody Soho *lose* money?'

'Lots of ways,' Roche replied, 'especially if they were sticking large quantities of coke up their noses every day.'

'I suppose.'

'Anyway, they wiped Leyne out. When he wouldn't come up with any more cash, Julian went round to threaten him, things got out of hand, yada, yada, yada . . .'

'Where did he get the gun?' Carlyle asked.

'That, he's not saying. But we've already got a match on the bullets that killed Leyne. Game, set and match.'

'His choice,' Carlyle grumbled. The Crown Prosecution Service could try and winkle that information out of him, to be taken into consideration at the time of sentencing, but that wasn't their problem. He glanced at the clock on the wall behind Roche's head. 'Shit! Time for Dugdale's kangaroo court.' He dropped the report on Roche's desk. 'You haven't had a date for your hearing yet, have you?'

Roche shook her head. 'Nope. My union rep says the longer they wait, the better my chances.'

That's handy, Carlyle thought suspiciously.

'Maybe they want to see how yours goes first.'

'Maybe,' Carlyle mumbled. 'Anyway, I'd better get going.'

'Okay,' said Roche, finishing her coffee. 'I'll see you up there.'

The disciplinary hearing was held in a large meeting room on the top floor of the Charing Cross station with a view across Trafalgar Square. Carlyle arrived five minutes before it was due to begin, to find Superintendent Rebecca Buck sitting on the far side of a long table, her back to Nelson's Column, busily scribbling notes on her set of papers. Next to her, with a large chocolate doughnut in his hand, was Ambrose Watson.

Taking a seat opposite the portly investigator, Carlyle gave him a cheery nod. 'Morning, Ambrose.'

Ambrose nodded sheepishly. 'Good morning, Inspector.' Buck half-looked up from her papers and grunted. Ambrose quickly took a large bite out of the doughnut to avoid having to say anything else.

Wishing he'd brought in a coffee, Carlyle drummed his fingers on the table and looked around the room. Behind him, the door opened. A moment later, Carlyle's Union rep, Geoff, appeared, looking like he'd just got out of bed, which he probably had. At least he had made the effort to put on a suit and tie, which made him look slightly more like a grown-up. After shaking the inspector's hand, he placed a Tesco plastic bag on the table, pulling out a sheaf of papers. *Jesus*, Carlyle thought, *thank God I don't actually need you here.* He made a vow that if Geoff opened his mouth in the actual hearing, he would get a swift and violent kick under the table.

By the appointed hour, the room was quite full, the atmosphere professionally grim. At the far end of the table, a stenographer had taken up position to record the minutes. Roche and Simpson had taken seats behind him, around the wall, as had Abigail Slater, looking at her most demure in a grey trouser suit, with minimal make-up. As far as Carlyle could see, the only person missing was Dugdale. *Doubtless struggling in with his usual hangover*, Carlyle thought sourly, as he played with his BlackBerry.

'Use of electronic equipment in this room is not permitted,' Buck said snidely.

Carlyle gave her a blank look. 'Have we started? I thought we were still waiting for your chairman.'

Superintendent Buck glanced at her watch and sighed. 'I am sure he will be here in a moment.'

'I will go and see if I can find out where he is,' Ambrose mumbled, wiping the doughnut crumbs from his shirt as he stood up. Lumbering round the table, he fled the room.

'I've tried his mobile,' Roche piped up. 'It's going to voicemail.'

'He's only a few minutes late,' Buck snapped. 'I'm sure that he is on his way.'

'If he doesn't turn up,' Geoff said cheerily, 'the hearing will have to be rescheduled.'

'I'm aware of that,' Buck retorted, looking up at Ambrose as he reappeared.

Ambrose shook his head. 'Can't get hold of him.'

'We'll give him half an hour,' said Geoff, putting as much authority into his voice as he could manage.

Carlyle went back to surfing the net. He had just finished reading a story about the latest government peer accused of tax dodging when a mobile phone started ringing behind him.

'Commander Simpson . . . yes, I see. Where? Okay, I will be right there.' Ending her call, Simpson got to her feet and stepped forward to the desk, to address Buck and Ambrose Watson. 'I am afraid that Commander Dugdale will not be coming this morning,' she said, placing a hand on Carlyle's shoulder, 'so this hearing will need to be rescheduled.' Not waiting for a response, she turned to Carlyle. 'Inspector, I need you and Sergeant Roche to come with me now, please.'

Five minutes later, the three of them were squashed into the back seat of a police BMW, moving slowly through the semi-gridlocked London traffic.

Stopped at a red light, the driver turned to face Simpson. 'I'll get us on to the Embankment and go along the river.'

'Fine,' the Commander nodded. 'Do the best you can. We're not in that much of a hurry.'

'Where are we going?' Roche asked.

'Docklands,' said Simpson. Before she could elucidate, her phone started ringing. While she answered it, the inspector stared out of the window at the barely moving city, letting his mind go blank as he did so.

Having taken off from City airport moments before, the British Airways jet sailed steadily past the window on its way to God knows where. On the thirtieth floor of the Norman Beresford Tebbit Tower in West India Quay, Carlyle watched it head south and wondered how long it would be before he could get back to ground level. Not a great one for heights, he looked down across Canary Wharf, Margaret Thatcher's Gotham, and shuddered. Moving back from the floor-to-ceiling windows, he retraced his steps across the carpet of the sixty-five-foot reception/dining room and hovered outside the nearest of the four bedrooms. Inside, the forensics guys were still busy doing their thing.

'You would have thought that they would have cut him down by now,' said Roche, not quite managing to keep the amusement from her voice.

'Yeah.' Carlyle glanced back inside the room at the body of Gavin Dugdale and winced. The Commander had been tied with what looked like electrical flex to a ten-foot wooden cross, in the shape of an X, which stood against the back wall. Dugdale's head was slumped against his left shoulder and there were traces of vomit around his mouth. The smell of different bodily fluids hung in the air and the area around the body looked like it had been hurriedly cleaned up. The rest of the room was strewn with various rubber accessories of different shapes and sizes.

'Fat, naked and dead is not a good look,' Roche murmured.

'Not really,' Carlyle agreed, disconcerted by the fact that he didn't feel happier at Dugdale's demise. Even though he was relieved to see the back of him, it was a terribly undignified way to go.

Roche's smirk somehow made him feel worse as she gloated. 'I guess his Press Officer won't be trying to spin this one.'

'No. Where is she?'

Roche nodded in the direction of the next bedroom. 'She's still next door. The forensics boys want her pink PVC underwear, so she's getting changed before they take her away for questioning.'

'Judith Mahon,' Carlyle sighed. 'Met Press Officer by day, Mistress Nikita by night.'

'Who'd have thought it?' Roche laughed. 'Such a mousey girl and she turns out to be the self-styled "most perverted dominatrix" in London. You should check out her website.'

'No, thanks,' Carlyle groaned. 'I think I'll leave that to you.'

Roche pulled out her BlackBerry and read from the screen. 'It says here that she charges two hundred and fifty pounds an hour to inflict "extreme pain, humiliation and torture" on clients.'

'I wonder if Dugdale got a mate's rate?'

'Maybe. Anyway, Mistress Nikita claims to be very good with CP – that's Corporal Punishment to you – and an expert on bondage with ropes, leather, rubber and clingfilm.'

Carlyle frowned. 'Clingfilm?'

'Yeah,' said Roche, affecting an insouciant tone. 'There's a vacuum machine in one of the other bedrooms for wrapping clients up in airtight clingfilm.'

He thought about this for a moment. 'Why?'

Roche shrugged. 'Fuck knows.' She returned to reading from the screen. ' "Beware, I am not a softie. I'm sadistic, intelligent and perverse. I'm a sadist of the worst kind. I have lots of tools to help me be creative to make each session one you will never forget".'

'On reflection,' Carlyle remarked, 'sounds like it might be worth a try.'

Roche dropped the BlackBerry back into her bag. 'At the end of the day, it's just a job, isn't it? A way to make a living.'

'It's good to have something to fall back on,' Carlyle grinned, 'particularly at times like this.'

Simpson appeared from down the hallway. 'I'm glad you two find this amusing.' However, her stern words were undermined by the smile dancing around her lips.

Carlyle shrugged. 'Funny old world.'

'They were taking part in a torture session, apparently,' said Simpson evenly, as if it were the most common thing in the world, 'with another dominatrix who did a runner when our man pegged out.'

'They did at least call 999,' Roche interjected.

'We think he may have choked on a rubber ball,' Simpson continued, 'or died after taking nitrous oxide.'

And when Carlyle looked mystified, Roche cheerily informed him: 'It's used as an anaesthetic to make sex sessions last longer.'

Carlyle felt his buttocks involuntarily tighten. 'Nice.'

'He was found wearing a leather "gimp" mask with a ball on a chain around his neck,' Simpson said. 'That was taken off when the ambulance crew tried to resuscitate him. Anyway, we'll have to wait for the results of the post-mortem examination to know precisely what caused his death.'

'Will the, erm, ladies be charged with anything?' Carlyle asked.

'That,' said Simpson, 'will ultimately be a matter for the CPS. If they've got any sense, they'll not pursue it, but you never know.'

'I wonder if his wife knew about his penchant for S&M?' said Roche.

Simpson, herself well aware of the vagaries of married life, gave a sad smile. 'Mrs Dugdale lives at the family home in Surrey; Gavin spent most of his time in London. I think they had been living separate lives for quite some time.'

'Maybe,' Roche replied, 'but this is still gonna be a hell of a shock.'

Simpson gave her a *shit happens* shrug. 'I think we need to take a look at how this will impact on your various ongoing investigations,' she said.

'Does this mean you're coming back?' Carlyle asked.

'Looks like it.' Simpson didn't sound too happy at the prospect. 'I've already been told by the higher-ups that that is the plan. I was due to go back to Canada at the weekend, but that's now on hold.'

'Great,' said Carlyle happily. He quickly ran her through where they were on their different cases.

'I'm hungry,' said Roche when he'd finished. Hoisting her bag over her shoulder, she headed for the door. 'Time for lunch.'

'You've got to be kidding,' Carlyle objected as he followed her out, unable to imagine his appetite returning for quite some time.

FORTY-FOUR

Francis McGowan lit up a Dorchester Superking and started puffing vigorously.

Taking a step away from the smoke, Abigail Slater shot him an irritated look. 'I didn't know that you smoked.'

'I have many vices,' said the priest grimly.

Slater took a seat in one of the pews, shivering against the cold. 'Are you even allowed to smoke in here?'

McGowan shrugged and took another long drag on his cigarette. 'I can't believe they didn't sack that policeman,' he said bitterly.

'Don't fret,' Slater told him. 'The hearing was postponed because one of the panel didn't turn up. They'll reschedule it in another week or two.'

'I could be in jail by then.'

Most probably, thought Slater. 'Possibly. But there's no point in worrying about that right now.'

'That's easy for you to say.' After taking a final drag, McGowan tossed the butt onto the flagstone floor and stubbed it out with the toe of his shoe. Bending down, he picked up the remains of the cigarette and placed it carefully in the pocket of his trousers. 'They'll put me in with the kiddie-fiddlers.'

Slater yawned. 'You should have thought about that before you paid a fifteen-year-old boy to give you oral sex. I am sure we will be able to get this all sorted,' she said, trying to sound as if she was still interested in her client. 'The policeman will be discredited and we will get the charges against you dropped.'

'But how?' McGowan wailed. The door to the church opened and a gaunt and tired-looking young woman appeared. Nodding nervously at McGowan and Slater, she hurried past. McGowan waited for her to light a candle and begin her prayers before turning back to Slater. 'Even if you do,' he breathed, 'Wagner says they will kick me out of here.'

'What?'

'The Monsignor has told me that it is time to move on.' McGowan gave her a pained look. 'It is not right.'

Slater half-suppressed a snort of laughter. The capacity of some people for self-delusion never ceased to amaze.

'I have been here almost twenty years,' the priest continued, his voice rising. 'This is my home. I am too old to go anywhere else.'

'The Monsignor has to look at the interests of everyone.'

'But it is just not right!' McGowan repeated, going red in the face. Reaching into his pocket, he took out his cigarettes again and fumbled with the packet before pulling one out and sticking it in his mouth. 'You must speak to him.'

Slater looked at him expressionlessly.

'You must!' McGowan hissed, still searching for his lighter. A look of desperation – or was it low cunning? – appeared in his eyes. 'Otherwise,' he croaked, 'who knows what I might have to say to the police?'

'Okay,' Slater sighed, struggling to believe that the devious old sod was trying to strong-arm her. 'I will see what I can do.'

The inspector reluctantly followed Roche to a Costa Coffee on Canary Wharf's North Colonnade, cradling a double espresso while his sergeant tucked into an oversized ham and egg bloomer awash in tomato sauce.

'All in all, that's a bit of a result,' said Roche, swallowing the last of her sandwich and wiping the corners of her mouth to remove stray traces of ketchup.

'The sandwich?' Carlyle asked obtusely.

'No,' Roche said primly, taking a mouthful of her latte. 'Dugdale's Jesus impersonation.'

'I think it was more like St Andrew,' Carlyle corrected her, thinking of the Patron Saint of Scotland, crucified on an X-shaped cross, or saltire, as he deemed himself unworthy to be crucified on the same type of cross as the Son of God.

'Who?'

'Never mind.'

'Whatever. His timing was perfect.'

Carlyle shrugged. 'Bit of a sad way to go.'

'I can think of a lot worse,' Roche protested.

'Yes, but even so.'

Roche frowned. 'But you hated the bastard.'

'Yeah,' Carlyle nodded. 'But I don't need to hate him any more – do I?'

'Doesn't sound like you,' Roche grunted.

Carlyle rubbed a hand over his face. 'There's a saying that if you sit by the side of the river long enough, you'll see the bodies of your enemies floating by.'

Roche almost choked on her coffee. 'How very . . . *philosophical* of you,' she said.

'I've found it a very helpful thought down the years,' Carlyle explained, ignoring her sarcasm. 'They float away and you forget about them. It's better than revenge. The inevitability of the process makes it very soothing.'

'If you say so, Chief.' Roche grinned. 'The question is: what will it mean for your disciplinary hearing?'

'Simpson will sort it out.'

Roche looked at him carefully. 'You two are quite close, aren't you?'

Suddenly Carlyle felt quite defensive. 'I wouldn't say *close*,' he replied, 'but we've worked together a long time.'

'She seems to put up with a lot of your crap.'

Carlyle smiled. 'She's a smart officer, just like you.'

Roche stared into her empty latte glass. 'Now who's taking the piss?'

Carlyle finished his espresso, placing the demitasse back on its saucer.

'Anyway,' said Roche slowly, still not looking up, 'Dugdale did do one thing before heading off to the great sex dungeon in the sky.'

'Yeah?' Carlyle asked, knowing what was coming next.

Finally looking up, Roche gave him an apologetic smile. 'My move to SO15 has been confirmed.'

'Congratulations.' Leaning forward, Carlyle patted her on the arm. 'Well done. I know that's what you wanted.'

'My start date is still to be confirmed, but I should be moving in something like six weeks.'

'Okay.'

'You're not pissed off?' She sounded a little miffed that he was taking it so calmly.

'Nah. You told me it was on the cards. It's good. I'm happy for you.'

'Thanks.'

The awkward silence was broken by Carlyle's mobile, which started vibrating in his pocket. Grabbing the handset, he opened the text message that had just arrived in his inbox. *I know you've been trying to get hold of me. Am at the usual spot.* Carlyle reread the message and laughed. 'That's ballsy,' he said to himself.

'What?'

'Nothing,' he said, getting to his feet. 'Got to run. Something's come up. I'll see you back at the station.'

Crossing her arms, Abigail Slater scanned the room, letting her gaze glide over the blank face of Eddie Wood and the slightly more reptilian features of Monsignor Joseph Wagner. This was a meeting she knew that she didn't want to be in. Annoyed at herself for being in the room, she toyed with the idea of just getting up and walking out. But she felt crippled by an unusual indecision, mixed with morbid curiosity.

Looking at Slater, Wagner cleared his throat. 'Edward . . .'

'Eddie,' the boy corrected him, sucking greedily on a can of Sprite as he leaned backwards on his chair.

'Eddie. I know that this has been a difficult time.'

Eddie shrugged, as if 'difficult' was simply his lot.

'And I know that the way the police have abused your trust must make it very hard for you to engage with reputable figures of authority.'

Eddie gave him an uncomprehending look.

This is not going to work, Slater thought, relaxing a little.

Wagner took a deep breath and ploughed on. 'But we are entering a very important time.'

Slowly, Eddie sat back upright. 'How much?' he said, scowling.

Wagner frowned. 'What do you mean?'

Eddie came up with his best attempt at a smile. 'You want me to withdraw my statement and bugger off, don't you?'

'Father McGowan,' Wagner said quietly, 'will be retiring soon. It is surely best for all concerned that we deal with this matter with the minimum of fuss. You should take time to think things through before deciding whether or not to go public with any lurid claims.'

Eddie let out a loud burp. 'How much?'

Wagner took an envelope from his pocket and placed it on the table. 'I am authorized to offer you five thousand—'

'Ten!' Eddie shouted gleefully.

Exasperated, Wagner looked at Slater. The lawyer gave him a wry smile. 'It looks, Monsignor,' she said, 'as if you have a negotiation on your hands.'

Jumping to his feet, Eddie reached across the desk and grabbed the envelope. 'Five now, five this time next week. I'll lie low until then, and if you come up with the rest of the cash, I'll go and tell Plod that I'm withdrawing my statement.' Stuffing the envelope into the front pocket of his jeans, he offered Wagner a hand. 'Deal?'

Ignoring the hand, the Monsignor signalled his assent with the curtest of nods.

'Good.' Eddie slouched his way towards the door. 'Ten grand – sweet!' He winked at Wagner. 'Keep up your end and I might even throw in a free blowjob.'

As Eddie disappeared into the night, Wagner shook his head. 'What kind of a child is that? With the morals of the gutter . . .'

Slater was already on her feet, about to make her exit. 'That's the kind of child that you're doing deals with,' she said contemptuously, 'to protect yourself from the truth.'

'The world,' Wagner smiled sadly, 'is a complicated place.'

'Yes,' said Slater, 'I suppose it is.' At the door, the lawyer remembered her promise to McGowan to raise the issue of his proposed banishment from London. Pausing, she half-turned back towards Wagner.

'Is there anything else?' the Monsignor asked.

Slater thought about it for a heartbeat. 'No,' she said. 'I think we've got everything covered.'

Standing by Regent's Canal, Carlyle nodded at the lone angler sitting on the towpath. Eating a cheese sandwich, the man eyed him suspiciously and didn't return the greeting. Realizing that he'd been sent on a wild-goose chase, the inspector stood pawing the stone while a pair of cyclists wobbled past. Undecided as to his next move, he watched a Capital Waterbus open-topped narrowboat pull up to a nearby stop on its journey west towards Little Venice. There were a grand total of four passengers on board, and it was only when the boat had come to a stop that he realized that one of them was gesturing at him, telling him to get on. He was an old guy, sitting alone at the back, wearing a quilted Barbour jacket and a West Ham baseball cap pulled down low. Frowning, the inspector hesitated. When, exasperated, the man pushed up the peak of his cap to reveal his face, Carlyle finally recognized him.

Digging a fiver out of his pocket, he handed his fare over to the boat's skipper and scrambled on board. Buttoning his jacket up against the cold, Carlyle made for the rear of the boat. 'I thought you weren't coming,' he said, belatedly wondering if he should have arranged for some back-up.

'That would have been a bit rude, wouldn't it?' Trevor Cole pulled his hand far enough out of the pocket of his jacket for Carlyle to be able to clearly see the grip of his semi-automatic. He gestured at the bench in front of him. 'Sit there.'

Carlyle sat down, immediately feeling the barrel of the gun pushed

270

firmly into the small of his back. 'Put that away,' he said as casually as he could manage. 'Otherwise you'll just cause panic.'

'Okay.'

Carlyle felt the pressure on his spine lift. 'Thanks.'

'Keep your eyes front and don't turn around. We're just gonna have a little chat. There's no reason why you shouldn't be able to behave yourself.'

Carlyle took a deep breath. 'No.'

Cole breathed into his ear as the boat resumed its journey: 'Now, first things first. Give me your phone, please.'

After the slightest hesitation, Carlyle reached into his jacket, pulled out his private handset and handed it over. Cole looked at the cheap, pay-as-you-go phone with dismay. 'You would have thought the police could afford something better than that,' he quipped.

Shrugging, Carlyle said nothing.

'Ah, well, at least it won't cost so much to replace.' Casually leaning across the side of the boat, Cole let the handset fall into the scummy water.

Carlyle shifted in his seat. He wondered what his chances were of reaching back and punching Cole's lights out before he could get off a round. Reluctant to risk getting his nuts – or anything else – shot off, he settled for a question instead. 'Is that the gun you used to shoot Kristin Lagerbäck with?'

'Come on, Inspector,' Cole scoffed. 'This isn't a Q&A session.'

What is it then? Carlyle wondered. He looked around. They would be approaching Camden soon. More people would be getting on the boat. He had to try and get this nutter off the water and into custody without causing a fuss. 'So what are we doing here?'

'Another question,' Cole sighed. 'But I'll indulge you. Let's put it this way. I think you're a good guy. You deserve to be told what happened.'

But I know what happened, Carlyle thought. *You just want to show off.*

'When I get off this boat,' Cole continued, 'that'll be it. I'm off. No more London. I'll enjoy a quiet retirement far away. Gotha Insurance will pay out on the shortfall and everyone will move on.'

'Apart from the three people who died,' Carlyle mused.

'The girl from the store – well, that was an accident; not my fault. Carla deserved it – she was always a pain in the arse. Why my brother ever married her, I'll never know. And as for that idiot boy of hers . . .'

'He rolled over on you, by the way,' Carlyle lied.

'That doesn't surprise me. No backbone at all. The same goes for his idiot friend for that matter.'

Not going to disagree with you on that one, Carlyle thought.

'But,' Cole continued, 'as you would expect, I factored that into my planning. If I'd been relying on Colin to keep his mouth shut, I would have deserved to get caught.' As the boat approached the stop at Camden Lock, Carlyle saw a small knot of half-a-dozen tourists waiting to get on. Following his line of vision, Cole gave him a sympathetic pat on the back with his free hand. 'Just sit tight, Inspector. This is not your stop. And, remember, don't try anything funny. "Canal-boat slaughter" wouldn't look too good on your CV, would it?'

Despite everything, Carlyle chuckled. 'No. I suppose not.'

Leaning forward, Cole grinned happily. 'You are a very pragmatic man, Inspector. That is why I thought we should have this meeting. I knew that you would take it all in good spirit and not try anything silly.'

FORTY-FIVE

Camden Lock was its usual dirty, tourist-infested self. Carlyle watched the new passengers clamber on board and waited for them to set off again. The boat was quite full now, with a couple sitting next to him chatting away happily in Spanish and a woman with a young boy of maybe six or seven in a row on the other side of the aisle. His window of opportunity, if it had ever existed, had gone.

Turning his head slightly towards Cole, he lowered his voice until it was barely audible over the spluttering engine. 'I can hardly take three murders in good spirit.'

'I explained the first two,' said Cole huffily. 'Miss Lagerbäck was, I admit, more gratuitous. I suppose I should have walked away, but she was always such an irritating cow, I just felt like it. Did you see that picture she had in her office? What a total narcissist.'

Great arse though. 'And the jewels?'

'They were all pre-sold long before Colin and Damian went any-where near St James's. That's the thing about my line of work – you have to know all the villains.'

Carlyle folded his arms. 'Same for me.'

'Exactly,' said Cole, with the cheery air of a bloke enjoying his first good man-to-man chat in ages. 'You didn't do me any favours by recovering so much of the stuff. But my needs are modest and I've got more than enough to see me through the rest of my days.'

A thought struck Carlyle. 'What about Mrs Cole?'

Cole grinned. 'She's under the floorboards in the kitchen, at home.'

'What?'

The insurance man's grin grew wider. 'Only joking! Only joking! Mrs C and I got a divorce – ooh, must be more than twenty years ago now. Last I heard, she'd moved to Norwich.'

Poor woman, thought Carlyle, genuinely horrified at the thought of anyone having to live beyond Zone One of the tube map. Up ahead, the huge aviary cages of London Zoo appeared on either side of the canal. Cole tapped Carlyle's foot with the toe of his shoe. 'This is your stop,' he said. 'I'll be staying on. Don't make a fuss and I won't have to shoot anyone by accident.'

'Understood,' said Carlyle.

'Good,' Cole said cosily. 'I'm glad we had this little chat. Aren't you?'

Carlyle grunted. 'Sure.'

'I wanted to be able to give you closure.'

Maybe it's a cry for help, Carlyle thought. *Maybe he wants me to throw him in the canal so he can get caught on a shopping trolley and drown.*

'Here.' Cole reached over the inspector's shoulder and pressed something into his hand.

Carlyle looked down at what looked like a little bug jewel. 'What's this?'

'It's a small gift for you – a memento of our little adventure – an eighteen-carat gold, diamond and ruby bee brooch. That would set you back the best part of nine grand, retail price. Mrs Carlyle will love it.'

Happily, thought Carlyle as he pocketed the brooch, *my wife isn't that kind of woman.*

The boat pulled up at the Zoo stop and people started getting off. Cole shooed him away. 'Now off you go, before I start shooting.'

'Eh?' Carlyle hesitated and immediately felt the barrel of the gun against his spine once again.

'Go on,' Cole hissed. 'And don't even think about trying to get help. You really don't want to piss me off. There are still women and children on this boat.'

'Okay, okay.' Getting to his feet, the inspector joined the queue of passengers disembarking, shuffling along the length of the boat and stepping onto the concrete jetty. A path led up a small wooded incline, leading to the zoo. Checking that Cole hadn't followed him, he jogged up the path, jumping behind the first big tree he could find. Pleased with himself for carrying two phones, he pulled out his BlackBerry and found Roche's number. Hitting call, he heard it ring twice before he dropped off the network. 'Shit!' Realizing that he only had one bar of signal, he sprinted up the hill and tried again. This time, the call went straight to voicemail. 'Fuck!' Ignoring the dirty look of a woman passing with her kids, he ended the call and hit the number for the desk at the station.

He listened to it ring for what seemed like an eternity. 'C'mon! C'mon!'

Finally, someone picked up. 'Charing Cross police station,' said a weary voice.

'Who's that?' Carlyle demanded.

There was a pause. 'What?'

'This is Carlyle,' he said angrily, struggling to keep his frustration in check. 'Who am I speaking to?'

'Oh, okay, Inspector. This is Butler.'

'Butler,' Carlyle sighed. Sergeant Robert Butler was a Brummie who had been stationed at Charing Cross for a little over six months. It was a fate that seemed to bemuse and dismay him in equal measure, as if he had landed in London by accident and couldn't manage to find his way home. Even by the standards of the Metropolitan Police, he was somewhat thick. Telling himself to speak clearly and s-l-o-w-l-y, Carlyle took a deep breath. 'Listen carefully. We have a very serious situation. This is what I need you to do . . .'

Putting the phone down on the sergeant, Carlyle wondered what *his* next step should be. As he did so, his phone went off in his hand. When he saw it was Simpson, he answered. 'We've got a big problem,' he said immediately. Before she could say anything, he quickly outlined the situation. As he did so, he saw another narrowboat approaching the jetty.

'I'll get straight over there,' said Simpson.

'See you there.' Skipping back down the hill, the inspector jumped onto the jetty as the bright red boat, with *Bert's Boat Trips* emblazoned on the side, pulled up. Happily, there was no one else waiting to embark. Carlyle counted six passengers, plus the skipper, or whatever he was called, already on board. Pulling out his warrant card, he leaped on board.

The boatman, a middle-aged guy in a green jumper and Breton cap, waved at him furiously with one hand while keeping the other on the tiller. 'Hey!' he shouted. 'What are you doing?'

'Police!' Carlyle shouted, waving the warrant card above his head. 'Everybody off! Now!'

A couple of passengers who were getting off anyway quickly shuffled onto the jetty. The remaining group, four women who appeared to be together, sat there like lemons.

'I'm sorry,' said Carlyle, trying not to sound too short, 'but I need the rest of you to get off as well, please.'

'What's going on?' the skipper demanded, still controlling the tiller.

Carlyle held up a hand. 'I'll explain in a moment, sir,' he said, trying, and failing, to muster a smile. 'First, I need to get these people off the boat.'

'But we've paid to go all the way,' a woman protested.

Carlyle grimaced. 'I'm sorry, madam, but this is a police matter.' He shoved his ID in front of her face. 'We are very grateful for your cooperation. I am sure we can sort out a refund later.'

'This is outrageous,' the woman harrumphed, taking to the role of ringleader like a hippo to water.

Carlyle changed tack, trying the obsequious approach. 'I'm very sorry. It is an emergency.'

The woman couldn't have looked any more irritated if someone had just taken her lunch away from her. With much huffing and puffing, she got to her feet. 'C'mon, girls,' she said with a weary shake of her head. 'If the *policeman* says we need to get off, we'd better get off.'

'Don't want to get arrested, do we?' one of her friends said.

Fatso glared at Carlyle. 'No, we wouldn't want that at all.'

Ushering them off, Carlyle moved to the back of the boat.

'You'd better have a good explanation for this,' complained the skipper.

'You're not gonna believe it,' said Carlyle with a wry grin. 'Get me to Maida Vale, full steam ahead, and I'll explain on the way.'

Feeling like a complete idiot, Carlyle stood next to the skipper as they chugged along in 'hot pursuit' of Trevor Cole. 'How fast does this thing go?' he asked over the spluttering engine.

'Top speed?' the skipper asked. 'Maybe twelve miles an hour.'

Great, thought Carlyle, tapping his foot nervously against the deck. *That's just fucking great.*

Twelve miles an hour proved to be somewhat ambitious. In the event, it took them just over fifteen minutes to reach the end of the line. As they approached the Maida Vale stop, Carlyle studied the scene of confusion and felt a chill run through his guts. The jetty had been sealed off, and heavily armed police were holding everyone on the Capital Waterbus boat. He could see at least two passengers half out of their seats filming the scene on their mobile phones. For all he knew, the whole fucking thing could be going out live on Sky News. But, try as he might, he couldn't make out Trevor Cole and his West Ham United baseball cap. He signalled to the *Bert*'s skipper to pull up and let him off as far away from the other craft as possible. To say that the situation needed careful handling was a bit of an understatement. Another fiasco was the last thing he needed right now.

Jumping onto the wooden jetty, Carlyle skirted round the cordon until he found a burly sergeant with a spectacular handlebar moustache who seemed to be overseeing the operation. Flipping out his ID, he introduced himself.

The sergeant pointed to a slim blonde woman standing by the boat with her back to them. 'DI Kent is in charge,' he said gruffly.

'Thanks,' said Carlyle, heading off towards the woman. Hands on hips, Kent was wearing jeans and a leather biker jacket. He was just contemplating her arse when she turned towards him, a grim smile on her face.

'Carlyle?' She offered him a firm handshake, 'I'm DI Kent. It looks like your guy is not on board. The skipper says he jumped off just after they left the Zoo. We've sent some people over there to take a look.'

'Shit!'

'A preliminary search of the boat has found no weapons,' Kent continued. 'We will, of course, take statements from all of the passengers, but no one seems to have seen a man with a gun.'

'Okay,' Carlyle nodded. 'We need to make sure that all airports and ports are alerted about this guy. I am sure he will try to leave the country as soon as possible.'

'Already done.' Carole Simpson appeared at his shoulder and introduced herself to Kent. 'All the necessary authorities have been alerted. I'm sure we will have Mr Cole in custody in short order.'

Carlyle wasn't sure about that at all, but he kept his peace.

'So,' said Simpson, smiling at Kent, 'I am sure you can handle things here. I need Inspector Carlyle to come with me.'

Clearly not happy at being left to clean up someone else's mess, Kent said stiffly, 'Of course. Thank you, Commander.'

'Good,' said Simpson. Taking Carlyle by the arm, she wheeled the inspector around and led him off the jetty at a brisk pace.

Sitting in the back of Simpson's staff BMW, Carlyle turned to his boss. 'Thanks for getting me out of that.'

'It's my pleasure,' Simpson said wryly. 'A key part of the job description.'

Carlyle stared out of the window. It had started to rain and London was at its grim, grey worst. 'The guy had a gun. I don't know what else I could have done.'

'The question is more why you went for a rendezvous with a suspected murderer on your own,' Simpson observed, '*without* any back-up.'

'Mm.'

'But,' the Commander sighed, 'we won't go there.'

'Thank you.'

'No need for thanks. It's nice to come back and know that some things never change.'

'How do you mean?'

Simpson laughed. 'I come back from Canada and Inspector John Carlyle is still pushing back the boundaries of modern policing.'

He gave her a quizzical look.

'Who else can say they've ever had a barge-chase?'

Carlyle grinned. 'I think you'll find that they were, in fact, narrowboats.'

'Either way,' chuckled Simpson, 'it was quite an achievement, even by your standards.'

Carlyle laughed along with her.

'I had a call from Superintendent Buck this morning,' said Simpson, moving the conversation on. 'Your hearing is now going to take place the week after next.'

'Conveniently after the Pope has been and gone.'

Simpson shook her head. 'I know you have a very high opinion of yourself, John, but I don't think you were ever going to have much impact on a state visit by His Holiness.'

'Maybe not,' Carlyle conceded.

'Anyway,' Simpson continued, 'it is totally in the IIC's hands, now that Dugdale has shuffled off his mortal coil. I presume that means it will be Buck's show. Hopefully, Ambrose will still be in attendance.'

Carlyle coughed. 'Do I have anything to worry about?'

Simpson looked at him carefully. 'Not if you didn't beat up your suspect, no.'

FORTY-SIX

Purring with delight, Christian Holyrod fell back onto the bed and gazed up at the ceiling. The Royal Suite of the Savoy was very much to his taste. One of the great London landmarks, a hundred-million-pound restoration of the Edwardian and Art Deco hotel provided him with an oasis of elegance and glamour that was truly worthy of his new paramour. Unzipping his trousers, he pulled out his flaccid penis and began masturbating lazily.

A look of disgust flashed across Abigail Slater's face. 'You never stop, do you? Put that bloody thing away!'

Holyrod forced himself upright. 'What's wrong?' he asked, dick still in hand.

'I want a drink.'

'Fine.' If Holyrod felt rather miffed by her attitude, it didn't seem to bother his cock, which was now almost good to go. He gestured towards the mini-bar. 'Help yourself. But I've only got half an hour.'

Turning away from him, Slater grabbed a couple of miniatures of Smirnoff Black and dumped the contents into a 50ml glass. Throwing back her head, she downed the contents in a single gulp.

'Feel better now?' Holyrod asked hopefully.

Looking at him in the mirror on the wall above the mini-bar, she shook her head. 'I just don't feel in the mood.'

Holyrod began to soften. 'What?' he said, a hint of desperation entering his voice. 'Not even a quick blowjob?'

With no more vodka on hand, Slater started on the Gordon's. 'You didn't sort out the policeman,' she said abruptly.

'For God's sake!' Holyrod threw himself back onto the bed in exasperation. 'I'm the fucking Mayor!' he spluttered. 'I don't go round interfering with police investigations just because . . . because . . .'

'Because I'm a good shag?' said Slater angrily, attacking the gin with gusto.

'Hah!' Holyrod laughed. 'I've had better,' he said meanly, immediately regretting the lie.

'Fuck you!' Slater screamed, hurling the now empty glass at his head. Taking evasive action, he fell off the bed just as the tumbler smashed against the headboard.

Lying on the carpet, he listened to her storm out of the suite. 'That went well,' he said to himself, as the door clicked shut. Slowly, he got to his feet. Tucking himself back into his trousers, he opened the mini-bar to see what was left to drink.

Tomorrow is the day, Carlyle thought nervously, as he gazed at Helen sitting on the sofa, concentrating on her Sudoku puzzle. *Either we get the all clear, breathe a sigh of relief and get on with our lives or . . . not.*

If it turned out that Helen didn't have the faulty BRCA2 gene, Carlyle knew that, for him at least, the whole thing would be ancient history in a matter of days.

On the other hand, if she did have it, he would plough on trying to fight the problem head on.

But what if they fought and lost?

Looking up from the paper, Helen caught him staring. 'Stop spying on me,' she ordered. 'I'm not a bloody invalid.'

'N-no, of course not,' he stammered, embarrassed. He pointed at her empty mug on the coffee table. 'Want some more tea?'

She shook her head. 'For God's sake, John! Just leave me in peace. Go to bed . . . or go and find something to do.'

Without another word, he padded into the kitchen and filled the kettle. While he waited for the water to boil, he checked out the back cover of the latest Commissario Brunetti novel, which he had been saving for a moment when he could give it the attention that it deserved. The prospect of a couple of hours in Venice before bed filled him with some kind of happiness, and he managed a half-smile as he placed the book on the worktop and pulled a bag of green tea from the box on top of the microwave. Dropping the bag into a chipped Fulham FC mug, a Christmas present from his daughter several years earlier, he added boiling water. Just as he was removing the bag, his phone started ringing. Tossing the bag into the sink, he pulled the handset out of his pocket.

'Carlyle.'

'John, it's Rose Scripps.' The background traffic noise told him that she was out on the street.

'Hi.'

'Apologies for calling you so late.'

'No problem.' Carlyle took a sip of his scalding tea and winced. 'What can I do for you?'

'I'm at the church. McGowan's on the roof. He's threatening to jump.'

Carlyle thought about that for a moment. 'Nice one. If he doesn't bottle it, see if you can record the action on your mobile for me. Make sure you get a nice close-up of the mess on the road.'

'I'm serious,' Rose said sternly.

'So am I.'

'Look, you have to get down here.'

Carlyle slurped his tea noisily. 'I'm busy.'

'Inspector, we have a very serious situation here. The man says he is going to kill himself and he is demanding to speak to you.'

Carlyle let out a deep breath. 'For fuck's sake!'

'Commander Simpson is on her way. And I've already seen that lawyer woman skulking about.'

'Fine,' said Carlyle huffily. 'I'll be there to see the whole damn freakshow in person. See if you can keep him from taking a dive for the next ten minutes or so. If I'm coming down, I don't want to miss the action.' Ending the call, he leaned back against the sink while he finished the last of his tea. Placing the mug next to the used tea bag, he glanced over at his book. 'Looks like Venice will have to wait,' he mumbled to himself, as he headed off to explain to Helen where he was going.

The slate roof of St Boniface's fell away steeply to a lead-lined gutter about ten inches wide. Between the gutter and the edge of the building was a stone parapet about a foot high and the same again wide. Illuminated by spotlights that had been part of the church's earlier refurbishment works, McGowan stood swaying on the parapet, at a point just below the spire. Just looking at him made Carlyle, who had no head for heights whatsoever, feel physically sick.

'How did he get up there?' Simpson asked.

'You can access the roof via a skylight on the other side.' Rose Scripps pointed at a figure crouching in the gutter at the other end of the roof. 'That's how our negotiator got up there.'

Carlyle looked around at the assembled circus: three police vans, two ambulances, two television trucks, a dozen or so uniforms and a growing crowd of gawkers. 'Who is it?'

'He's called Angel,' Rose said. 'Sergeant Fletcher Angel. A very experienced guy, apparently.'

'You can't go wrong with an Angel,' Carlyle quipped. 'How's he doing?'

'Okay, I think,' said Rose. 'It's hard to communicate with McGowan because he won't let anyone get too close and he doesn't have a mobile or anything,'

'Well, at least he hasn't jumped,' said Simpson.

At that moment, there was an incomprehensible cry from up above. The crowd gasped as all eyes turned to the heavens. For a moment, McGowan seemed to teeter on the edge before stepping off the parapet back into the gutter.

'Not yet, anyway,' said Rose.

Carlyle gestured at Abigail Slater, pacing up and down behind the police cordon, talking animatedly into a mobile phone. 'The best result would be if he did jump and landed on his bitch of a lawyer.'

Simpson and Scripps both shot him disgusted looks.

'Hey,' Carlyle shrugged, 'you can't blame a boy for dreaming, can you? It would solve the problem of my hearing.'

Simpson gestured to the heavens with her chin. 'Are you going up?'

'Looks like it. Do we know what has prompted this little drama?'

Rose shook her head. 'I asked the lawyer but she said she didn't know. I'm sure she's lying but there's nothing I can do about that.'

'Okay,' said Carlyle, reluctantly deciding to bite the bullet. 'Wish me luck.'

Not waiting for a response, he strode off in the direction of the church.

What was it Roche had told him? You need to put your chimp back in the box. The chimp theory might be bullshit, but if there was ever a time to give it a go, this was it. Now was not the time to get carried away with emotion, unless you wanted to risk crashing to your death. Taking a couple of slow, deep breaths, he closed his eyes and imagined locking away his inner primate. Putting the key safely in his pocket, he opened his eyes and blinked twice.

'*Ready?*'

'Ready.' With his heart hammering inside his chest, the inspector stepped out onto the roof. Almost immediately, he was hit by a gust of wind that caused him to sway alarmingly. At least, for once, he had dressed for the occasion. Zipping his Berghaus Parka all the way up to his chin, he edged his way round the side of the building to where the police negotiator was crouched in the gutter.

'Angel?' Perching on the inside edge of the parapet, his feet firmly planted in the gutter, Carlyle shook the sergeant's hand. 'I'm John Carlyle.' He nodded at the figure of McGowan, who was twenty yards away. 'He asked for me?'

'Yeah,' Angel said.

'And it's safe for me to go along there?' Carlyle asked, praying that the answer would be 'no'.

'Yeah,' Angel grinned. 'Just stay in the gutter, take it nice and slow – and don't look down.'

'Jolly good,' said Carlyle grimly. Immediately disobeying and looking down, he was suddenly struck by just how much he liked the feeling of firm ground under his feet.

'Good luck,' Angel smiled.

'Thanks.' Another gust of wind cut through them and Carlyle was sure that, at any second, he was about to meet his Maker.

'If he decides he wants to come down,' Angel said, apparently unperturbed, 'we've got a cherry-picker on the way. If you're worried about being stuck, just sit tight.' With his back against the roof, he manoeuvred past Carlyle, leaving the inspector free to continue on his journey.

'Will do.' Shuffling along on his haunches, with one hand on the parapet and another on the roof proper, Carlyle slowly made his way towards the priest. After five minutes, he had gone about halfway but McGowan, in his suicidal funk, showed no sign of acknowledging his presence. A thought suddenly hit him: what if Helen and Alice were watching this live on TV, right now? Unable to resist another peek down, he could clearly make out the lights of the TV camera pointed in his direction. The sheer bloody stupidity of what he was doing almost overwhelmed him and he stopped to fight for a few breaths before continuing on his way.

'Stop! Don't come any closer!'

Less than five feet from McGowan, Carlyle did what he was told. For a few moments the two men eyed each other warily. McGowan's eyes were bloodshot and wild. At his feet was an almost empty bottle of Famous Grouse whisky. *Not my first choice for a final tipple*, thought Carlyle, *but what the hell.* 'It's fucking freezing up here,' he shouted, gesturing at the scotch. 'Can I have some?'

McGowan looked down at the bottle as if he'd never seen it before and kicked it in Carlyle's direction. It came to rest against the parapet a foot away. Slowly, keeping his eyes on McGowan, Carlyle moved towards the bottle. Picking it up, he wedged himself into the gutter, with his back against the parapet, unscrewed the top and took a long mouthful.

'Thanks,' he sighed, and McGowan nodded.

Carlyle offered him the bottle back but the priest shook his head. Carlyle put the cap back on and placed the Famous Grouse upright in the gutter between them. The whisky was already having the desired effect, putting some warmth in his belly and taking the edge off his fear. 'You wanted to talk to me?'

Taking a couple of steps closer, McGowan sat down tentatively on the parapet. There was now only a couple of feet between the two men. The priest went to say something, but all that came out was a loud burp. He held out a hand. 'Pardon me.'

A bit late for manners, Carlyle thought, already eyeing the rest of the Famous Grouse. He turned his head towards the roof. The folks down on the ground wouldn't be able to hear him, but he didn't want any lipreading going on either. 'What do you want, Francis?'

'You have ruined me!' the priest lamented.

'Me?' This time Carlyle did grab the bottle.

'They are sending me away.'

I bloody hope so, Carlyle thought. 'Nothing to do with me,' he shrugged. Another long swig left the Famous Grouse almost finished. No point in leaving such a small amount, he mused, sucking down the remainder greedily.

'It was you,' McGowan groaned. 'You chased me down; you tried to kill me.'

Carlyle thought about throwing the bottle at one of the TV crews below, but commonsense prevailed. Tossing it back into the gutter, he wiped his eyes and yawned.

'You wanted me dead,' the priest repeated.

Yes, I did, Carlyle thought. The parapet was cutting into the small of his back, forcing him to shift position. He looked searchingly at McGowan. 'And what about Simon Murphy? Who killed *him*, you old bastard?'

The priest looked at him blankly.

Carlyle sighed. 'Let's get down from here.'

McGowan gestured out into the illuminated night and the crowd below. 'You have to admit your l-lies,' he stammered.

'What lies?' Carlyle snorted.

'You have to tell them I am innocent.'

'But you're not innocent.' Carlyle could feel his mobile buzzing in his jacket pocket, but he ignored it. 'You're as guilty as sin.'

286

'I'll jump!'

Carlyle shrugged. 'Be my guest.'

'You must repent.'

'Fuck off,' Carlyle said angrily. 'Look, either you jump or we get down from here right now.' A thought popped into his head. 'Anyway, I believed that taking your own life was a sin.'

'It is,' McGowan panted. 'Of course it is.'

'Well then,' said Carlyle, wondering if he should maybe try and brain the crazy old bastard with the bottle, 'that's this little problem sorted. Let's go and get another drink.'

Half-standing, McGowan looked as if he was going to lunge at Carlyle. 'You . . . must . . . repent.'

Oh fuck, Carlyle thought, *what do I do now?* Trying to wedge himself as deeply as possible into the gutter, he grimaced as the priest took a step towards him then side-stepped off the parapet and into thin air. His brain flipped between a freeze-frame image of McGowan there and one of McGowan gone. Even as the screams reached him from down below, he wasn't sure which picture was real.

The view from the gutter was not great. No London landmarks were visible; all you could make out was the light pollution from dozens of office buildings and hundreds of streetlights. But the polluted orange glow was at least the polluted orange glow of home and he was a man – a rather pissed man – at peace with his surroundings. After an indeterminate amount of time he became aware of a mechanical noise coming from somewhere below him. Shortly afterwards, a man's head appeared beyond the parapet. Carlyle did a double-take before he realized it was the smiling face of the cherry-picker operator, come to rescue him.

'Inspector?'

Carlyle nodded.

'Don't worry, sir,' the man said cheerily. 'We'll have you back down on the ground in no time.'

'Thank fuck for that.'

After manoeuvring the small platform into place, the man opened a small gate and helped him to clamber on board. Holding onto the railings for dear life, Carlyle concentrated on breathing deeply while studying the cityscape in the middle distance to avoid looking down.

'A word to the wise, sir,' the operator said as they approached the ground.

'What's that?' asked Carlyle, cheered by the realization that he probably was going to make it back down alive. Below them, he could see McGowan's body being loaded into an ambulance which then began slowly moving away down the street. As it did so, he caught a glimpse of Slater stealing away into the night.

'Your wife is waiting for you down there.'

'Oh fuck.'

'I think I heard her say something about you "not answering your bloody phone".'

'Mm.' Looking down, it didn't take him long to pick out his wife and daughter. Alice waved at him cheerily and he almost felt like crying with gratitude. Helen's expression, however, was a different matter entirely.

FORTY-SEVEN

'What the hell were you playing at?' Pushing her way past Simpson and Rose Scripps, Helen rammed an angry index finger into his chest. Carlyle reached over to give her a hug, but she brushed him away. 'You stupid bloody bastard!' she shouted, almost sobbing with rage, pointing to the skies. 'What the fuck were you *doing* up there?'

Alice appeared at her mother's side, giggling. Helen was not given to such foul-mouthed tirades and her daughter couldn't help but be amused. 'Dad!' she shouted. 'You were on the telly!'

The adrenaline was rapidly wearing off and Carlyle felt weary to his bones. 'Let's talk about it on the way home,' he said, bending down to kiss his daughter.

Stepping closer, Helen sniffed him theatrically. 'Have you been drinking?'

Carlyle frowned. 'Not here. I'm fine. Everything else we can talk about in private. Let's go home.' He glanced over at Simpson, who nodded her agreement. 'See?' he grinned. 'You can't get this kind of excitement in Canada.'

Simpson laughed. 'I'm on the first flight out of Heathrow tomorrow.'

'Yeah, right. I'll see you tomorrow.' Taking Alice's hand, Carlyle forced a reluctant Helen to take his arm. Together, the three of them marched through the police cordon and off into the London night.

As he approached the front desk the next morning, Carlyle saw Roche engaged in an argument with a scruffy-looking kid. Nodding at his sergeant, Carlyle approached warily. 'Everything okay?'

'I want my money!' said the boy, stamping his foot in a way that made Carlyle want to laugh.

'Inspector,' said a weary-sounding Roche, 'this is Sam Smallbone. He wants to claim a reward for information provided regarding the St James's Diamonds robbery.'

'I want my money!' Smallbone repeated.

Carlyle tried to look thoughtful. 'Isn't that a matter for the insurance company, Sergeant?'

'Yes, sir,' said Roche, playing along. 'I've been trying to explain to Sam – er, Mr Smallbone – that that is how it works but . . .'

'I'll never get nuffink from those bloody crooks!' Smallbone protested.

Not an unreasonable assumption, Carlyle thought. 'What information did you actually provide?' he asked.

Smallbone gestured at Roche. 'Tell 'im.'

With a sigh, Roche explained what had happened. When she had finished, Carlyle rubbed his chin thoughtfully. 'Well, sir,' he said finally, 'first, I have to thank you on behalf of the Metropolitan Police . . .' Fearing the brush-off, Smallbone made to protest, but Carlyle held up a hand. 'And I am sure that we can come up with something suitable. If you wait here for ten minutes, the sergeant will be back to see you.' Smallbone looked doubtful, but he gave a small nod of agreement.

Taking Roche by the arm, Carlyle began walking her down the corridor, into the station proper.

'What are you going to do?' she asked, once the boy was out of earshot.

'I'll do what I said,' Carlyle replied, 'get him a few quid. Go upstairs and I'll swing by your desk in a few minutes.'

'There you go.' Tossing a small brown paper envelope onto Roche's desk, the inspector said, 'There's two hundred and fifty quid in there. That's the best I could do.'

Roche looked at the envelope. 'I don't think that's quite what he had in mind.'

'Well, it's all he's gonna get. Tell him it's better than nothing.'

'Fair enough,' Roche said. 'Where did it come from?'

'I signed it out as a payment for one of my CIs.'

'God bless Confidential Informants,' Roche grinned. Getting to her feet, she grabbed the envelope. 'I'll go down and give Sammy Boy the good news.'

Carlyle nodded at the black bin-liner by her chair. 'Clearing out?'

'Yeah,' said Roche sheepishly. 'I start in SO15 in a couple of weeks but I'm gonna take some time off, so this is my last day in Charing Cross.'

'Oh.'

'I'll be having a leaving drink, of course,' she added, 'but I haven't sorted that out yet.'

'Sure,' Carlyle smiled. 'End of an era.'

'Yeah.' Roche stared at her shoes. 'I do have something for you, though.' Pushing her chair away, she reached under her desk and pulled out Helmut Newton's outsized print of the young Katrin Lagerbäck. 'I know you were a big fan. Here.'

Reluctantly, Carlyle took the print. 'Isn't that evidence?' he asked.

'Her firm threw it out when they closed down the office. I rescued it from the trash.'

He blushed slightly. 'Thanks. Not sure where I'll put it, but it was a nice thought.'

'My pleasure.' She waved the envelope. 'Let me go and give Sam his reward. I'll see you later.'

It took Carlyle less than fifteen minutes to bash out a short account of his escapade on the roof of St Boniface's Church the night before. He was just printing out a copy when Simpson appeared. 'Good timing,' he told her, gesturing in the direction of the printer. 'That's my take on what happened.'

'Your "take" on what happened,' Simpson said as she plucked the single sheet of A4 from the printer. 'You never oversell yourself, do you, Inspector?'

Carlyle gave the smallest of bows. 'I try not to.'

Simpson scanned the text. 'Anyway, it's not like there's anyone who's going to be able to contradict you about what happened up there.'

'No.'

'There was some film producer once,' Simpson mused, 'who had a great line: "there are three sides to every story – yours, mine and the truth".'

Carlyle laughed. 'Not in this case.'

'No, I suppose not.'

'No Hollywood endings for us.'

'No.'

Carlyle looked up at his boss. 'Will McGowan's skydive have any impact on the hearing?'

'Not as far as I know,' Simpson told him, 'although the whole thing does seem a bit cursed. Assume it's still on and I'll let you know if I hear any different.' She watched a doubtful look cloud his face. 'Don't worry, John. It will get sorted.'

'Okay.'

Simpson gestured at one of the various piles of papers on his desk. On the top of this one was the letter from HR about his redundancy terms. 'You're not still thinking about that, are you?'

'What? Early retirement? No.' Reaching over, the inspector grasped the letter and tore it up, tossing the pile of scraps back on his desk. 'Not at all.'

'Good.' Simpson looked pleased. 'By the way, I saw Alison Roche downstairs. I hear that you'll be needing a new sergeant.'

'Looks like it.'

'Shame,' said Simpson. 'I know you rated her.'

'These things happen,' Carlyle said philosophically. 'It's what she wants to do.'

'Any ideas on who you'd like as a replacement?'

He shook his head. 'Nope.'

'Okay. Let's think about it.'

'Yeah.'

'Meanwhile, I do have one bit of good news for you.'

'Oh yes?'

'Trevor Cole was caught this morning, trying to get on a ferry at Dover.'

'Excellent.' Carlyle half-heartedly waved a triumphant fist in front of his face. 'At least that's a result . . .' Suddenly remembering the diamond and ruby bee brooch, he pulled it from his pocket and tossed it underarm to Simpson, who caught it at the second attempt. 'Cole gave me that as a memento yesterday,' he explained, getting to his feet. 'Can you deal with it for me?'

A look of annoyance appeared on Simpson's face, but it quickly passed. 'Of course.'

'Thanks,' said Carlyle, grabbing his jacket from the back of his chair, ' 'cos I've got to run.'

FORTY-EIGHT

Despite the gusting wind and the threat of rain from a darkening sky, they chose to sit outside, on Lamb's Conduit Street. Two tables down, the Goodfellas regulars were still discussing football and fiddling with their roll-ups. A white delivery van came along the road and pulled up by the kerb. The driver jumped from his cab, trotted to the back and pulled out a tray of fresh pastries. As he tracked the progress of the cakes inside, the inspector noticed a flyer taped to the café's window and let out a small laugh. Having survived their brush with SO15 in the Strand underpass, the Eternity Dance Troupe was going to perform a gig in Red Lion Square.

'What's so funny?' Helen squeezed his arm as she stared into the middle distance.

'Nothing.' Massaging the back of her hand, he let his gaze shift to the other side of the road. The undertaker's immediately opposite showed no sign of life. In the flower shop next door, an elderly sales assistant was making up a large bouquet of lilies while chatting cheerily to a customer, a middle-aged man in a red windcheater. Leaving them to their conversation, Carlyle glanced at his watch. In less than fifteen minutes, they would be sitting in a consulting room round the corner in Great Ormond Street. Helen would be told whether she had the cancer gene, BRCA2. 'We should get going.'

'We've got plenty of time,' she replied, seemingly reluctant to move.

'But, still. There's no harm in being a little bit early.' Pushing back his chair, he got to his feet, gently kissing the top of her head before helping her up. Oblivious to the minor domestic drama nearby, the regulars continued their conversation about the appalling standard of referees in the Premier League. Skipping out of the café, the van driver jumped back into his cab, started up the engine and headed off. After a few moments, the customer came out of the flower shop carrying his lilies. Zipping up his jacket, he headed off briskly, in the direction of Holborn.

Carlyle took a deep breath. 'You okay?'

Helen nodded.

'Good.' Taking his wife's arm, he did his best to smile. Together, they began walking slowly down the street.